Lost Soul

Tessa Knox

Published by Tessa Knox, 2024.

This is a work of fiction. Similarities to real people, places, or events are entirely coincidental.

LOST SOUL

First edition. November 10, 2024.

ISBN: 979-8227658647

Written by Tessa Knox.

Chapter 1: The Dare That Brought You Here

The floorboards creaked beneath me as I stepped inside, and the scent of dust and salt settled over me like a second skin. Shadows stretched and pooled in the corners, giving the place a kind of haunted dignity, and though I laughed it off in front of my friend, I could feel the steady pound of my pulse in my wrists, in my throat, as if the mansion had its own heartbeat that synced with mine the moment I entered. A dare, I kept reminding myself, just a dare. But as I looked around, I couldn't shake the sense that this house—no, this entity—was daring me right back, taunting me to stay just a little longer, to see just a little more.

The air was thick with stories that seemed to hum in the walls, each worn, floral wallpaper panel holding the weight of a hundred whispers. I'd heard the stories, of course; everyone in town had. Rumors of the house's former owners, tales of a love gone wrong, and whispers of visitors who'd come here on a whim and never quite left. But all of that felt like old folklore, fragments of a mystery I couldn't quite believe until I was standing here, feeling the chills skittering up my spine.

I clutched my suitcase tighter, scanning the hall for any sign of life, but the house was still. There was a staircase just ahead, winding up into darkness, and to my left, a door ajar, leading into what looked like a grand parlor. I made my way toward it, the muted glow from a stained glass window casting jeweled colors over faded rugs and cracked wood. Just as I reached the door, a faint creak echoed from above, and I froze, my heart leaping in my chest.

"Is someone there?" My voice, brittle and small, sounded strange in the quiet. Silence answered, heavy and almost smug. It was as though the house was watching me, assessing, as if weighing my worth.

Shaking off the feeling, I forced myself to take a step into the parlor. The room was cold, and the weight of disuse hung over everything, from the dust-veiled piano in the corner to the forgotten portraits on the walls. Each face seemed to watch me, their eyes a bit too lifelike, their expressions trapped somewhere between boredom and disdain. One painting in particular caught my eye—a woman in a deep emerald gown, her lips curved in a faint, mocking smile, her eyes flickering with a knowing glint. She looked like she could tell secrets, ones meant to be kept.

"Who were you?" I whispered, as if the canvas could answer. But the figure just stared back, her painted gaze unyielding, daring me to find out for myself.

As I moved farther into the room, a faint breeze brushed against my cheek, stirring the edges of the musty drapes, though there were no open windows. The scent of lavender—fresh, startlingly real—wafted through the air, so out of place it was almost jarring. It was the same scent my grandmother used to wear, a fragrance that felt like a memory half-forgotten, clawing its way back to me in this strange, forgotten house.

Another creak from the hall snapped me back to the present. My pulse quickened, and I spun around, half-expecting to see someone—or something—looming in the doorway. But the hall was empty, the silence pressing in again. There was no one there. I tried to convince myself it was just the old wood settling, but deep down, I knew better. The house had its own way of speaking.

I exhaled, letting go of the tension that had twisted my shoulders into knots. Just an old house, I reminded myself, nothing to be afraid of. But as I turned back toward the room, a voice cut through the silence—soft, barely a whisper, yet unmistakably close.

"Well, are you staying or running off, darling?"

I froze, my heart hammering so hard it felt like it would leap right out of my chest. I whipped around, scanning the room, but there was no one. Just the portraits, the piano, and the drapes still whispering in the phantom breeze.

"Who's there?" My voice came out shakier than I'd have liked, but I couldn't help it.

A laugh, rich and sardonic, echoed around me, seeming to come from every shadow at once. It was a voice like honey poured over gravel, smooth but edged with something sharp, something that promised secrets I might not want to know.

"Oh, come now," the voice drawled. "You didn't think you'd be alone here, did you? That would be far too kind of me."

It took every ounce of courage I had not to bolt. I squared my shoulders, trying to muster some semblance of bravery.

"I don't know who—or what—you are, but this house doesn't scare me."

A snort echoed through the room, the sound somehow managing to be both amused and incredulous.

"Doesn't scare you?" The voice sounded almost delighted now. "Oh, darling, I do hope you're here for a good time, then. Because I assure you, this house is going to take everything you think you know about fear and turn it on its head."

My palms began to sweat as I looked around, scanning every inch of the room, searching for the source. But the voice seemed to move, dancing from corner to corner, a phantom presence with a laugh that brushed against my skin like a ghost's fingers.

And then, just as quickly as it had come, the voice was gone, leaving behind only silence and a gnawing curiosity that I couldn't shake. I took a shaky breath, the room settling back into stillness, the shadows once again draped over the furniture like shrouds. The air was thick with anticipation, as though the house itself were waiting, daring me to continue.

The air was dense and still, pressing in like the walls themselves were breathing, subtly shifting with each silent inhale. I took another hesitant step, trying to shake off the prickling at the back of my neck. The house, or whatever presence was within it, had settled back into that thick silence, though I could still feel the aftermath of that voice winding its way through my thoughts. It clung to me, tugging at the corners of my mind like a tune you can't quite place.

I moved farther into the room, fingers brushing over the dust-laden surfaces. Every step felt like a negotiation, a silent agreement between me and this house to move without disturbing whatever lay dormant. The low evening light filtered through the stained glass, casting colors that felt almost alive. They painted strange, spectral patterns across the walls, and as I stood in the midst of it, I felt like I'd stepped into some strange, otherworldly dance hall, like a guest to a party that had ended long ago but still lingered in spirit.

A cough behind me made me jump, and I whirled around, clutching my suitcase like a lifeline. There, standing in the doorway, was a man—a real, actual human, though he looked only marginally less ghostly than the portraits lining the walls. He was tall, his face framed by unruly dark curls, and his clothes had the slight disarray of someone who'd been caught by surprise. I could tell by the faintly amused quirk of his mouth that he was no stranger to the peculiarities of this house.

"You must be the latest unfortunate soul lured in by that ridiculous dare," he said, his voice low and smooth, with a trace of something unplaceable—an accent, perhaps, or just the remnants of sarcasm barely hidden. He had a look of someone who found the world amusing in all its absurdity.

I raised an eyebrow, doing my best to seem unruffled. "It was hardly a 'lure,'" I replied, my voice firm despite the quiver threatening to sneak in. "More like... a friendly suggestion that I decided to take seriously."

"Is that what they're calling dares these days?" he asked, stepping into the room. His gaze flicked from my face to the suitcase still clutched in my hand, and he gave a soft chuckle that held a faint edge of pity. "Do you even know what you're getting yourself into?"

"Oh, please," I scoffed, though the feigned bravado sounded thin even to my own ears. "It's just an old house. Dusty, sure. Maybe a bit drafty. But hardly the set of a horror movie." I tried to sound casual, as if my heart weren't pounding against my ribs.

He gave me a knowing look, the kind of look one gives a child who insists the shadows hold no monsters. "Old house," he murmured, his tone laced with irony. "Yes, let's call it that."

He extended his hand, his eyes narrowing in what I could only describe as polite curiosity. "Nicholas," he said. "I'd say it's a pleasure, but I think we both know that would be a lie."

I took his hand, surprised by the warmth and solidity of his grip. "Nice to meet you, Nicholas. I'm Elise. And I wouldn't worry about politeness," I replied, finding a flicker of confidence. "We both know neither of us is here for pleasantries."

Nicholas's gaze sharpened, his eyes holding mine a beat too long before he released my hand. "A realist, are you?" he asked, his tone light but probing.

"Just practical," I replied, though I could feel my pulse thrumming. "So what are you doing here, anyway? Do you make it a habit to skulk around in haunted mansions?"

"Skulk?" He raised an eyebrow, a faint smile tugging at his lips. "I prefer to think of it as... studying. This house has a certain charm, wouldn't you agree? A certain... character."

I bit back a laugh. "That's one way to put it. Though I'd wager most people would call it 'creepy' or 'possibly cursed.'"

"Ah, but that's the beauty of it," he replied, crossing the room with an ease that made him look right at home amidst the dust and shadows. "Not everyone appreciates the allure of a house like this. The quiet, the sense of mystery. It's a rare soul who doesn't immediately turn tail and run."

"Good to know I'm a rare soul," I said, forcing my voice to stay steady. "Though I can't say the appeal is exactly overwhelming so far."

Nicholas laughed, a soft, rich sound that reverberated in the quiet room. "Give it time, Elise. This place has a way of revealing itself, bit by bit. The trick is to listen closely. The house speaks, you know. If you're patient enough."

I shivered, though I tried to hide it. "And what exactly is it saying right now?"

"Wouldn't you like to know?" he murmured, his voice dropping as he leaned just slightly closer. "Let's just say it's noticed you." His gaze flicked to the portrait over my shoulder, the woman in the emerald gown, her eyes watchful and knowing.

"Are you going to keep talking in riddles all night, or do I actually get a straight answer out of you?" I challenged, trying to ignore the goosebumps prickling my skin.

He grinned, looking both infuriatingly amused and faintly impressed. "You're braver than you look. But maybe that's why you're here." He moved past me, brushing a faint trail of dust from the piano as he did. "Come on, then. Let me show you the rest of this charming, potentially cursed mansion. Since you're not one for running away."

I hesitated, glancing back at the door, at the rapidly darkening sky outside. But curiosity won over caution, and I found myself following him, suitcase and all, as he led me through the winding halls. The rooms seemed to shift in the dim light, their features distorted, familiar yet unsettling.

We moved through a library filled with books whose spines were faded with age, a dining room where the chandelier hung at a slight tilt, catching the light in strange ways, and finally to a grand ballroom, its floorboards polished but worn, the echoes of old music clinging to the silence like smoke.

Nicholas stopped in the center of the room, his gaze sweeping over it with a strange mixture of reverence and regret. "This house isn't just old," he said, almost to himself. "It remembers things. Things most people would rather forget."

I studied his profile, catching the faintest trace of something guarded, almost vulnerable, beneath his cool composure. "You speak as if you know that firsthand."

His gaze flicked to me, sharp and assessing. "Perhaps I do," he said softly, his voice barely a whisper. "Perhaps we all have things we'd prefer remain buried."

A chill crept over me as his words sank in, but before I could respond, a low creak sounded from somewhere above us, like the groan of an old hinge or the distant footfall of someone—or something—that shouldn't be there.

The creak overhead lingered, stretching the silence like a taut wire waiting to snap. I felt a faint prickle at the base of my neck, the kind of feeling that told you someone—or something—was standing just out of sight, watching. But when I looked at Nicholas, he was still, his face impassive yet somehow tense, as though he, too, had heard it but was pretending otherwise.

He offered me a wry smile, one that didn't reach his eyes. "The house likes to make itself known," he murmured. "Especially to those who aren't used to listening."

I forced a laugh, the sound hollow in the vast, empty room. "Well, I can hear it just fine. I think it's trying to tell me this was all a very bad idea."

"Oh, it absolutely was," he replied, amusement flickering back into his expression. "But you're here now. Leaving without understanding what you've started would be a shame, wouldn't it?"

The words hovered, their weight pressing down on me, daring me to argue. But I couldn't seem to summon a single reasonable objection, not with him standing there looking so infuriatingly calm, like he'd seen and heard worse than this mansion's creaks and whispers. I could feel his gaze settle on me, studying my expression like he was looking for something, and for a strange, unguarded moment, I felt like he could read every thought that crossed my mind. Every fear.

He turned, gesturing for me to follow. "Come on. There's a spot upstairs I think you'll appreciate. Consider it part of the... initiation."

I hesitated, glancing back at the door, but his look held a challenge, one that clawed at my pride. Besides, I was hardly about to admit that I was nervous. So I squared my shoulders, willing myself not to feel every creak of the floorboards as an omen, and followed him out of the ballroom and up the winding staircase. As we ascended, the house grew darker, the light from below slipping away until it felt like we were moving through a deep, murky shadow, each step an act of blind faith.

Nicholas stopped at a door at the end of the hallway, a heavy, dark wood that looked somehow older than the rest of the house. He placed his hand on the doorknob, looking back at me, a small smirk on his face as if daring me to guess what lay behind it.

"Ready?"

I nodded, even though every instinct screamed that I should be anything but ready.

The door creaked open, revealing a small, dim room filled with the faint scent of wood smoke and something faintly floral. The walls were lined with shelves, each one cluttered with an odd assortment of objects—a tarnished silver mirror, a tiny glass vial filled with an iridescent blue liquid, an old-fashioned pocket watch, its hands frozen at midnight. It was a collection of strange artifacts, each more intriguing and peculiar than the last.

"What is all this?" I breathed, moving closer to a delicate lace glove lying atop a small wooden box. It was strange, almost beautiful, in a sad, forgotten way.

"Memories," Nicholas replied, his voice soft. "Or at least, that's what they feel like. Things people leave behind, remnants of their time here. Each one holds... something."

"Something?" I raised an eyebrow, though I couldn't help the curiosity gnawing at me. "You mean like ghosts?"

He tilted his head, a faint smile teasing at his lips. "Not quite. More like... echoes. Pieces of a story that never fully left."

I reached out, my fingers brushing the lace glove, half-expecting it to feel icy, but it was warm, almost pulsing beneath my touch. An odd sensation tingled up my arm, a whisper of something half-formed—a laugh, a soft voice, the faint scent of lavender. Startled, I jerked my hand back.

Nicholas chuckled. "Sensitive, aren't you?"

I shot him a glare. "And you're awfully smug for someone who lives in a house filled with 'echoes.'"

"Someone has to appreciate it," he replied, unperturbed. "If you can't learn to listen to the past, you'll never really understand a place like this."

I ignored him, drawn instead to the pocket watch. It lay open, the unmoving hands pointed sharply at midnight. I picked it up, feeling the cold metal against my palm, and for a fleeting second, the world shifted. I was no longer in the dim, dusty room but in a brighter place, the sound of laughter echoing in my ears, a woman's voice soft but urgent, saying a name I couldn't quite catch.

I blinked, and the room snapped back into focus, the vision fading, but the echo of that voice lingered, settling into the air like a ghostly sigh.

"Did you...?" I began, looking up at Nicholas, but his face was impassive, as if he'd seen it all before. Maybe he had.

"You're not the first to feel it," he said, as if reading my thoughts. "And you won't be the last. This place has a way of opening itself to those who dare look."

I dropped the watch, letting it fall back onto the shelf with a soft clink. "Well, it's certainly full of surprises."

"Surprises are just the beginning," he murmured, his gaze distant as if he, too, was seeing something I couldn't. "This house has stories in every corner, every shadow. Most of them... aren't finished."

A chill ran down my spine, and for once, I didn't try to shake it off. There was something about the way he spoke, the certainty in his voice, that made me feel as though I was only just scratching the surface of whatever lay hidden here.

Just then, a loud crash sounded from somewhere below us, reverberating through the walls with a force that made the shelves rattle. My heart jumped, and I looked at Nicholas, but his expression remained oddly calm.

"Stay here," he said, his tone firm, commanding. Before I could respond, he'd slipped through the door and down the stairs, leaving me alone in the strange, dark room with nothing but the ticking silence for company.

I swallowed, suddenly feeling the weight of the shadows pressing in, thick and watchful. The air felt colder, as if whatever warmth had existed in this room was leaking away, leaving me surrounded by something... hungry.

As I glanced back at the pocket watch, its hands still frozen, a strange thought prickled at the back of my mind. What if these echoes weren't just memories? What if they were something far more aware, something that could reach out to those who dared touch them?

The glove on the shelf seemed to twitch, just the tiniest movement, but enough to send a shiver down my spine. I backed away, inching toward the door, a sense of dread pooling in my stomach. But as I reached the doorway, something cold wrapped around my wrist, holding me in place.

I gasped, looking down to see... nothing. Just the faint impression of fingers, pressing into my skin like a whisper turned physical.

My heart hammered as I struggled to pull away, but the grip only tightened, a silent, invisible force holding me in place, relentless and unyielding.

Chapter 2: Shadows of a Stranger

He was there again, as if summoned by some forbidden part of my soul. The night was thick with shadows, dancing across the walls, flickering with the golden light from the fireplace. The man was tall, his outline strong yet softened by a kind of melancholy grace, a silhouette woven from shadows and longing. He moved toward me, the light catching his eyes—a shade of blue so deep it was almost violet. I knew those eyes, knew them as surely as I knew my own heartbeat, though I'd never seen them in daylight. They held stories, secrets that twisted in my gut like half-remembered dreams, and as he extended his hand toward me, I felt an ache—a yearning that seemed to belong not only to me, but to the very air we shared.

I tried to speak, to demand answers, but my throat closed, the words tangled in fear and fascination. He pressed a finger to his lips, a silent command, and suddenly, my hand was in his, my fingers lost in his cool grasp. He guided me forward, his touch steady, grounding. I couldn't resist, couldn't even fathom wanting to. We moved in a rhythm only we knew, an ancient dance that pulled me under its spell, coaxing out secrets I didn't know I had. His eyes held me, unwavering, and as we spun in the quiet, an inexplicable peace wrapped around us. But just as I felt him soften, felt some unspoken promise rise between us, his grip slackened, his form melting back into the darkness, leaving me gasping and alone as I reached out to catch hold of him.

Morning was relentless, dragging me from the remnants of sleep with an unapologetic brightness that felt like betrayal. I rubbed my eyes, trying to shake the haunting vision, but fragments of the night clung to me like mist. There was a strange, lingering scent on my skin—something woodsy, touched with spice and smoke. Impossible, of course, just as the man himself was impossible. And yet, as I moved about my room, each footstep felt like an intrusion, as though I were a trespasser in my own space. I glanced around, half expecting him to materialize out of thin air, laughing at my foolishness. But all I found was silence, a stillness that was somehow too heavy.

Determined to shake off the feeling, I pulled on a shawl and made my way to the library, hoping that burying myself in the solace of well-worn pages would quiet my thoughts. The room was one of my favorites, lined wall-to-wall with books in every shade of leather, their spines polished by years of eager hands. The high ceilings and intricate moldings had always lent it a dignified charm, a timelessness that felt grounding. But today, something was different. A draft brushed my cheek, the air somehow charged, like the hush before a storm.

And then, there it was again—that faint trace of cologne, lingering in the air, impossible to ignore. It was warm, earthy, but with a bite of something dark, something forbidden. I froze, my heart pounding so loudly it nearly drowned out the silence. My mind raced, trying to conjure a reasonable explanation, but each rational thought crumbled as I saw a flash of movement in the corner of my eye.

In the shadowed recess between two shelves, he stood, solid and present, his gaze locked on mine with an intensity that stole my breath. The fear that should have seized me was strangely absent; instead, a thrill rippled through me, a pulse of recognition that bordered on madness.

"I don't understand," I whispered, my voice barely audible even to myself.

He tilted his head, a slight smile pulling at his lips, as if he were amused by my confusion. Then he took a step forward, and another, until he was close enough that I could feel the warmth radiating from him, close enough that I could see the fine lines etched into his skin—a detail too vivid for any dream.

"You've been searching," he said softly, his voice carrying a warmth that was both soothing and unnervingly familiar. "Even if you don't know it yet."

My chest tightened, the unspoken truth of his words wrapping around me, drawing me closer. "Searching for what?" I managed to ask, my voice a rough whisper.

"For yourself." His answer hung in the air, as if it were a secret shared in the quiet stillness between breaths. His eyes never wavered, each word a quiet conviction that stirred something buried within me, something I had long ignored.

I opened my mouth to argue, to tell him he was mistaken, but the words dissolved on my tongue. In that instant, a fragment of a memory surfaced—foggy and distant, like a faded photograph left too long in the sun. I remembered standing alone, a vast sky above me, stars scattered like spilled sugar, and a feeling of weightlessness, of endless possibility. I remembered reaching out, calling for...someone. Something. An answer.

Before I could grasp it fully, the memory slipped away, leaving only a hollow ache in its place. The man reached up, his fingers grazing my cheek, and the gesture was so tender, so achingly familiar, that I shivered. He leaned closer, his breath warm against my skin.

"You're close," he murmured, his voice a low whisper that held both promise and warning. "But you must keep going."

And just as quickly as he had appeared, he withdrew, his hand slipping from my cheek, his form blending into the shadows, dissolving as if he'd never been there at all. I was left alone in the library, my skin tingling where he'd touched me, my pulse racing with the thrill of his words—a promise I didn't yet understand.

I stood there for a long time, unmoving, as if the very air might hold some clue, some piece of the puzzle I was now helplessly caught in. Finally, I pulled myself from the trance, clutching at reality, telling myself it was only a dream. But even as I forced myself back into the routines of the day, a part of me lingered in that shadowed library, listening, waiting, and hoping for his return.

I found myself lingering in the study, the shadows pooling under the dim glow of the desk lamp. The room felt oddly close, as if it held its breath, waiting. It was absurd, truly, this sensation of being haunted by a man who—surely—did not exist. And yet, here I was, clutching my shawl around me as though that would protect me from my own mind. But even the shawl, wooly and familiar, offered no comfort. Every time I thought of those eyes—so familiar, yet utterly foreign—I felt a peculiar tightening in my chest, a pull I couldn't define or dismiss.

"Well, this is ridiculous," I muttered to myself, though the silence was somehow less comforting than it should have been. There was no answer, of course. Not even the usual creaks and groans of an old house settling in the night. Just silence. A heavy, echoing silence that settled around me like a smothering blanket. The shadows seemed to stretch, curling into shapes that hinted at something hidden, something that might have a heartbeat of its own.

A noise from the hallway—faint, almost too faint to notice, yet enough to prick every nerve in my body into a sharp, thrilling alertness. I held my breath, straining to hear, to pick apart the familiar sounds from the unfamiliar ones. It was a soft footstep, or perhaps just the shuffling of air. But it was there. And it was close.

"Is anyone there?" I called out, hoping my voice held more authority than my shaking hands did.

No answer. But I could feel it again—that sense of presence, close enough to feel but impossible to see. I pressed my back against the wall, scanning the room, searching for some kind of explanation, though what sort of explanation would fit was beyond me. Perhaps a mouse? But no mouse had ever left a trail of cologne or filled my dreams with strange visions.

I stepped into the hallway, half-expecting to see nothing, half-prepared to confront whoever—or whatever—had taken up residence in my home. But it was empty, just as I knew it would be. And yet, that unmistakable scent lingered in the air, intoxicating, drawing me forward, teasing me. It was a game, I realized, a slow unraveling of mystery designed to draw me in inch by inch. And heaven help me, I was following, spellbound and unable to stop myself.

I continued down the hallway, the house quiet, the wooden floors creaking beneath my bare feet. The air grew colder the further I went, a chill that seemed to seep into my skin and settle in my bones. A strange flicker of movement caught my eye from the drawing room—a shadow, soft and ghostly, as if something or someone was watching me from just beyond the edge of the doorway.

"Who are you?" I demanded, my voice little more than a whisper.

The silence was maddening. And then, a soft chuckle, low and rich, carried from the shadows, sending a thrill through me. There was no form, no face to attach to the sound—just that dark, velvet voice that seemed to come from nowhere and everywhere all at once.

"Do you really want to know?" he asked, his tone as smooth as silk, as dangerous as broken glass.

I swallowed hard, the question twisting inside me like a dare. Did I want to know? Or was this some strange, twisted game, one that would leave me lost, wandering in my own memories? But curiosity was a fierce thing, gnawing away at my hesitation until I found myself nodding.

"Yes," I whispered, surprised by the conviction in my voice.

A pause, long enough for me to feel the weight of it pressing down on me, filling the room like smoke. And then he was there, stepping forward from the darkness, his face half-shadowed, half-lit by the faint glow of the drawing room lamps. He was... achingly familiar. The lines of his face, the tilt of his mouth, the intensity in his eyes—everything about him felt like it belonged in some hidden, forbidden part of my mind.

"I'm only a memory," he said softly, his gaze never wavering from mine. "A piece of something you left behind."

"That's impossible," I whispered, though even as I said it, I felt the truth of his words burrowing into my skin, rooting itself in my mind. "I would remember you."

He smiled, a wry, almost bitter smile that made my heart ache in a way I couldn't quite understand. "Would you? Memories have a way of slipping away when they're too painful to keep. And you..." His gaze dropped, his voice thick with something I couldn't name. "You were always good at forgetting."

My breath caught, my mind spinning as I tried to grasp what he was saying, to find some anchor in the midst of the dizzying storm of emotions his words had stirred up. "What does that mean?" I demanded, my voice sharp, desperate.

He looked at me for a long moment, his expression unreadable. And then he took a step back, his form blurring, fading into the shadows once more. "It means that some things can't be forgotten," he said softly, his voice lingering in the air long after he'd disappeared.

I stood there, alone, his words echoing in my mind, twisting around my heart like a thorny vine. A piece of something you left behind. I couldn't shake the feeling that he was right—that there was something I had buried, something I had chosen to forget. And now, whatever it was, it was rising to the surface, clawing its way back into my life, refusing to be ignored.

That night, I lay in bed, staring up at the ceiling, my mind too restless for sleep. The shadows seemed to dance across the walls, shifting and changing, teasing me with half-formed memories and flashes of faces I couldn't quite place. I closed my eyes, forcing myself to breathe, to find some semblance of calm.

But sleep didn't come easily. My dreams were tangled, a maze of twisted corridors and flickering lights, each turn leading me deeper into a memory I couldn't quite grasp. And in the midst of it all, he was there, watching, waiting, his gaze full of a sadness that made my heart ache even as it sent a thrill of terror through me.

When I woke, the room was bathed in the first light of dawn, pale and cold against the shadows that lingered in the corners. I felt hollow, as if some part of me had been peeled away, leaving me raw and exposed. I pulled the blanket tighter around me, the memory of his touch still lingering on my skin, warm and solid, too real to be a dream.

And as I lay there, caught between sleep and wakefulness, I knew one thing with a certainty that terrified me. Whoever he was, whatever he was, he wasn't just a figment of my imagination. He was real. And he was here, waiting for me to remember.

That evening, a storm swept over the house, thickening the air with the scent of rain and damp earth. Lightning flashed beyond the windows, casting wild shadows across the walls, and with each thunderous rumble, the walls seemed to close in a little tighter. I told myself it was just the storm rattling my nerves, that this was simply another evening. But as I crossed the hallway, drawn inexplicably toward the drawing room, I knew I was lying to myself.

The room was dim, filled with an odd glow from the fireplace, a fire I hadn't lit. The flames danced, casting flickering orange light on the high ceiling, sending shadows sprawling across the plush armchairs and the faint outlines of paintings I rarely paid attention to. And there, in the midst of it all, he stood—no longer a faint impression of a man, but clear and solid, his gaze as piercing as the strike of lightning outside.

"Of all the places I thought I'd find you," he said, his voice soft yet filling every corner of the room, "this isn't one of them."

I felt a flush creep up my neck, as if I'd been caught somewhere I shouldn't be. "Excuse me?" I managed, surprised by the bite in my voice. "You're the one haunting me, remember?"

He tilted his head, a slight smirk playing at the corner of his mouth. "Am I?" he mused, as though I were the unreasonable one. "Or maybe you're haunting me."

I opened my mouth to retort, but the words tangled in my throat. Haunting him? The very idea seemed absurd. "How can I be haunting you when you're the one appearing out of thin air?"

He took a step forward, his eyes catching the firelight, making them gleam with an intensity that felt almost predatory. "You called me, remember? Whether you meant to or not, you reached out, searching."

A cold trickle of recognition ran down my spine. I tried to push it away, to dismiss it as some foolish notion, but something in his gaze told me I couldn't. "Searching for what?"

"Yourself," he answered, his voice so steady, so certain, it sounded like the toll of a distant bell. "You've hidden so much of yourself, buried it under years of trying to be something else. And now," he paused, his gaze locked on mine, "it's all starting to unravel, isn't it?"

I clenched my fists, a surge of frustration welling up in me. "You don't know anything about me."

"Don't I?" he murmured, stepping even closer, until I could feel the heat radiating from him, warm and grounding, as if he were something real, something solid that I could hold on to. His voice dropped, softened, "Tell me you don't remember."

The challenge in his eyes was unmistakable, and a small, reluctant part of me knew what he meant. But I pushed it down, the way I'd pushed down so many other things. I'd spent years carefully crafting myself into someone practical, sensible—someone who didn't believe in dreams or ghosts or hidden pieces of lost memory. I couldn't let one unsettling figure in the dark tear that all apart.

He watched me, waiting, as though he could see each thought flitting across my mind. And then, slowly, he reached out, his fingers brushing my cheek. His touch was startlingly warm, real in a way that jarred against every instinct I had. I felt a strange pull toward him, a faint tug that whispered of something I couldn't quite name.

"You're not real," I whispered, though my voice wavered, the words faltering in the thick silence that filled the room. "You're just...something I dreamed up."

A flicker of pain crossed his face, so swift I almost missed it, but it was there, real and raw, like an old wound suddenly reopened. "Oh, I'm real," he replied, his voice laced with a quiet intensity. "Real enough to haunt you, to pull you back to what you've forgotten. The question is, are you real enough to face it?"

A thousand questions tumbled through my mind, each one more tangled than the last, but I couldn't make myself ask a single one. Instead, I found myself holding his gaze, mesmerized by the sadness lurking there, as if he carried a burden I couldn't even begin to understand.

"What is it I've forgotten?" I asked, barely recognizing my own voice.

A ghost of a smile tugged at his lips, bitter and almost broken. "Everything, my dear. Everything."

And with that, he turned, his form fading into the shadows, leaving me standing alone, the chill of his absence like a blade cutting through the heat of the fire.

The storm outside raged on, but it was nothing compared to the storm churning within me. His words echoed in my mind, twisting and turning, as if they were alive, reshaping themselves with each beat of my heart. Everything. What did that even mean? What was there to forget?

I sank into the armchair, staring into the fire, my thoughts a tangled web of doubt and fear. His presence had felt so real, so unshakably solid, that it left a hollow ache in my chest. And that look in his eyes—a mixture of sorrow and tenderness that felt both foreign and painfully familiar—haunted me, curling around my thoughts like smoke.

A flicker of movement caught my attention, a soft rustling sound from the hallway. My pulse quickened, but I forced myself to stand, stepping out into the corridor. The shadows were thick, almost tangible, pressing in around me as I made my way down the hall, my heart pounding in my ears.

I turned the corner, my breath catching as I saw him standing there once again, his back to me, his form half-shrouded in darkness. He didn't move, didn't even turn as I approached, but I could feel his awareness of me, as if he'd been waiting all along.

"Why are you here?" I asked, my voice barely more than a whisper, thick with the weight of unspoken questions.

He was silent for a long moment, and then, finally, he turned, his gaze locking onto mine with a fierceness that stole my breath. "Because," he said softly, each word carrying the weight of something ancient and unyielding, "I'm the part of you that you can no longer hide from. And I won't rest until you remember."

The intensity in his eyes was unnerving, a spark that flickered and danced, as if something untamed lurked just beneath the surface. But before I could respond, before I could even take a step back, his hand shot out, clasping mine with a grip that was both gentle and unbreakable. The room seemed to spin, the walls blurring and fading, the shadows swirling around us in a dizzying whirlwind.

I felt myself falling, my vision narrowing as the world dissolved into darkness. And just as I was about to succumb, his voice echoed in my mind, a faint whisper that sent a shiver down my spine.

"Remember," he murmured, his words the last thing I heard before everything went black.

Chapter 3: The Portrait in the Parlor

The portrait's eyes followed me, an accusation, or perhaps an invitation; it was hard to tell in the wavering candlelight. Shadows danced along his face, cast by the flickering glow, as if he might blink at any moment, step out of that frame, and demand answers from me. I felt a chill run through me, a thrill almost, though I scolded myself for romanticizing the eerie charm of an old, abandoned house. Rationality had been my refuge for as long as I could remember—clear-cut facts and hard truths kept me grounded. And yet, here I was, feeling the weight of something I couldn't rationalize; this portrait seemed to hold an answer I was desperate to find.

The parlor itself seemed intent on keeping secrets, the air thick with the scent of aged wood and something earthy that clung to the dust motes swirling in the weak light. Dark, heavy furniture surrounded me like solemn guardians of this relic from another life. This was the only room left untouched by the renovations I'd seen on the tour, kept in some odd state of reverence. Perhaps out of respect—or fear? The housekeeper had given a sharp little warning when she saw my eyes lingering on the closed door to this room. "No one goes in there," she'd said, with a tone that almost dared me to break her rule. And now, here I was, curiosity winning over caution.

There was something about the man in the portrait, something unyielding in his expression. He wasn't handsome, exactly—not in a traditional sense, at least. His face was sharp, angular, with a storm in his dark eyes, a recklessness that mirrored the parts of me I had spent years tempering. I couldn't pinpoint why his image unnerved me. All I knew was that I'd seen those eyes before, in dreams that lingered like smoke, slipping away each morning as I woke, leaving behind a faint impression, like the memory of a melody I couldn't quite place. I reached out, fingertips brushing the frame, and for a moment, it felt warm, as if the wood had absorbed years of warmth and was releasing it just for me. Absurd, I know, but in that moment, I couldn't shake the feeling that I wasn't alone.

A loud creak from the hallway snapped me back to my senses, and I dropped my hand, heart hammering. I wasn't supposed to be here. I'd slipped from my room when sleep refused to claim me, driven by something unnamed, some pull stronger than reason or caution. The mansion was quiet, the kind of quiet that only old, massive houses know, filled with secrets and long-gone lives. The walls here had seen more than I could imagine, and yet, as I backed away from the portrait, I felt a strange resistance, as though leaving meant abandoning something important, something waiting just out of reach. My breath caught as I turned to leave. I heard a faint whisper, too quiet to make out, and before I could talk myself out of it, I bolted down the hall, retreating to the safety of my room, pulling the door shut behind me as if it might keep whatever lurked in the shadows at bay.

Back in my room, I tried to slow my breathing, lighting the small lamp on the bedside table as if it might chase away the sense of foreboding lingering over me. I slipped into bed, telling myself that what I'd felt was nothing more than an overactive imagination, too many hours spent in the isolation of this vast estate. But the mystery of the portrait gnawed at me, its image burned into my mind. I closed my eyes, hoping that the soft warmth of the blankets might lull me to sleep, but every time I drifted off, there he was, waiting in the darkness of my dreams, his eyes locked onto mine with an intensity that left me breathless.

I awoke before dawn, the faint light of early morning casting pale, hesitant shadows across the room. There was no escaping it now—I had to know who he was. Still, it would take subtlety, something that had never come easily to me. I'd arrived as the new caretaker, tasked with restoring the gardens, fixing the property's tarnished charm in time for the tourist season. Hardly a job that warranted prying into the family's dusty secrets. But it wasn't just curiosity, I told myself. I had to make sure this place was, well...safe.

I hurried to dress, tugging on a coat to ward off the chill as I made my way downstairs. I was greeted by the skeptical eyes of Mrs. Haverton, the housekeeper. She was the only one left in this house older than the wood beams themselves, her sharp gaze assessing as she caught sight of me. "You're up early," she noted, her voice edged with a subtle warning. If she had even the faintest inkling that I'd been in the parlor, she didn't let on.

"Couldn't sleep," I replied, keeping my tone light, innocent. "The house has...an energy, doesn't it?" I gave a soft, unassuming laugh, hoping to draw her out without giving myself away. She eyed me for a moment longer than I liked, her lips pressing into a thin line before she sighed, shaking her head.

"That's what they all say, miss. Always too curious for their own good," she muttered, a strange hint of resignation in her tone. For a moment, I thought she might go on, but she merely busied herself with a tray of cups, her silence heavy with what she wasn't saying. The familiar frustration of running headfirst into a wall of unspoken truths gnawed at me, but I managed to hold my tongue, giving her a polite nod before turning toward the garden door. But before I could step outside, her voice stopped me.

"They say," she began, her tone low and conspiratorial, "that he was a man of fire, of passion. Too much for this house, for this family. They buried his memory like they buried him, deep and out of reach." She paused, a faint glimmer of something in her eyes as she looked at me. "Be careful, miss. This place doesn't like people digging too deep." And with that, she turned back to her work, leaving me standing there, the morning light creeping in, casting long shadows that only deepened the mystery I'd stumbled into.

The chill of dawn settled over the garden, casting an eerie calm over the statues and stone benches lined up like silent sentries. Mist clung low to the ground, and the flowers I'd spent hours tending felt strangely surreal in the muted light, their colors softened to pale ghosts of themselves. Every leaf and petal seemed to hold its breath, as if waiting for something—or someone. I shivered, pulling my coat tighter as I surveyed the sprawling estate, wondering what secrets lay just beneath the surface.

It was easy to imagine the house as a living thing, one that watched and whispered, silently tracking my every move. The windows glinted, glancing down at me like narrowed eyes. As I walked, I couldn't shake the feeling that I was being observed—not just by the ever-watchful Mrs. Haverton but by the very walls themselves. It was as though the house held memories in its bones, memories it had no intention of surrendering easily.

As the morning stretched on, I found myself distracted, torn between my duties and the relentless pull back to the parlor. The face in that portrait haunted me, slipping into my thoughts no matter how hard I tried to focus on the tasks at hand. I was trimming the hedges, and every snip of the shears seemed to echo louder than it should have, a rhythmic, insistent beat that matched the pulse of questions in my mind. Who was he? And why did I feel as if some part of him was waiting for me to remember?

"Daydreaming again, are we?" A voice interrupted my thoughts, startling me so badly I nearly snipped through a rosebud. I looked up to find James, the gardener's assistant, grinning at me with that irritatingly knowing smile of his. He was one of those effortlessly charming types, the kind who assumed everyone must be dying to hear his latest adventure. But today, I wasn't in the mood for his antics.

"Just...thinking," I replied coolly, trying to shake the lingering tension from my shoulders.

"Dangerous pastime, that," he teased, leaning against the garden wall, twirling a bit of twine between his fingers. "Thinking's the last thing you want to do around here. It only leads to trouble."

"Oh? And you're the expert on trouble, are you?" I shot back, unable to resist a smirk. "Enlighten me."

He chuckled, clearly enjoying himself. "Oh, I know my fair share. But it's different here. There's a reason people avoid the west wing after dark. And that parlor you were poking around in last night? Best not to let Mrs. Haverton catch wind of it, or she'll have your head faster than you can say 'ghost stories.'"

I stiffened. "How did you know I was in the parlor?"

He shrugged, an infuriatingly casual gesture that only made me more suspicious. "This house has eyes, doesn't it? Windows everywhere. Walls that carry sound like a rumor. And besides, you're not the first person drawn to that portrait. They say he was quite the charmer, back in his day."

The air between us grew thick with unspoken things, and for a moment, I felt as though I'd wandered into one of those old tales where curious girls find themselves caught in webs spun long before they were born. "What do you know about him?" I asked, careful to keep my voice light, as if I were merely making polite conversation.

James glanced over his shoulder as if to ensure no one else was listening, then leaned in, his voice dropping to a conspiratorial whisper. "They call him the Lost Lord," he said, eyes gleaming with mischief. "Said he had a wild streak, couldn't be tamed. The family tried to erase his memory, scrubbed him right out of the history books. But some memories aren't so easy to bury."

I frowned, unsure whether to believe him or to dismiss it as one of his tall tales. "So, what happened to him?"

James shrugged, the glimmer of a smirk lurking at the corner of his mouth. "Depends on who you ask. Some say he disappeared in the night, never to be seen again. Others claim he haunts the house, waiting for something...or someone."

I let out a laugh, more out of nervousness than amusement. "You don't really believe that, do you?"

"Believe it?" He raised an eyebrow, looking far too pleased with himself. "No. But I'd be careful if I were you. It's easy to get caught up in things you don't understand, especially when they're as old as this place. The Lost Lord has a way of weaving people into his story."

With that, he sauntered off, leaving me to stare after him, the weight of his words settling heavily in the pit of my stomach. As much as I wanted to dismiss it as nonsense, something in his tone—and the way he'd looked at me, almost as if he pitied me—left me unsettled.

By the time I finished my work, the sun had climbed higher, casting the estate in a bright, indifferent light that felt oddly at odds with the shadowy whispers lingering in my mind. I couldn't resist one last glance at the west wing as I made my way back inside, half-expecting to see some sign of the Lost Lord staring back at me. But all that greeted me was the steady creak of floorboards as I walked down the hall, each step leading me closer to the truth I was beginning to fear as much as I craved.

I found Mrs. Haverton in the sitting room, her eyes narrowing as I approached, as if she could read the questions I hadn't yet asked. "Something I can help you with?" she asked, her voice as crisp and unyielding as the starched collar of her blouse.

I hesitated, choosing my words carefully. "I couldn't help but notice the portrait in the parlor," I began, watching her reaction closely. "It's...striking."

Her gaze turned colder, a flicker of disapproval passing over her face. "Best not to dwell on that. The past is best left where it belongs."

"Does that apply to all of us?" I asked, a hint of defiance slipping into my tone. "Or just those who've been forgotten?"

She straightened, her hands smoothing her apron as she met my gaze with a look so sharp it could cut glass. "The family has its reasons. Not all history is meant to be remembered. Some things are forgotten for a purpose."

Her words were like a lock closing, a barrier placed firmly between me and the secrets lurking within these walls. But I'd come too far to be dismissed so easily. "I don't think he wants to be forgotten," I said quietly, watching her reaction.

For a moment, she was still, her expression unreadable. Then, without a word, she turned and walked away, leaving me standing there, heart racing with the certainty that I'd brushed against something forbidden, something that had lain hidden for far too long. And as her footsteps faded, I felt it again—that pull, the undeniable sense that the Lost Lord's story was far from over...and that somehow, I was now part of it.

The air in the parlor was thick, heavy as if it had absorbed too many secrets, too many whispered words left hanging in the shadows. I could feel the pull of the portrait, calling me back into its haunting gaze, daring me to face whatever lay hidden within those dark, penetrating eyes. But this time, as I stood alone in the early evening hush, the quiet stretched, pressing against my skin with a weight I couldn't ignore.

With no one around to witness, I let my guard slip. I reached out to touch the edge of the frame, fingers brushing along the intricate, almost baroque carvings that lined the wood. Beneath the layer of dust, I could feel a peculiar warmth, like a pulse, and I jerked my hand back, my heart pounding at the odd sensation. It was almost as if the frame itself was alive, as though it had waited all these years for someone to come along and listen.

"Curious, isn't it?" A voice cut through the silence, and I jumped, my hand flying to my chest. I spun around to find James, his usual smirk replaced by an unsettlingly serious expression. He leaned against the doorframe, arms crossed, his eyes fixed on me with a mixture of amusement and something darker, something that made me wonder if he, too, had once felt the same pull. "Most people would've let it be by now, you know."

"Most people aren't me," I replied, struggling to regain my composure. "Besides, you can't deny there's something strange about him. It's like he's—"

"Calling to you?" James interrupted, his smirk returning, though it didn't reach his eyes. "Careful with that kind of talk. The last person who felt that way...well, let's just say they didn't stick around long."

He was teasing, but the words lodged in my mind, unsettling me more than I cared to admit. "Is that supposed to scare me off?" I asked, raising an eyebrow, trying to keep the tremor from my voice.

"Just a friendly warning," he replied, stepping into the room, his gaze flicking to the portrait. For a moment, his expression softened, almost as if he, too, felt some connection to the Lost Lord. But just as quickly, his usual nonchalance returned. "Though I can't say I blame you. There's something...magnetic about him, isn't there?"

I glanced back at the portrait, half expecting to see a new expression on the Lost Lord's face, some acknowledgment of our shared intrigue. But he remained as he was, silent, mysterious, a relic of a life that had been erased. I wondered if he had known what would become of him, if he'd sensed that his very existence would be scrubbed from the walls, reduced to a single, overlooked portrait in a forgotten room.

"He was a troublemaker," James said suddenly, as if reading my thoughts. "Or at least, that's what the rumors say. A wild one, they called him—reckless, impossible to control. Not exactly the kind of man you'd expect to find preserved in a place like this."

I crossed my arms, intrigued despite myself. "So, what did he do? Steal the family fortune? Break hearts? Or was it something darker?"

James chuckled, though there was a hardness to it. "All of the above, if you believe the stories. He was a bit of a renegade, from what I've gathered—never could play by the rules. And apparently, that didn't sit well with the family. Or with certain...members of the household."

I caught the hesitation in his voice, the way he glanced at the door as though checking for eavesdroppers. "You mean Mrs. Haverton," I guessed, watching his reaction closely.

His smile slipped. "She's been here a long time. Some say longer than any human should be. Knows things most people would rather forget. If anyone understands the mysteries of this place, it's her." He met my gaze, a silent warning lurking in his expression. "But you won't get much out of her. She's as tight-lipped as they come."

A low creak echoed through the hall, and we both froze, glancing toward the door. It was nothing but a house settling, I told myself. But the uneasy silence that followed made my skin prickle, as though the house itself was listening, waiting for us to say too much.

James straightened, his casual demeanor slipping. "Listen," he said, his voice low, urgent. "If you really want to understand him, you'll need more than just a few stories. There's a...a book, somewhere in the old library. It's hidden—locked away, actually. But it has everything the family tried to erase. His letters, his journals. It's like a blueprint of his life, every wild, rebellious thing he ever did."

I blinked, my heart racing. "And you're just telling me this now?"

He shrugged, giving me a lopsided grin. "I didn't think you were serious. Most people who poke around lose interest pretty quick. But you—you're stubborn. I can see it in your eyes. Same fire he had, probably."

"Flattery will get you nowhere," I shot back, though I felt a faint flush of pride, mingled with excitement. "So, how do I get this book?"

James hesitated, his gaze flicking toward the portrait as if weighing his answer. "There's a key," he said finally. "An old skeleton key, hidden somewhere in Mrs. Haverton's quarters. It's the only way to unlock the case that holds the book."

My stomach dropped at the thought of sneaking into Mrs. Haverton's quarters, her eagle-eyed gaze and sharp tongue flashing before me. "Are you suggesting I break into her room?"

He grinned, a wicked gleam in his eye. "I'm not suggesting anything. Just thought you might like to know. What you do with that information is up to you."

I opened my mouth to protest, but before I could form a response, a sudden gust of cold air swept through the room, extinguishing the candle on the mantle and plunging us into near darkness. I gasped, my skin prickling as a shiver ran down my spine. For a split second, I could have sworn I heard a faint whisper, an echo of words that melted into the shadows before I could grasp their meaning.

James shot me a wary glance, his bravado faltering. "I should go," he muttered, heading toward the door. "Just...be careful, all right? This house has a way of taking what it wants."

And then he was gone, leaving me alone with the portrait and the lingering chill that seeped into my bones. I stood in silence, my thoughts racing, a thousand possibilities swirling through my mind. The book. The key. The mystery of the Lost Lord and the secrets he had carried to his grave. I was on the cusp of something, something that felt dangerous and exhilarating all at once.

As I turned to leave, I heard it—a soft, barely audible sound, like the rustle of fabric, the faintest sigh of breath. I spun around, eyes scanning the shadows, half expecting to see a figure standing in the doorway. But the room was empty, silent, save for the ticking of the grandfather clock in the corner.

My pulse hammered in my ears, a frantic beat that seemed to grow louder with each passing second. And then, just as I began to convince myself that it was nothing, that my mind was playing tricks on me, I felt a hand on my shoulder, firm and unmistakably real.

I froze, heart pounding, every nerve on edge. I wanted to scream, to turn and face whoever—or whatever—had found me in the dark. But before I could summon the courage to move, a voice, low and familiar, whispered in my ear, sending a chill through me that rooted me to the spot.

"Some things aren't meant to be found."

Chapter 4: The Dance Beneath the Moonlight

The garden was a world apart from the house, a retreat of twisted vines and shadowed alcoves that seemed to lure secrets from every corner. It wasn't just the hum of crickets or the scent of night-blooming jasmine that made the place so intoxicating; it was as though each leaf and petal held its breath, suspended in anticipation. The air itself felt charged, heavy, as if holding back some secret waiting to break free. As I wandered further from the safety of the patio lights, the melody floating on the night breeze grew clearer, its lilting notes curling like fingers, beckoning me forward.

The music seemed to come from everywhere and nowhere all at once, an unseen orchestra playing just for me. It was achingly familiar, and yet I couldn't place it—a haunting tune that tugged at forgotten memories, luring me with its strange, bittersweet promise. The sound led me past the old oak, its branches stretching like skeletal arms in the moonlight, and over the dew-damp grass until I reached the edge of the lawn. There, framed by the ghostly glow of the moon, stood a figure so still, so silent, he might have been a part of the shadows themselves.

Tall and lean, he was dressed in clothes that seemed to shimmer between old-fashioned elegance and the dark, rebellious edge of something timeless. His face was partially obscured, yet I could make out the hint of a smirk on his lips, a glint of amusement in his eyes that flickered as he noticed my approach. His hand extended toward me, fingers open, palm up, an invitation I felt compelled to accept. My heart raced, each beat a question, every step toward him a choice I didn't fully understand.

His touch was warm, grounding in a way that both anchored and unsettled me. He said nothing, nor did I, as if words might shatter the delicate, almost ethereal silence binding us. The music continued to swell around us, and slowly, we began to move in a silent, graceful rhythm, our bodies turning and swaying beneath the stars. I wasn't sure where I ended, and he began, only that we were bound in a dance as old as time, as natural as breathing. The scent of the jasmine thickened, mingling with something warmer, more intimate—the faint, lingering aroma of sandalwood and cedar.

His gaze held mine, unwavering, as if he could see past the surface, through every carefully guarded piece of myself to the places I kept hidden even from me. There was a warmth in his eyes that promised understanding and a wildness that whispered of things just out of reach. His movements were effortless, every step precise, but unhurried, as though we had all the time in the world beneath the silver sky. I found myself losing track of time, my awareness shrinking down to the soft press of his hand, the steady beat of his heart against my palm.

And yet, an unease prickled at the edge of my mind, a reminder that something this perfect rarely lasts. I couldn't shake the feeling that this moment, this dance, was borrowed, a dream on the brink of breaking. My fingers tightened around his, and he smiled—a small, sad smile that left me wanting to demand answers I wasn't even sure existed.

In a motion almost imperceptible, his hand slipped from mine, our fingers parting like the last threads of a frayed rope. I blinked, and he was gone, leaving me in the middle of the garden, the music fading into the night air as though it had never been. The space around me felt emptier, the shadows deeper, the garden suddenly cold without his presence. I touched my fingers to my lips, as if I might catch some lingering trace of him, something real, but all I felt was my own skin, my own pulse beneath the surface.

I don't know how long I stood there, waiting for the impossible, for some sign that it had been real. The moon hung bright and indifferent, casting long shadows across the lawn, each one a reminder of the absence he left behind.

The night hung heavy around me, thick with the scent of damp earth and blooming jasmine, yet it felt emptier now, as though he had taken something irreplaceable with him. I found myself reaching out into the dark, hoping my hand would brush against his warmth again. But the air was cold and unyielding, leaving me with nothing but the whisper of night sounds and the echo of that haunting music fading into silence. A part of me wanted to laugh at the absurdity, at how thoroughly he'd managed to unsettle me with just a glance, a touch, a fleeting dance under the moon. But the ache gnawing at my chest was too real, too sharp to dismiss.

A sudden rustling snapped me out of my daze, and I whirled around, half-expecting to see him there, stepping out from the shadows with that maddening smile. But it was only the wind stirring the leaves, the garden a symphony of shadows and quiet murmurs. Still, a prickling at the back of my neck told me I wasn't alone. I took a deep breath, fighting the urge to call out into the night, demanding answers I wouldn't know how to frame. My cheeks burned, more from frustration than embarrassment, and I clenched my fists, suddenly acutely aware of how foolish I must look—standing alone in a garden, yearning for someone who may or may not have even been real.

"You know," came a dry voice from behind me, "most people prefer to have their midnight breakdowns indoors."

I spun around, heart stuttering, and found myself face-to-face with a figure leaning against a stone pillar, arms folded, a bemused glint in his eyes. Tall, sharp, and dressed in dark clothing that blended effortlessly into the shadows, he seemed to appear from nowhere, his features only half-lit by the moonlight. His smile was crooked, lazy, and entirely too knowing.

"Didn't mean to interrupt," he continued, the hint of a smirk playing on his lips. "But it looked like you could use the company."

I crossed my arms, feigning a calmness I didn't feel. "Funny. I didn't think company included lurking in the dark like some kind of... garden specter."

He chuckled, the sound low and warm, drifting toward me like smoke. "Well, if I'm a specter, then you're the only one who can see me. Which makes you..." he paused, looking me over with a grin, "...the mysterious midnight wanderer."

I rolled my eyes, though I could feel the corners of my mouth twitching. "Oh, please. I was just... admiring the garden."

His gaze flicked over my shoulder, as if to examine the garden himself, before returning to me, arching one skeptical eyebrow. "Funny thing to do in the dead of night."

I swallowed, trying to keep my composure. "I like the quiet," I managed, though the words felt hollow. Even I wasn't sure if I believed them. He tilted his head, and I felt myself shift under the weight of his stare, a mixture of amusement and something else—something that seemed to see more than I intended to show.

"Well, in that case, far be it from me to interrupt your contemplative solitude," he said, voice thick with playful sarcasm. He made an exaggerated show of retreating a few steps, arms raised in mock surrender.

"Wait," I called out before I could stop myself, hating how desperate it sounded. He paused, a glimmer of satisfaction crossing his face.

"Yes?" He drew out the word, his grin widening as he turned back, and I felt a surge of frustration bubble up.

"Who are you?" The question slipped out, raw and blunt, and I realized I needed an answer more than I cared to admit.

He shrugged, feigning casualness, but there was a flicker of something guarded in his eyes. "Just a visitor, passing through," he replied, voice softening, almost wistful. "The garden drew me in, same as it did for you."

"Right." I bit back a laugh. "Just another aimless wanderer with a taste for moonlit gardens?"

His gaze met mine, unflinching. "You'd be surprised how many of us there are," he murmured, and there was a weight to his words, an edge of truth that made the hairs on my arms stand up.

Before I could pry further, he pushed away from the pillar and began to walk past me, his steps silent, blending with the shadows as if he belonged to them. My heart lurched, and I reached out, fingers brushing his sleeve. He paused, looking down at my hand, then back at me, his expression unreadable.

"Wait," I said again, hating the vulnerability in my voice but too curious to care. "What... what was that?"

His smile softened, a touch of sadness ghosting over it. "Just a dance," he replied. "One you may forget by morning, if you're lucky."

I let out a shaky breath, feeling the truth of his words settle somewhere deep, somewhere tender. "And if I don't want to forget?"

He laughed softly, the sound tinged with something bittersweet. "That's the trouble with these things," he said, voice almost a whisper. "The more you hold on, the harder it is to remember. Sometimes, the best way to keep something is to let it slip through your fingers."

I opened my mouth to protest, but he was already stepping back, fading into the shadows like a ghost in the moonlight. I blinked, and in the heartbeat it took me to look around, he was gone, as though he had never been there at all. The garden was empty, silent, and for a moment, I wondered if I'd imagined the whole thing, if the dance and the stranger were just figments of a restless mind.

But as I stood there, I felt the echo of his warmth on my skin, the soft brush of his hand lingering in the air, and I knew, deep down, that it had been real—no matter how impossible it seemed.

The garden seemed to stretch on forever as I stood, breathless, the fading warmth of his touch still tingling on my skin. My heart, still pounding in erratic rhythms, begged for sense, for reason, but the more I tried to gather my thoughts, the less they made sense. His presence had been so vivid, so undeniably real, and yet the moment I opened my eyes—he was gone, swallowed by the night as if he were nothing more than a dream conjured by moonlight.

I stood there, rooted to the ground, staring at the space where he had been. The air felt thick now, laden with unspoken words, with the faint trace of cologne lingering like a whispered secret. Had he truly been there? Or had my mind, too starved for something—anything—gone astray in the quiet of the evening? But that touch, that warmth. It felt too real to be a figment.

I shook my head, pulling myself from the clutches of confusion, my eyes scanning the garden. Shadows twisted around the trees like silent, knowing sentinels, and the leaves, silver under the moon, seemed to hold their breath. The stillness was unnerving. For a moment, the world felt too vast, too empty, as though something was waiting in the silence, its gaze fixed on me.

The soft trill of crickets, once a comforting backdrop, now seemed like a distant murmur compared to the pounding of my heart. I turned, suddenly aware of how cold the night had become, the chill seeping through my thin dress, and walked briskly toward the house, eager to escape the gnawing sensation that something had shifted—something irrevocable.

Inside, the house felt quieter than ever, the walls pressing in, their ancient timbre full of secrets. I wandered through the darkened halls, the faintest trace of moonlight seeping through the windows and casting long, jagged shadows across the polished floors. The house, which I had once known so well, now felt foreign to me, a place out of time, a space filled with echoes of things past.

As I passed the old library, I paused. The door was ajar, a sliver of light escaping through the crack, beckoning me. I hesitated, a small spark of curiosity igniting within me. The library had always been a place of quiet refuge, filled with the scent of aged paper and leather-bound treasures that whispered of forgotten histories. But tonight, there was an odd pull, an unspoken invitation, as if the room itself had secrets it was waiting to share.

Pushing the door open, I stepped inside, the air thick with the musk of old books. The light came from the far corner, where the fireplace glowed faintly, casting a warm, flickering light over the shelves. But it wasn't the fireplace that caught my attention. It was the figure sitting by the window, facing away from me, their back to the room.

I froze. My breath hitched in my chest as I recognized the figure. Him.

The man from the garden.

I had no words, no breath, as I stood there, my mind racing for any explanation, any logic that could make sense of this. How was it possible? How was he here, in my house, in this room, sitting so calmly as though our encounter had never ended? As though it had been nothing more than a passing moment, easily forgotten.

He turned then, slowly, his gaze locking onto mine. His eyes, dark as the night itself, gleamed with an emotion I couldn't name. A faint smile tugged at his lips, the corners of his mouth lifting just enough to be playful, but not quite enough to reassure me.

"Did you enjoy our dance?" His voice was soft, but there was a weight to it, a depth that made every word feel like it carried a thousand meanings.

I opened my mouth to speak, but no sound came out. How could I ask him what was happening? How could I demand an explanation when everything about him—everything about this—was impossible?

He stood up slowly, as though time moved differently for him, and the movement was so fluid, so graceful, that it only unsettled me further. He walked toward me, each step deliberate, as though he were savoring the moment. My mind screamed for me to run, to retreat to the safety of reason, but my body refused to obey. I was rooted to the spot, caught in the orbit of his presence.

"Who are you?" The words slipped out, a whisper, as though speaking too loudly might shatter the fragile illusion.

He stopped just a breath away from me, and for a moment, I thought he might touch me again, that warmth returning with the promise of something I couldn't quite understand. But instead, he simply tilted his head, as if studying me with a curiosity that mirrored my own.

"I could tell you," he said, his voice now tinged with amusement, "but I think you'd prefer to discover it for yourself."

Before I could respond, before I could even process what he had said, there was a sudden shift in the air—an unspoken tension thickening the space between us. His eyes narrowed, a shadow flickering in them, and I felt a cool draft brush across the room, as though something had moved too quickly to be seen.

Then, without warning, the door slammed shut behind me with a force that rattled the walls. My heart jolted in my chest, and I spun around, frantic. The room, once warm and familiar, had become a trap. The light from the fireplace flickered once, twice, then died completely, plunging the room into darkness.

I heard him laugh—low, soft, and full of something unspoken.

And then, the room was silent again.

Except for the soft, unmistakable sound of footsteps approaching from the darkness.

Chapter 5: The Letter Left Unread

I ran my finger over the edge of the yellowed paper, the texture rough beneath my skin, almost as if it carried the weight of all the years it had been tucked away in the forgotten corners of time. The letter trembled in my hands, but not from any breeze or draft—no, this was a tremor born from something deeper, something older. There, etched in the delicate script, was my name. But this wasn't just any letter—it felt like a confession, like a promise, like a plea.

The words spoke of passion, of a connection that seemed to pulse from the ink itself, soaking into the crevices of my mind as though it had always been there, buried somewhere deep.

"My dearest, I cannot see the world beyond your eyes. They hold the secrets of the universe. Your touch lingers with me, even in the absence of your presence. I swear, I will come for you, even if the heavens themselves forbid it. This love, as strange as it may seem, binds us across time and tide. And when I return, as I surely will, I will be yours forever."

I had to steady myself against the heavy oak desk, my knees buckling as though the room were suddenly tilting. The words blurred, threatening to pull me under. They sounded familiar, and yet foreign. How could this be? How could a letter, written in another era, speak so directly to my heart, as though it knew the very essence of me?

I closed my eyes for a moment, willing myself to breathe, to gather the fragmented pieces of my thoughts. My heart thudded in my chest, a rhythm that felt too frantic, too wild for a single, solitary moment. The letter wasn't just addressed to me—it spoke of me, as though it were written for me, from a past I had no memory of. The ink, once dark, had bled with age into a hazy shade of brown. But the words—they were alive. They were unmistakably real.

I shifted, the air thick with the scent of dust and wood, and glanced around the library. Bookshelves stood like silent sentinels, each row stacked high with yellowed pages and forgotten stories. The silence felt oppressive, like the room was holding its breath, waiting for something. For me, perhaps? But the question was too large, too far-reaching. I couldn't afford to entertain such thoughts, not yet. There were facts to uncover, and truth had a way of dancing just beyond my reach.

I unfolded the letter completely, trying to decipher the rest of the text, but the final words ended abruptly, as if torn from the paper itself. The ink splattered at the end, like the last remnants of his soul had been spilled across the page, never to be written again.

"I love you beyond measure—"

And that was it. No farewell, no explanation. Just an unfinished sentence hanging in the air like a song that had been cut short.

My hands shook, my breath shallow as I sat back in the armchair that felt too soft, too heavy for my frame. This couldn't be real. But then again, could it? I had felt that pull before—hadn't I? That unmistakable ache deep within me, the sensation that somehow, somewhere, I had known something like this. This man. His words. It was as though the very fabric of time had stretched, bent, and then snapped back, creating a rift that allowed our worlds to touch.

I shook my head. "No. No, this isn't possible. It's just a coincidence. A prank, perhaps, or some strange twist of fate that has nothing to do with me." But even as the words left my lips, I knew they were hollow, meaningless.

I dropped the letter onto the desk and pressed my fingers to my temples. The faint scent of ink and old paper lingered in the air, weaving into the fabric of the room like a memory I couldn't quite catch. I needed answers—desperately.

Standing up, I paced the library floor, the hardwood creaking beneath my feet with each step, a rhythm that seemed to mirror my frantic pulse. I wasn't sure how long I had been standing there, trapped in the moment, before the sound of footsteps interrupted the silence.

I froze, heart lurching in my chest.

It was only then that I realized I had been alone when I entered the room. I hadn't heard anyone approach. And yet—

The door creaked open, and a figure stood in the threshold, just beyond the faint slant of afternoon light. A tall, broad-shouldered man, his features obscured by the shadows, yet somehow unmistakably familiar. His eyes locked with mine, and in that instant, my breath caught in my throat. There was a flicker of recognition in his gaze, a flicker that quickly disappeared, masked by a cold, unreadable expression.

He stepped forward, his presence commanding, filling the space with an unspoken tension.

"You've found it," he said softly, his voice low and smooth, like velvet brushing against the air.

I swallowed hard, my throat dry. "What do you want?" I whispered, barely able to form the words.

His lips twitched, as though suppressing a smile—or perhaps a grimace.

"That, my dear, is the question, isn't it?" he replied, his eyes never leaving mine.

The room seemed to narrow, closing in on me as the weight of his gaze pressed down, suffocating in its intensity. The letter, forgotten for a moment, lay discarded on the desk between us, a silent witness to the storm that was about to unfold.

The man didn't move, but the air seemed to constrict around us, thick with unspoken understanding. His silence was a weight, pressing in on the edges of my mind, coaxing the question I didn't want to ask. Who are you? But I didn't speak the words out loud—couldn't—because, for some inexplicable reason, I already knew the answer. He was the man from the letter. The ink may have faded, but the pull of his presence was unmistakable. It was as if the very room, the very house, had conspired to bring him here.

His lips twitched again, not quite a smile, but the curve of it was dangerous, promising something wild. The dim light caught his hair, making it appear darker than it actually was, a deep, rich brown that softened the sharpness of his features. His eyes—God, his eyes—were dark, not just brown, but the kind of dark that seemed to pull in all the light, making everything else around him fade.

"You look like you're trying to remember something," he said, his voice thick with something I couldn't quite place. "It's a curious thing, isn't it? Memory."

I swallowed, trying to loosen the vice that had gripped my chest. "I'm not sure I understand what you mean," I said, though my voice sounded small, even to my ears.

"Oh, but I think you do," he said, his tone teasing, though there was an edge to it. He stepped closer, his boots making no sound on the hardwood. "You've read it, haven't you? The letter."

I couldn't answer right away, because what could I say? The letter felt like a secret that had always belonged to him, one I had no right to uncover. And yet, here I was, standing before the man whose words had been scrawled in ink, meant for a version of me that existed in another time. I folded my arms, trying to shield myself from the tension coiling in the pit of my stomach.

"I don't even know who you are," I said, the words coming out sharper than I intended, but I wasn't sorry for it.

He nodded slowly, his lips pressing together in something like amusement. "No. You don't. But you will. Or at least you'll come to understand. After all, we've met before. In another life, perhaps."

I scoffed, though it came out as more of a laugh, nervous and strained. "You're not serious. This isn't some... romantic fantasy, if that's what you're after."

He tilted his head slightly, studying me as though I were an artifact he couldn't quite place. "And yet," he said, his voice lowering, "you feel it, don't you? The pull. The connection. The feeling that we were supposed to cross paths again. That it's inevitable."

I blinked rapidly, trying to steady my racing thoughts. My hands—how had they gotten so cold? I forced them into my pockets, feeling the crinkle of the letter inside, as if it were somehow connected to him, to everything swirling around us.

"It's all too much," I muttered to myself, but the words seemed to echo off the walls, betraying the panic I was trying so hard to keep contained.

He stepped forward, close enough now that I could feel the heat radiating off him. "Is it? Or are you just afraid of the truth?"

"I don't know you," I said again, this time with more force, though my voice wavered. "And this whole... thing—this strange letter, this house—it's too much."

He stopped just short of me, his presence so commanding I couldn't think straight. But his next words were soft, almost gentle. "Maybe it's meant to be too much."

And that was when I felt it—the shift in the room, the sudden tension that wasn't just from him but from the space itself. The air grew heavier, the light in the room dimming just slightly. The shadows seemed to stretch unnaturally along the walls, creeping toward us, as if they were alive, as if they were part of the story unfolding.

"I don't believe in fate," I said, trying to reclaim control, but my voice faltered at the end.

He smiled, that wry, dangerous smile. "You will."

I wanted to step back, to retreat into the safety of the familiar, to escape this strange, magnetic force that seemed to be wrapping around me. But I couldn't. I was rooted to the spot, my feet unwilling to move. It wasn't just his presence—it was something deeper, something ancient that made my heart race and my pulse quicken. I had the strangest sensation that if I tried to move, I would only end up somewhere else entirely, like the world was already shifting, like the reality I knew was slipping away.

"Who are you?" I whispered, the words spilling out before I could stop them. "Who are you?"

He didn't answer at first, and I thought maybe he wouldn't. But then he leaned in, his face inches from mine, his breath warm against my skin. The world outside the room seemed to vanish, leaving only us, suspended in time.

"I'm someone you've been waiting for," he said softly, his voice a caress, but there was something in the finality of his words that made me shiver. "I'm the one you've always known, but have never truly seen."

The words didn't make sense, not really. But in that moment, they felt like the only truth in a world of chaos.

I opened my mouth to respond, but before I could speak, there was a loud noise from upstairs. The floorboards creaked ominously, and the sound of something—someone—moving swiftly through the hallway echoed down the stairs. The moment snapped.

And just like that, he was gone.

I stood there, dumbfounded, the faint scent of him still lingering in the air, as if he had never been there at all. I blinked several times, trying to clear the fog from my mind, but it was as if the world around me had changed, and I hadn't been given the map to find my way back.

I felt the weight of the letter in my pocket again, its edges soft against my skin. And I knew—without a doubt—that my search had only just begun.

The house was unnervingly quiet in the wake of his sudden departure. The very air felt charged, as though the walls had absorbed something intangible, something that could not be shaken off with a mere breath. I stood motionless in the center of the room, the weight of his absence pressing down on me just as heavily as his presence had. But he was gone. Vanished. As if he'd never existed.

I thought of the letter crumpled in my pocket, its edges soft from the nervousness with which I'd pressed it to my side, as if somehow keeping it close could stave off the questions swirling around my mind. Questions I couldn't answer. I hadn't wanted to ask him—What are you? What do you want from me?—because somewhere in my gut, I already knew the answer. And it terrified me.

My legs felt like lead, but I forced them to carry me back toward the desk, to where the letter had been tossed aside, as if I could make sense of the senseless. My fingers grazed the surface of the desk, and my eyes flicked over the familiar objects scattered about—the collection of old books, the antique clock, the faded maps of places I didn't recognize. They were just things, relics of a time I couldn't touch, much like the letter.

I retrieved it carefully, unfolding the yellowed paper once again, as if by sheer repetition I could bring some clarity to the overwhelming fog of confusion clouding my thoughts. The words blurred in front of me, the promise of his love and his absence all too real. But what was I supposed to do with that?

"I love you beyond measure," I whispered aloud, the words feeling strange in my mouth, heavy and foreign.

The echo of those words lingered in the room, a reminder of something I couldn't quite place. The ink had bled, but the sentiment remained intact. I set the letter down, letting the silence wrap around me once more. How was it possible? To be tied to someone I had never met, or had I?

The house seemed to mock me with its secrets, its history, as if it were made up of nothing but whispers of the past. I glanced toward the staircase, as if expecting him to appear again, but nothing. Just the quiet creak of the old beams overhead. The shadows in the room seemed to lengthen, stretching toward me, curling in on themselves.

And then there was that noise again. A faint scraping sound, as if someone—something—was moving upstairs.

My heart slammed against my chest, and I instinctively backed away from the desk, my pulse quickening. It wasn't the wind. It wasn't the house settling. No, this was something else, something deliberate.

The hair on the back of my neck stood up, and I turned toward the door. Every instinct in me screamed to run, to leave this place and never look back, but something rooted me to the spot. I couldn't leave. Not now, not when I was so close. The threads of the past were pulling too strongly for me to ignore.

"Who's there?" I called out, my voice steady despite the rising panic in my chest.

For a long moment, there was only silence. The stillness of the house was so deep it felt almost suffocating, pressing in from all sides. Then, the unmistakable sound of footsteps, slow but measured, crept down the hallway.

My breath hitched. My fingers curled into fists at my sides, but I couldn't move. I wanted to—God, I wanted to—but something about the way the footsteps came closer kept me rooted. They weren't hurried, weren't rushed, as if whoever it was had all the time in the world. Time that didn't belong to me.

"Show yourself," I said again, a little louder this time, hoping my voice would carry a command I didn't feel.

The footsteps paused, just beyond the door. A heavy silence stretched between us, thick and suffocating. My chest tightened, my throat dry. I took one shaky step forward, but before I could reach the door, the knob turned. Slowly. Creaking with a sound that seemed louder than it should be.

The door pushed open.

There, standing in the doorway, was the last person I expected.

He was tall, broad-shouldered, and looked as though he had stepped out of another time altogether. His eyes, dark and fathomless, were fixed on me with an intensity that made the room feel even smaller, the air even thicker. His face was hard to read, but there was a quiet strength about him that made my breath catch.

"Did you think I wouldn't find you?" he asked, his voice low and steady, with a touch of amusement.

I couldn't speak at first. My mouth was dry, words failing me in the face of the overwhelming presence before me. I had thought—no, I had hoped—that I'd be alone in this, but now he was here, standing in front of me, with a look on his face that suggested he'd been waiting for this moment far longer than I had.

"Who are you?" I finally managed to whisper, my voice barely audible.

He smiled, but it wasn't a comforting smile—it was the smile of someone who knew things I didn't. Of someone who had seen the way the world tilted and fallen into place around them.

"Do you really need me to answer that?" he asked, a challenge in his voice.

My mind raced, the words I love you beyond measure looping in my thoughts like a broken record. The pull—the connection—was undeniable. My heart hammered in my chest as I stared at him, at the man who seemed to be carved from the same fabric as my past, someone who had waited for this moment, just like I had. But he was no stranger.

"You've been waiting for me," I said, the words falling from my lips before I could stop them.

His gaze softened for a fraction of a second, and in that brief moment, I saw it—something that looked like regret.

"Yes," he said quietly, his voice barely above a whisper. "And so have you."

The tension in the room was palpable, a storm building in the space between us. I felt the weight of the moment pressing down on me, suffocating me with its intensity. Then, without another word, he stepped toward me.

And just as his hand reached for mine, the lights flickered and went out.

Chapter 6: The Secrets We Keep

I sat at the edge of the couch, my fingers nervously tracing the rim of my coffee mug, the porcelain cool against my skin. The silence that stretched between us felt thicker than the humid air outside, like it had been suffocating us for hours. Outside, the world went on—cars passing, people laughing, the occasional dog barking in the distance—but here, inside this small, claustrophobic living room, time seemed to stand still. I didn't know what to say, didn't know if I was even supposed to say anything at all. Words had lost their meaning when he walked through that door.

"I didn't think you'd come back," I finally managed, my voice barely above a whisper, cracking on the edges like old wood under pressure.

He leaned against the doorframe, his hands shoved deep into the pockets of his jacket, his jaw tight. "What was I supposed to do, Daisy? Leave things like this?"

Things like this. He was talking about the mess we'd made of each other's lives, the wreckage we'd left behind in a mad dash of emotions neither of us had been prepared to handle. He hadn't even touched the couch, choosing to stand as though the space between us was sacred. Or dangerous.

I swallowed hard, the words coming slower now, like they had to fight their way through my chest. "I thought you'd have figured it out by now. You know, whatever it is you think we're doing here."

He snorted, a bitter laugh that echoed too loudly in the empty room. "You think I don't know? You think I haven't spent the last week trying to piece this together?" His eyes met mine, dark and intense, filled with something that I couldn't quite read. "The more I try to understand, the less sense it all makes. But it doesn't stop me from wanting to know. I can't... I can't walk away, Daisy."

His words were a punch to the gut, but they weren't the worst part. The worst part was that I couldn't walk away either.

I could feel the tremor in my hands as I set the coffee mug down on the table, too hard, too fast. It tipped over slightly, the dark liquid spilling onto the wood with a soft hiss. I didn't reach for a napkin. I didn't even flinch. Instead, I stared at the spill as though it held all the answers, or maybe all the questions.

"What do you want from me?" The words escaped before I could stop them, the vulnerability of the question hanging in the air, heavy and unspoken. It wasn't just a question about us—it was about everything. About the shattered pieces of my life, about the lies I told myself, about the ghosts that had been haunting me since the day I walked into that room with him.

He pushed off from the doorframe, his movement smooth and deliberate. "I want the truth, Daisy. I want you to stop pretending like you don't feel this." He took a step toward me, then another, until we were only a breath apart. His voice was low now, almost dangerous in its intimacy. "I want to know what's so goddamn important that you can't just let go of the past."

I inhaled sharply, a spike of panic shooting through me. The truth? How could I give him that when I was still trying to make sense of it myself? The lies, the secrets, the memories I'd buried so deep beneath layers of fear and shame—they had a way of resurfacing when I least expected them.

"Maybe I don't know how," I whispered, my voice trembling despite my efforts to sound certain. "Maybe I don't even know where to start."

His gaze softened, just a fraction, but it was enough. Enough to break something in me, something that had been locked up tight for far too long. The weight of his stare was like a warm, invisible hand pressing against my chest, unraveling me thread by thread.

"I don't need you to have all the answers, Daisy," he said, his voice rough but kind. "I just need you to stop hiding from me. Stop hiding from yourself. We both know you're carrying something—something that weighs you down every day. But you won't let me in. You won't let anyone in."

I wanted to push him away. I wanted to say something sharp, something cutting, to shut him down before he got too close. But the words wouldn't come. The truth was that he was right. I was terrified of letting anyone see the real me. Terrified that if I did, I would shatter into a million pieces, beyond repair.

"I'm not hiding," I said, but the lie was weak even to my own ears.

He gave a humorless laugh. "No? Then what do you call this?" He gestured around the room, at the space between us. "What do you call this constant tug-of-war? This push and pull where you won't let me help?"

"I'm not asking for help," I snapped, surprising myself with the venom in my voice. "I'm trying to protect you. From me. From everything that's coming."

He didn't flinch at my words, didn't back away. Instead, he closed the distance between us, standing so close now that I could feel the warmth radiating off his body. I fought the urge to step back, but my feet refused to move.

"I don't need protection, Daisy," he said softly, his voice low and dangerous. "Not from you. Not from anything."

And that's when I realized—he had already seen the parts of me I'd tried so desperately to hide. He had seen them, and he wasn't running. Not yet, anyway.

"Why?" I asked, the word almost breaking. "Why are you still here?"

His gaze never left mine. "Because I need the truth. And I think, deep down, you do too."

I pulled my hands into my lap, willing the tremor in my fingers to stop, but it didn't. It was as if every nerve in my body was humming in dissonance, at odds with the stillness of the room. He watched me, his eyes unblinking, like he was waiting for some kind of signal, some move I'd make to let him in. But I wasn't ready for that. Not yet. The walls I'd built around myself were sturdy, like an old stone house weathering a storm. It had been easier, simpler, to lock everything inside and pretend the world beyond my doorstep didn't exist.

He shifted, the faint creak of his boots on the hardwood floor too loud in the silence. "You keep saying that you're protecting me, Daisy," he said, his voice a mixture of disbelief and frustration. "But you're not. You're suffocating yourself. And me. And—" He broke off, his gaze flicking to the window as if the answer might be out there, hiding behind the closed blinds.

"And what?" I challenged, my voice sharper than I meant it to be. "You think I'm lying to you? You think I'm keeping something from you on purpose?"

The hurt flashed across his face too quickly for me to miss, but he masked it just as fast. "No," he said, voice low, like he was testing the waters. "I don't think you're lying to me. I think you're lying to yourself."

I sucked in a breath, his words hitting their mark, even though I wanted to deny them. How could I not? The thought of facing the truth was like staring into an abyss I wasn't sure I could crawl out of. It wasn't just about us anymore. It was about everything I had kept locked away for years, everything I had buried so deep that I couldn't remember where it ended, or even if it ever would.

I ran my hand through my hair, tugging at the strands in frustration. "You don't understand," I said, the words escaping before I could stop them. "You don't know what it's like, to live with this... this thing, always in the back of your mind, gnawing at you. I can't let you in, not when I can't even face it myself."

He exhaled slowly, his breath like a soft gust of wind. "Then let me help," he said, his voice almost a plea. "We're in this together, Daisy. You don't have to do this alone."

The words should have been comforting, maybe even reassuring. But they felt like a challenge. A test I wasn't sure I was ready to face.

"You don't get it," I said, standing up too quickly, the sudden motion unsettling. "You think it's just a matter of telling you everything, but it's not. You can't just—"

"Can't just what?" he interrupted, a small frown playing at the corners of his lips. "You think I'm going to run? You think this—" He gestured between us, a sweeping motion that somehow encapsulated everything in the room, everything we had been through, everything we hadn't said yet. "This is something I'm going to walk away from?"

I didn't answer. I couldn't. The silence between us was charged, crackling like the air before a thunderstorm. His gaze softened, though, and I could see the raw vulnerability in his eyes, the look of someone who wasn't sure whether to fight or surrender.

"I'm not asking for you to open up all at once," he said, his voice gentle now, as though he were trying to coax a frightened animal out of hiding. "I just want you to know I'm here. I'm not going anywhere."

I swallowed the lump in my throat, feeling like I might choke on the words that had been building inside me for days, weeks, maybe longer. He didn't know. How could he? I had spent so long convincing myself that the past was buried, that I had moved on. But it had a way of creeping back in, finding cracks in the walls I'd built and slithering through, like the shadow of something I couldn't outrun.

"There's nothing to fix," I said quietly, my eyes not meeting his. "There's nothing you can do to make it go away."

"That's where you're wrong." His words were soft, but firm, and they hit me harder than any accusation could. "It's not about fixing anything. It's about being honest. With yourself. With me. With everyone who's waiting for you to come back."

I let his words settle, the weight of them sinking deep into me. He was right, but I wasn't ready to admit it. Not yet.

He took a step forward, and I instinctively stepped back, the movement involuntary but telling. It was like we were playing a game neither of us wanted to win, a delicate dance where each of us was trying not to make the first move.

"I'm not pushing you," he said, his voice quieter now, almost a whisper. "I just need to know that you're not shutting me out completely."

The words hung in the air, delicate and fragile, as if the slightest movement might make them crumble to dust. I wanted to respond, to tell him that I wasn't shutting him out, that I wasn't trying to push him away. But I couldn't. Not yet. I wasn't ready to let go of the things I had kept hidden for so long.

I turned away from him, unable to meet his gaze, the weight of his presence pressing against me like a physical thing, like a storm gathering on the horizon.

"You can't keep running, Daisy," he said, his voice rough with something I couldn't name. "You can't keep pretending like nothing's wrong. You can't hide forever."

And there it was. The truth, staring me in the face, daring me to see it. But I wasn't ready to look. Not yet.

I could feel the silence press in around us, thicker than the humid air that clung to the city outside, smothering everything in its path. I wasn't sure if it was the weight of his words or the heaviness of the room itself, but it felt like something was on the verge of breaking. The sharp click of the front door closing behind us was all I could hear, followed by the soft thud of my heart in my chest.

"You can't keep avoiding this," he said, his voice a mixture of frustration and something softer, something vulnerable. He took a slow step toward me, his gaze steady, unwavering, like he had already decided what the truth was—and now it was just a matter of getting me to admit it.

I stood there, my arms crossed defensively, but it wasn't enough to protect me from the quiet intensity in his eyes. The air between us had shifted, the old familiar walls I had put up crumbling under the weight of everything unspoken. He wasn't just some guy standing in my living room anymore. He was a reminder of everything I had spent years trying to bury. And in that moment, I realized—he wasn't going anywhere. Not until I faced it. Not until I faced him.

"What do you want from me?" The question came out sharper than I intended, but the desperation I felt had a way of pushing me past the point of civility. "What is it you think you're going to find here?"

His jaw tightened, and for a moment, I thought he might leave, take that step back out the door, and disappear again. But then he shook his head slowly, like he had already made up his mind about something that neither of us were ready to face.

"I want you to stop pretending you don't need me," he said quietly, his words a soft challenge, something meant to get under my skin and make me feel it. The truth. The truth I had been running from. "You keep pushing me away, but you're just pushing me into the silence. I won't be silent anymore, Daisy."

I could feel my pulse quicken. That wasn't something I'd expected him to say. Not that way, not with that certainty in his voice. It was as if he knew something I didn't, something I couldn't see. Something that I had to let in, whether I was ready or not.

"You don't know me," I snapped, but my voice wavered. "You don't know what it's like to live in the past, to carry the weight of something that shouldn't even exist anymore."

His eyes darkened, the hint of understanding behind them unmistakable. "I know enough to know that this isn't about the past. It's about you. About your fear. About the walls you've built up to keep everyone out, including yourself."

The words stung more than I cared to admit. He was right, of course. I had spent so long hiding, so long pretending I wasn't afraid of what would happen if I let the walls come down. I had convinced myself that if I could just hold on tight enough, if I could just keep pushing forward, everything would eventually settle. But it wasn't. And the harder I tried to outrun it, the closer it got.

"Why now?" I asked, my voice barely a whisper. I wanted to sound strong, defiant, but the vulnerability in my chest was choking me. "Why after all this time? What made you think this was the right moment?"

He closed the distance between us, the air around us growing thick with something unspoken. "Because I know you," he said simply, like that was the answer to everything. "I've always known you. I've seen the way you fight, the way you bury yourself under a hundred different things, pretending like nothing matters. But I know it does. It always has."

My heart was racing, each beat echoing in my ears like a drum, louder than the words between us. He was too close now, too close for comfort, but I couldn't make myself move away. There was something magnetic about him, something undeniable, like a force I couldn't resist. I wanted to step back, to slam the door between us and shut him out once again, but instead, I stood there, rooted to the spot, feeling every inch of his presence invade my space.

"You think you can fix me?" I spat, the bitterness in my voice betraying the fear I couldn't hide. "You think you can just waltz in here and put everything back together? It's not that simple."

"I never said it was simple." His voice was low, serious, his gaze unwavering. "But I'm not going anywhere. And I'm not going to leave until you let me help."

I swallowed hard, my throat dry, as his words settled over me like a heavy blanket. Part of me wanted to scream, to tell him to leave, to tell him to forget about me and walk away while he still had the chance. But another part—one I wasn't sure I could control—wanted to collapse into him, to let him in and take the weight of everything I had carried for so long.

I took a step back, away from him, but the movement felt like I was retreating into the past, into all the things I had buried, all the things I had tried so hard to forget. And in that moment, something inside me snapped. The dam I had built up, brick by brick, for years finally cracked, and the flood of emotions I had spent so long keeping at bay surged forward, threatening to drown me.

"Daisy," he said softly, his voice a steady anchor in the storm. He reached out, his hand hovering in the air like he was waiting for permission to come closer. "Let me in."

But I couldn't do it. Not yet. Not when everything I had ever believed was crumbling around me.

The phone rang, its shrill tone slicing through the moment like a knife. I glanced at the screen, the name flashing in front of me—Mom. And for the first time in what felt like forever, I knew the answer would change everything.

Chapter 7: A Love Torn Apart

It was the smell that hit me first. The distinct scent of pine and something far sweeter, like the sticky-sweet tang of honeyed tea left to steep too long. It mingled with the damp earth, the kind of damp that clung to your skin and worked its way under your nails, as though the forest was determined to hold you in its embrace forever. I stood on the porch of the old house, fingers gripping the wooden railing so tightly that my knuckles ached, feeling like I might fall forward into the mist at any moment.

The trees stood like sentinels, dark and towering, surrounding the house like ancient guardians. They whispered in the wind, and if you listened closely enough, you could almost make out words—things about the house, about the land, about the curse. But what was most curious of all was the silence within. The windows of the house were dark, hollow, as though they too had learned to forget. Everything here had learned to forget, except for one thing. Him.

My breath caught in my throat when I saw him standing there in the doorway. He wasn't a ghost, not exactly. But he sure as hell wasn't real, not in the way I knew people to be. He was more like a phantom pulled from the edges of my memory, a dream stitched together with fragments of half-remembered touches and conversations that I couldn't quite place.

His face was sharper now, older, more worn by time and regret than I ever remembered it being. His eyes, though, those eyes—still the same eyes. They held the same weight of something unspoken, something buried deep beneath the surface, like they'd been carrying the same unshakable secret for lifetimes. The kind of secret that gnawed at your insides, reminding you that no matter how far you ran, it would always follow.

He wasn't supposed to be here. Not now. Not after everything.

I hadn't expected to find him in this place, of all places. There were so many ways to hide from the past, to bury it deep enough that it couldn't claw its way back into your life. And yet, here he was, standing in the threshold of the house I had inherited, the house that I had no choice but to return to. The house that had called me back with its dark corners and restless energy.

"Why are you here?" My voice cracked as I spoke, the words slipping from my lips like a secret I didn't want to share.

He didn't answer right away. Instead, his gaze softened, just slightly, and he stepped forward. His boots made a quiet sound on the worn wooden floorboards, the only noise in the stillness of the room. For a moment, I forgot how to breathe.

"I never left," he said, his voice rough, as though it hadn't been used in years. "I've been waiting for you."

I blinked, unsure whether to laugh or cry. Waiting for me? After all this time? He had left me once—left me to pick up the pieces of my life, left me to figure out how to keep breathing when all I wanted was to crumble. He had promised me then that it was only temporary, that the separation wouldn't last. But I had learned the hard way that promises meant nothing when they were spoken by people who couldn't keep them.

"You didn't wait for me," I said, my words sharper than I intended, each one stabbing like a needle through the fragile veil of my composure. "You left me to face it alone."

He flinched, the faintest tremor running through him, and I regretted it the moment the words left my mouth. He hadn't left because he wanted to. He hadn't had a choice. Not really.

"I know," he said, his voice barely a whisper now. "But I didn't mean to. I never meant for any of this to happen. I thought I was protecting you."

"Protecting me?" I scoffed, shaking my head, feeling the old anger stir. "You thought pushing me away was protecting me?"

He closed his eyes, as though the weight of the years pressed down too hard for him to bear. When he opened them again, there was something in them that sent a chill running through me. It wasn't fear, exactly, but something darker, something heavier. "I couldn't risk you getting hurt. You deserve more than this life. More than what I can give you."

I swallowed hard. More than what he could give me. The words had a bitter edge to them, the same kind of bitterness I had tasted in the pit of my stomach when I had realized I would never see him again. Not after everything. Not after the things we had done to each other in the name of love.

"You still don't get it, do you?" I took a step back, feeling the cold of the house seep into my bones, the walls pressing in on me. "I never wanted more than you. I never wanted anything but you. But you—" I stopped myself, because there were too many things unsaid, too many words I wasn't ready to admit to myself, let alone say out loud.

He took a step closer, his hand reaching out, as though he could somehow bridge the gap between us with the simple act of touching me. I wanted to step away, to pull back, to hold onto the bitterness and the anger that had kept me warm all these years. But there was something about him, something that drew me in, even though I knew better. Even though I knew nothing would change. The past would always remain between us, a wall we couldn't tear down.

And yet here we were, standing on opposite sides of it, as though time itself hadn't torn us apart.

"I didn't want to lose you," he said, his voice ragged, the words coming out in a rush, as if he couldn't contain them any longer.

But I was already shaking my head, already pulling away, because the truth was, I wasn't sure if I could afford to let myself fall in love with him again. Not when I knew how the story would end.

I turned, abruptly, the heat of his gaze still lingering in the space between us like an invisible thread pulling at me. The floorboards creaked under my weight, as if the house itself was reminding me that every decision I made here would echo through its walls forever. It was so absurd, the way everything felt like it was coming back to life. It wasn't just him—it was the house, the smell of pine, the dampness in the air, the hum of memories that hadn't quite been forgotten.

I wasn't ready to face him—not like this. Not with the ghosts of what we once were still hanging in the air.

"I need some air," I muttered, as if that could somehow shield me from the inevitable collision of past and present. Without waiting for a response, I strode out of the room, my boots pounding against the floor. The door swung open with a creak, the night air biting at my skin, and I stepped outside, the world stretching wide and silent before me.

The darkness wrapped around me like a blanket, heavy with secrets I wasn't sure I wanted to know. I could hear the soft rush of wind through the trees, their branches swaying like ancient arms, reaching for something they couldn't grasp. The house behind me was quiet now, as though it too was holding its breath, waiting for me to make the next move. But I wasn't ready to decide. I wasn't ready to let go of everything that had built up in my chest over the years.

I wasn't sure how long I stood there, staring out into the blackness, trying to let the air clear my head. The sound of footsteps behind me was unmistakable, but I didn't turn around. I knew it was him before he even spoke.

"Don't walk away from me again," he said, his voice low and firm, and I could feel the weight of those words settle into the pit of my stomach.

I closed my eyes, the temptation to turn and face him almost overwhelming. But I didn't. Because if I did, I was afraid I might fall apart. If I looked at him again, I might remember everything I had lost, everything I still wanted. And I wasn't sure I could handle that.

"You don't get it," I said, the words tumbling out, raw and jagged. "You don't get to just come back after all this time, after what happened, and expect me to—"

"To what?" His voice was a sharp edge cutting through the night. "To forgive you? To forget?"

I let out a breath, forcing myself to turn and face him, my heart thrumming in my chest like a drum. The moonlight caught the angles of his face, casting him in a stark light that made him look more distant, more unreachable than he had in all the years I had spent without him.

"No," I said softly, but firmly, the weight of it pressing down on me. "I can't forget, and I can't forgive. Not when you left me with nothing but silence and a broken heart."

He stepped closer, but I didn't retreat. "I didn't want to leave you," he said, his voice cracking in a way that made me pause, just for a second. "I never wanted to hurt you. I thought I was doing the right thing—keeping you safe from... everything that was coming."

I shook my head, my hands balling into fists by my sides. "You didn't keep me safe. You kept me in the dark, and that was worse. You let me think I was the problem. That I wasn't enough. But I—I was fine without you. I made my own life. I built something for myself. I don't need you to come back and undo all of that just because you can't face what you did."

I could feel the pressure of his gaze, like it was reaching right through me, pulling at the cracks I had so carefully hidden away. But I wasn't going to let him see. Not this time.

"You think I didn't want to come back?" His voice was low now, almost a whisper, but it carried across the distance between us like it was meant to cut through the very air. "You think I didn't fight with every part of myself not to show up on your doorstep? To beg you to let me explain?"

"Explain?" I spat the word, each syllable sharp. "Explain what? That you left because you couldn't handle being in love with me? That you couldn't keep your promises?"

"I couldn't protect you," he said, his voice breaking, but I wasn't sure if it was from regret or something darker. "I couldn't protect us. There was too much at risk, too much at stake, and I didn't know how to make it right. I still don't."

There was something raw in the way he spoke—something I hadn't heard from him before, something that made the walls I'd built around myself begin to crack, just a little. I wanted to hate him. I really did. But there was no hate. Not when he looked at me like that. Not when the person standing before me was someone I had once loved more than my own heartbeat.

The silence stretched between us, thick and suffocating. I could hear his breath, shallow and uneven, and I realized, for the first time, that maybe he hadn't walked away from me because he didn't love me. Maybe it had been the opposite.

Maybe he had loved me so much that he had believed leaving was the only choice he had.

I could feel the tears prick at the corners of my eyes, but I refused to let them fall. I couldn't be that vulnerable again. Not after everything.

"Why now?" I asked, my voice quieter this time, a thread of confusion leaking through. "Why come back now, when everything is so... tangled?"

His eyes were searching mine, as if he could see into the very heart of me. "Because I never stopped loving you," he said simply, the words heavier than any promise could ever be. "And I'll keep waiting until you're ready to face that truth. I've waited this long. I can wait longer."

The earth beneath me felt unsteady, as if the ground might give way at any moment. I wasn't sure if he was being brave or foolish. But I wasn't ready to find out. Not yet.

I stepped back, feeling the weight of his words press into my chest. The chill of the night seemed to wrap tighter around me, as if the air itself were holding me here, forcing me to face the past I had been trying so hard to outrun. The distance between us was palpable, like a canyon that neither of us could cross. But still, he stood there, his eyes locked on mine with the same desperate intensity that had once made me feel like the only thing that mattered in the world.

I shook my head slowly, taking a step back. "You can't just show up and expect everything to fall back into place like it's some fairy tale. Life doesn't work like that."

He flinched, the muscles in his jaw tensing, but he didn't step back. He was standing there, stubborn as ever, as if he was convinced I could still be swayed. "I'm not asking for a fairy tale," he said, his voice steady now, though it still carried a trace of the rawness that had been there moments before. "I'm asking for a chance to make things right."

"Make things right?" I repeated, a bitter laugh escaping before I could stop it. "How exactly are you planning to do that, huh? By offering me more broken promises? By giving me more of the same silence and regret you left me with before?"

His expression faltered, and for a brief moment, I thought I saw something like pain flash across his face. But it was gone so quickly, I wasn't sure if it had even been there at all.

"I didn't want to leave you," he said again, like repeating it would somehow make it true. "I never wanted any of this. I never wanted to hurt you."

I wanted to scream at him. I wanted to tell him how much I had hurt. How I had spent years trying to forget him, trying to move on, only for him to waltz back into my life like nothing had ever happened. But the words didn't come. Instead, all I could do was look at him and feel the ache in my chest that had never quite disappeared.

"You should have told me the truth," I said quietly, forcing my voice to stay steady. "If you had just told me the truth, maybe... maybe I could have understood. But you didn't. And now I'm supposed to just forget everything that happened?"

He didn't answer immediately. Instead, he ran a hand through his hair, looking up at the sky as if the answers might be hiding in the stars. "I didn't tell you because I was trying to protect you," he said finally, his voice softer now. "I thought... I thought if I left, if I stayed away long enough, you'd be safe. That you wouldn't have to be involved in all of this."

I narrowed my eyes, my mind racing. "Safe from what?" I asked, my voice laced with suspicion.

He hesitated, his gaze flickering to the trees at the edge of the yard, then back to me. There was something in his eyes now, something darker than I had ever seen before. "From the danger I was in," he said, his voice barely a whisper. "From the things I got tangled up in. Things that I couldn't pull you into."

I felt a chill crawl up my spine. "What things, Jake? What are you talking about?"

He closed his eyes for a moment, as if trying to find the right words, or maybe trying to build the courage to speak them. When he finally opened them again, his face was set, determined. "There are things that are bigger than us, things that we can't outrun. And I've been trying to protect you from them. From the people I pissed off. From the mistakes I made."

I swallowed hard, the knot in my stomach tightening. "What does that even mean? Are you telling me you're in trouble? With people? Real trouble?"

He nodded slowly, his jaw clenched. "I didn't know what else to do. I thought if I stayed away long enough, maybe the danger would pass. But it didn't. It only got worse."

I felt like the ground had shifted beneath me. "And now you're back?" I whispered, a sharp edge creeping into my voice. "To drag me back into whatever mess you're in?"

"No," he said quickly, taking a step toward me. "I'm not dragging you into anything. I just need you to listen. The only reason I came back was because I didn't know where else to turn. The people I pissed off—they're getting closer. They know about you."

I froze. My heart stuttered in my chest. "What do you mean, they know about me?" I asked, my voice tight with fear.

Jake's eyes darkened, his face drawn. "They know we were together. They know I cared about you." He paused, his voice growing rough again. "And they're going to use that against me."

The words hit me like a physical blow. My mind raced, trying to process what he was saying. "Who are these people, Jake? What did you get yourself into?" My voice trembled, betraying the fear that was now bubbling to the surface.

"I can't tell you everything," he said, his voice low and urgent. "Not yet. But you have to trust me when I say this: they're dangerous. And they won't stop until they get what they want."

I shook my head, my thoughts swirling. "What could they possibly want from you? What do they want with me?"

"They want leverage," he said, his face grim. "They want to make me do things. Things I can't do. And they'll use you to make sure I do."

I took a step back, my mind racing. "And what, you think I'm just going to sit here and let you drag me into this?" I demanded, the anger surging in me now. "I'm not some pawn for you to play with, Jake. I'm not your—"

Suddenly, the distant sound of a car engine cut through the tension. My heart skipped a beat as headlights flashed through the trees, cutting the night open. I turned, panic rising in my chest, and I could hear Jake curse under his breath.

"They're here," he said, his voice barely audible. "And we don't have much time."

Before I could say anything, he grabbed my arm, his grip tight, and began pulling me toward the house. My heart was pounding in my chest, my breath coming in shallow gasps. I wanted to fight him off, to demand answers, but the fear in his eyes was enough to silence me.

"Come on," he urged. "Now. We don't have much time."

As we ran toward the house, I could hear the sound of the car drawing closer, and I realized, with a sinking feeling in my stomach, that I wasn't just running from him. I was running from something much worse.

Chapter 8: The Watcher in the Woods

The forest was a labyrinth, the trees reaching their gnarled limbs toward the sky like silent sentinels. Their shadows danced in the late afternoon light, thick with mystery, just as the whispers of the town had suggested. I'd heard the stories—chilling, fragmented tales of a figure who watched, always just out of sight. The Watcher. The name hung in the air like a forgotten dream, one that clung to the back of your mind, refusing to let go. No one knew who he was, not exactly, but everyone seemed to agree on one thing: if you ventured too far into the woods, you'd encounter him. If you were unlucky enough, he'd speak to you, and when he did, you wouldn't forget it.

I didn't believe in ghosts, not in the sense of floating sheets or chains rattling in the night. But there was something about this place, something undeniably alive in the air, that told me I wasn't entirely wrong to listen to the stories. Maybe it was the way the old house at the edge of the woods seemed to sigh with the wind, or how the ground trembled beneath your feet when you walked through the overgrown garden. There were remnants of something here, something heavy, tethered to the land in a way I couldn't quite understand.

I found him where the town's paved roads melted into the dirt paths leading into the forest. There was a small clearing there, a forgotten place where time seemed to lose its grip. The scent of wet earth and moss clung to everything, and the air was thick with the kind of stillness that makes you forget how to breathe. That was where I saw him—a figure draped in dark cloth, a hood shadowing his face, standing at the edge of the trees, unmoving.

The world held its breath as I approached, my boots crunching on the dry leaves, the only sound in an otherwise silent world. He didn't turn to face me, didn't acknowledge my presence at first. It was as though he was waiting for me to step closer, to prove that I was worthy of whatever he had to offer. My heart thudded in my chest, but curiosity drove me forward.

"I need answers," I said, my voice unsteady but determined. "I've been looking for someone who knows what's going on, who understands what's happening to this place."

His voice came, low and rough, as though it had been unused for years. "Answers? Ah, yes. You want the truth, but the truth is a heavy thing, isn't it? Most people would rather live with their lies than face what's real." He finally turned, and the movement was so smooth, so fluid, it took me by surprise. His face was hidden in shadow, but I could feel the weight of his gaze, like a pressure on my chest.

"I'm not afraid of the truth," I lied, my words barely above a whisper.

The Watcher chuckled, a sound that sent a shiver crawling down my spine. "Everyone's afraid of the truth, child. They just don't know it until it's too late." He stepped closer, the ground seemingly parting beneath him as he walked, the space between us growing narrower with every step. "You're chasing ghosts. And ghosts... they always have a story to tell."

I swallowed hard, fighting the urge to take a step back. "I'm not here to chase anything," I said, more forcefully this time. "I need to understand what's happening to the house. I need to know what happened to her."

His eyes glinted beneath the hood, catching the dying light of the sun. "Ah, yes, her." He tilted his head, his expression hidden in the folds of his cloak, but I could feel the weight of his focus. "She was never really gone, you know. Not entirely."

I froze, my blood turning to ice. "What do you mean? Who was she?"

"The house doesn't forget, you see. It remembers all who've walked through its doors, especially the ones who never left," he said, his voice almost a whisper now, as though the trees themselves were eavesdropping. "There was love, once. And betrayal." He paused, the tension in the air thickening. "And when betrayal is involved, the cost is always steep."

The world seemed to tilt on its axis, the edges of my vision blurring. "You're saying there's something... alive in there?"

He gave a slow nod, his face still obscured in shadow. "Oh, it's alive, alright. The house is full of unfinished business. Souls that didn't get their closure. Lovers who never made it right. And when that kind of energy builds up... it becomes something more."

The words hung between us, thick and foreboding. "And what about me?" I asked, my voice barely audible. "Why do I feel like I'm part of this, like I'm being pulled into it?"

The Watcher's smile was all teeth, though I couldn't see them clearly. "Because you are," he said simply. "The house called to you. And you answered. That means you have a role to play in this story. Whether you like it or not."

My breath caught in my throat as his words settled like a weight on my chest. "So, what do I do now?" I asked, though I already knew the answer. Whatever it was, I couldn't turn back. Not now.

"You'll find your way," he said. "But be careful. There are things in the woods that aren't as easy to outrun as you think." With that, he turned away, disappearing back into the shadows of the trees, leaving me standing alone in the fading light.

I didn't know whether to follow him or turn back to the house. But I knew, with a sudden certainty, that my search for answers had just begun.

I walked back to the house with the taste of the Watcher's words still lingering on my tongue, sour and unsettling. The air around me felt heavier now, as though the woods had exhaled a warning, a breath that hung in the sky like a storm waiting to break. The house loomed ahead, its silhouette sharp against the dimming sky, and for the first time since I'd arrived, I questioned my decision to stay. What was I really searching for? Answers? Or had I already known the truth the moment I stepped foot into this forsaken place?

I paused at the threshold, my hand on the door, but the hesitation was brief. There was no turning back. Not now. The Watcher's cryptic warnings echoed in my head—"You have a role to play." What role? I wasn't sure. But I was beginning to sense the pull of something deeper here, something that wasn't going to let me leave until it had its say.

Inside, the house was just as it had always been—quiet, its silence stretching long enough to feel oppressive. The creaking floorboards groaned underfoot as I walked toward the staircase, but it was the feeling of being watched that sent a chill racing up my spine. It wasn't just my imagination; I could feel it. The air seemed to shimmer with anticipation, like the house itself was waiting for something. I glanced over my shoulder, half-expecting to see a figure standing in the hallway, but no one was there. Still, the sensation gnawed at me, relentless.

I decided to start at the top, where I'd felt the strongest pull—the old room at the end of the hall. The one that had always been locked, the one that no one talked about. My hand hovered over the doorknob, trembling slightly, though I wasn't sure if it was from fear or excitement. I hadn't dared to open it before, but now, I was almost desperate to see what lay inside.

The door creaked open, revealing a room that had been preserved in time. Dust hung in the air like a fog, settled thick over the furniture, the drapes, the once vibrant tapestries that now appeared as faded as the memories they were supposed to hold. The room was a mausoleum of a life long gone, and yet it felt alive. I stepped inside, the floorboards groaning under my weight, my footsteps muffled by the heavy silence.

It was the portrait that caught my eye. The woman in the painting was striking—her dark eyes sharp, her lips curved in a faint, knowing smile. She was dressed in a gown so elaborate, so rich with detail that it seemed to almost breathe with the fabric's texture. But it wasn't the gown that drew me in—it was the feeling of recognition. I couldn't explain it, but the longer I stared at her, the more certain I became that I knew her. That I should know her.

I took a step closer, drawn by an invisible force, my pulse quickening as I traced the lines of her face with my gaze. She looked so familiar, but the name escaped me, dancing just out of reach like a forgotten dream. A shiver skittered up my spine when I realized that her eyes weren't fixed on the viewer—they were locked on something else, something behind the painting, something deeper.

I reached out instinctively, my fingers brushing the cold surface of the frame. The moment I touched it, the room seemed to shift. The air thickened, and the shadows deepened, curling at the edges of my vision like smoke. The floor beneath me trembled ever so slightly, a low vibration that reverberated in my bones. The room was alive, and it was aware of me.

A voice broke the silence—soft, barely a whisper. I turned quickly, my heart slamming against my ribs. "You shouldn't have touched it," the voice said, low and malevolent.

I spun around to find the source, but the room was empty. My breath caught in my throat. I was alone, or at least I thought I was. The shadows were thicker now, gathering at the edges of the room, creeping forward with a hunger I couldn't explain.

"Who's there?" I called, my voice far more trembling than I would have liked.

A laugh echoed in response—low, cruel, and unhinged. It felt like it came from all directions, as if the house itself was mocking me.

I stumbled backward, my hand still gripping the frame of the painting, trying to steady myself. I wanted to run, to flee from whatever had just happened, but something kept me rooted to the spot. Was it fear or something else? Perhaps it was the same thing that had kept me in the house in the first place—an unrelenting pull to uncover what had been buried, to understand what had gone wrong.

Then, I heard it again. A voice, but this time clearer. A woman's voice. "It wasn't supposed to be this way."

I turned toward the sound, my heart pounding in my chest. "Who are you?" I whispered, the question trembling on my lips.

The shadows seemed to writhe in answer, and for a moment, the woman's figure took shape within the darkness. She was slender, her face obscured, but her presence was undeniable. She was there, just out of reach, hovering between the known and the unknown. I could feel her sorrow, her rage, and something else—something cold, a depth of loss that threatened to swallow me whole.

"You don't belong here," she murmured, her voice a faint echo of something lost. "But neither do I."

Before I could respond, before I could process the enormity of her words, she vanished—dissolved into the air like a wisp of smoke. I was left standing in the room, shaking, my heart a chaotic rhythm in my chest.

I knew, with terrifying clarity, that the Watcher's warning was only the beginning. I wasn't just looking for answers anymore. I was tangled in something far darker, something that had been waiting for me long before I ever stepped foot in this house.

I sat in the dim light of the kitchen, the flickering glow from the stove casting shadows against the walls. My fingers traced the rim of my mug absentmindedly, the warmth of the coffee a small comfort against the chill that had settled into my bones. The house was quiet now, eerily so, as though the entire place had exhaled and held its breath, waiting for something to happen. I had thought I'd be able to ignore the creeping unease, the whispers that followed me like a shadow. But now, after hearing the woman's voice in the room, it was clear that I couldn't escape the pull of whatever was lurking here. The truth was tangled up in this house, and every step I took seemed to bring me closer to something I didn't fully understand.

I had thought, foolishly, that all it would take was a little investigation—a few conversations with the locals, maybe a bit of history digging—and I'd uncover whatever had happened here. But now I realized, with a sickening clarity, that I was in over my head. The house wasn't simply haunted by ghosts. It was haunted by something more ancient, more insidious. Something that was feeding on the past, pulling its tendrils into the present, forcing me to play my part in a story that was far from finished.

My thoughts were interrupted by a sharp knock on the door. I froze, the mug in my hands trembling as the sound echoed through the house. The town was small, and I couldn't think of anyone who would come calling at this hour. I stood slowly, the sense of dread rising in my chest like a tidal wave. When I opened the door, I didn't expect to see him. But there he was—the Watcher, standing in the doorway, his face obscured by the same dark hood from earlier.

"Looking for answers, are we?" His voice was gravelly, but there was a slight amusement in it, as though he knew I would be exactly where I was, doing exactly what I was doing.

I didn't invite him in. I didn't even speak at first, just studied him, trying to piece together the puzzle of who he was and why he had come. "You said I had a role to play," I finally managed, my voice tight, the words heavy with unspoken questions.

"And you will," he replied, his head tilting slightly, as if savoring the moment. "But you're not ready for it yet. The house isn't finished with you." He stepped closer, and though I didn't want to let him in, something about his presence was magnetic, pulling me toward him despite myself.

"I don't know what you want from me," I said, my voice catching in my throat. "What does any of this have to do with me? Why am I even here?"

The Watcher's eyes glinted from beneath the shadow of his hood, and for a moment, I could have sworn there was a flicker of something ancient in them. "You're a part of the story," he said simply, as though that should answer everything. "And when the house calls, there's no ignoring it. Not unless you want to become another ghost of its past."

I flinched at the thought, the image of the woman in the painting flashing before my eyes. I wasn't just being haunted—I was becoming part of the haunting, a thread woven into the fabric of something much darker than I had ever imagined.

"You have to understand," he continued, his voice low, "the house doesn't just keep memories—it traps them. People come and go, but the energy they leave behind doesn't fade. It lingers. And sometimes, it finds a way to make people stay. You're connected to something here, whether you want to be or not."

My breath caught. "And how do I break it?"

He didn't answer immediately. Instead, he glanced over his shoulder, his gaze drifting toward the dark woods that loomed beyond the yard. The wind rustled the leaves, a sound that seemed almost like a whisper. "You can't break it. Not alone, anyway."

I opened my mouth to protest, but before I could speak, the Watcher raised a hand, silencing me. "But there is something you can do. The house has a way of drawing people in, but it also has a way of letting them go. If you can find the right thread, the right place to pull, maybe you can undo what's been done. But it won't be easy."

"Undo what?" I asked, my voice barely above a whisper. I wasn't sure I wanted to hear the answer, but I needed to know.

"The curse," he said simply, as though it were the most obvious thing in the world. "There's a reason the souls of this house won't rest. Love, betrayal, unfinished business. All of it is tangled up together, waiting for someone to set it right. And you're the one who's been chosen to do it."

"Why me?" I demanded, my patience snapping. "I didn't ask for this. I didn't come here to play some part in some twisted game."

The Watcher's lips quirked upward in a faint, almost pitying smile. "You didn't choose it, but you're here now. And the house knows it. It's been waiting for someone like you. Someone who can see beyond the veil, someone who isn't afraid to look at the dark corners of this place and ask questions."

I stepped back, feeling the weight of his words settle heavily on my chest. "So what now?"

He didn't answer immediately. Instead, he stepped closer, his eyes boring into mine with an intensity that made the air around us feel thick. "Now, you find the truth. You dig through the layers of this house, through its walls, its memories, its ghosts. And when you do, you'll find what you're looking for. But be warned: Not everything that's buried wants to stay hidden."

Before I could ask another question, the Watcher turned, his figure blending into the shadows like smoke, vanishing as quickly as he had appeared. I stood there, in the doorway, my heart pounding, the taste of fear sharp on my tongue. The house was waiting for me, and now I knew it wasn't just the past that needed to be uncovered—it was the future, too.

A crash shattered the silence from somewhere deep within the house. The sound of breaking glass. The unmistakable sound of something—or someone—moving inside.

My heart skipped a beat. It was time to go in.

Chapter 9: The Glass Shattered

I stood in the doorway, my heart pounding like a drumbeat in my chest, threatening to escape, or worse, shatter under the weight of the words I had been holding in all this time. The house felt different tonight, its creaks and groans whispering secrets I couldn't hear clearly but knew deep in my bones. The night air wrapped itself around me like a lover's embrace, sweet but suffocating, and the moonlight filtered through the cracks in the curtains, casting odd shadows on the floor. I could feel him here—closer than I'd ever felt him before, his presence pressing against the walls, against me.

But I needed the truth. I needed to know why he'd come to me, why he'd chosen me out of everyone, why he lingered in this fractured world when all others had long moved on. I could barely breathe for the weight of it, the tension crackling in the air like the electric charge before a storm.

"Why?" The question slipped from my lips before I could stop it, a raw rasp of disbelief. I hadn't meant for it to sound so weak, but there it was—shaking and brittle. "Why didn't you tell me? Why didn't you warn me?" The silence stretched between us, thick with secrets, thick with the weight of everything unsaid.

His form emerged slowly from the shadows, like a specter returning to its place in a forgotten story. He was a ghost, yes, but no ordinary one. He wasn't like the ones you read about, drifting aimlessly, bound to a place or a time. No, he was alive—or had been. Alive, in the way the dead dream of being, living in the gaps, where life and death overlap. His eyes locked onto mine, and for a moment, all the world faded into nothing. It was just the two of us, tangled together in this fragile reality, spinning and collapsing, like stars burning out too soon.

He opened his mouth to speak, and his voice was as broken as I felt, a tremor running through the words that he must've long practiced in silence. “I never wanted this for you,” he said, each syllable drawing tighter around my chest. “But it was never about wanting. It was about needing.”

There it was again, that word. Need. I’d heard it so many times in the last few weeks, but never like this. It was almost a curse, a bond that kept us tethered together despite the impossible distance between our worlds.

“You don’t owe me anything,” I whispered, as though saying the words would make them true. But deep down, I knew the truth. I was the one who had been chasing him from the moment he’d appeared, chasing the pieces of him I couldn’t quite catch, no matter how fast I ran.

He took a step forward, the floorboards groaning under his weight, and for the briefest of moments, I felt it—a flicker of warmth, a fleeting sense of something real. But then his eyes—those eyes, dark and fathomless—shifted, and the world around me shifted with them. His gaze turned sharp, distant, cold. And in that instant, I felt the world break apart, like glass shattering beneath the weight of a thousand tiny cuts.

The sound was deafening, like every fragile thing in the house crumbling in a single moment. The windows vibrated violently, and the walls seemed to pulse with an energy that made the very air feel too thick to breathe. I stumbled back, my heart clenching in terror as his figure began to fracture, splintering like shards of glass in a million directions. Pieces of him scattered across the room, dissolving into the darkness like smoke.

“No!” I cried out, my voice cracking with desperation. I reached for him, my hands shaking as if the very air itself was trying to keep me from him. “No, don’t leave me like this.”

But it was too late.

The room was cold—colder than I’d ever felt it—and all I could see was the void where he had once stood. The silence around me was suffocating, a silence so deep and final it threatened to drown me. For a moment, I was certain I had lost him, that whatever fragile thread had bound us together had finally snapped. My knees buckled, and I sank to the floor, the cold seeping into my skin, my bones.

Then, as though the universe had decided to test my limits, I heard it.

A soft whisper, like the rustling of paper or wind in the trees. The sound of something breaking, reforming, and then... him. Slowly, like a figure emerging from a fog, his form reassembled before me. But this time, it was different. It wasn't just the pieces coming back together—it was him, but not him. His edges were sharper, his body more defined, his face... distant. His eyes locked with mine, and they weren't filled with the warmth I had come to crave. Instead, there was something cold in them, something almost cruel.

"You shouldn't have asked," he murmured, and the words felt like a slap, their sting lingering long after they were spoken.

I opened my mouth to speak, to demand an explanation, but the words failed me. My throat tightened, and for the first time, I wondered if I had made a mistake. If I had pushed too far, too fast, and broken something that could never be fixed.

His gaze never wavered, his expression unreadable, as though he was seeing me for the first time—not with longing or affection, but with a cold, calculating detachment.

And just like that, I knew. I knew that nothing would ever be the same again.

The air hung heavy between us, the kind of air that thickens with unspoken words and things that should never be said. He stood in front of me, still whole but so far removed from the person I thought I knew that I couldn't help but flinch. His eyes, those haunting eyes that used to hold secrets only I could understand, now looked past me. Like he was seeing me for the first time, but with a new clarity that sliced through me like a blade.

"Why did you do that?" I whispered, barely able to form the words through the tightness in my chest. "Why did you leave me like that?"

He didn't answer right away. Instead, his gaze drifted around the room, lingering on the shattered remnants of glass, the broken pieces that once held him together like fragile moments in time. His face was unreadable, but the tension in his shoulders, the clenched fists at his sides, told me more than any words could.

"You're still here," I said, my voice shaking despite my best efforts to steady it. "After everything. You're still here."

"Not by choice," he muttered, a harsh edge to his tone that made my heart flutter in confusion. "You don't know what it's like. You can't understand what it feels like to live between worlds, to be neither dead nor alive, not truly belonging anywhere."

His words hit me harder than I expected, each one a tiny echo of my own fears, my own doubts that I had been trying to ignore. I stepped forward, feeling the space between us closing with each hesitant movement. His eyes followed me, his lips pressing together as if he were holding back something dangerous.

"I think I do know," I said softly, my voice barely above a whisper. "I've been trapped in a place like that before, in a life that wasn't mine to begin with. I've been stuck, between who I was and who I was supposed to be. But somehow, I'm still standing here. Still breathing. I'm still here, just like you."

He shook his head, the motion swift and full of impatience. "You don't get it. You're alive. You have the chance to change things, to move on, to let go. I don't have that. Not anymore."

The finality in his words hit me like a punch to the gut. There was no hope in them, no flicker of the man I had once known. The ghostly lover who had walked into my life with promises wrapped in mystery had been replaced by someone unrecognizable, someone whose pain seemed too much for anyone—least of all me—to bear.

I swallowed, trying to find the words that might bridge the distance between us. But there was nothing. He had been shattered, and I didn't know how to put him back together. I couldn't even begin to understand what had happened to him. He was no longer a ghost I could touch. He was something else, something far darker, more dangerous than I ever could have imagined.

"You don't have to do this," I said, trying once more to reach him. "You don't have to push me away. We can figure this out. Together."

The corner of his mouth twitched, like he almost wanted to smile but couldn't bring himself to. "Together? You want to fix me? Do you think you're the first one to try?" His voice was low, almost mocking, and it sent a chill through me. "You think this is something that can be fixed with a few kind words or a touch of your hand? I'm not a puzzle you can put back together."

I flinched at the coldness in his tone, at the finality in the way he spoke. He was right, of course. I couldn't fix him. But I had always believed there was a way out of darkness, a way to find light, even in the deepest parts of the night. I just had to reach him. Somehow.

"I don't want to fix you," I said, my voice shaking but firm. "I just want to understand. I want to know why you came here. Why you found me." I took another step forward, willing my legs to carry me closer to him despite the dread pooling in my stomach. "You don't owe me anything. But I deserve the truth."

His eyes flickered, just for a moment, like he might finally break, might let the walls he had built around himself crumble. But then, just as quickly, his expression hardened again, his features sharpening like the edge of a blade.

"You want the truth?" he asked, his voice icy. "The truth is that I didn't come here for you. I didn't come to be with you. I came to warn you."

I froze, the words hitting me like a sudden punch to the chest. "Warn me?" I repeated, disbelief flooding my veins. "Warn me about what?"

"About what you've gotten yourself into," he said quietly, his gaze finally meeting mine with something that wasn't quite anger, but something darker. "I didn't come to be your lover, to live out some tragic romance. I came because you're in danger now. And I've been trying to keep you safe from the very thing I am."

I couldn't breathe. The air seemed to press against my lungs, squeezing out all the oxygen I needed to function, to process what he had just said. Danger? Safe from what? The words didn't make sense, but the tension in his voice—the urgency in his eyes—told me this wasn't something I could brush off.

"From you?" I asked, the question slipping out before I could stop it.

He didn't answer immediately. Instead, he looked away, his jaw tightening as if the weight of the truth was too much for him to bear. Finally, he exhaled sharply and nodded, but it wasn't a simple confirmation. It was an admission that sent a chill running through my veins.

"Yes," he said, his voice barely above a whisper. "From me."

The room seemed to constrict around us, the air so thick it felt like it was suffocating me. I couldn't tear my eyes away from him, from the shattered fragments of his figure that had begun to reform, each piece clicking back into place like a jigsaw puzzle I wasn't sure I had the pieces for. It wasn't him, not the way he used to be, but I didn't know what to do with the version of him standing before me. The broken parts—those jagged edges that had once been familiar—seemed sharp enough to wound if I reached too close.

His gaze swept over me again, but this time it wasn't with affection. No, there was something colder, something calculated in the way he looked at me. As if he had just now realized the price of whatever this was between us. The connection we shared was slipping through my fingers like sand, and I wasn't sure if it was my fault or his, or maybe a mix of both.

He opened his mouth, but for a moment, the words didn't come. Instead, there was a long, drawn-out silence, thick with tension, heavy enough to make the air crackle with its unspoken weight.

"You don't understand," he finally said, his voice rough, tinged with something I couldn't quite place—fear, regret, maybe both. "I never wanted to drag you into this. Into me. Into what I am."

"You didn't drag me into anything." The words came out sharp, but I could barely believe them myself. The truth was, I had followed him every step of the way, through every shadowed doorway, every unanswered question. "I chose to be here."

His eyes flickered, a brief flash of something—guilt, maybe, or just the remnants of the man I thought I knew—but it was gone as quickly as it had come. "That's just it, isn't it? You don't know what you've chosen. You think you do, but you have no idea what it means. What I'm capable of." His words were low, dangerous even, but they were real, and that made my stomach turn.

I swallowed hard, taking a step back, feeling the cool hardwood floor beneath me. "What are you talking about?" I asked, though part of me dreaded hearing the answer. I had been living in this in-between world with him for so long now, hadn't I earned the right to know what I was actually dealing with?

"I told you," he said, a bitter laugh slipping from his mouth. "I didn't come here to be with you, to give you whatever fairytale you had in your mind about this—about us. I came here to warn you. To keep you from the thing that follows me, the thing that..."

His voice faltered, like the words he wanted to say couldn't quite form. A flicker of hesitation passed across his face, and I felt my pulse quicken. The thing that follows him? What was he talking about? This wasn't about love or some doomed romance, was it? No, there was something else in the air now, something heavier, something darker.

"You're not the only one who's haunted," he muttered, almost to himself, and it sounded like a confession—or maybe a plea. "I didn't ask for this. I didn't ask to become a target."

"Target?" I echoed, but the word was so far from anything I'd expected that it hung in the air, disjointed. "What the hell are you talking about? A target? You came into my life and broke everything into pieces and now you want me to run away?"

He closed his eyes for a long moment, his fists clenched at his sides. "You can't run away. It's already too late."

I took a step forward, bracing myself against the panic rising in my chest. "What's too late? What is it? Tell me the truth."

His gaze flickered to mine, and for the first time, I saw something—something real. He wasn't a ghost anymore, not in the way I'd understood him. No, he was something else entirely. He was dangerous. And that terrified me, more than I wanted to admit.

"I didn't want to be the thing that destroys you," he said, his voice cracking, raw. "But I can't stop it. I can't stop them."

"Who? Who are you talking about?" The words spilled from me in a rush. "Who is coming after you? After us?"

The room seemed to tighten around us again, and the shadows shifted in a way that made my skin prickle with a sudden, eerie coldness. The house itself groaned as if it could feel the weight of the words hanging in the air.

"The thing that follows me is older than time," he said softly. "Older than this house, than the things you believe in. It's not just a curse. It's a contract, and it's been signed for centuries."

My breath caught. I reached out for him, grabbing his arm, trying to hold onto some shred of hope that whatever this was, whatever darkness he carried with him, wouldn't be enough to tear us apart. "Tell me. Please."

But instead of answering, he flinched away, his eyes now filled with something I couldn't bear. Not pity. Not fear. But something far worse—resignation. "There's nothing you can do. Nothing anyone can do. It's already begun."

Just then, the house trembled again, harder this time, as if the foundation itself was being shaken. The windows rattled in their frames, and the floor beneath my feet seemed to sway, as though the world itself was shifting beneath me. The air grew colder, and I could feel the change before I even saw it.

It happened so fast—too fast to react.

The door to the hallway slammed open with a force I couldn't explain, and a gust of wind, sharp and foul, poured in. The shadows lengthened, stretching toward us like fingers, clawing and reaching.

I took a step back, my heart pounding in my chest. "What's happening?"

He didn't answer. He was looking at the door, his face paling as he stepped in front of me, shielding me. His eyes locked onto something in the dark hallway, something I couldn't see, but I could feel it—feel it, like a presence, a malevolent force gathering, waiting.

"We need to leave. Now," he said, his voice tight. "Before it's too late."

But before we could move, a figure stepped into the doorway, and I froze, my blood turning to ice. The figure was cloaked in shadows, too tall, too wide to be human, and as it advanced, the temperature in the room plummeted, sending a chill deep into my bones.

And then the voice came, cold and smooth, echoing in the silence: "I've been waiting for you."

Chapter 10: The Mark of a Past Life

I stared at the mark, its heat still lingering, a strange warmth that spread beneath my skin, reaching down to the bone, settling into my very soul. It was a faded scar, but it pulsed with a life of its own, like it had been waiting for me to wake up. My heart skipped a beat, not out of excitement, but from the unsettling feeling that something ancient, something more than just me, was tied to it. As if the universe had tattooed its secret on my wrist—proof of something I hadn't yet fully understood.

It had come in the night, while I was tangled in the depths of sleep. I hadn't noticed the first time, too exhausted to stir from the haze of dreams. But now, in the quiet of the early morning, the mark burned with a clarity I couldn't ignore. The symbol—a jagged line with two loops at its ends, sharp and unexpected—looked like something I'd seen before, only in the pages of old, weathered books. I'd thought it was a relic of myth, a fantasy scribbled down to sell a few copies. But now, it was a reality pressed into my skin, the truth of it settling in like a stone lodged in my throat.

I ran my fingers over it, still not fully understanding, but instinctively feeling the connection to something deeper than the words of the letter he'd left behind. The memory that had haunted me for weeks flickered again—us, a different time, a different world. There, we had stood side by side, faces locked in silent promise, the air thick with the scent of rain-soaked earth. A world that seemed so far away, so impossible. Yet the vividness of it clung to me, unshakable.

What was it? A dream? A vision? Or perhaps something older? A past life that lived just below the surface, surfacing now because of him? And why had it appeared now, as though we were both waiting for this moment?

I shook my head, pushing the thoughts away. There was no time for wondering about past lives, not when the present felt so pressing. But the mark was a constant reminder—a tether, an anchor to something I wasn't ready to understand.

I stood from the bed and glanced at the letter again, its words still fresh in my mind. "I'll find you. You know I will. And when I do, nothing will stand between us, not even time itself." His promise had been clear, but the words were laced with an urgency I hadn't quite grasped until now. It was almost as if he knew this would happen, as though he had prepared me for the inevitable. That thought sent a shiver up my spine. Could he have known? Could he have felt it too?

I turned to the window, the soft gray light of morning spilling in, the streets below still damp from the night's rain. A quiet hum of city life began to stir, but it felt distant, muffled—like the world itself had paused, waiting for the next step. My hand rested on the windowpane, and for a moment, I considered everything that had brought me here: the strange dreams, the pull I had felt when I first met him, the undeniable connection that had built between us.

But those were things I couldn't explain, things that didn't belong in this world.

And yet, the mark on my wrist burned brighter, reminding me that it wasn't just something I could ignore. It was real. It was happening.

"Get it together," I muttered to myself, a quiet laugh escaping my lips as I rubbed my temples. "You're not going crazy. Not yet, at least."

But the doubt still lingered, threading through the words like a dark cloud.

I grabbed a sweater, pulling it over my head as I headed for the door. My fingers brushed against the mark again, the sensation sharper this time, a twinge of something—guilt, fear, longing—flaring up in me. This wasn't just a symbol. It was a curse, or at least, that's what I suspected. Something that could ruin everything, yet tie me to him irrevocably. The idea of a curse had never felt so real until now.

The world felt heavier as I stepped outside, the air cool and crisp, brushing against my skin like the softest kiss. But even that couldn't ease the ache in my chest. My heart kept drumming, louder now, in sync with the thrum of the world around me. It felt like I was waiting for something to break. I wasn't sure what. But I had no choice but to move forward, even if my feet were unsure of the path.

I wasn't going to let whatever this was control me—not yet. I couldn't afford to.

The city moved around me, oblivious to the turmoil inside me. People rushed by, their faces full of their own quiet battles, their eyes fixed on destinations I couldn't see. They passed me without a glance, but I noticed them all—the young couple laughing under the weight of something unspoken, the old man walking with a slow, deliberate step, as if each moment mattered more than the next. It made me wonder what they all carried. What burdens. What desires. What secrets. I was no different. But in that moment, I wanted to believe that I could hold on to mine for a while longer.

I didn't know what the mark meant, what the memories of the past meant, or how I would untangle the knots of time. But I couldn't ignore it any longer. There was a road ahead of me, and somehow, it was already marked—by him, by us, and by a past I hadn't yet lived.

I pressed my palm to my wrist again, the heat still radiating from the mark like an echo of something far too ancient to make sense of. The sensation was both intimate and ominous, as though the burn had been branded by hands that weren't entirely my own. Every shift of my fingers across the skin beneath it seemed to whisper fragments of forgotten things—visions of him, of us, in a time where we weren't so caught up in the mundane mess of now. I had no idea how or why this had happened, but the weight of it sat squarely on my chest, a pressure I couldn't shake.

I turned from the window, my gaze lingering on the rainwater that clung to the glass like tiny, hesitant beads of sorrow. I didn't need the weather to mirror my mood, but it seemed to understand better than I did. The truth was, the mark wasn't the only thing plaguing me. I was haunted by fragments of that memory—the flash of his face, familiar yet distant, a sense of endless loss mingled with an almost suffocating certainty that we had been together once before. That knowledge should have been comforting, like a warm hand guiding me back to him, but instead it felt like a tether pulling me toward something dangerous.

I should have gone to work, should have forced my feet to follow their usual rhythm, but the idea of stepping into that world again—into the same routine I had followed for years—seemed impossible. The mark on my wrist was not something that could be ignored over an iced coffee and a spreadsheet. There was no room for normality when the supernatural was slamming into my life with the force of a speeding car.

And then there was him. His words from the letter were never far from my mind: "When I find you, nothing will stop us." Nothing. Not time. Not death. Not fate. It made my heart ache just to think about it. We had been so certain, once, in another life, and yet here we were—pulled together by forces we didn't fully understand, tied by something far older than either of us could fathom. Was love truly enough to break the curse? Or was it merely the start of something far worse?

I slipped my coat on with more force than was strictly necessary, the fabric too tight across my shoulders, as if my body knew it had been pretending for too long. I couldn't keep this up—this façade of being okay. I couldn't walk around pretending I wasn't terrified of what was happening to me, to us. As if I could step back into my old life after all of this, as if nothing had changed. No one ever tells you how quickly things fall apart once you start uncovering the truth. One day, you're just a regular person, and the next? You're marked.

The door clicked shut behind me, and I walked down the narrow corridor of my apartment building, the walls closing in like they had a mind of their own, making me feel trapped in a maze of choices I didn't understand. A choice. I had the power to make one, didn't I? I could walk away, I could forget the mark, the dreams, the pull of the past. The question was, could I forget him?

The soft chime of my phone vibrating against my coat pocket pulled me from my spiraling thoughts, and I glanced down. It was a message from a friend. Not just any friend, but Riley—someone I hadn't spoken to in weeks. My thumb hovered over the screen, hesitating. Should I reply? Was there even a point? The old me would have dove right in, typing back with that casual ease I had perfected, the kind that said everything and nothing at the same time. But this me—the one who had the mark of a past life etched into her wrist—had become unsure of everything, even the easy things.

I unlocked my phone, swiping quickly.

"Hey, are you okay? You seemed off last time we talked."

It was a simple question. One I had no answer for. Off? Was that how I'd seemed? Disjointed, like a broken puzzle trying to fit the wrong pieces together? Maybe. Probably. The truth was, I didn't know how to explain any of this to Riley, let alone anyone else. Not when I couldn't even explain it to myself.

I typed back quickly, trying to bury the cracks beneath a layer of false normalcy.

"Yeah, just busy with work. You know how it goes. I'll catch up soon."

I hit send before I could talk myself out of it, locking the phone and slipping it back into my pocket.

But as I rounded the corner toward the café, a feeling tugged at me, a sense that something—someone—was watching me. It was the kind of feeling you get when you're walking down a dark alley, knowing full well there's no one behind you but still hearing the echo of footsteps in the distance. My skin prickled, and I stopped dead in my tracks, glancing over my shoulder.

There, standing under the awning of a shop, was a man I didn't recognize. His face was partially hidden by a dark hoodie, the kind that did nothing to obscure the sharpness of his features—features that, despite their unfamiliarity, felt hauntingly familiar. His eyes locked with mine, and for a split second, I swore I saw recognition in them. A sense of something unspoken, a connection that hit me like a wave, too swift and powerful to avoid.

I blinked, and he was gone.

No trace. No echo. As if he had never been there at all.

But I knew, deep in the pit of my stomach, that he had been. And I knew that he had been watching me for far longer than just today.

I hurried across the street, the damp pavement slick underfoot, the soft patter of rain tapping against my coat like the world was trying to get my attention. My mind was tangled in a mess of thoughts, the mark still fresh and pulsing with a strange heat that seemed to follow me wherever I went. The figure I had seen earlier—the one who had disappeared as quickly as he appeared—lingered in my mind. Who was he? Why did I feel like I should have known him?

The air around me was thick with something I couldn't name, a pressing weight that seemed to follow my every step. I shook my head, pushing the thought away. I wasn't going to be one of those people who thought they were being stalked by shadowy figures. That would be insane. It was already enough that I felt like I was losing my grip on reality. My feet picked up pace, instinctively heading toward the café, a place that had always felt safe, even when everything around me seemed to be shifting.

The bell over the door chimed softly as I stepped inside, the warmth of the café wrapping around me like an old, familiar embrace. I could feel the weight of the outside world, with its strange symbols and unexplainable encounters, drop away as I walked up to the counter. The barista, a young woman with an easy smile, didn't seem to notice the slight tremor in my hands as I ordered my usual—a steaming cup of chai latte, the spice soothing in its comfort.

"Rough morning?" she asked, her tone light but sharp, a glint of curiosity in her eyes.

I managed a half-smile, the kind that was supposed to assure people I was fine, when I was anything but. "You could say that," I replied, a bit more truthfully than I had intended.

She gave me a knowing look but didn't press, probably used to the quiet stories the café's regulars left untold. As she handed me my drink, I felt the warmth seep into my fingers, but it couldn't quite chase away the chill that had settled inside me. I turned to find a table by the window, the small glass pane fogging up as I settled into the worn leather chair.

The world outside moved at its usual pace, but inside, the noise seemed muffled, like I was watching everything through the wrong end of a telescope. The thought struck me again, sharp as a knife—what if everything I had ever believed was wrong? What if this mark, this connection I felt to him, was more than just some wild coincidence?

I rubbed the space on my wrist where the symbol was, the faint heat still simmering just beneath the surface, and I couldn't shake the feeling that I was being led somewhere. Not by my own hands, but by something far older, far more powerful.

As I took a sip of my chai, the smooth liquid warming me from the inside, I tried to focus on the task at hand: finding answers. I wasn't about to sit idly by while everything around me turned into some surreal dream. I had spent too long being the person who stayed in the background, watching others chase their futures. This was my future now, whether I liked it or not.

My phone buzzed in my pocket, and I glanced down, my heart skipping when I saw the name on the screen.

It was him.

The message was short, but my pulse raced as I read it.

"I know you've felt it too. It's starting. Meet me tonight."

There was no name, no explanation. But I didn't need one. His words hit me like a physical blow, a jolt that ran from the top of my head to the tips of my toes. The memory of his face, his voice, those eyes that had locked with mine in some other life, rushed back, overwhelming me.

I felt a strange mix of relief and fear, as if I had been waiting for this moment, and yet, I wasn't ready for it at all. He was coming for me, and in a way, I was coming for him, too. But was I truly prepared for whatever this was? Whatever we were?

I quickly typed out a reply.

"Where?"

I hit send before I could second-guess myself, setting the phone down on the table with a soft thud. The wait stretched out in front of me, too long, too uncertain, and I found myself staring at my reflection in the café window. There was something different about me now—something I couldn't explain. The eyes looking back at me didn't seem entirely like my own. They were darker, more haunted, as if I had already seen too much.

The phone buzzed again, snapping me from my thoughts.

"The old library. Midnight. Don't be late."

The message was final, as if he was certain I would follow.

I stood up, my chair scraping noisily against the floor, the noise drawing a few glances from the other patrons. The weight of the moment settled back in, pressing harder than ever. The old library. It wasn't far from here, tucked between the rows of shops on the quieter side of town. I'd passed it a hundred times without ever considering it anything more than a crumbling relic of the past. But tonight, it would hold something far more important—answers, maybe, or something far more dangerous.

I finished my drink in a few long gulps, then grabbed my bag, the strap slinging over my shoulder with a quiet snap. The air outside had become colder, the sky darkening in the distance like the world was closing in on itself. There was no turning back now.

I could feel the pull of the past in my bones, urging me forward, to the library, to him. I didn't know what awaited me there, but there was only one way to find out.

I wasn't the only one carrying a secret anymore.

As I made my way down the street, the soft echo of my footsteps following me, I realized the danger wasn't in what I knew—it was in what I was about to learn.

And as the old library loomed into view, the air around it felt heavy, charged, as if the walls themselves were waiting for something, too.

Something was coming. Something I wasn't prepared for.

Chapter 11: The Price of Remembering

The wind had a way of picking up in the mornings, like it had somewhere else to be. As I walked along the shoreline, I could feel it in my bones—shifting, tugging at my coat, reminding me of something I'd forgotten long ago. The waves broke rhythmically against the rocks, but it wasn't the ocean that held my attention. It was the way the sea foam kissed the sand, curling like the edge of a forgotten memory, fading and yet lingering.

I had always thought of myself as someone who could handle the truth. That was before I learned that truths have a way of sticking with you like gum on your shoe, impossible to scrape off no matter how hard you try. The more I delved into the past, the more I felt it—those old ghosts, whispering their secrets into my mind, one after another, faster than I could process. They weren't mine, I knew that. But they didn't care. They still came for me, like a tide that didn't know the meaning of retreat.

I hadn't meant to remember him. I hadn't meant to dig up the twisted pieces of what we were, what we had been, but curiosity has a way of eating you alive. It starts as a dull ache, a longing for answers you can't explain, and before you know it, you're deep in the dark, clawing through the rubble of a life that's no longer yours. Or maybe it never was. I didn't know what was real anymore.

Every day felt like walking through a fog, half-remembered and half-dreamed. Sometimes, I'd catch myself in the mirror, eyes wide, lips parted, like I was waiting for something. Something, or someone. His name lingered on my tongue like an echo, an ache in the very core of me. I had loved him, hadn't I? More than anything.

But there was a cost. Oh, there was always a cost.

I stood there now, watching the waves crash against the rocks below me, the cold seeping through my boots, my fingers trembling as I clutched the letter. I had come all this way to meet him. I had been chasing shadows, yes, but they were shadows I had known once. They knew me too. It was as if the past and the present had collided, blurring into something that hurt to touch, but I couldn't let go.

"Isn't this where you belong?" His voice was a whisper, carried on the wind, but I knew it wasn't the wind. It was him.

My heart skipped, my pulse quickened, and I spun around.

There he stood, but not in the way I remembered. His form was more like a wisp, as if the world itself was trying to swallow him up again. His features were faint, a cloud of memory hanging on the edges of the reality around us. But I knew him. I knew those eyes, that crooked smile that never quite reached his eyes.

"You're... here?" I wasn't sure if I was asking him or myself. My voice cracked, an echo of something too familiar.

He didn't answer at first, just stared at me with those impossibly deep eyes. Eyes that had once been a map of everything I ever wanted, everything I ever feared. They still held that same pull, but there was something darker now, something deeper, like the abyss.

"You've been looking for me, haven't you?" His voice was the same, but the words carried weight now, a heaviness I wasn't ready for.

I nodded, the lump in my throat growing larger by the second. "I didn't mean to. I didn't mean to remember."

His expression softened, but the flicker of something darker passed through it before it was gone, like a shadow passing over the sun.

"It's never a choice, is it? What we remember, what we forget." His hand reached out, and for a split second, I thought I could feel the warmth of his touch, but then he pulled it back, as if he had realized the gesture meant more than either of us was prepared for.

The wind howled louder, tugging at my hair, pushing me back from him. I resisted, not wanting to retreat, not wanting to lose this fragile moment between the two of us.

"We weren't meant to be torn apart," I whispered, my voice barely audible over the crashing waves. "You said we would never be apart. You promised me."

He winced, like I'd struck him. His eyes darkened, and for a moment, I saw something so raw, so painful, that I felt my own heart squeeze with it.

"I never wanted to leave you," he said, his voice raw, like he hadn't spoken in a long time. "But sometimes... the price of remembering is too high."

I couldn't breathe. I couldn't think. The words were like shards of glass sinking into my chest, and I wanted to scream, wanted to run. But I couldn't move. I couldn't turn away from him, not now. Not when I had come so far.

"What do you mean?" My voice broke on the last word, desperate for the answer I feared.

He seemed to hesitate, then took a slow, deliberate step toward me, the air between us crackling with something electric, something dangerous.

"You have to understand," he said softly, his voice thick with regret. "Some things are better left forgotten. Some truths... they have a way of destroying everything they touch. Especially love."

The words struck me like a thunderclap, sending a tremor through my entire body. It felt like a warning. But to what? What was I supposed to do with this knowledge?

His eyes locked onto mine, and I saw the truth in them—the truth I had been running from. I knew then, in the deepest part of me, that our reunion wasn't a blessing. It was a burden. And I wasn't sure I was strong enough to bear it.

"Are you ready to pay the price?" he asked, his voice barely a whisper.

And I knew, then, that I wasn't.

I stood there, frozen in place, as the cold wind swept around us, biting at my skin, pulling at my coat like it was trying to tear me away. His eyes were still on me, and I couldn't look away, even though I could feel the weight of everything I wasn't ready to face pressing down on my chest. My heart pounded, not from fear—though there was plenty of that—but from something deeper, something more tangled. Something like love, something like loss.

The moment stretched between us like an old song, familiar yet suffocating. Every time I thought I understood him, I discovered there was more—more pain, more truth, more of him buried beneath layers I wasn't prepared to uncover. He had been a shadow, a whisper in my mind, a dream I could almost touch but could never fully hold. Now, here he was, standing in front of me, and I didn't know how to breathe through it.

"Is it always like this?" I asked, the words tumbling out before I could stop them. "Always so... heavy?"

He tilted his head, a faint smile playing at the corner of his lips, though it didn't quite reach his eyes. It was the same smile he had worn years ago, but there was a sadness in it now, as if the world had worn him down to something unrecognizable.

"Life has a way of being heavy when we're not careful with it," he said, his voice a mixture of tenderness and something darker, something I couldn't quite place. "But it's easier to bear when we don't try to remember everything at once."

I could feel the weight of his words like they were etched into my skin. But it was too late for that, wasn't it? I had already started down this path, digging up pieces of myself I had forgotten, or maybe never really knew. And now, in front of me, stood the answer to all the questions I had been asking.

"But I can't forget," I whispered, my voice trembling with something between fear and desperation. "Not when I feel like there's something I've lost. Something... we lost."

His gaze softened, but only for a moment. Then, he looked away, his expression hardening. "Some things are better left buried," he said, his tone clipped. "Some things, once unearthed, don't stay quiet."

The air between us seemed to thicken, like we were standing on the edge of something we couldn't see but could feel closing in on us. The memories, those fragmented shards of a past that wasn't mine, flared up again. I could see flashes—his hand in mine, his face so close I could taste him, and then the flash of pain, the snap of something breaking, and then nothing. Darkness. And him, fading away.

"You don't know what you're asking for," he said, almost as if he was talking to himself. "You're not prepared for the cost of remembering."

The words struck me again, that feeling of something just out of reach, the pain of it, sharp and raw. I knew what he meant. I had seen it in those fragments, in the moments that slipped through my fingers like sand. There was a reason we had been torn apart, a reason I had been forced to forget.

But I couldn't stop myself. I had to know. The question burned in my chest, so hot it threatened to consume me.

"Then why are you here?" I demanded, my voice rising, desperate for something more. "If it's so dangerous, if it's so painful, why are you here? Why did you come back?"

He flinched, his eyes flashing with something I couldn't quite read. Anger? Regret? Maybe both. He stepped closer, closing the distance between us, but there was no comfort in his proximity, only the cold chill of inevitability.

"Because you're asking the wrong questions," he said, his voice low, dangerous. "You should be asking if you're ready to pay the price for the answers. Not whether or not you can live with the pain of remembering."

I felt the ground shift beneath my feet. The world seemed to tilt, and for a moment, I was no longer standing on the shore, but somewhere much darker. The air grew thick, suffocating, as memories—his memories, my memories—flooded me again. Each one sharper than the last, more vivid, more intense.

I gasped, my breath catching in my throat as a vision of that night—the night we had been torn apart—flashed before my eyes. I saw the storm, the chaos, the finality of it. I saw him, standing there, helpless, his face a mask of regret, and then—nothing. The world fell away, and the memory shattered, leaving me breathless, my chest aching.

"Stop," I choked out, my hands shaking as I pressed them to my temples, trying to block it all out. "I can't... I can't do this."

But he didn't pull away. Instead, he stepped closer, his presence overwhelming, impossible to escape.

"I know you think you can handle it," he murmured, his voice rough, like gravel being scraped across stone. "But you can't. Not yet."

I shook my head, refusing to look at him, to listen to him. "I have to. I have to know."

He sighed, a sound filled with so much weight, so much history, that it nearly brought me to my knees.

"Then you're already too far gone." His voice was quiet, resigned, and there was a strange sadness in it, like he had already lost me.

I didn't know what to say to that. The truth was, he was right. I had already crossed some line I couldn't uncross, and now, there was no turning back. The memories would keep coming. The questions would keep piling up. And I would be left to sort through the rubble, piece by piece.

But even as the weight of it all settled into my bones, there was something else, something deeper that pulled at me—something that made me reach for him, despite everything. Because even in the darkness, even in the pain, I still felt him. I still wanted him.

And that, I realized, was the price of remembering.

I tried to breathe, but the air felt heavier than it should have, thick with the weight of things I had no name for. He was still there, standing too close now, a mere breath away, and yet still not fully real. His edges blurred like a mirage, like he might vanish if I blinked. It was like standing in the middle of a dream, a dream I wasn't sure I wanted to wake from or to sink deeper into. I knew better than to reach out, but my hands betrayed me, fingers twitching toward him as if by instinct.

"You're not real," I whispered, the words clinging to my lips as soon as I said them. "You can't be. I'd have known... I would've known."

He didn't answer immediately, just watched me with those eyes, dark pools of unspoken stories. The silence between us thickened, charged with a tension that crackled like static in the air. Finally, after what felt like an eternity, he took a step back, his expression unreadable.

"Does it matter?" he asked quietly, his voice low but clear. "Does it really matter if I'm real or not, if I'm here or not?"

I stared at him, my mind whirling, caught between the fear that this was all slipping away from me and the aching need to understand. "If you're here, then what does that mean? Why now?"

"You're the one asking the questions you're not ready for," he said, his mouth twisting into something that was neither a smile nor a frown. "You dug up things you didn't want to remember. And now you're asking why they're showing up."

His words sliced through me, cutting through the haze that had clouded my mind. I knew the answers, or at least I thought I did, but they were scattered, fragmented, like pieces of a shattered mirror. Every time I tried to grasp one, it slipped away from me, leaving nothing but emptiness.

"I didn't ask for this," I said, my voice catching in my throat. "I didn't want any of this. I didn't want to remember."

His gaze softened, but there was a hardness underneath it, a deep-set resignation that made my chest ache. "And yet, you've been digging for the truth, haven't you? You've been chasing ghosts. You were always going to find them."

The words sank into me like stones, heavy and cold. I wanted to deny it, to tell him that I hadn't been looking for ghosts, that I was just trying to make sense of the disjointed memories that plagued me. But that would have been a lie. I had been searching for something—someone—and I had known it all along.

I was still trying to make sense of what I had uncovered, but the more I pieced together, the more it felt like the world I had built for myself was coming apart at the seams. My heart raced as the memories hit again—fragments of a night that felt more like a bad dream than reality. The violence of it, the fear, the sudden coldness between us.

"We didn't just... fade away," I said, my voice trembling despite myself. "Did we?"

He shook his head slowly, almost regretfully. "No. We didn't fade. You've got it wrong. You're seeing things, but not the way they happened. You don't remember the truth yet."

The words punched through me, sharp and biting. I didn't want to know the truth. I didn't think I was ready to face it. The thought of it, of the reality that was slipping through my fingers like sand, was terrifying. But deep down, in the place where the fear couldn't reach, I knew I needed to know.

"Then what am I missing?" I demanded, my voice cracking with the weight of the question. "What am I supposed to remember?"

He took another step closer, his presence overwhelming, filling the air with something I couldn't name. For a second, the world seemed to still, as though it was holding its breath. Then, just as quickly, he turned away, his face hardening.

"You're asking the wrong questions again," he said, his voice a low murmur. "You're asking for answers, but answers come with consequences. Do you think you can handle it?"

My pulse hammered in my ears, and a cold shiver ran down my spine. I wanted to say yes, to demand that he tell me, to force the truth out of him. But something in the pit of my stomach told me I wasn't ready for it.

"I have to know," I whispered, more to myself than to him.

He turned back, his eyes dark, unreadable. "You think you're strong enough? You think knowing will make you feel better?"

"I don't know what I think anymore," I said, my voice barely a whisper. "But I know that if I don't get the truth, I'll lose myself completely. And if I lose myself..."

He stepped forward, closing the distance between us until his breath was warm on my face, his hand raised but not quite touching me.

"You're already lost," he said softly. "You just don't know it yet."

I could feel the weight of his words settle over me like a shroud. The tension in the air was suffocating, and I felt the walls closing in, pushing me closer to him, closer to the truth I wasn't ready for. My mind raced, heart pounding, as I tried to piece together what he was really saying. But the more I tried to understand, the more elusive it became.

And then—just as quickly as he had appeared—the air shifted. A gust of wind tore through the space between us, and I felt something change. My heart stopped, just for a moment, as the ground beneath me seemed to tremble, as if the very earth was giving way. The air turned cold, biting, sharp enough to cut through the haze that clouded my thoughts.

I reached out instinctively, but he was gone.

Just like that. Vanished.

I was left standing on the edge of something I couldn't understand, the questions swirling around me, unanswered. I took a step forward, only to feel something sharp press into my side. I looked down.

A note, folded and crinkled, was wedged between my ribs like it had been there for a long time. I pulled it out slowly, heart pounding. My hands shook as I unfolded it, reading the single, cryptic sentence scrawled in jagged letters:

The truth is waiting for you, but you're not ready to see it.

And then, everything went black.

Chapter 12: The Choice of Forever

The shadows of the day stretched long, curling their fingers through the trees, as I stood on the porch, watching the sky deepen from gold to rose to violet. The air had that particular stillness, thick with the promise of something that could change everything. I had felt the shift in the atmosphere for hours, like the quiet hum of a storm that hadn't yet made itself known. But I couldn't tear my eyes away from the horizon. There was something about the way the sun sank, as if it were offering one last gift before it disappeared entirely. One last piece of hope before the dark swallowed it whole.

My thoughts, ever restless, swirled around a familiar man who had already come and gone from my life twice. Each return was like a magnetic pull that I couldn't ignore, no matter how I fought it. The first time, I hadn't known him for what he truly was—his name a mystery, his presence an enigma that seemed to materialize out of thin air. The second time, I'd recognized the truth, and I had been terrified. But now, standing on the edge of another revelation, I found myself wondering if I was the fool to hesitate.

The creak of the garden gate broke my reverie, followed by the soft padding of footsteps across the gravel driveway. My breath caught, just for a moment, before I turned. There he was—Jack, his silhouette framed by the fading twilight, his presence filling the air like a breath held too long. His dark hair tousled by the wind, his expression a blend of longing and something else... something far more dangerous.

He was close now, close enough that I could see the muscles in his jaw clench, the lines around his eyes deepen as he tried to make sense of the storm raging inside him. And, for the first time in the months we'd spent skirting around the edges of a future together, he looked truly uncertain.

"Jack," I whispered his name, the syllables tasting like honey on my tongue, even though my heart twisted with uncertainty. "What is it?"

His lips parted, but for a long moment, no words came. I watched as he battled with himself, his gaze flicking to the sky, then back to me. There was a sadness there, a quiet sorrow, that clung to his every movement like a shroud.

"I've been thinking," he began, the rasp of his voice feeling like a jagged edge against the smooth calm of the evening. "About us. About what this is... and what it could be."

I frowned, stepping down from the porch and crossing the space between us. "What do you mean?" I asked, my voice steady but the fluttering in my chest betraying me.

He sighed deeply, a sound that seemed to carry the weight of years—years I hadn't shared with him, but now found myself wishing I had. "I've been living in this world for a long time, Sienna. A long time, and the truth is... I can't keep pretending it's enough. It's never been enough. Not for me. And not for you."

I shook my head, unwilling to accept where this was going. "Jack—"

"No," he interrupted, his hands reaching for mine, holding them with a quiet desperation that sent a shiver through me. "I need you to listen. You deserve a choice. The kind of choice I never gave you before."

I swallowed hard, trying to make sense of his words. "A choice? What are you talking about?"

The air around us grew thick with tension, a tangible thing that made the ground beneath my feet feel unstable, as though the world was tilting on its axis. "If we're to be together, truly together... I need you to leave behind everything you know. The world of the living, everything you've built, everything you love."

I stared at him, as if his words had been written in a language I could almost understand, but not quite. "What are you saying?" My voice was barely above a whisper now, the weight of his confession settling over me like a heavy fog.

He closed his eyes, as if the truth pained him too much to speak it, but when he opened them again, there was a rawness there that I had never seen before. "I'm not a man, Sienna. Not like you. And if you want to be with me—if you want this—you'll have to give up your life. The one you've known, the one you've built. You'll have to step into my world. The world of forever."

My heart stopped in my chest, the silence stretching out between us like an endless chasm. I couldn't breathe. I couldn't think. All I could do was stare at him, willing the words to make sense, willing the pieces to fall into place.

"You want me to leave behind everything?" My voice cracked, the pain of the thought searing through me. "My family? My friends? My life? Everything?"

His hands tightened around mine, pulling me closer, the desperation in his eyes mirroring my own. "I wouldn't ask if it weren't the only way," he said, his voice soft now, as though he were confessing something sacred. "But if you stay... if you remain in this world, I can't promise you the life we both deserve. We can't have what we want if you stay here. I need you to choose, Sienna. Choose me, or choose your life."

His words fell heavy, each syllable a weight that pressed down on my chest, threatening to crush the air from my lungs.

The air around us seemed to freeze in place, as if the earth itself were holding its breath. Jack's eyes—those deep, endless eyes—searched mine, his hands trembling just enough that I could feel the slight shift in his grip. It wasn't from cold, but something deeper, more profound. It was fear. He was scared, but not of me. Of what he was asking, of what this might mean. And somewhere, in the pit of my stomach, I knew that this was the moment that would decide everything. No turning back.

"I don't know if I can do that," I said finally, my voice thick with the weight of the words I had to speak. "How can I leave everything behind, Jack? You don't understand—my life is here. My family, my friends. It's all I know. How could I just... give that up?"

He stepped closer, the intensity of his gaze now pinning me in place. His brow furrowed, his lips tight as though every word he was about to speak was going to cost him a piece of his soul.

"I don't want you to give anything up," he said softly, the words almost pained, as though he were saying goodbye before the words had even left his mouth. "But you already know. You've always known. Since the first time we met, it's been building to this moment. And now... it's your choice."

I wanted to scream, to ask him how he could stand there and ask me to walk away from the only world I had ever known, but I couldn't. His expression, so open and vulnerable now, silenced every retort I could have mustered. Instead, I felt a wave of something unfamiliar wash over me—an unsettling mix of longing and loss. Because he was right. Deep down, I had always known this moment was inevitable.

"Is that really it, then?" I asked, voice barely above a whisper. "I choose you, or I choose them? There's no middle ground? No other way?"

"No middle ground," he confirmed, his tone low and resigned. "This world, this life, doesn't work that way. It never has. Not for me, not for anyone like me."

I clenched my fists at my sides, the urge to lash out like a flare in the dark, lighting up everything in its path. It was so unfair. To ask someone to leave behind everything they loved—to walk away from all the faces, the moments, the places that shaped them into the person they were. I wasn't sure I could. And yet, as I looked at Jack, there was a part of me that felt something I couldn't explain. A part of me that would follow him into the unknown, because the idea of never seeing him again was too much to bear.

I sucked in a shaky breath and took a step back, the weight of my decision sinking into my chest like stones in water.

"What happens if I don't choose?" I asked, my voice thin, like I was testing the waters before I jumped.

His gaze darkened, and for the first time, I saw a flicker of something harsh, something cold. "You stay in the world you know. You stay, and you forget about me. Or at least, you try to. But nothing will be the same. Not after this. Not after us."

I stared at him, the reality of what he was saying settling in. It wasn't just a choice. It was a consequence. A line in the sand that once crossed, could never be uncrossed. I would either step forward into his world, leaving my old life behind, or I would remain in the life I knew, knowing that I would always be missing a part of myself, a part of my soul.

The silence between us was thick, punctuated only by the sound of the wind rustling the trees, the faint chirping of crickets in the distance. I was trapped in the eye of a storm, with no way of knowing which direction the winds would carry me. And yet, despite the fear gnawing at the edges of my mind, there was a strange sense of calm that washed over me. Because for the first time in months, I was looking at Jack—not the man I had been chasing, not the mystery I had fallen in love with, but the real man, the one who stood in front of me now, vulnerable and raw.

"I can't promise you forever," I said softly, lifting my chin to meet his gaze. "But I can promise you right now. That I'm not walking away from you. Not tonight. Not yet."

He inhaled sharply, like he'd been holding his breath since the moment I'd answered him. And then, as if a weight had been lifted from his shoulders, his expression softened, the tension in his body easing, just for a moment.

"I never wanted to put you in this position," he said quietly, his voice cracking just a little. "But I had to give you the choice. It's yours to make, Sienna. No one else can make it for you."

I nodded, not trusting myself to speak. What could I say? I had already made my decision. My heart, that reckless, stubborn thing, had already chosen him.

But even as I made the choice in my mind, something dark and murky began to churn deep within me. Because as much as I wanted to believe I had control, that I could choose this life, this love, I couldn't ignore the nagging voice in the back of my mind. The one that asked, What happens if I'm wrong? What happens if there's no coming back?

And yet, standing there, in the soft glow of the setting sun, with Jack's steady gaze fixed on mine, I couldn't imagine walking away. Maybe it wasn't just about choosing him or my life. Maybe, I thought, it was about finding a life worth living—one I could face with him, whatever it looked like.

"Okay," I said finally, my voice barely audible, but the decision clear. "Okay. I choose you."

I didn't know how long we stood there in the thickening dusk, Jack's hand still wrapped around mine as though it could anchor me to this moment, to this decision that I had just made. My heart pounded, erratic and unsure, but there was something else, too. A strange, thrilling weight, like I was finally stepping into the life I was always meant to lead, even if I didn't fully understand it yet.

I swallowed hard, willing myself to breathe, because right now I was certain I was holding my breath, terrified of what might come next. Jack's eyes were softer now, a mixture of relief and something else—something that made my pulse race faster. I wasn't sure if it was love or guilt, but whatever it was, it was something that bound us together, that pulled us even closer.

"I never thought you'd say yes," he admitted, his voice soft but charged with an unspoken intensity. "But now that you have..." He trailed off, as if trying to find the right words, the ones that would make sense of the tangled mess between us.

"Well, maybe you don't know me as well as you think," I shot back with a wry smile, my words cutting through the tension, though my throat still felt thick, as though I were trying to speak around a lump that wouldn't go away.

Jack chuckled, the sound low and rich, but there was something fleeting in his smile. "I don't know you as well as I'd like to. Not yet, anyway."

"Maybe we'll fix that," I said, not realizing until it was out of my mouth that the words held more truth than I had intended. Maybe this was the beginning of something more than I could understand right now. Maybe it wasn't about choosing him or my life, but about finding a new life, one I could share with him.

But just as quickly as the thought came, doubt followed. The kind that crept in from the corners of my mind, nagging at me like an itch I couldn't scratch. I had chosen him, yes, but what did that really mean? What was I walking into? What if there was no going back from this world he spoke of—the one that had always seemed so distant, so unreal? What if I had made a mistake?

Jack must have sensed the shift in my energy because he stepped closer, his hand gently cupping my cheek. "Don't doubt this. Not yet. Not when we've barely even begun."

I wanted to believe him. I wanted to trust that this decision would somehow lead to something better, something more than I had ever known. But what if I was wrong? What if there was no way to turn back?

“I need you to promise me something,” I said suddenly, my voice tight. “Promise me that when we step into your world... we won’t lose who we are. We won’t forget where we came from.”

His brow furrowed, and I could see the wheels turning behind his eyes as he considered my request. For a moment, he said nothing, his gaze never leaving mine. The world felt strangely suspended in that instant, as if everything, all the noise and the chaos of the world, had quieted down, and it was just the two of us standing at the edge of some great unknown.

“I can’t promise you that,” he finally said, his voice tinged with sadness. “I can’t promise that we won’t change. That’s the price we pay for stepping into this life, Sienna. Everything changes when you cross over. But... I can promise you that I’ll be with you every step of the way.”

Every step of the way. It was a promise that should have comforted me, but instead, it only made the weight of my choice heavier. Because what did it really mean? How far would I have to go to truly be with him?

“I don’t know if I can do this,” I said, the words tumbling out of me before I could stop them. “I don’t know if I can become part of your world, Jack. I don’t know if I’m strong enough for that.”

His eyes softened, and for the briefest moment, the fierce determination in his expression wavered. “You’re stronger than you know. You always have been. And if you weren’t, I’d never ask you to make this choice. But we’re already in this, Sienna. Whether you want to be or not.”

I felt a shiver run down my spine as the full weight of his words hit me. It wasn’t just about the world I was stepping into. It was about the world I was leaving behind. And as much as I wanted to ignore the ache in my chest—the guilt, the fear—I couldn’t. I couldn’t forget the people I would lose, the life that would never be the same again.

"You say it's my choice," I said, my voice barely above a whisper. "But how much of it really is?"

His face hardened, and for a moment, I saw something flicker in his eyes—a glimmer of something dark. "What are you asking, Sienna?" he asked, his voice edged with something almost dangerous. "Do you think I'm asking you to give up everything just because I want you with me? Do you think I want to be alone in this world?"

The sudden intensity in his tone caught me off guard, and for a split second, I wondered if I had made the wrong decision altogether. But then, just as quickly, the tension between us dissolved, leaving only the quiet murmur of the evening breeze.

"I don't want to be alone either," I whispered, almost to myself, the words carrying more weight than I had intended.

Jack didn't respond immediately, his gaze unreadable, like he was piecing together something that I wasn't seeing. Then, without warning, he stepped back, his hand slipping from my cheek as if he were pulling away from something too fragile to hold.

"Then come with me," he said, his voice low and steady, but with an undeniable edge. "But know this—there's no turning back from here."

I nodded, heart pounding in my chest, as I realized that I wasn't just making a decision for now. I was stepping into something that could change everything forever.

But just as I was about to take the first step toward whatever future awaited us, I felt it—a cold rush of air, sharp as a knife, slashing across my skin.

And then I heard it.

The sound that would change everything.

Chapter 13: A Door Half-Open

The air in the hallway was thick with dust, the kind that hung in the corners like it had settled in for a long, lazy nap. My bare feet made no sound on the wooden floor, each step silent, as if the house itself was holding its breath. I couldn't sleep—couldn't find the peace I'd been chasing for weeks. It was always the same: when the night fell and the world went quiet, I was left with nothing but the sound of my own heart thumping in my chest. I had never been good at ignoring things, and it was growing impossible to ignore him, or the pull of the decision I couldn't make.

Him.

It wasn't that I didn't love him. Oh, I did. I loved him more than I had ever known how to love, in ways that made my skin burn and my heart skip. But somewhere in the tangled mess of emotions and desires, I'd forgotten what it meant to love myself. Every moment we spent together felt like I was fading into him, becoming someone I wasn't, someone I didn't want to be. And then there were the nights, like this one, when I lay beside him in our bed, only to feel the coldness creeping into my bones, the weight of something unspoken pressing on my chest.

The door had always been there, right in front of me. Just a door. But tonight, with the house dark and still, it seemed to have a life of its own. I'd passed it countless times without ever thinking twice. A door that was half-open in the cellar, old wood chipped and worn by time. I'd heard whispers about the cellar, vague stories that hinted at things that should be left alone. But curiosity, like the tide, had pulled me in.

I approached it now with a kind of wary reverence, the cold draft tugging at the hem of my nightgown. It was strange—the door had always been there, yes, but tonight it felt different. The air around it was thicker, heavier, as if something was waiting on the other side, holding its breath, waiting for me to move. The light from the hallway spilled over the threshold, casting eerie shadows on the stone floor. There was no sound except the rush of my pulse in my ears and the soft creak of the house settling around me.

I reached for the knob, and it turned under my hand with a gentle, almost reluctant ease. The room beyond it was dark, swallowed up by shadows that seemed to stretch farther than they should. There was no immediate sense of danger—just that old, suffocating feeling that something was wrong, something I couldn't quite place. And then I heard it. A voice, a whisper, barely more than a breath against my skin. It wasn't his voice, not the deep, calming timber I had grown so familiar with. No, this voice was different. It was softer, sweeter, and yet it carried the weight of something ancient. Something I couldn't ignore.

"Come in," it said, the words wrapping around me like a shroud. "Come find what you seek."

I hesitated, my heart in my throat, but the pull was undeniable. Something was inside that room. I could feel it—could almost taste it on the back of my tongue, like salt in the air before a storm. My feet moved of their own accord, and I stepped over the threshold into the dark. The door closed behind me with a soft click, cutting off the comforting light of the hallway. I was swallowed whole by the darkness.

For a moment, I couldn't see a thing. I blinked, trying to adjust, but the dark didn't give. The silence was oppressive, thick as smoke, and the air felt colder here—colder than I ever remembered it being. And then I felt it again. The voice. Not just the whisper now, but a presence, something that had been waiting for me, watching me as I approached.

"You've come," it said, this time with a sense of knowing, a satisfaction that sent a shiver down my spine.

I tried to speak, but my voice failed me, choked off by the sudden tightness in my throat. My feet moved again, guided by some unseen hand, toward the far corner of the room where a faint glow flickered. It wasn't much—just a pale light, barely enough to make out shapes.

And there he was.

But not him.

A figure stood there, half-hidden in the shadows, his features obscured by the soft light, his body trembling with some invisible energy. His back was to me, but there was no mistaking the way he held himself—tall, proud, and somehow... not quite right. A chill ran up my spine as I stepped closer, unable to stop myself, my legs carrying me toward him with a purpose I didn't understand.

I reached out, my fingers brushing against the air, feeling the tension in the room like a live wire. The figure turned slowly, revealing a face I knew all too well, yet not at all. His eyes were darker, more hollow, as if something had drained the life out of him, leaving only the shell behind.

He wasn't my him.

This wasn't the man I'd loved, the one who held me at night and whispered promises in my ear. This was something else, something ancient and broken, something that had been waiting for me.

My breath caught in my chest. "Who are you?" I whispered, not even sure I wanted the answer.

His lips parted, but it wasn't his voice that answered.

"You're not ready to know yet," it said. "But you will be."

I should have known. I should have turned around the moment I felt that voice, or maybe even earlier when the temperature dropped just enough to make the hairs on my arms stand on end. But curiosity, that wretched thing, kept pulling me closer. It wasn't just the air, thick and musty, that made my breath hitch. It was the promise of something that felt like an answer—something that could tie together all the loose, frayed threads of my life. Because nothing else made sense, not anymore. Not the endless nights of tangled sheets and whispered regrets. Not the way his eyes looked at me, full of longing, but distant—like he was staring through me, into something else, something I wasn't allowed to see.

The glow in the corner flickered again, casting strange shadows that twisted and buckled like something alive. And that's when I realized—the figure before me wasn't just an echo of him. It wasn't even a reflection of him. It was something else entirely. This wasn't the man I had shared a life with. No, this was something darker, something older, and it had been waiting for me.

"You shouldn't be here," the voice rasped, though it came from the figure's mouth, not his. I barely had time to process the words before a low chuckle—too deep, too knowing—rumbled through the room, making my skin crawl.

My mouth went dry. "What are you?" I demanded, trying to steady my voice.

The figure took a slow step forward, its gaze sharp, almost too sharp. "I'm what you're afraid to see," it murmured. The air grew colder still, and for a moment, I thought I might freeze in place, paralyzed by the weight of that statement. My heart hammered against my ribs, but I refused to let it show. No, I couldn't let it. Not now.

The floor beneath me groaned as I stepped back, the weight of the moment sinking in. It wasn't just fear anymore, it was... confusion. And betrayal. How long had this thing been here, behind the door, lurking in the shadows? How long had it been waiting for me to find it?

A cold laugh sliced through the tension. It wasn't a laugh of amusement; it was one of recognition. Recognition that, despite the terror gripping my heart, I was right where I was meant to be.

"Is this what you wanted?" I asked, unable to stop myself. My voice came out sharp, more defiant than I felt.

The figure tilted its head, the glow around it pulsing softly, like it was alive. "Oh, darling," it said with a smile that made my stomach churn, "you've been wanting this longer than you know."

And then, before I could protest, the figure stepped forward again, and this time, the glow in the room flared. My vision blurred, and for a heartbeat, I couldn't breathe. The room around me bent, warped, as if the walls themselves were shifting and stretching. I reached out, hands trembling, searching for something to hold onto.

That's when I heard him.

Not the voice I'd been listening to for weeks, full of softness and promises. No, this was different. This voice was familiar, but strained—like he was calling to me from a great distance.

"Don't," he said, his voice urgent. "Don't let it take you."

I spun, the room spinning with me. The walls were closing in. I reached out to him, but he wasn't there. Not in the way I expected. The figure smiled wider, its eyes now gleaming with a knowing that sent a new wave of terror crashing through me.

"You're too late," it whispered, and then it reached out with a hand, cold as the grave, and touched my arm.

I screamed, but the sound was smothered before it could leave my mouth. The world around me shuddered, and for a moment, I thought the floor had opened beneath me. The cellar, the stone walls, the distant hum of the house above—it all vanished.

I was falling.

It felt like I was being pulled into something vast, something that stretched far beyond the cellar. It wasn't just the room that had changed, it was me. I wasn't sure where I was anymore, or what I was becoming. The darkness had a pulse of its own, alive with a rhythm that seemed to be matching the frantic beat of my heart. I tried to call out, but no sound escaped. I tried to move, but my body felt like lead.

Then, suddenly, everything stopped.

I was back in the room. The walls were solid again, the stone floor beneath my feet. But the air was thick with something else now, something that tasted like dust and regret. The figure was still there, watching me with its too-knowing eyes, and I could feel its presence like a weight pressing on my chest.

"I told you," it said softly, "you were always meant to be here."

I clenched my fists, trying to steady my breathing, but the air was thick, heavy. Something inside me recoiled, something I couldn't name. But there was a flicker, something deeper, a piece of me that wasn't willing to just give up.

"No," I said firmly, my voice shaking. "I don't belong here. Not with you."

The figure's smile faltered, just for a second. But it was enough. Just enough for me to see the cracks, the lie.

"You really think you can leave?" It stepped closer again, and this time I didn't step back. "You think you're free of this? You're already ours."

I swallowed hard, fighting the rising panic in my chest. No. Not this time. Not now.

And then, in that moment of panic, I felt it—a tug, deep in my gut. Something pulling me, guiding me away from the figure and the suffocating room. Without thinking, I turned. I didn't know where I was going, but I knew I had to go.

The door.

It was there, standing wide open in the distance, the faintest sliver of light spilling through. And without a moment's hesitation, I ran.

My heart thundered as I sprinted toward the door, my feet skimming across the cold, damp floor, driven by some primal instinct that refused to be ignored. Every step felt heavier, like the walls were pushing in on me, trying to hold me back. But I couldn't stop. The pull was too strong. The shadows seemed to stretch longer with each stride, threatening to devour me whole. I didn't dare glance over my shoulder, not when I could feel the figure's eyes burning into the back of my skull, its voice echoing in my head.

"You can't outrun this. You're already part of it."

The words, laced with dark promises, reverberated through me, but I shoved them aside, focusing solely on the light spilling from the open doorway ahead. That sliver of light was my salvation, or so I convinced myself. I pushed forward, my breath ragged, my mind swirling in confusion. What had I just witnessed? What was that thing in the corner of the room, that dark figure with a smile that twisted something inside me?

The door was within reach now, the cold wood beckoning me like an old friend. My fingers brushed against the handle, icy to the touch, and for a moment, I hesitated. I'd never been this close to the edge before—never this close to whatever lay beyond that door. And what if—what if opening it meant leaving behind everything I'd known? What if the world I was running toward wasn't one of safety, but one of endless dark and whispers?

But then, that voice again, the voice that had been my constant companion for so long, the one that still haunted the edges of my thoughts.

"Don't turn back now."

I didn't need to be told twice. With a force that surprised even me, I wrenched the door open and stumbled into the light.

The world shifted, and I was no longer in the cellar. The room around me was unfamiliar, the air warmer, almost comforting. It was a stark contrast to the chill I'd just left behind. The walls were lined with old bookshelves, heavy with the weight of forgotten knowledge, and the faint smell of lavender lingered in the air, as if this place had been untouched for years.

I spun around, scanning my surroundings, and froze.

He stood there, waiting.

But this time, it wasn't the man I had known. No, this was something else, something far more dangerous. His eyes locked onto mine, glowing with an intensity that made my stomach drop. There was no love in those eyes, no warmth—only a raw, unrelenting hunger. His lips curled into a smile that didn't reach his eyes.

"You shouldn't have come," he said, his voice smooth but chilling.

"Where are we?" My voice cracked, betraying the unease bubbling up inside me. My chest tightened, my breath shallow. The room—the light, the air—none of it felt real.

He didn't answer at first. He simply stepped toward me, the soft scrape of his boots on the floor echoing in the silence. My pulse quickened, and I fought the urge to step back. There was nowhere to run, no way to escape.

"You've been running for so long, haven't you?" he murmured, his voice like silk, but his words like a blade to the heart. "You think there's a way out of this. That you can hide in some corner of your mind and forget. But you can't. You never could."

I swallowed, trying to maintain control, to keep the terror from consuming me. "What do you want from me?"

He took another step, and I couldn't help but flinch, my mind reeling with the implications of his words. You've been running for so long. Had I? Had I been trying to escape something? Or someone?

His gaze never left mine as he reached out, fingers brushing the air just in front of me, as if testing to see how close he could get before I crumbled.

"I don't want anything," he said, the words twisting like poison. "I just want you to see. To understand."

He was so close now that I could feel the heat radiating off him. I wanted to back away, but my feet felt rooted to the spot, as if some invisible force had shackled me to the ground. He smiled again, his teeth sharp and gleaming in the dim light.

"See what?" I whispered, my throat dry, the words barely escaping.

He tilted his head, the glint of amusement flashing in his eyes. "See the truth, of course. The truth you've been hiding from all along."

And then, before I could even process what he meant, he reached out and touched my arm.

The moment his fingers made contact with my skin, a jolt of electric pain shot through me, sharp and fierce. I gasped, my body jerking back instinctively, but it was no use. His grip tightened, and suddenly, I was there—no longer standing in the room with him, but... somewhere else entirely.

It was a place of shadow, where nothing seemed real. The air was thick with static, buzzing against my skin, and the ground beneath my feet felt unstable, as if it might crumble away at any second. The only thing that was solid, that was real, was him.

"You were never meant to stay in the light," he whispered, his voice a low growl, and the world around me seemed to pulse with the force of his words.

I opened my mouth to speak, to demand answers, but the words caught in my throat. I couldn't breathe. Couldn't move. It was as if I was trapped in a dream, a nightmare, but it was too real to escape.

"You wanted to know what lies behind the door, didn't you?" he continued, stepping closer until his breath was warm against my ear. "Well, here it is. This is where you were always meant to be."

My heart raced, panic rising like a tidal wave. I could feel the walls closing in on me, but no matter how hard I tried to struggle, no matter how hard I tried to move, it was as if I was glued to the spot.

And then, in the midst of the darkness, I saw something. Something that shouldn't have been there. A door—slightly ajar. A familiar draft, the same cold that had lured me to this place.

The door was waiting.

But was it the way out, or was it another trap?

The moment I reached for it, I felt his hand close around my wrist, his grip like iron. "You're not going anywhere," he said, his voice low and final. And for the first time, I felt the real weight of his power.

Everything went still.

Chapter 14: The Woman Who Waited

The air in the attic was thick, musty, and tangled with the scent of dust, forgotten years, and old wood that creaked like it was warning me to turn back. But I wasn't about to listen. The world down there, below me, had been too small for too long. The house felt like a trap, its walls closing in, whispering their secrets through cracks in the floorboards. I needed to find something. Anything that might explain the ghosts that still haunted me, like the echoes of footsteps that sometimes followed me down the hall when I was sure I was alone.

I pushed the door open, the hinges groaning in protest, and stepped into the room. The air was heavy with the scent of mildew, but beneath it, there was something more, something familiar. A strange feeling washed over me as my fingers grazed the edge of a dusty trunk. The worn leather looked as though it had been touched by countless hands, its surface faded, almost apologetic. It didn't take much to lift the lid. My hands moved of their own accord, the slow, deliberate motion betraying my eagerness. Inside, a jumble of forgotten relics lay scattered: letters tied with a ribbon, a tarnished locket, a dress folded carefully in the corner, as though someone had tried to preserve it in the best way they knew how—like they were preserving me.

I reached for the locket first, my fingers trembling slightly as I unclasped it. It was lighter than I expected, colder too. Inside, a faded photograph of a man stared back at me, his features soft with age but unmistakable. His eyes, dark and unwavering, locked onto mine. It was him. The man who had been a ghost in my life, always just out of reach, always slipping away when I needed him most. The man I had spent years waiting for. The man whose promises had never quite matched the reality of his absence.

The locket clicked shut as though it were trying to protect me from the memories it held. I tossed it aside for the moment, my eyes scanning the letters that lay tangled beneath it. I untied the faded ribbon, the paper inside brittle and yellow with time. I unfolded it carefully, as though it might crumble in my hands if I wasn't careful enough. The ink was smeared in places, but the words were still legible—barely.

My darling,

I hope you know that I love you more than words can say. I know this is a difficult time, and I can't explain why I must leave, but I swear to you, I'll come back. Please don't doubt me. Please don't doubt us. You're the only thing keeping me grounded, keeping me alive, and I will find my way back to you, no matter what.

Yours, always...

The letter dropped from my hands, its words still echoing in my mind. I will find my way back to you. How many times had I read those words, written in a shaky hand, in the dead of night when the loneliness felt too overwhelming? How many nights had I waited by the window, staring out into the empty street, hoping to see him return, just like he promised? How foolish I'd been, waiting for someone who never really came back—not the way I needed him to.

I sighed, and for the first time in a long while, I let myself sit down. I let the dust settle around me, the weight of it all pressing in, and I let myself feel the bitter sting of it. The woman who had written these letters was someone I couldn't quite recognize anymore. She was naïve, desperate, clinging to promises made in the quiet moments of a life that had long since been abandoned. She had loved him with every inch of her being, had built a life around a man who could never quite be hers in the way she needed.

And yet, as much as I hated to admit it, a part of me still loved him. Or rather, loved the idea of him. The man I had waited for was as much a figment of my imagination as he was a reality. He was a collection of memories and promises, words that wrapped themselves around my heart like vines, suffocating everything else.

I reached for the dress next, its delicate fabric soft and worn with time. It was beautiful, though—fragile and almost too perfect for a woman like me. I slipped my arms into the sleeves, the cool silk brushing against my skin, and stood in front of the mirror. The reflection that stared back at me was familiar, yet foreign, as if the woman in the glass didn't quite know who she was anymore.

It was me. But it wasn't.

I ran a hand through my hair, pushing it back from my face, and caught a glimpse of the locket once more. The man's eyes seemed to follow me, his presence weighing heavily in the room. I thought about the life I had lived, the woman I had been, and the one I had become in the years since he had vanished. I had built walls around myself, walls so high I'd forgotten what it felt like to be vulnerable, to hope for something more than what I had. I had convinced myself that I didn't need him anymore, that I was stronger than the woman who had waited for him.

But there was still a piece of her inside me, still a part of me that was waiting. Waiting for something I couldn't name, something I wasn't sure I was even worthy of anymore.

I folded the dress carefully, placing it back into the trunk. As I closed the lid, the room felt smaller, the air heavier. I wasn't sure what I had been expecting when I came up here, but it certainly wasn't this. The past had a way of creeping up on you, didn't it? It was never as far behind as you liked to think. I had been holding onto something that wasn't mine to keep anymore. And now, there was nothing left to do but let it go.

I dropped the last letter onto the floor, the fragile paper crinkling as it fluttered to a stop. There was something undeniably poetic about the way it had fallen. As if the words inside had finally been set free—no longer waiting to be read, no longer holding onto the past, but free to scatter with the dust that clung to the corners of this forgotten room.

A soft knock at the door startled me. My heart lurched in my chest, a knee-jerk reaction I couldn't suppress. I stood there for a moment, frozen in place, wondering if I'd somehow conjured that knock with the memories I had unearthed. The only sound now was my breath, quick and shallow, matching the rhythm of my thudding pulse. I didn't answer. No one else should have known I was up here. I had never told anyone about this room, about this attic. It was my secret, my place where the past still lingered like perfume that refused to fade away.

The knock came again, more urgent this time, a single rap followed by a hesitant pause. It was as though the person behind the door had reconsidered, unsure of what they might find, unsure of whether they should even proceed.

"Let it go," I whispered to myself, but the words didn't carry any conviction. The past was like an invitation that demanded to be opened, a sealed letter you couldn't resist reading. So, I answered it.

The door creaked open slowly, my hand instinctively gripping the handle as if the brass might slip from my grasp. Standing in the doorway was a silhouette, shadowed and indistinct, yet unmistakably familiar.

"Sarah," I breathed, the word slipping out before I could catch it.

She looked every bit the same, and yet, not. The years hadn't been kind to her. There was something in her eyes now—more guarded, more worn—that hadn't been there the last time I'd seen her. She was still the same woman who once laughed at my ridiculous attempts to bake chocolate chip cookies in a kitchen that wasn't mine, but now, she was different. More serious, more guarded.

"You've been avoiding me," she said, her voice tinged with the frustration that had been simmering between us for months now.

She stepped into the room with a quickness that surprised me, her boots scraping the old wood floor as she moved toward the trunk I had just closed.

"I've been busy," I replied, leaning against the doorframe, suddenly very aware of the disarray in the attic. It felt like a strange violation, having her here. As if I had been caught somewhere I wasn't supposed to be. The silence stretched between us, thick with things unsaid.

Sarah raised an eyebrow, her lips curling into a wry smile. "Busy? Or just hiding?" Her eyes flicked to the trunk, her gaze narrowing when she saw the faded ribbon, the creases in the paper that spilled from it like secrets begging to be heard.

I shifted uncomfortably, the weight of the room pressing down on me. I could feel the pulse of old regrets beating between us, heavy and suffocating. "It's not what you think," I muttered, hoping the explanation would feel as convincing to me as it might sound to her. But of course, it didn't.

"What's not to think?" Sarah's voice softened now, a tinge of something that might have been sympathy flickering behind the sharpness. "You've been holding on to something that's long gone. You know that, right?"

I swallowed hard, my throat tight. She was right. I had been holding on. But how could I let go of something that had been so central to everything I had built my life around? How could I simply toss away the memories that had made me who I was—who I'd been?

"I'm not holding on to anything," I lied, my voice betraying me with its tremor. I could hear the accusation in my own words, but I refused to acknowledge it. Instead, I focused on her—on the way she shifted uncomfortably from one foot to the other, as if unsure of her place in my world anymore.

Sarah's eyes softened just a little, but her words were no less direct. "You've been waiting, but for what? Him? The same man who left you without a word and who won't ever be the person you want him to be?" She sighed, and for a moment, her gaze softened. "I just don't get it, you know? You deserve more than this."

Her words hit harder than I expected. I had always thought Sarah was the strong one between us, the one who always knew how to cut through the bullshit and speak the truth when I was too afraid to. It was one of the things I loved about her—and resented about her in equal measure.

"I'm not like you," I said, the words slipping out before I could stop them. "You've always known what you wanted. You've always known how to get it. Me? I've just... I've just been waiting for something that may never come." I felt a bitter laugh bubbling up inside me, but I swallowed it down. It was all I could do to hold back the flood of emotion threatening to burst out.

"I don't know if I even remember what I was waiting for anymore," I continued, my voice small. "But I keep hoping—hoping I'll wake up one day, and everything will make sense."

"Hope is a funny thing," Sarah said, her tone now almost wistful. "Sometimes, it keeps us going. And sometimes, it keeps us stuck."

She was right. Hope had kept me moving for so long, but it had also anchored me in a past that wasn't mine anymore. It had kept me in a place where I could still pretend, just a little longer, that I hadn't been forgotten. Forgotten by the man who had promised to come back. Forgotten by a life that no longer seemed to fit.

"I don't know how to let go," I admitted, the words hanging in the air between us like a confession. And, for the first time in a long time, I wasn't sure if it was something I could do alone.

The weight of Sarah's words settled on me, pressing against my chest with an uncomfortable insistence. Her voice, always so direct, had cracked through the layers of silence I had carefully built, the walls I had spent years constructing to protect myself from the inevitable truths I refused to face. I could feel the sting of her gaze, sharp and unyielding, as she waited for me to respond.

I shifted uneasily on my feet, the clutter of the attic surrounding me like a maze of forgotten moments. The only light in the room came from a sliver of sunshine peeking through the half-open window, casting everything in a soft, muted glow. For a second, it felt like the room itself was watching me—waiting, just as Sarah had said. Waiting for me to make a decision I wasn't sure I was ready to make.

"You don't get it," I said finally, my voice catching in my throat. It wasn't the answer I wanted to give her. It wasn't even the answer I believed, but it was the one that felt easiest. "I don't know how to stop."

Her face softened for a split second, but there was no pity in her eyes, only understanding. "You think I've never been there?" she asked, her tone shifting into something warmer, more familiar. "I've spent my share of nights wishing for a life that wasn't mine. For things to be different. But you can't keep waiting for someone else to change your life for you. Not him. Not anyone."

I shook my head, though her words felt like they were starting to unravel something inside me. "You make it sound so simple," I said, trying to keep my voice steady. "Like it's just a switch I can flip."

"It's not simple," she replied, her eyes meeting mine with a sharpness that nearly made me flinch. "It's the hardest thing in the world. But it's the only thing that will set you free."

I didn't know how long we stood there, our silent war of wills hanging in the air, thick as the dust that clung to the beams above. Part of me wanted to retreat back into the memories that still clung to me, into the small, quiet spaces where I could keep pretending that everything was still as it had been, that the man I had waited for might still find his way back. But another part of me—an unfamiliar, almost unrecognizable part—began to wonder if Sarah was right.

"I didn't think you'd come here," I said quietly, my words tumbling out before I could stop them. "I thought maybe I could just... leave it all behind. Close that door and never come back to it."

Her eyes softened, but there was no judgment in her gaze, only a quiet understanding that made the room feel smaller, somehow. "And what would that have solved?" she asked. "Would it have fixed anything? Would you have felt better for running away from it?"

The question hung in the air between us, unanswered, as though it was one of those rare, unspoken truths that could only be realized when you were finally ready to hear it. The silence stretched out, thick with the weight of what I hadn't said, what I hadn't allowed myself to feel.

"I don't know," I whispered, more to myself than to her. "Maybe it wouldn't solve anything. But I thought it might give me a little peace."

"Peace doesn't come from running," Sarah said, her voice softer now, almost gentle. "It comes from facing the things that scare you the most. It comes from choosing to live in the present instead of the past."

I wanted to argue, wanted to tell her that she didn't understand, that it wasn't that simple. But the words stuck in my throat. I could feel the truth of what she was saying sinking in, like the steady drip of rain on a roof that had been dry for too long. Slowly, relentlessly.

A sharp noise interrupted the quiet, the sound of something shifting in the corner of the attic. I spun toward it, heart racing as I searched the dim space for the source of the noise. My breath caught in my throat as I spotted something—no, someone—standing just beyond the farthest beam of light.

"Who's there?" I called out, my voice steady despite the sudden surge of panic. My eyes strained to make out the figure, but all I could see was a shadow—tall, looming, like it didn't belong.

For a long moment, the room fell silent. The only sound was my own breathing, shallow and quick. And then, the figure stepped into the light.

My stomach dropped as recognition flooded me.

He was here. The man I had once loved. The man I thought I'd buried along with everything else in this room. He stood there, his face as unreadable as the day he left. His hair was longer now, but it was him. There was no mistaking those eyes. Those eyes that had once made promises they could never keep.

"What the hell are you doing here?" My voice came out in a harsh whisper, as if speaking too loudly might break the fragile reality I was standing in.

He didn't answer right away. Instead, he just stared at me, as though the years between us hadn't existed at all.

"I've been looking for you," he said finally, his voice low, rough in a way that sent a chill down my spine.

"Looking for me?" I echoed, incredulous. "After all this time? You just... show up?"

He stepped closer, and I could feel the room shrink around me, the air growing heavy with all the things left unsaid. "There's a lot I need to explain," he said quietly, his eyes never leaving mine.

I swallowed, my heart racing. I wanted to say something, anything, to push him away—to keep him at arm's length. But as I opened my mouth, the words wouldn't come. Instead, I just stood there, frozen in place, as the past I had thought I'd buried came crashing back into my life.

Chapter 15: A Fire Rekindled

The air in the room hummed with something heavy, something unsaid. We sat side by side, my hand tucked in his, the warmth of it both foreign and familiar. There was a quiet intensity that had settled between us, like the calm before a storm that was always on the edge of breaking. I couldn't tell if it was the quiet in his eyes or the way the world outside felt distant, like I was floating in some kind of waiting space, suspended between then and now.

His fingers brushed over mine in slow, deliberate motions. I could feel the calluses on his skin, the rough edges of time spent building things, fixing things—always the fixer, never the one in need of fixing. It made sense, in a way. People like him didn't need saving. They just needed someone to stand by them when the walls started crumbling. And I, foolishly, had always been the one to run when things fell apart.

But that was before. Now, as I sat there, I could feel the weight of the years pressing in on us. Time had never been our ally, always slipping away like sand through our fingers. I thought I had forgotten him, buried him deep in the corners of my mind. Yet, here he was, more vivid than ever, every laugh, every word we shared, all coming back with an intensity I wasn't prepared for.

"Do you remember the rain?" His voice, low and rough, broke the silence, pulling me back to that time.

I closed my eyes, the memory of it flooding over me. It had been our secret weather, hadn't it? The rain that was never just weather. The rain that meant something—somewhere between the start of our relationship and the end of it, we'd shared those days drenched in the sound of thunder, soaked in quiet understanding. But now, the memory felt different, like a relic. A broken picture frame, but the picture wasn't entirely gone, just a little faded.

"I do," I said softly, shifting on the couch to face him fully. "I remember it like it was yesterday. The way it would fall, so steady, so sure."

He nodded, the corners of his lips lifting in a half-smile that didn't quite reach his eyes. "And you hated it. Hated the way it made everything feel heavy, like you were trapped under the weight of something you couldn't escape."

I swallowed hard. The truth of his words stung more than I wanted to admit. He was right. I had hated the rain—hated how it mirrored the heaviness of my heart at the time, how it was never just weather but a reflection of everything I couldn't bring myself to say.

"Did you?" I asked, keeping my voice steady, though my heart felt like it was beating in double time. "Did you really think that? That I hated it?"

He studied me for a moment, his gaze so intense it almost hurt. "I think you hated feeling trapped. And the rain made you feel like there was no way out."

The words cut through me, sharp as glass, and I couldn't help but wince. The truth was, I had felt trapped. But not by the rain—by him, by us. It had been too much, too fast, too everything, and I didn't know how to breathe without feeling like I was suffocating. I had pulled away, like I always did when things started to matter.

But that was the past, wasn't it? We couldn't live there anymore, not even in these moments of silence where every breath felt like a thousand unspoken confessions.

"I didn't know how to be what you needed," I whispered, the words slipping out before I could stop them.

He didn't answer immediately, his thumb tracing small circles on the back of my hand. I had the sudden urge to pull away, to break the contact, but I didn't. Instead, I held onto his hand like it was my lifeline, like it was the only thing keeping me tethered to the present.

"You were what I needed," he finally said, his voice rough with something I couldn't name. "You just didn't believe it."

I wanted to tell him he was wrong. I wanted to argue, to defend myself, but the words stuck in my throat. Because he wasn't wrong. I hadn't believed it. I had never believed it. Not when we were together, not when we were apart. The worst part was, I didn't even know why.

The silence stretched between us, thick and suffocating. I could feel him, feel the weight of his words hanging in the air like an unspoken promise. It was that same fire again, the one that had always been there, smoldering beneath the surface. Only now, it was different. It was real, more solid than it had ever been.

And yet, I wasn't sure if it was a fire I wanted to rekindle.

His gaze didn't leave me, his eyes dark and searching, like he was looking for something I wasn't ready to give. Maybe it wasn't about whether I was ready or not. Maybe it was about whether he was, whether we both were.

"I don't know what this is," I said, the words leaving my mouth before I could stop them. "I don't know what I'm doing here, what we're doing."

He didn't flinch. He didn't pull away. He simply watched me, his thumb continuing its steady rhythm against my skin.

"Neither do I," he said softly, "but maybe we don't need to know. Maybe we just need to stop trying to figure everything out."

His words lingered in the air, hanging between us like an invitation I wasn't sure I was ready to accept.

The night grew heavier, pressing down on the room with the weight of unsaid words. I shifted, trying to find a more comfortable position, but his hand never left mine. Each brush of his fingers, each subtle shift in the way he held me, felt like an anchor, keeping me rooted to this moment even as the past threatened to pull me under. The scent of him was intoxicating—earthy and familiar, like rain-soaked soil after a long dry spell, and it made my heart ache in ways I couldn't explain.

I glanced at him, really looked at him, and felt a flicker of something—longing, maybe. Or was it regret? He had always had a way of looking at me like I was a mystery to be solved, a puzzle he wasn't quite finished with. Now, I found myself wishing I could figure him out. He had changed in ways that were too subtle for me to grasp—more solid, more grounded—but the flicker of uncertainty in his eyes reminded me of the man I once knew. He was standing right in front of me, but he felt far away, and that distance between us was a chasm I couldn't cross, no matter how much I wanted to.

"You never did like being in the dark," he said, his voice so quiet that I almost missed it.

I blinked, unsure if I had heard him correctly. "What?"

He leaned forward slightly, his forehead just barely grazing mine, and I caught the glimmer of something in his eyes—was it amusement? "You always hated not knowing everything, not having control. But look at us now. We're both floating in the unknown, aren't we?"

His words hit me harder than I expected. They were true, painfully so. I had always craved control, certainty—both things that had slipped through my fingers like water through a sieve. The irony was thick, but I didn't know if I could laugh about it yet. Not now. Not when everything felt like it was hanging by a thread.

"Maybe I've learned to live with it," I muttered, but the words felt hollow, empty. A defense mechanism. I had spent so long telling myself that uncertainty wasn't my enemy, but in this moment, it was all I could feel. And I hated that.

He didn't respond right away. Instead, his hand slid from mine, but he didn't pull away entirely. His fingers, still warm, hovered just an inch above my skin, like he was giving me a choice, waiting for me to reach for him. But what did I want? What could I want? The fire between us was blinding, but it burned too brightly, too painfully. I didn't know if I could stand the heat again.

"You never did learn how to ask for what you wanted, did you?" he said, his voice low, but the edge of his words cutting through me.

I let out a sharp laugh, but it wasn't anything close to joyful. "And you never learned how to take no for an answer," I shot back, my tone sharper than I intended. But it was true. He had always wanted more from me than I could give, always pushed me toward a future I wasn't sure I wanted. It was easier to retreat, to keep things at arm's length. But in doing that, I had let everything slip away.

He looked at me then, really looked at me, and the silence between us stretched, thick and uncomfortable. "You're still running, aren't you?" The words weren't accusatory. They were just a statement, a quiet truth that settled into the room like a cloud I couldn't shake off.

I swallowed hard, refusing to look away. "I'm not running." My voice was unsteady, and I hated how fragile it sounded. "I'm just..." I trailed off, searching for the right words. Searching for something that made sense of what had happened between us. But nothing did. Not really.

He took a deep breath, as if collecting himself, and then he reached out, his hand resting on my shoulder, gentle but firm. "You don't have to run anymore," he said quietly. His thumb brushed over my skin in a slow, soothing motion, and for the first time, I didn't feel like I had to pull away. I felt... safe, strangely enough. Safe in his presence, in the weight of his touch. But even as my body softened in response, I couldn't quite shake the fear that had always been there—the fear that, in the end, we would never be able to bridge the gap between us.

"We can't go back," I said before I could stop myself. The words had been burning on the tip of my tongue, and once I said them, they hung in the air, the undeniable truth of it all.

"No," he agreed, his voice just a thread above a whisper. "We can't. But that doesn't mean we can't move forward." His gaze was steady now, unwavering, and I could see that he wasn't looking at me with the same uncertainty I felt. He wasn't afraid of what was coming next.

But I was.

I wanted to believe him, to believe in the possibility of something more, but there were too many pieces missing. Too many gaps in the story that I didn't know how to fill.

"Forward?" I echoed, raising an eyebrow. "And where exactly is forward?"

He grinned, a glimmer of mischief flickering in his eyes. "I'm not sure yet. But I'm willing to find out." He paused, his smile fading just enough to make me wonder if he was taking a step back, too. "But you've got to stop running for me to do that."

I opened my mouth to respond, but no words came out. What could I say to that? Could I really stop running? Could I risk everything, even my own heart, for a chance at something that might not last? A fire rekindled is still a fire, after all—it can burn you just as easily as it can warm you.

I tried to focus on his words, but my thoughts were scattered, like pieces of a puzzle I couldn't quite fit together. The way he spoke, the way he looked at me—it was almost as if he hadn't changed at all. As if I hadn't either. And yet, the space between us, the chasm that had grown over time, felt insurmountable. Maybe that was the trick, I thought bitterly—he'd never needed the distance, never needed to build the walls that I had. For him, this was all just a moment we could step into, and for me, it felt like an abyss I'd have to crawl out of if I wanted to find any peace.

"You still don't get it, do you?" he said, breaking my thoughts like a glass shattering on the floor. His voice was low but firm, tinged with something like frustration—frustration I wasn't sure was aimed at me or at something neither of us could articulate. "You still think there's a right time, a perfect moment for all of this to make sense. But there isn't. There's just now."

I wanted to argue with him, wanted to throw back a dozen reasons why this couldn't work, why it would only end the way it always had. The pattern of us—of me pulling away when the heat became too much, when the fire burned too hot, too bright. But I didn't argue. Instead, I found myself watching him, watching the way his eyes softened, the way the tension in his jaw seemed to ease. It was almost as if he had already accepted the inevitability of what we were—and what we weren't.

"I don't need things to make sense," I said, and the words tasted like rust on my tongue, harsh and real. "I just need to know if I'm brave enough to face them."

He was quiet for a moment, his thumb still tracing invisible patterns on my skin. I thought for a second that he might laugh, might dismiss me like he always did when I tried to be vulnerable. But instead, his expression shifted, a shadow crossing his features.

"Brave enough?" he repeated, almost to himself. "Maybe that's all we have left."

I wasn't sure if he meant it as a challenge or a concession, but I felt it all the same. That quiet truth that I wasn't sure how to react to. The truth that whispered of all the things we had never said, of all the things we would never say. And yet, the silence between us had shifted, deepened. It wasn't awkward, not exactly. But it wasn't comfortable either. It was that space you find between longing and fear, between knowing and not knowing, and it made my chest tight with something I couldn't name.

I pulled my hand back, not entirely sure why I did it. Maybe I was afraid he would feel the weight of my doubt in the simple act. Maybe I was afraid of what would happen if I didn't pull away.

His eyes tracked my movement, but he didn't try to stop me. Instead, he stood, his posture stiff for just a moment before he relaxed. "I think we both know what's at stake here," he said, his voice rougher than before, as if the words had dragged something from deep within him. "But that doesn't change the fact that we're standing at the edge of something that could either break us or build us back up."

His words hung in the air like smoke, shifting in all the right ways, but not landing in my heart the way they were meant to. Because I wasn't sure I wanted to be built back up.

"I don't know if I can do it again," I said, my voice quieter now, almost fragile, as if the admission was something too heavy to carry.

He looked at me then, really looked at me, his gaze searching, but not judgmental. "Then don't," he said simply. "Do it for yourself. Not for me."

That made me laugh, the sound a little too bitter for my liking. "It's never just for myself, is it?" I didn't mean it to sound like an accusation, but the words left my mouth before I could stop them. The truth was, nothing had ever been just for me. Not when it came to him. Not when it came to us.

"Maybe it is," he said, leaning against the back of the chair, his hands in his pockets. "But you'll have to decide that. No one else can do it for you."

I opened my mouth to respond, but the words died on my lips as a knock echoed from the door. A sharp, insistent knock, followed by the faint sound of a voice from the other side. My stomach dropped, that familiar sense of dread settling over me.

"You expecting someone?" he asked, his tone light but with a hint of suspicion.

I shook my head. "No." But I didn't move. There was something about that knock, something that felt wrong, off in the way it interrupted the delicate tension we'd built.

The knock came again, more urgent this time, followed by a muffled voice. "We need to talk."

My pulse quickened, and I felt a sudden, jarring shift in the room. The fire that had been smoldering between us felt like it had gone out, replaced by an unshakable unease. I glanced at him, and in his eyes, I saw the same flicker of concern, the same instinctive awareness that something had just changed.

"Who is it?" he asked, the calm in his voice belying the tension I could feel in the air.

"I don't know," I whispered, barely able to breathe. My heart was racing, and every instinct I had was telling me that whatever was waiting for us on the other side of that door was not something either of us were ready for.

The knock came again, louder this time.

And then, I heard the words that stopped my heart entirely. "Open up. It's about her."

Chapter 16: The Veil Weakens

The first time I noticed it, I thought it was a trick of the light. A flicker in the hallway, just at the edge of my vision—barely enough to be sure of. I chalked it up to the long hours and the sleep-deprived haze I had been slipping into lately. But then it happened again. And again.

It was a chill at the back of my neck, like someone was standing too close, but when I turned, the hallway was empty. The walls seemed to hold their breath, and the air in the house had taken on the texture of something waiting. Waiting for what, I couldn't say. But I felt it—the pull, the insistence. And I knew, in some strange, primal part of me, that it was connected to him.

I wasn't sure when it started, when the feeling of his presence shifted from unsettling to familiar, but it had. His shadow was no longer a specter that darted from corner to corner but something that seemed almost tangible, like a thread pulled tight across a canvas, taut and purposeful. He would be there, when I least expected him, perched in a corner of the room, his dark eyes fixed on me with an intensity that made the hairs on my arms stand on end. And I—foolish as I was—began to welcome it.

It wasn't love, not in the way I would have recognized it. There were no flowers, no tender touches, no soft whispers in the night. But there was something there, something magnetic, pulling me closer with a force I couldn't fight. He was a presence, a lingering warmth, something in between the living and the dead, something too dangerous to ignore. Yet every time he appeared—whether standing motionless in the doorway or vanishing into the shadows—I felt that familiar tug, like gravity itself had bent around him and drawn me into his orbit.

The house, too, was changing. I could feel it in the creak of the floorboards beneath my feet, in the heavy silence that settled over the rooms when the wind outside stopped blowing. It seemed to respond to him, to us. The walls groaned, like they were waking from a long, uneasy sleep, and I could hear faint whispers echoing through the rooms, voices just out of reach. The air smelled different, too—musty, like the forgotten corners of an attic, mixed with something faintly metallic, like blood. It was in the way the light shifted in the mornings, casting eerie shadows that didn't seem to belong. The more I let him in, the more the house seemed to merge with him, as though the boundaries were blurring and pulling us both into something bigger, something darker.

I couldn't pull away, not now. Not after everything that had already happened, after the way he had made me feel. Not after the way his cold fingers would brush the skin of my wrist, like a reminder that he was here, that I wasn't alone, not anymore.

But that, too, was a lie. Because with him came the feeling that I was more alone than I'd ever been. There was no one left to understand the tension in my bones, the way my body thrummed with the pulse of something foreign and ancient. When I looked in the mirror, I no longer recognized the person staring back. My eyes were too wide, too haunted, my skin too pale, my lips too red, too full. I wasn't sure if I was becoming part of him or if he was becoming part of me. Either way, I could feel it. The weight. The change.

And yet, there was a kind of sweetness to it. A lullaby beneath the horror. The way he would stand there, silent, watching me, never speaking, just waiting. For what, I wasn't sure. But I could sense that he, too, was caught in this web, this strange tangle of time and space that neither of us understood.

It was impossible to tell how much of this was me and how much was him. How much of this was the house and how much of it was simply the weight of all the things we had yet to uncover. Because there was still so much that I didn't know. There were secrets buried in this house, secrets tied to him, secrets tied to me. The longer I stayed, the more I felt the weight of that knowledge pressing against me, urging me to dig deeper, to unravel it all.

But I wasn't ready. I wasn't sure if I ever would be. The closer I got to the truth, the more it seemed to slip through my fingers like water, as though it were meant to stay hidden, meant to stay buried. I couldn't let it go. I couldn't turn away from him.

I stepped into the parlor, the dim light from the setting sun filtering through the dusty curtains, casting long shadows that stretched across the floor. It felt colder in here, somehow, more oppressive. As if the air itself had grown thicker, more charged. And there he was, just standing there in the doorway, his presence filling the room in a way that made the space feel smaller, tighter.

His gaze was intense, unwavering, and I felt the familiar pull, the irresistible desire to close the distance between us. But I couldn't. Not yet. There was something stopping me, something in the way the room seemed to be holding its breath, waiting for me to make the next move.

His lips parted, but the words that fell from them weren't what I expected. "You're running out of time."

The voice was low, raspy, a whisper that seemed to echo in the very bones of the house, vibrating through the floor beneath my feet.

I didn't know what he meant. Not yet. But I felt it, deep in my gut—the certainty that whatever was coming, I wouldn't be able to stop it.

I knew I should've been scared. The rational part of me—well, the part of me that was still a bit too attached to this world, to logic and reason—told me I should be terrified of what was happening. Objects shifting on their own, doors creaking open when no one was around, that unnerving whisper that seemed to slither under the surface of every conversation. But all I could do was lean in, closer and closer, like I was listening for a secret that could only be understood by walking deeper into the dark.

Maybe it was the way he looked at me. There was something magnetic about it, something that felt like an invitation I couldn't refuse. Every time I caught his gaze—dark, unreadable, yet unmistakably intense—I couldn't help but wonder what it would feel like to cross that line. To step into whatever world he came from, where the rules of time and space didn't quite apply.

The house was changing, yes, but I was changing, too. I could feel it in the air, thick and heavy with something unspoken. The walls themselves seemed to be reaching out, inch by inch, creeping closer until I could feel the pulse of the house in the pit of my stomach. And him—always just there, always hovering at the edge of my consciousness—was at the center of it all, like a storm that had somehow taken root in the foundation of this place.

But it wasn't just him, not entirely. It was the way the house responded to him, to us. The once quiet corners of the house had taken on a kind of living quality. I'd catch glimpses of movement—shadows that didn't belong, objects that shifted when I wasn't looking. I'd hear footsteps, echoing down empty hallways, always one step behind me. And yet, every time I turned around, I'd find nothing but empty space. The veil was thinning, I realized, and not just between me and him. It was between this world and the next.

I'd begun to wonder, in the quiet hours of the night, what would happen if I didn't pull back. If I didn't fight whatever this was that had wrapped itself around me, pulling me in, inch by inch, until I was so far gone I couldn't see where reality ended and the impossible began.

"Are you afraid?" he asked, his voice low and smooth, sliding into my thoughts like a forgotten melody. I didn't need to see his face to know he was there, standing just behind me, too close to be comfortable.

I paused, considering the question. I wanted to say yes. I wanted to scream that I was terrified, that this whole thing was madness, that the house was falling apart at the seams and that I couldn't keep up with the changes. But instead, I just shook my head. "No. I don't think I am."

There was silence, then a soft laugh, like he found the answer both amusing and strangely satisfying. "You should be. Fear is the only thing that keeps you from falling too far."

Falling. I couldn't help but wonder if that was exactly what was happening to me. I felt like I was slipping, like every moment I spent in the house was another step into a place I could never return from. It was like treading water, just barely keeping my head above the surface, but each wave felt stronger, more insistent, as though it was trying to pull me under.

I could feel the shift in the air, the weight of his presence pressing against my skin. It was becoming harder to separate myself from it, from him. When I closed my eyes, I saw nothing but darkness, a thick, swirling fog that made me dizzy. When I opened them again, I would find him—always there, always watching. His eyes burned with an intensity that left me breathless, like he was studying me, like I was a puzzle he was slowly, deliberately solving.

I didn't know what he wanted from me. And I didn't know if I wanted to find out. But there was no going back now.

The house seemed to pulse with a kind of energy, a silent warning that reverberated through every room. The walls, once comforting in their stillness, had taken on an ominous tone. It was as if the house was aware of everything I was going through, every thought I had, every decision I was too afraid to make. There was a tension in the air, a feeling of something about to snap. It was in the way the wood groaned beneath my feet, in the way the light flickered at odd moments, casting shadows that danced on the edges of my vision.

And then, one evening, as I sat by the fire in the drawing room, staring into the flames, the house let out a sound—a low, almost imperceptible moan that echoed through the floors, as if the very foundation of the house was shaking. It was the kind of noise you'd expect from a place on the edge of collapsing, as though the weight of time had finally taken its toll. I looked up, expecting to see him, but he wasn't there. Instead, the room felt... different. Cold. The fire, once crackling with warmth, now seemed distant, its heat just beyond reach.

I stood, walking toward the window, my hand trailing along the smooth surface of the glass as I peered out into the darkened garden. The trees outside were still, their branches stretching like gnarled fingers into the night sky. But something was different. The wind had died, and the air outside felt charged, like the calm before a storm.

I couldn't help it—I had to know.

Turning away from the window, I walked to the door, my feet moving almost of their own accord. I hadn't planned on leaving the house tonight, hadn't even thought about it. But the pull was undeniable. It was as if something in the very air was calling me, beckoning me to step outside, to cross over into whatever lay beyond the house's threshold.

The door creaked open as I stepped into the night, and the air, cool and sharp, hit me like a slap to the face. The garden was quiet, unnaturally so, and I couldn't shake the feeling that I wasn't alone. I wasn't sure why, but I knew, deep in my bones, that I was being watched.

And then, from the corner of my eye, I saw him.

I wasn't sure when the house stopped feeling like a home and started feeling like a cage. The change was subtle at first—just the creak of floorboards in the dead of night, the occasional chill that skittered up my spine. But the longer I lingered here, the more I felt the walls pressing in, as though they were closing ranks, tightening around me like a noose. The air was heavier now, thick with something ancient, something old. And every time I reached out, touched the cold stone walls or breathed in the musty air, I could feel it. The house wasn't just an inanimate structure; it was a living thing. Alive with secrets. Alive with the past.

I had convinced myself, at least for a while, that it was nothing more than my imagination. I tried to push the thoughts out of my head—tried to ignore the whispers that seemed to follow me from room to room, the shadows that stretched just a little too far, that flickered at the corners of my vision. I told myself it was normal. I wasn't losing my mind. This house, this place, had been here far longer than I had. Maybe it was simply settling, stretching into itself, trying to adjust to the lives it had taken in over the years. But deep down, I knew. I knew there was something more. And the more I tried to deny it, the more it wrapped itself around me.

And then there was him.

It was impossible not to feel him—impossible not to sense the way he lingered in the corners of the room, watching, waiting. His presence was palpable, thick in the air like smoke, curling around me in ways that made my skin prickle. But it wasn't just his nearness that unsettled me. It was the way the house seemed to change when he was near. The walls seemed to lean in, listening to his every word, every breath, and I couldn't help but wonder if the house itself was aware of him, as though it was just as trapped in whatever this was as I was.

He had never told me his name. Not that I could ask him. The words never seemed to form properly in my mouth when I was around him. He didn't need to speak, though. His silence was louder than anything he could have said. But even in that silence, I could feel the tension between us, like a string pulled taut, ready to snap.

"You're still here," I said, my voice strangely calm, even though I could feel the pulse of panic just beneath the surface.

I had gone out into the garden to escape the house for a moment, to breathe, to remember what it felt like to exist outside of this place. But the moment I stepped back inside, I found him. Standing in the doorway, half in shadow, half bathed in the soft light from the hallway.

"I never left," he replied, his voice low and effortless, like he had all the time in the world.

There was something unnerving about the way he spoke, as though he existed outside of time. But his words weren't what unsettled me the most. It was the way his eyes looked at me, like he knew everything I was thinking before I even had the chance to fully form the thought. Like he could hear the rhythm of my heartbeat, understand the tremor in my hands before I even noticed it.

"You can't keep doing this," I said, my voice barely above a whisper. The words were barely my own, tumbling out of my mouth like something I wasn't ready to admit.

He didn't move, but there was a shift in the air. It was subtle, but I felt it—like the world around us had exhaled, taking a breath it had been holding for far too long. "Doing what, exactly?" he asked, his eyes never leaving mine.

I swallowed hard, trying to gather the courage to speak, to say the words I had been avoiding for days. "This," I said, gesturing between us. "The house. You. Me. This... whatever this is."

His lips curved into a smile, the kind of smile that didn't reach his eyes. "I told you. You're the one who invited me in."

The words stung more than I expected. I had been the one to open the door, to let him cross the threshold. I had let him in because I thought I could control it—because I thought I could manage whatever this was. But now? Now I felt as if I were drowning, sinking deeper and deeper into a world that didn't belong to me.

"And yet, you're still here," he added, his voice tinged with something like amusement.

I wanted to say something—anything—to push him away, to break the tension that had grown between us like a storm cloud. But nothing came. I couldn't move. I couldn't think. All I could do was stand there, caught in the gravity of his presence, knowing that whatever was happening, it was bigger than either of us.

A sudden, sharp crack split the silence.

I jumped, instinctively reaching for the doorframe to steady myself. My heart raced, the blood rushing in my ears as the room seemed to tilt, the walls stretching and bending in ways they shouldn't have. For a moment, everything felt wrong. The very air seemed to shimmer, like heat waves rising from the floor, warping the space around us. The light flickered and dimmed, casting long, twisted shadows that seemed to crawl along the walls. The house groaned again, louder this time, like a beast waking from a long, troubled sleep.

"I think it's time," he said, his voice barely audible over the rising noise. His words were thick with an urgency I hadn't heard before.

"Time for what?" I whispered, my throat dry, every instinct screaming at me to run.

But before he could answer, the door slammed shut behind me with a deafening bang.

And the room—no, the entire house—felt like it was holding its breath.

Something was coming. Something I had no way of stopping.

I turned to face him, but the space where he had been was empty.

Chapter 17: The Hidden Staircase

The fog, thick and stubborn as an old argument, clung to the ground in layers, muffling the world around me. The sun, just beginning to stretch its fingers over the horizon, barely made a dent in the oppressive silence. In the dim light of the library, the air smelled like dust and musty paper, a scent so familiar it had become part of me, seeping into my skin, settling in my bones. It was the kind of morning that made the world feel smaller, quieter, like something unsaid was hanging in the air, waiting to be revealed. And reveal it did.

I had always found comfort in the library. The heavy oak shelves stacked with books, the ones I had read and the ones I hadn't, their spines lined up neatly, each one holding a secret waiting for the right moment to be unearthed. But on this particular morning, a curiosity tugged at me, pulling me toward something that had never caught my attention before. It was the tapestry, a faded thing that hung by the back wall, its intricate pattern of dark blues and golds a stark contrast to the room's usual dull lighting. I had passed it countless times, always distracted by the far more important business of sorting through old manuscripts or hunting for the next forgotten gem. But today, it seemed to hum with a faint energy, as though something was waiting just behind it.

I tugged at the edge of the tapestry, more out of instinct than reason, and my fingers brushed against something cold and smooth. The wall was not quite a wall at all, but a thin, hidden doorway. The hairs on the back of my neck prickled. I should have stopped. The rational part of me screamed that this was a mistake—this was a place no one was meant to find—but the other part, the one that lived for the mystery, urged me forward.

The door creaked open, groaning like an old woman roused from a deep sleep. It revealed a narrow, spiraling staircase that seemed to dive into the belly of the earth itself. The air that leaked from the gap was damp, heavy with the smell of stone and something ancient. My pulse quickened as I hesitated at the threshold, the flickering candlelight casting strange shadows across the walls. I had no idea what I was walking into, but something told me that there was no turning back now.

The staircase was steep and uneven, each step seeming to creak louder than the last as I descended. The stone underfoot was slick with age, a thin layer of moisture clinging to it like a warning. The further I went, the colder it became, until the air felt like it had a bite to it, a sharpness that made my breath come out in shallow bursts. My fingers brushed against the walls as I navigated the tight turns, feeling the smoothness of the stone, rough in some places and smooth in others, as if worn down by hands long forgotten.

It felt like hours before I reached the bottom, though it could have been mere minutes. Time seemed to twist in the depths of this place, warping in ways I couldn't explain. The chamber that awaited me was vast, its stone walls etched with symbols that seemed to pulse with a strange energy. They were old, impossibly old, each one more intricate than the last, winding in spirals and loops that made my head spin if I stared at them too long. The air here was thick, almost too thick, like it was waiting for something—or someone—to arrive. I could almost hear it, the hum beneath the silence, a sound so faint I wondered if it was merely the echo of my own thoughts.

At the center of the room stood a stone pedestal, its surface worn smooth by time, and around it, scattered like broken promises, were artifacts I couldn't begin to identify. Some were small, delicate objects, their surfaces tarnished by centuries of neglect, while others were large, imposing pieces that seemed to belong to a different age altogether. But it wasn't the artifacts that caught my attention, not immediately. It was the feeling that settled in the pit of my stomach, a feeling I couldn't name but knew well enough by now. It was the feeling of something meant for me. For us.

The realization hit me with the weight of a stone falling from a great height. This room—this hidden, forgotten chamber—had been waiting. Waiting for me to stumble upon it. To find the pieces of a puzzle I hadn't even known I was meant to solve. The knowledge didn't come in a rush, but rather in a slow, creeping wave, as if the air itself was sharing a secret with me, one I had been avoiding for too long.

I stepped forward, drawn to the pedestal like a moth to flame, my fingers trembling as I traced the worn stone surface. I wasn't sure what I expected to find, but the moment I touched the pedestal, I felt it—something ancient, something powerful. A jolt of energy, of life, ran through me, quick and sharp, leaving me breathless. The symbols on the walls seemed to shimmer, as though they were alive, responding to the disturbance.

This was no ordinary room. This was a place of power, a place where things could be bound or freed, where the course of fate could be altered—or sealed forever. I wasn't sure if I was meant to understand it yet, or if this was simply the beginning. But I knew one thing: I had crossed a threshold, and there was no going back.

The silence of the room pressed down on me, thick and suffocating, as if waiting for me to make the next move. And I knew, deep down, that whatever I chose to do next would shape everything to come.

I stood there, in the middle of the chamber, my heart thudding in my chest, the weight of the air pressing against my skin. The dim glow from the candlelight barely reached the far corners of the room, leaving parts of it shrouded in a creeping darkness that felt alive in its own right. The symbols on the walls twisted and curled like the remnants of some forgotten language, the edges almost indiscernible as though they had been etched by hands both skilled and desperate.

They didn't just decorate the walls—they seemed to whisper, beckoning, urging me closer, though I was reluctant to listen.

My fingers brushed against one of the carvings, a series of jagged lines that circled a central point, and for the briefest moment, I felt a shiver of recognition. It was as though the walls themselves were breathing, exhaling in rhythm with my own shaky breath. I pulled my hand back, startled, but the lingering sensation of a connection—something older than time itself—lingered at the tips of my fingers.

For a moment, I considered retreating. Climbing back up the narrow staircase and slamming the tapestry back into place as if nothing had happened. Maybe that would be the safest option. After all, some things were best left undiscovered. But then I remembered the way the room had felt when I touched the pedestal—how the air had thrummed with an energy I could neither name nor explain. Whatever this place was, it wasn't just for show. It wasn't just a relic of the past meant to gather dust. It was waiting for something, and, in some strange way, I was the one it had been waiting for.

I glanced at the pedestal once more, a simple stone structure, unremarkable in form yet somehow impossibly significant. Its surface was worn smooth by centuries of use, and I wondered—no, I knew—it had been touched by others before me. I wasn't the first to come here, though I might be the first to truly understand it. The thought was both thrilling and terrifying in equal measure.

A creak from behind me made my heart leap into my throat. I spun, half-expecting the shadows to shift, to reveal something lurking just out of sight, but there was nothing there. Just the same oppressive silence. But the air had changed. It was thicker now, and I wasn't sure if it was the weight of my own thoughts or something far more tangible. Something was coming.

I wasn't alone in this room. I could feel it, a presence like an echo pressing against the edges of my mind.

"You're still here, I see," came a voice, low and disembodied. It echoed from the far corner of the room, though there was no visible source.

I froze, my breath catching in my throat. The words seemed to materialize out of thin air, not a sound but a vibration that settled in the back of my skull. It was not a voice I recognized, not a voice that belonged to the world I knew.

"Who—?" I started, but the words caught in my throat. I had to swallow twice before I could continue. "Who are you?"

The silence stretched long enough that I began to wonder if I had imagined the voice. But then it spoke again, this time closer, almost at my ear, its breath cold and ancient.

"I am what you have been searching for, and what you have feared. You've crossed the line now. You cannot unsee what you've seen."

I stumbled back a step, the words sinking in, like sharp stones dropped into water, creating ripples that seemed to touch every part of me. It was true. I had crossed something. This room, this staircase—it was all more than just a place. It was a boundary, one I had been too careless to notice.

"I didn't mean to," I said, my voice trembling, unsure if I was speaking to the air or to the presence that seemed to hang like a thick mist around me. "I just... I was curious."

The air shifted again, thickening with a hum of energy that buzzed in my veins. And then the presence spoke once more, its voice quieter now, but full of a quiet intensity that made my bones ache.

"Curiosity is a dangerous thing, child. It's always the first step toward something much larger than you can control. What you have found here is not meant for you to understand. Yet, it seems fate has its own plan."

I felt a chill run down my spine, as though I had been branded by the weight of those words. Whatever this was—whatever I had stumbled into—there was no undoing it now. It was more than a matter of curiosity. It was about power. Power that I wasn't sure I could handle.

The room suddenly felt smaller, suffocating. I could hear my own heartbeat in the silence, each thud loud enough to drown out any remaining thoughts. My eyes locked on the pedestal again, my instincts screaming at me to move closer. I didn't understand why, but it was as though something was calling me. The air around the stone seemed to shimmer, like heat rising from the pavement on a summer day, but it was cold. So cold it numbed my skin.

Before I could stop myself, my hand reached out toward it, a magnetic pull stronger than any will I could muster. As soon as my fingers brushed against the stone, the ground beneath my feet shifted. Not in the way stone settles after centuries of age, but in the way a heartbeat races, in the way the earth trembles just before something is about to break open.

The symbols on the walls blazed to life, glowing faintly at first and then, with an intensity that made my eyes sting, they burned like the sun. They danced before me, each one spinning in an intricate pattern, moving faster and faster, until I could barely follow them. The room was alive, thrumming with a power I couldn't grasp, a power I was suddenly afraid to touch.

And then, just as quickly, everything stopped. The glow faded. The hum of energy ceased. The room fell silent once more. But in that silence, I knew something fundamental had changed. I had crossed a line, and there was no going back.

The presence was gone, leaving nothing but the echo of its words hanging in the air like a warning.

The silence hung like a heavy curtain, muffling everything except the sound of my own unsteady breathing. The symbols on the walls flickered, almost like they were watching me—no, waiting for me. I wasn't sure what had changed in the room, but something had.

The air itself felt different now, pregnant with something I couldn't name, a tension that seemed to stretch, pulling at the very edges of the room.

I blinked, unsure of what to do. I was standing at the pedestal, my hand still hovering over it, feeling its cold surface beneath my fingers like the last breath of a dying thing. The moment I'd touched it, the energy had surged through me, but now that rush was gone, replaced by an eerie calm that was even more unsettling. It was as if the world had stopped—paused for just a moment to breathe, and in that space, everything felt more fragile. I wanted to turn away, to run back up those narrow stairs and lock the door behind me. But deep inside, something—someone—was pulling me forward.

I took a step closer to the pedestal, my breath shallow, a faint trembling coursing through my fingertips. The room around me seemed to grow colder with every passing second, the shadows shifting, stretching longer than they should. And then I noticed something else—an inscription, barely visible beneath the stone's surface, as though it had been etched there only moments ago.

I leaned down, my eyes narrowing in an attempt to make sense of it. The letters were old, the language unfamiliar, but there was something in the way the symbols were arranged that made the hairs on the back of my neck stand on end.

The words twisted in my mind like a riddle I couldn't solve, but as I stared at them, a strange sensation took over—like I wasn't looking at them, but rather into them.

"You've found it," a voice whispered. The words were thick with a strange, guttural quality, as if they had been spoken through the earth itself.

I jumped back, heart racing, every muscle tensing, expecting to see someone—him, the presence I had felt before. But there was nothing. No form, no figure, just the oppressive silence that seemed to echo in the hollow spaces between my thoughts.

"Who's there?" I demanded, my voice sharp, more out of fear than defiance.

For a moment, nothing happened. The room was still. And then—then—the air shifted. The ground beneath my feet groaned, the walls groaning in response as though the very building was alive, reacting to something deeper. I could feel it now, this undercurrent of power thrumming beneath my skin.

"You mustn't be so hasty," the voice said again, its tone almost playful now, as if it knew something I didn't. "The answers you seek are not so easily claimed."

I glanced around wildly, my breath coming in quick gasps. This was madness. Whatever this place was—whatever had been waiting for me here—it wasn't just a forgotten relic. It was a living thing.

I turned my attention back to the pedestal. The symbols still glowed faintly, now pulsing with the same rhythm as my heartbeat. The longer I looked at them, the more I felt something stirring within me, something ancient and bound up in these walls, waiting for me to make the next move.

And then it came to me: I was the one meant to move. I had always thought of myself as a passive observer, someone who watched the world unfold rather than shaping it. But standing here, in this room, surrounded by this strange, pulsing energy, it was impossible to ignore the growing awareness within me. The decision—whatever it was—lay with me.

But the realization was a bitter one. Because as the room pressed in closer, I knew—knew—that whatever I chose now would change everything.

The ground rumbled beneath me, and the walls shuddered in a way that made my teeth rattle. I grabbed onto the pedestal, steadying myself, trying to ground myself in something solid, as the room seemed to tilt. The symbols on the walls blurred, the faint light dancing around them in erratic bursts as if the very air was alive with electricity. And there it was again, the whisper, this time louder, closer—so close I could feel the words vibrating in my bones.

"Let go of it," the voice hissed. "Let go, and it will all be over."

I froze. I didn't understand. I didn't want to understand. This place, this power—it was too much, too much for someone like me. I had no right to be here, no business meddling with whatever dark force had been buried in these walls for centuries. But the pull of it—the pull of something I couldn't name, something deep and ancient—was overwhelming. The desire to know, to see, to touch, to claim it for myself.

But something else stirred inside me then. A warning. A primal instinct, buried beneath my curiosity. The last remnants of self-preservation. It wasn't too late, I told myself. I could walk away. Leave it all behind. But even as I thought it, I felt the truth slither through me like a serpent. It was already too late.

A sudden, sharp crack rang through the room, so loud it made my ears ring. The walls groaned as if the earth itself was being torn open. The symbols—those cursed symbols—flared to life again, brighter this time, their light stabbing into the darkness. A voice rang out—no, screeched—from the shadows. It was so loud, so fierce, that I clutched my head, as though trying to block it out.

The pedestal began to shake violently, the stone vibrating beneath my hands, sending tremors up my arms. The air around me grew thick, suffocating, and with a final, ear-splitting crack, the pedestal split in two.

I stumbled backward, my breath catching in my throat. And then, from the cracks in the stone, something rose. Something that wasn't human. It was a shadow at first, a ripple in the very fabric of the room, but then it solidified, revealing a figure. A figure I knew all too well.

I froze, my heart in my throat, as the figure turned toward me, its eyes—his eyes—locking onto mine.

"You shouldn't have come," he whispered, a dark smile curling on his lips.

And then, the world went black.

Chapter 18: The Pact

The moonlight filtered through the ancient stone archway, casting soft patterns on the floor, its light muted and gray against the deep shadows. The chamber felt smaller than usual, as if the walls were pressing in, closing the distance between me and everything I thought I knew. In the center of it all, he stood, as if summoned by the very air around him. His presence filled the space, not just in body but in the very fabric of the room itself, weaving into the cold stones like a whisper of fate I could no longer ignore.

His gaze met mine, steady and searching, as if he too could feel the pull between us, the invisible thread that stretched taut across the chasm of time and memory. He didn't speak at first. There was no need for words. The silence between us hummed, thick with the weight of years, of regrets, of choices both made and unmade. It was always like this with him—everything felt like it had been leading to this moment, this tension that could either break or bind us forever.

I stood there, frozen for a heartbeat, my breath coming shallow and quick. There was a chill in the air now, seeping into my skin, mingling with the rush of heat that seemed to rise from the very core of me. The world outside—distant, unreachable, a mere shadow of what it once was—seemed to blur into nothingness, until there was only him, only us, here in this room, facing a choice neither of us was prepared to make.

"Are you afraid?" His voice was low, a familiar melody that wrapped itself around me, tugging at the edges of the restraint I'd forced upon myself for so long. The question hung between us, heavy with the weight of our shared history, a history that was never supposed to happen. I had made my peace with the idea of being alone, of walking away from everything I'd once thought I needed. But the truth? The truth was I had never stopped wanting him.

"I'm not afraid of you," I said, my voice steadier than I felt. I forced myself to meet his gaze, to ignore the trembling in my fingers, the unrelenting surge of fear and longing that wanted to overwhelm me. "I'm afraid of what we've become. Of what this is. Of what it means."

His lips twisted in a smile that was at once bitter and knowing. "You think I haven't wondered the same thing?" He took a step forward, and the air around us seemed to grow thicker, denser. It felt like the room itself was holding its breath. "You think I haven't spent every moment since the last time we met asking myself the same question—whether we could survive this. Whether what we have is even real, or just some cruel illusion, a trick of fate that's destined to ruin us both."

I took a step back, pressing my palms against the cold stone of the wall. "It's not just us anymore," I said, my voice quiet but firm. "There's something else here. Something darker, older. Something that wants us to fail."

He nodded slowly, the weight of his expression making me feel the truth of his words. "I know," he said, and there was a vulnerability there, one I hadn't seen in him before. A crack in the armor that had always shielded him, an invitation into a part of him that had been hidden, even from himself. "I can feel it too. It's like a shadow that follows us wherever we go, a weight pressing down on us, pushing us toward an end we can't escape. But you're wrong about one thing."

"What's that?" I whispered, the words barely forming on my lips as I struggled to breathe through the rising tide of uncertainty.

"The choice isn't just yours," he said, his voice almost a whisper now, as if the room itself might be listening. "It's ours. We either choose to fight this together, or we let it tear us apart. There's no in-between, no escape."

A sudden gust of wind swept through the chamber, rattling the ancient stones and sending a chill down my spine. I didn't flinch. If anything, the cold seemed to crystallize my thoughts, to bring them into sharp focus. He was right. There was no escape. There never had been.

And then, in that moment, I realized what I had to do.

I had spent so long running from this, from the fire between us, from the pull that always drew me back to him. But I couldn't outrun it anymore. Not this time.

I took a deep breath, my heart pounding in my chest, and stepped forward, my feet moving of their own accord. The distance between us, once a chasm, now felt so small. So insignificant. When I reached him, I didn't wait for him to speak, didn't wait for him to make a move. I pressed my palm against his chest, feeling the steady beat of his heart beneath my hand, and whispered the words I had kept locked inside for far too long.

"I choose you."

For a moment, the room seemed to hold its breath, the tension palpable, suffocating. Then he placed his hand over mine, his touch warm, grounding, as if he had been waiting for this moment just as much as I had.

"I choose you too," he whispered, his voice a promise, a vow, something far deeper than just a simple declaration.

And then, without another word, we bound ourselves to each other, not with chains or oaths, but with something far more powerful—our love, our trust, our shared understanding that no matter the cost, no matter the darkness that threatened to consume us, we would face it together.

And in that moment, I knew that whatever lay ahead, we were ready.

I felt the weight of his words settle deep in my chest, each syllable a reminder of everything we had shared—and everything that had been lost. The pull between us hadn't diminished; if anything, it had only grown stronger with each passing moment, each beat of our hearts aligned in a rhythm that seemed destined for destruction.

We had chosen this, or perhaps fate had chosen it for us, like the fickle hand of a player pushing us to the edge of the board. I wasn't sure anymore. The room around us seemed to blur as I gazed at him, the edges of reality softening, slipping into the space between breaths. The tension in the air crackled, invisible but undeniable, like the charge before a storm. He had always been like this—everything he did, every glance, every word, pulled me into a world I couldn't fully understand, a world where I had no choice but to follow him.

"I hate this," I muttered, more to myself than to him. "You know that, right? This... this curse we've wrapped ourselves in." My voice was sharper than I intended, but it didn't matter. He wasn't offended. He never was.

"I know." His answer was a low murmur, the sound of a man who had known the same bitterness, the same weariness, in his own soul. He leaned in, his breath warm against my ear, and for a moment, I almost believed he was going to tell me something that would change everything. But instead, he whispered, "But we don't have a choice anymore."

I pulled away from him, my chest tight, but I couldn't tear my gaze from him. His words, their finality, hung in the air like a challenge. We didn't have a choice, did we? Not anymore. Not after everything we'd done to get to this point, everything we'd sacrificed just to find each other again.

There was a rustle behind me, faint but distinct, and I spun around, half-expecting to see some new threat creeping out from the shadows. But it was nothing, just the old tapestries swaying in the breeze, the remnants of a place that had long been forgotten by time, by the world outside. And yet, even now, it seemed like something was watching, waiting.

I turned back to him. "We should leave. We should walk away. You said it yourself—there's nothing but darkness here. Why can't we just..." My voice faltered, the words sticking in my throat. How could I ask him to walk away from this, from us? From the love that had never truly left us, even when we'd tried to bury it under years of silence and distance?

"Because I won't," he interrupted, his hand coming up to cup my face, his thumb tracing the curve of my jaw in a gesture so intimate, so familiar, it made my stomach twist. "I won't leave you. Not now, not after everything we've been through. Not when we're so close to ending this—for good."

"And what if we're wrong?" I shot back, my voice a little sharper than I intended, but I couldn't help it. "What if this is all a mistake? What if fighting it only makes it stronger?"

His lips pressed together in a thin line, and for a moment, I thought I saw a flicker of something like regret in his eyes. But it was gone before I could fully recognize it, replaced with something far darker. "I can't live with the idea of us not trying. Not after all this time."

There it was. That damnable hope that had always been there, buried beneath his cool exterior. The same hope I couldn't resist, even when I wanted to. It was as if, by some cruel twist of fate, our souls had been intertwined long before we even realized it. And that was why we couldn't let go. Why we couldn't walk away. Because we had already crossed that line. The one where there was no turning back.

I swallowed hard, my heart pounding in my chest, and took a step closer to him, the words I needed to say on the tip of my tongue. "But what if it's already too late? What if we're already too far gone?"

He shook his head, his eyes darkening with determination. "It's never too late. Not for us. Not when I know what's at stake. And what we're fighting for."

I wanted to believe him. I did. But the gnawing doubt at the back of my mind refused to go away. It wasn't just the darkness that we had to contend with. It was the fact that love—our love—was always so fragile, so easily shattered. We had been torn apart once before. What was to stop it from happening again?

Before I could voice my thoughts, a loud crack echoed through the chamber, followed by a rush of air so cold it left me breathless. The room shuddered, as if the very foundations of the world were beginning to collapse around us. I looked at him, my heart leaping into my throat.

"Do you feel that?" I whispered, barely able to keep the panic from my voice. The ground beneath us trembled, a low, menacing growl rising from deep within the earth itself. Something was coming. And it wasn't something we could fight with just our love.

"I feel it," he said, his voice tight. "And I'm not running from it. Not again."

He grabbed my hand, pulling me toward the door, and for a moment, everything that had held us apart—the fear, the doubt, the darkness—seemed to fall away. It was just him and me now, together in this fight, whatever it might be. I didn't know what we were facing, but in that instant, I knew one thing with absolute certainty: we were in this until the very end.

The walls of the chamber seemed to breathe around us, their ancient stones pulsing with an almost malevolent energy. I could feel the air thickening, pressing down on my chest like a weight, making each breath harder to take. The flickering torches cast strange shadows, dancing like wraiths across the floor, and every step I took felt like a defiance of the forces stirring beneath the surface.

His grip tightened on my hand, his fingers warm against mine, grounding me in a way I hadn't realized I needed. There was no escape from what was coming—whatever that was—but if I had to face it, I would do so with him by my side. The way he held me, the strength in his touch, didn't make it easier, but it made it bearable.

"Do you ever wonder if we're just... pushing it all further down?" I said, my voice soft, the words escaping before I could stop them. "All this power, this darkness—it's not just a curse. It's us. It's what we did. What we created."

His expression didn't change, but his eyes softened just enough to show he understood. "Maybe," he said, his voice low and steady. "But it's too late for that. You can't bury something that's already been born."

The words hit harder than I expected. It wasn't just what had happened between us, but everything—this ancient force, whatever it was, that had been unleashed. It was in the very air, swirling around us, lingering like a storm waiting to break. I didn't know what it wanted from us, but I felt its hunger, felt its desire to tear through everything we'd built, everything we'd fought for.

We were standing on the precipice now, and there was no easy way back.

"We can't fight this forever," I murmured, more to myself than to him. "I can feel it—like a fire that we're feeding every time we come closer to it. But how long before we burn ourselves alive?"

He stepped closer, his body pressing against mine, the heat of him seeping into my skin like a promise, an anchor. "We don't have to fight forever," he said, his breath warm against my ear. "We just have to survive long enough to make sure it doesn't consume us completely."

His words, though meant to reassure, felt like the promise of something inevitable. We were too far gone, standing at the edge of something that couldn't be undone. But in that moment, with him this close, his scent mingling with mine, I couldn't help but want to believe him. I didn't want to be the one to let go. Not when we had come this far.

I stepped back, breaking the connection for just a moment to breathe, to think. "How do we fight something we don't even understand?" My voice cracked, betraying the vulnerability I'd been desperately trying to suppress.

"We don't fight it," he said, his eyes burning with an intensity that shook me to my core. "We outlast it. We prove that we're stronger. We prove that we're not the same people who set this in motion."

"And how do we do that?" I shot back, a bitter laugh escaping me. "How do we prove something to a force that's been here long before either of us?"

"By making the choice to be better than what's come before. To be better than this." His voice grew firmer with each word, his resolve filling the space between us. "We have the power to shape what happens next. Together."

For a moment, I almost believed him. That was the problem. He made me believe. But something in the back of my mind screamed that we were only delaying the inevitable, postponing the confrontation we were meant to have with this darkness. It had already marked us. We had already chosen it when we allowed ourselves to rekindle this flame.

I turned my gaze to the far corner of the chamber, where the shadows seemed to grow thicker, darker. The air around us shifted, the temperature dropping several degrees. It was subtle, almost imperceptible, but it was enough to make the hairs on my neck stand on end.

"We're not alone," I whispered, my heart pounding in my chest.

He stiffened, his eyes scanning the room, the muscles in his jaw tightening. There was no denying it now. The presence was undeniable, like a weight in the room, an oppressive force that we couldn't see but could feel pressing in from all sides.

"We need to leave," I said, the urgency in my voice not matching the calm I tried to project. I turned back toward the exit, my feet moving instinctively, but before I could take a single step, the door slammed shut with a force that shook the very foundation of the chamber. The sound echoed through the room like thunder, and I spun around, my pulse racing.

He reached for me, his grip firm and steady. "It's not letting us go," he said, the finality in his words making my stomach churn. "We have to face it."

The temperature continued to drop, and a low, guttural sound reverberated from the walls, filling the room like a distant growl. I could feel it now—something dark, something ancient, stirring within the very stone of the chamber. It was alive, aware, and it was coming for us.

I took a deep breath, my thoughts racing. "What is it?" I demanded, my voice trembling despite myself. "What do you think this is?"

"I don't know," he said, his jaw clenched, his eyes narrowing as he scanned the shadows. "But whatever it is, we're about to find out."

Before I could respond, the air thickened, a suffocating presence filling the space, and the ground beneath us began to tremble once more. The shadows seemed to writhe, stretching toward us with unnatural speed, closing in on us from every direction.

And then, just as I opened my mouth to speak, I heard it.

A voice. Faint at first, almost a whisper, but unmistakable.

"Leave... before it's too late."

I froze. The voice was low, gravelly, as if it came from deep within the earth itself. It was both a warning and a command.

And for the first time, I realized I didn't know if we were strong enough to fight it.

Chapter 19: The Shadows of Betrayal

The candles flickered in the stillness of the room, their flames quivering like fragile little sparks of life. The air smelled of lavender and something more acrid, like burnt offerings or the last remnants of a lost dream. I could feel the weight of it, the scent of magic thick and suffocating, as if the room itself was holding its breath, waiting for something. I glanced at him, his form just beyond the reach of the dim light, the shadows stretching long across the floor between us. His silhouette seemed so familiar, but not in the way I wanted it to be. Something about him was off, like a melody played slightly out of tune.

He met my gaze, and for a moment, there was nothing but the raw, unspoken tension between us. His lips curved into a smile, but it didn't reach his eyes. I had seen that smile before, many times, but never under these circumstances. Never when the air was thick with the ghosts of our past lives.

"I know what you're thinking," he said, his voice low, as though he were trying to soothe a restless beast inside me. But there was something in his tone that made my skin crawl, something too smooth, too practiced. It wasn't the comfort I sought, but a challenge I wasn't sure I was ready to face.

"I doubt you do," I answered, my voice sharper than I intended, but it came out as the truth. The truth that had been festering inside me, buried deep under the weight of everything he'd done—and everything I hadn't known. I swallowed hard, pushing the bile of doubt back down my throat. "What makes you so sure? You've lied to me before."

He stiffened, the sharpness of his reaction more revealing than anything he could have said. I saw it then—glimpses of the man who had stood in front of me, swearing promises he never intended to keep, hiding the secrets that had eventually torn us apart. The memories flashed in front of me: the whispered conversations behind closed doors, the lies that had slipped so easily from his lips, the absence when I needed him most. I had trusted him once, blindly and without question, but that trust had been shattered—fragmented beyond repair.

"You think I lied to you?" His voice, now softer, almost tender, sent a chill through me. It was the voice of a man who had been wronged, who was playing a game he had no right to win. "What do you remember of our past? What are these... things you keep thinking of?"

The question hung in the air, a dangerous thread that threatened to unravel everything. I could feel it, like the pull of a riptide, dragging me back into the depths of a life I no longer understood. I didn't want to answer him, didn't want to give him the satisfaction of knowing that I remembered everything—the betrayal, the hurt, the way it had all ended before we were given this second chance. This time, I wouldn't be fooled.

"I remember a lot more than you think," I replied, the words tasting like ash on my tongue. "I remember you leaving me. I remember the darkness that swallowed me whole when I found out everything you kept from me." My eyes narrowed as I took a step forward, the floor creaking under my weight, as though even the house knew the tension between us was too thick to bear. "Do you think I forgot, that I could just forgive you because of some... ritual?"

His eyes flickered, something close to regret flashing behind them, but it was fleeting, lost behind the walls he'd built up over the years. "I didn't leave you," he said, each word careful, deliberate. "I did what I had to do. What we both needed. You were safer without me."

"Safer?" The word felt foreign, alien coming from his lips. "You think you can hide behind that excuse forever?" My voice cracked, and I hated how easily the vulnerability slipped out. "You've always thought you knew what was best for me, but you never asked. You never once cared to know what I wanted."

His gaze hardened, and the room seemed to shrink, the air thicker with the weight of unspoken words. "Don't pretend you were innocent in all this," he shot back, his tone no longer soft, but razor-edged. "You think I didn't see it? The way you pulled away, the way you let the distance grow between us until there was nothing left but silence? You think I was the only one who made mistakes?"

I took another step forward, my heart pounding in my chest, the blood roaring in my ears. "You've made it all about me, haven't you?" I whispered, my breath hitching with the words. "But it's not about me. It's about you and your damn secrets. You've never told me the truth. Not once."

His jaw clenched, and for a brief, terrifying moment, I thought he might come at me, that he might break. Instead, he stood perfectly still, his fists clenched by his sides. "You wouldn't understand," he said, the weight of the words hanging heavy in the room. "You can't possibly understand what I had to sacrifice."

I laughed, bitter and low, a sound that made him flinch. "Sacrifice? You think I don't know about sacrifice?" The memories of my own choices—the ones I had made in the name of love, in the name of survival—burned in my chest. "I gave everything for us. For you. And you let me burn."

The silence between us stretched, thick and suffocating. It wasn't just the ritual anymore, the dark magic that had once bound us together—it was the truth, crawling out of the shadows, demanding to be seen. And as I stared at him, I realized something that made my blood run cold: The betrayal wasn't a thing of the past. It was right here, between us, waiting for me to confront it. To decide if I could trust him again. If I could trust myself to let him in.

But in that moment, all I could feel was the suffocating weight of doubt—and the certainty that nothing would ever be the same again.

The silence between us stretched, taut as a bowstring, until it felt like the very air around us was humming with unspoken words. His gaze never left mine, though there was something in it now—something that reminded me of a time long ago when his eyes had been full of promises. Back then, his presence had felt like home. It was a feeling I'd given up on long ago, buried beneath the weight of what had come after. And now, I wasn't sure if I wanted to dig it back up.

I turned my back to him, stepping toward the circle of chalk on the floor, each mark etched with purpose, each symbol a reminder of what had brought us here. The ritual. The promise that this time would be different. But nothing felt different. Nothing felt like it would ever be enough to make up for the years lost between us.

"You're doing it again," he said, the tension in his voice wrapping around the words like a noose. I could feel his presence, even without looking at him. His shadow clung to the edges of my thoughts, threatening to undo everything I was trying to hold together.

I froze, just for a moment. "What?" I asked, my voice sharp.

"You're pretending like I'm the only one who's changed," he said, his tone low, more resigned than accusatory. "I've spent every day since the last time we were together trying to figure out how to fix this, how to make up for everything. You act like nothing's different, like you've been waiting all this time for me to make things right."

I could hear the weight of those words, the unspoken plea buried beneath them. But I couldn't bring myself to acknowledge it. I had spent years convincing myself that I didn't need him, that whatever had gone wrong between us was a lesson learned and sealed away in the past. Yet here he was, forcing me to dig it all back up, turning the knife over in my gut and twisting it just when I thought I had finally healed.

"Maybe I have changed," I said, my back still turned, my fingers tracing the edge of the circle. "Maybe I don't want things fixed. Not like you think."

He stepped forward then, close enough that I could feel the heat of his body against my skin, even if he didn't touch me. "You think I want to go back to what we had?" he asked, his voice rough, almost breaking. "You think I want to live in the shadow of my mistakes forever?" His hand reached out, stopping just shy of my shoulder, like a question he wasn't sure how to ask.

The question hung in the air, suspended between us, heavier than the candles' flickering flames. I swallowed the words I wanted to say, the ones that would have torn the walls between us down. Instead, I turned slowly to face him, my eyes locked with his, and I allowed the silence to stretch longer than it should have.

"I don't know what I want anymore," I said, the words like an admission of failure. The truth stung, sharp and bitter, but there was nothing else left to say. We had been through too much to go back, too much to pretend that the weight of our history could be erased with a single touch or a single promise.

He seemed to take a breath, steadying himself, and for the first time, I saw something in his eyes that I hadn't noticed before—vulnerability. It was raw, unfiltered, and it made my heart ache in a way I hadn't expected. "Then let me help you figure it out," he said quietly. "Let me be the one who helps you heal."

"Help me?" The laughter that bubbled up from my chest was bitter, too bitter for comfort. "You think you can heal me? You think you can just waltz back into my life and make everything okay again?"

His jaw tightened, but there was no anger in his expression. Just that same quiet resolve that had always been there, the part of him that refused to back down. “I’m not asking for forgiveness. I’m asking for a chance to prove to you that I can be the man you need me to be.”

A hollow laugh escaped me, and I shook my head, the motion slow, almost painful. “The man I need you to be?” I repeated the words back to him, as if they were foreign, unrecognizable. “I don’t even know who that is anymore.”

He took a step forward, his eyes never leaving mine. “Neither do I,” he admitted, his voice low, raw. “But I want to find out. Together.”

And in that moment, the air shifted. I could feel it, the change, though I couldn’t place it. Maybe it was the way his words wrapped around my chest, squeezing so tight that I could hardly breathe. Maybe it was the flicker of something—something I didn’t want to name—rising in me. Hope? Hope felt like a lie, something too fragile to rely on. But maybe, just maybe, it was enough to make me question everything.

The candles flickered again, their flames dancing like nervous whispers in the quiet. My heart raced, unsure of whether it was racing toward something or away from it. Everything inside me wanted to pull away, to push him back into the shadows where I could keep him at a distance, where the pain wouldn’t feel so close. But there was something in his eyes now, something I hadn’t seen before—a vulnerability that mirrored my own.

“Don’t,” I whispered, though the word felt like it was meant for both of us. Don’t push me. Don’t force me to face this again. But as I said it, I realized the truth. It wasn’t him I was pushing away. It was me.

“I won’t make promises,” he said, his voice quieter now, but steady. “Not this time. But I’ll be here. No matter what you decide, I’ll be here.”

And with those words, I found myself standing on the edge of a choice I hadn’t been prepared for. Would I walk away, leaving the shadows of betrayal to swallow me whole? Or would I take the leap, trusting that whatever lay ahead was worth the risk? The truth was, I didn't know. I didn't know what I could trust anymore. But I knew one thing for certain: this time, I wouldn't make the same mistake twice.

The air felt colder now, the chill creeping up my spine as I watched the flickering candlelight twist into jagged shadows against the walls. It was as if the very room had become a living thing, breathing with anticipation, and every breath I took felt too shallow, too heavy with what loomed ahead. My fingers brushed against the ancient book that lay open on the altar between us, its pages cracked and yellowed with age, as if the weight of time itself was pressing down on us. I could hear the faint rustle of the wind outside, like a distant warning, but it did nothing to quell the rising tide of dread in my chest.

He moved closer, his presence filling the space between us, but even as he reached for my hand, there was a hesitation—something unsaid, something that clung to the edges of his every movement. His fingers grazed mine, warm against the cold air, and for a moment, I wanted to pull away. But I didn't. I couldn't. Not yet. Not when every part of me screamed to stay.

"This is it, isn't it?" I said, my voice low, almost too quiet to be heard over the sound of my heartbeat. "This is where it all changes."

He nodded, the tension in his jaw betraying his calm demeanor. His eyes met mine, but they weren't the eyes I remembered. They were darker, filled with a depth I couldn't quite read. "It's where it all ends," he whispered. The words hung between us like a dare, a challenge neither of us were ready to face, but here we were, unable to stop the inevitable from unfolding.

I should have been afraid. The rituals, the magic, the possibility of undoing everything we had fought for, everything we had rebuilt—it was all too much. Too dangerous. But the strangest thing was, I wasn't afraid of the ritual itself. I was afraid of what would happen after. Of what we would be once it was done, once we had crossed the line and could never go back.

My breath caught in my throat as I took a step back, my fingers tightening around the edge of the book. The symbols on the pages seemed to shimmer with a life of their own, a warning flashing in the corners of my mind. It was too much. Too much to ignore, too much to pretend we could control.

"What happens if we can't undo what's been done?" I asked, my voice suddenly trembling. It was a question I'd been avoiding, one I hadn't allowed myself to truly ask, but now, standing here with him, I couldn't pretend it didn't matter. "What if we fail?"

He reached out again, his hand hovering just inches from mine, but this time, I didn't pull away. I didn't flinch. Instead, I met his gaze, and for the first time in what felt like forever, there was no pretense between us. "Then we deal with it," he said, the words as steady as the ground beneath us, even as I could feel the earth beginning to shift.

The quiet hum of magic in the room grew louder, swirling around us, thickening the air. I felt it—like a weight pressing down on my chest, making it harder to breathe, harder to think. It was so much more than the ritual. It was the culmination of everything that had come before: the lies, the secrets, the things unsaid. The past we had tried so hard to bury now stood at the doorstep, demanding to be faced.

"I don't know if I can trust you," I said, the words tumbling out before I could stop them. "Not after everything. Not when I still don't know if I was the one who was wrong, or if you kept something from me, something that changed everything."

His eyes darkened, and he stepped back, though he didn't take his gaze off me. "I don't expect you to forgive me," he said, his voice rough, almost raw. "Not yet. But I'm asking you to trust me now. Just this once. Let me show you that I can be the man you need."

The silence that followed his words was thick, suffocating. My heart beat faster, my pulse a drumbeat of confusion and fear. I wanted to believe him. I wanted to trust him. But how could I, when every instinct inside me screamed that there was more to this story than either of us were willing to admit?

For a moment, I thought about walking away. About leaving him there, with all his promises and all his lies, and never looking back. But something stopped me. Something in the way he looked at me, the way his desperation bled through the cracks in his carefully constructed facade. It wasn't enough. But it was something.

"I don't know if I can," I said quietly, the words hanging in the air like a curse.

He didn't answer. Instead, he took another step toward me, close enough that I could feel his breath on my skin, close enough that I could taste the tension between us. The ritual was still waiting, still hanging over us like an unspoken demand. The moment was slipping away, and with it, every chance we had to make a choice.

But then, before I could make a decision, before I could even open my mouth to say anything else, a sharp crack pierced the air—a sound like thunder splitting the sky. My heart stopped, and for the briefest of moments, everything went still, the world frozen in time.

And then the walls began to shake.

The candles sputtered and went out, one by one, until the room was plunged into darkness. The air crackled with a new, unfamiliar energy, thick and charged with something I couldn't understand. It was as if the magic in the room had suddenly gone wild, uncontrolled, and I felt it—the rush of power, of something ancient and powerful, filling the space around us.

I reached for him instinctively, my hand finding his, but his grip was cold, too cold, and when I looked at him, his face was twisted in an expression of pure terror.

"What's happening?" I asked, my voice barely more than a whisper, but my words were lost in the chaos. The room began to pulse, the walls shuddering with each beat, as though the very earth beneath us was about to crack open.

And then, through the thick blackness, I saw it. The shadows that had been lurking at the edges of the room, the ones that had been waiting for this moment—rising, stretching, like dark fingers reaching toward us.

"No," I breathed, panic clawing at my chest. "This wasn't supposed to happen. It wasn't supposed to—"

But before I could finish, a scream tore through the room, a sound that was both human and something else entirely. And everything—everything—went black.

Chapter 20: The Whispering Walls

The house was more than a collection of brick and mortar; it was an heirloom of memories, its walls a tapestry of moments that no one could see but me. I had long since stopped fighting the truth that it was alive. It wasn't the creaking floorboards or the quiet sighs of settling beams that spooked me; it was the way the house seemed to know—know things that I didn't. It had lived through every secret we kept, every fight we had, and every soft confession whispered into the late-night air.

I stood in the middle of the kitchen now, the worn tile beneath my feet slick with the damp of an autumn chill that had crept through the cracks. The countertops, once gleaming, were now dull with age, their edges rounded with the passage of years. Still, the house had a familiarity to it, a strange comfort I couldn't shake, as if it were holding me in place, reminding me of something I had forgotten—or perhaps something I had buried.

The first whisper came as I stood by the window, staring out at the rain that had begun to tap on the glass. The breeze moved the drapes slightly, but it was more than that. It was a voice, soft and unsure, drifting from the walls themselves. "You never did understand him, did you?" The words were like a soft breath against my ear, pulling my attention toward the door where his jacket still hung, its worn leather gleaming faintly under the dim light.

I could almost hear his voice then, the way it would change when he was frustrated, or when he was lying—or perhaps when he truly believed what he was saying. But it wasn't just his voice. No, it was the house's too. It had learned his rhythms, absorbed his presence in a way I had never fully realized.

The voice grew stronger, more insistent. "You never listened." A rustling came from behind me, and I spun around, expecting to find a shadow or a draft. But nothing was there. The house was quiet again, as though nothing had happened. I could feel my pulse quicken, a pressure building in my chest that I couldn't quite explain.

The kitchen table sat untouched, a relic of breakfasts that felt like they were centuries ago. The chairs—once bright, now dulled—seemed to groan under the weight of their own memory. I reached out to touch the table's edge, feeling the smooth surface that had once been warm with the promise of shared meals, laughter, arguments, and silence. So many silences. I ran my fingers along the rim, tracing a deep gouge in the wood, a scar I hadn't noticed before.

It wasn't from me. I knew that. The memory stirred, unbidden. It was from one of the nights we fought, one of the nights he slammed his fist against the table, the echo of it reverberating through the whole house. I had stood there, frozen, unable to speak. The words were always harder to find in the aftermath of one of his rages. I had learned to bite them back before they could form, and yet the walls of the house seemed to hold onto those words, absorbing them, as though it could somehow keep them safe.

The air shifted again, cooler this time. A soft murmur followed—"You think you know the truth." It was as if the house was chiding me, reminding me that there were things I hadn't seen, things I hadn't wanted to see. The chill ran through me like the fingers of a ghost brushing across my skin. I felt the sting of betrayal again, but this time, it was sharper, more personal.

I closed my eyes, the world outside fading into the murkiness of memory. There had been so many moments like this—so many times I had stood here, caught between the man I had loved and the one I had lost. And now the house seemed determined to remind me of all the ways I had failed to understand him.

The whispers escalated, faster now, a chorus of voices rising from the walls. I could hear them now, fragments of conversations I had never fully processed. "I never wanted to hurt you." "You didn't listen to me." "You were always so busy."

I had heard those words before. They had been his defenses, his shield against the truth he couldn't face. But it was different now. The house, in its quiet wisdom, was showing me something I hadn't allowed myself to see before—his own fear. He had been afraid of being vulnerable, of being real with me, and in his fear, he had built walls that even I couldn't break down.

The air thickened, and I took a slow, trembling breath. A part of me wanted to flee, to escape the house that was so full of his memory, but another part—something deeper, more fragile—wanted to stay. I had always thought I was the one who had been wronged, that I was the one who had been betrayed. But in that moment, with the whispers pressing in on me, I began to wonder if I had missed something crucial. Perhaps, just perhaps, I had misunderstood everything.

The house wasn't asking me to forgive him. It was asking me to understand. To see the man I had loved—not just in the moments of passion, but in the quiet ache of his own regret. The walls, as silent as they were, had been his confessor. And they were waiting for me to listen.

But could I? Could I let go of the years of anger and resentment, of the betrayal that had burned so fiercely in my chest? The house, with its whispers, seemed to ask me that very question.

I pressed my palm against the table again, feeling the warmth of the wood beneath my fingertips. There was something in the touch—something familiar and full of longing. It was as though the house itself was offering me a way forward, if only I was willing to take it.

The whispers softened then, quieting to a near hum, and the house held its breath, waiting. And so did I.

I moved from the kitchen to the living room, the plush carpet beneath my feet a subtle reminder of all the times I had sunk into its softness after a long day, grateful for the sanctuary of this house. It had been a haven, once. The walls, once pristine with a shade of blue so calming it had almost felt like breathing, now seemed weighed down with too many things unsaid. I sank into the armchair by the fireplace, its fabric cool against my skin, and waited for the next whisper to find me.

The fire had long since burned down to embers, the soft crackle in the hearth almost mocking the silence that had settled between us—me and the house. I leaned back, crossing my arms, as if to shield myself from what it might reveal next. The air was thick, pregnant with the weight of what was unsaid.

Then came another murmur, but this time, it wasn't from the walls. It was from somewhere deeper, a voice wrapped in the rustle of old memories, thick with guilt. "You never understood why he left." The words fluttered around me, barely audible, like the echo of a dream I hadn't wanted to wake from.

I bit my lip, trying to keep the wave of emotion from overwhelming me. Of course, I understood. Or at least, I thought I did. It had been the easiest explanation—he left because we were too different, because we couldn't fix what had started to unravel between us. There had been no grand betrayal, no explosive confrontation. It had been the slow, inevitable drift of two people growing apart. The tragedy, however, wasn't the separation; it was the hollow, silent aftermath. The time between his departure and now had felt like waiting for something that was never coming back.

But the house... The house had a way of asking questions that dug under my skin, nudging at things I wasn't ready to confront. It whispered of things I had long since shoved into corners, buried beneath the busyness of life. He hadn't left because of something so simple, so explainable. No, the house seemed to suggest there was more, something I'd missed, something still hidden in the dark corners of that shared past.

I stood again, the floorboards creaking as I crossed to the door that led into the hallway. The familiar scent of wood polish and dust lingered in the air, a quiet reminder that I hadn't been paying attention to this house for far too long. The hallway stretched before me, its length marked by pictures I'd once lovingly hung—snapshots of happy days that felt more like they belonged to someone else now. The photo at the end of the hall was the one that caught my eye this time.

I walked toward it, the faintest shiver running through me. It was a picture of us, our smiles so wide, so genuine. I was leaning into him, his arm draped casually over my shoulders, his eyes bright with a spark I hadn't seen in ages. And yet, looking at it now, there was a weight in the photo, something that hadn't been there before. I couldn't explain it, but I felt it—like a silent alarm going off, warning me of something I wasn't prepared to face. I reached out and touched the glass, the cold of the frame sending a ripple of unease through me.

The whisper came again, sharper this time. "He didn't leave because of what you think."

I closed my eyes, willing the voice to fade, to leave me in peace. I knew what it wanted. It wanted me to understand, to see the truth I had been so desperate to avoid. But truth, I had learned, was often an unwelcome visitor, showing up uninvited, revealing things I was in no way prepared to hear.

I pulled away from the picture, turning toward the stairs. They loomed in front of me, their familiar creak underfoot a subtle reminder that I had spent countless hours here, moving through the space in search of comfort, in search of answers. I hesitated.

I had never ventured up here since that day. It had been years since I had set foot in the bedroom we had shared, where so many things had been said, and more importantly, where so many things had gone unsaid. The door at the top of the stairs was still ajar, the faintest sliver of light spilling through, casting long shadows across the floor.

I didn't want to go up there. I wasn't ready. But the house had a way of compelling me, and so I found myself climbing the stairs, each step creaking louder than the last. It was as if the house was watching me, urging me forward, forcing me to confront the past. The air grew thicker the higher I climbed, as though the very walls themselves were holding their breath, waiting for me to see what I had refused to acknowledge all this time.

When I reached the top, I stopped. The hallway stretched out before me, leading to the room that had once been our sanctuary, our safe place. The door was open wide enough to let in the glow of the hallway light, casting a faint golden hue across the room.

I hesitated for a moment before pushing the door all the way open. The room was as I remembered it, except for the absence of him. The bed was still unmade, the sheets rumpled from the last time I had been here—before the silence, before the distance. The walls were adorned with pictures, the same ones that had once made me smile, now only serving to remind me of the things we had lost.

And then, there it was—right on the nightstand, a single item I hadn't noticed before. It was a letter, folded neatly, as if waiting for me. I hadn't seen it in all the time I had been in the house, but somehow, it had appeared here, as if the house itself had decided that it was time for me to know the truth.

My hand shook as I reached for it, the paper crinkling under my fingers. I opened it slowly, careful not to tear it. His handwriting was immediately familiar, but the words were anything but.

"I didn't leave because of you, not because of us. I left because I had to. There's a part of me you'll never understand, but I need you to know that I never stopped loving you. Please don't hate me for it."

I felt the weight of the words settle into my chest, and I wondered if it was the house, or the letter, or something else entirely that was slowly cracking open the walls I had built around myself.

I sat on the edge of the bed, the letter still trembling in my hands as if it, too, were afraid of what it had unleashed. The words—his words—hung heavy in the air, circling like something both familiar and foreign. I had never been one to believe in fate, but there was something about the timing of this letter, its sudden appearance, that seemed too deliberate to ignore. Why had he left this here, hidden all this time, only to be found now? And why now, when the house was speaking to me in riddles I could barely comprehend?

I dropped the letter onto the bed, my fingers still numb with shock. The room seemed colder now, though the light outside had hardly shifted. The weight of his absence pressed in around me, and yet, his presence lingered—just out of reach, but palpable in the stillness.

The house shifted again, like an old man settling into his favorite chair, ready to tell a long-forgotten story. The floorboards groaned beneath my feet as I stood and paced, the edges of the room narrowing with each step I took, as though the walls themselves were pressing in, pushing me toward something I wasn't ready to face. But there was no escaping it now. The house wasn't letting me leave until it had told its story, until I had heard everything it had to say.

I stepped over to the window, the glass cold against my palms as I leaned forward, staring out into the gray, swirling sky. The rain had stopped, but the air was thick, heavy with an unsettled tension that mirrored my own. The wind had picked up, rattling the trees outside, their branches swaying in the dark. It was as if the world itself was holding its breath, waiting for me to make the next move.

But what was the next move? What was I supposed to do with this information? How was I supposed to move forward when the past felt like it had rooted itself too deeply in the foundation of this house, in my heart?

I closed my eyes, trying to silence the barrage of thoughts that had erupted inside my mind. "You never understood why he left." The words echoed in my mind again, the house's voice now like a distant hum in the background. But was that true? Did I really not understand?

The house had been a witness to everything. It had seen us at our best, at our worst. It had been a silent observer, holding the secrets we never voiced, the promises we never kept. I had blamed him for leaving, for walking away without warning, without so much as a decent explanation. But now—now that I was faced with the weight of this letter and the whispers that seemed to follow me everywhere—I wondered if I had ever really listened.

The truth was harder to face than I had imagined. The walls of this house, once a symbol of security, now seemed to be closing in on me, each one shifting, groaning under the weight of the past. And the more I tried to push against it, the more it became clear that there was no escaping the truth that had been here all along.

I turned away from the window, my gaze landing on the dresser across the room. The old, carved wood gleamed in the dim light, as though it, too, had a story to tell. It was there that I had found his watch—the one he had left behind all those years ago. I had never known what to do with it, but the house, like a patient parent, had held onto it, waiting for me to finally understand.

Without thinking, I crossed the room and reached for the watch. It was cold to the touch, heavier than I remembered, as though it had absorbed the years of silence, the weight of everything unsaid between us. I held it in my palm, the ticking of the second hand too loud in the quiet room, too deliberate.

As I turned it over in my hands, I saw the engraving on the back, the small inscription I had long since forgotten. It was simple, just a few words: “Always with you.” I had never asked him about it. I had never needed to. But now, staring at the faded letters, I felt a pang of something—regret, maybe, or maybe it was longing. Whatever it was, it was something I hadn’t felt in a long time.

I closed my eyes, pressing the watch to my chest. The house was still, too still, as though waiting for me to make the connection, to understand what had been right in front of me all this time. The air seemed to grow thicker, like the house itself was holding its breath, waiting for me to finally open my eyes and see the truth.

Suddenly, the floorboards creaked behind me. My heart leapt in my chest, my breath catching in my throat. I spun around, half-expecting to see someone standing in the doorway. But there was no one there. The room was empty, save for the shadows that seemed to stretch further into the corners, twisting like something alive.

I set the watch down gently on the dresser, my hands trembling as I tried to steady myself. I could feel the weight of the house’s gaze on me, the way it seemed to watch, to wait. I didn’t want to turn around, didn’t want to face whatever it was that had stirred in the dark corners of this place. But I had to. I had come this far, and there was no turning back now.

The whisper came again, clearer this time. “You think you understand, but you haven’t seen it all yet.”

A cold chill ran through me. The door behind me creaked again, but this time, I didn’t turn. Instead, I stood perfectly still, listening. And then I heard it—the sound of footsteps, soft but distinct, moving through the hall outside the room. My pulse quickened, and for the first time since I had stepped into this house, I felt a surge of fear.

There was someone here.

The question was—who?

Chapter 21: The Storm That Broke Us

The storm had arrived as though it had been summoned, each crack of thunder like a fist pounding against the earth. It rattled the windows and screamed through the trees, as if nature itself were bent on protesting the course we had chosen. But inside the chamber, all was calm—at least, for a time. The only sounds were the quiet murmurs of incantations, the sharp scent of incense, and the soft flicker of candlelight casting trembling shadows on the stone walls.

I wasn't sure why we thought we could control it. Magic—ancient, dangerous, unyielding—was never something to be tamed. Not by us, not by anyone. Yet there we were, standing in a circle, holding hands, hearts beating in synchrony as we began the ritual. The air was thick with anticipation, charged with a sense of expectation that made the hairs on the back of my neck stand at attention. We had done this before, many times, and nothing had ever gone wrong.

But tonight felt different. The storm outside seemed to echo the nervous energy that buzzed in the air, as though it could sense the stakes. A truth was about to come to light, one that none of us could have predicted, and it wasn't just the storm that was about to break. No, it was us—the fragile, delicate web we had woven over the years—about to unravel in a single, devastating moment.

When the first flash of lightning cracked through the sky, the power in the room surged like an electrical charge. I could feel it in my fingertips, in the very marrow of my bones, as the spell we were attempting to weave began to take shape. But it wasn't right. Something was wrong. The air became suffocating, thick with a pressure that squeezed my chest. The candles flickered violently, casting erratic shadows that seemed to dance with malevolent glee.

"Focus," a voice hissed, but I wasn't sure whose it was. It could have been anyone's—mine, his, hers—an indistinct blur as the world around us started to warp.

Then, the walls groaned, and the floor beneath our feet trembled as if the very foundation of the world were shaking. Objects began to levitate, swirling through the air like leaves caught in a whirlwind, shattering against the stone with deafening cracks. I couldn't focus. My vision blurred, my body shaking, my pulse hammering in my ears. There was a flash of light, blinding in its intensity, and I felt my knees give out beneath me. I was pulled to the ground, the cold stone beneath me grounding me in a way that did nothing to calm the rising storm inside me.

"Stop!" someone screamed, but the sound was lost in the cacophony of chaos. The storm outside howled, as though mocking our attempts to harness the power we'd so naively thought we could command. We were too small, too insignificant in the face of what we had unleashed.

And then it happened.

The truth.

A sharp, searing pain sliced through me, a pain that felt not just physical but internal, as though a piece of my very soul was being torn away. I gasped, clutching at my chest, trying to hold myself together as the world around me splintered into jagged shards of reality.

In the chaos, a voice broke through, low and guttural, shaking the very air as it filled the room. It was familiar—too familiar—and the words, though whispered, echoed in my mind with a clarity that made my stomach churn.

"You think you know who you are," the voice crooned, "but you're wrong. All of you are wrong."

My heart stuttered. I knew that voice.

I knew it all too well.

And with that realization came the crushing weight of betrayal.

I looked up, my eyes searching for him in the darkness, the flickering candlelight revealing his face—his twisted smile, his eyes cold and empty. But it wasn't just him. No, it was all of us. Each of us, caught in the web of our own lies, our own secrets. We had known something was wrong, had suspected it, but none of us had dared to speak it aloud. Not until now.

He had been a part of it all along. A part of the plan. A part of the lies. The very person I had trusted most, the one I had leaned on through every storm, every tear, every victory—had betrayed me. Had betrayed us all. And now, it was too late.

The pain inside me doubled, my breath coming in ragged gasps as the room spun wildly. The storm outside roared louder, the lightning striking so close that I could feel the heat of it on my skin. But it wasn't the storm that was breaking us—it was him. It was the revelation that shattered everything we had ever known. He was the storm. And in that moment, I realized with an eerie clarity that the power we had sought to control, the power we had sought to understand, had always been his to wield. We had been nothing but pawns in his game.

The candles flickered one last time before plunging the room into darkness. Silence fell, heavy and oppressive, broken only by the pounding of my own heart.

The silence after the storm was deafening. Not a single sound came from anyone—not the other members of the circle, not the cracking wood from the old beams above, not even the wind that had howled so ferociously moments ago. The air was thick, too thick, and it settled heavily on my chest. I wanted to scream, to tear it away, but nothing came out. I wasn't even sure I could move. I blinked, my vision slowly adjusting to the dark, but it didn't make the scene any clearer. The room seemed to stretch and shrink at once, the shadows dancing in ways that defied logic.

And him. He was still there, standing opposite me in the same position where we had started the ritual. The same place where I had thought—no, hoped—he would be my partner in all this. My rock. The one person I could rely on.

His face was a mask of calm, the same smile that had once soothed me now a distant, almost cruel curve. I wanted to believe it was all some twisted illusion, that the storm had somehow affected us all in ways I couldn't understand. But the icy weight in my gut, the sense of betrayal, was real. Too real.

I stood, my knees trembling beneath me as I pushed myself upright, the cold stone of the floor still pressing against the palms of my hands. The ritual, the magic we had tried to control, had pulled us into this mess, and now it was asking—no, demanding—answers.

"What did you do?" I barely managed the words, my voice thin, shaky, as though I hadn't used it in years. The energy between us was still there, crackling in the air, but now it was suffocating.

"I didn't do anything," he replied, his voice smooth, far too calm for the chaos that had just unfolded. "You all did it. This is on all of us."

I wanted to throw something at him, anything—one of the shattered remnants of a vase, the rusted ceremonial dagger that lay abandoned at the foot of the altar—but I couldn't move, couldn't even think straight. The room felt like it was closing in on me, and I was running out of breath to scream.

"You think this is on all of us?" My words finally spilled out, harsh and raw, like a wound that had been opened too suddenly. "You think I did this? We trusted you!"

His eyes didn't flicker. They never did, those cold, calculating eyes that I had once thought were the depth of everything I needed. Now they were just voids. "You think trust is what brought us here? You're wrong."

His words hit harder than any physical blow. They were the ones that unraveled the fragile thread of my composure. I staggered back, my feet stumbling over the debris from the ritual—broken pottery, twisted metal, the remnants of candles that had melted into pools of wax.

"This is what you wanted all along," I spat, my chest rising and falling with every sharp, angry breath. "All this time, I thought we were a team. But you've been playing us from the start, haven't you?"

"Look at yourself," he said quietly, tilting his head, his voice low, almost sympathetic. "You're no better than the rest of us. You didn't come here out of some noble sense of duty. You came here for power, for control, just like the rest of us."

I blinked hard, trying to clear the haze in my mind. His words were poison, but they were coated in just enough truth to make my skin crawl. Was it really so simple? Was I just like them, chasing after something I didn't fully understand, pulling at threads I couldn't hope to weave back together?

The realization hit like a slap across the face. My stomach churned. He was right. All of us, every last one of us, had entered this game thinking we could bend reality, that we could manipulate the forces of the universe for our own selfish reasons. The storm outside, the chaos we had unleashed, was nothing more than a reflection of the darkness inside each of us.

But I wasn't ready to give up. Not yet.

"You think you can just walk away from this?" I demanded, taking a step closer. My fists were clenched at my sides, the nails digging into my palms, but I didn't care. I was beyond caring.

"Of course I can," he said, as though it were the simplest thing in the world. "You can, too. But whether or not you want to is the question. The truth is, you've always known this day would come. You just didn't want to face it."

The air between us grew thick again, dense with tension, thick with all the words we hadn't spoken. Words we'd been too afraid to utter until now. I realized, with a horrible clarity, that this moment had been coming for a long time. Not just the storm—this conversation, this reckoning, this breaking point.

My heart was pounding in my chest, but the adrenaline had shifted into something darker, something colder. "I don't need you," I said, the words coming out before I could stop them. "I never did. I only thought I did."

For a split second, his mask cracked, his eyes flickering with something that could have been guilt. Or maybe it was just surprise. But it didn't matter. He had already gone too far. He had already taken everything we had, everything we could have been, and ripped it apart.

And I was done.

I took a deep breath and let the silence fill the space between us, the weight of my decision settling like a stone in my chest. I didn't know what the future held, didn't know what came next, but for the first time, I didn't care.

I walked away from him, or at least, I thought I did. My feet moved in the direction of the door, but my body felt like it belonged to someone else. I was no longer sure what I was running from—was it him, the ritual, or the shattering of everything I had once believed to be true? The air in the room pressed against me like an invisible hand, heavy and suffocating. Each step I took felt like a betrayal, a step away from the person I had been, a person who still believed in the idea of us, the promise of something better.

But the truth had sliced through me like a blade, and now I was left standing in the aftermath, bloodied and broken, trying to stitch together the remnants of what was left.

The storm outside had reached its peak, the wind rattling the walls of the chamber with such force that it felt as though the building itself might collapse around us. Thunder cracked so loudly that it seemed to reverberate in my bones, the lightning flashing like jagged teeth, tearing apart the night. It felt as though the storm was responding to the storm inside me, the one that raged between every breath, between every thought.

"Where are you going?" His voice was soft, almost too soft, but it carried through the tension in the air. It wasn't a question, not really. It was a command, the same way it had always been. And for a second, I almost listened. Almost.

"I'm leaving," I said, and the words were foreign even to me, as if someone else had spoken them. I paused, hand on the cold iron handle of the door. "For good this time."

"I knew you'd say that," he said, and I could hear the smile in his voice. The kind of smile that used to make my heart flutter. The kind that now made me want to choke on the bitterness rising in my throat.

I turned slowly, meeting his gaze once more. The flickering candlelight made his features appear almost otherworldly, his sharp jawline cast in shadows, eyes gleaming with that familiar coldness. He stood in the same spot he had been before, hands at his sides, the picture of calm control. But I knew better now. The cracks in the façade were there. I could see them. And they were deep.

"I told you," I said, trying to steady my voice, to find the strength that had once come so easily. "I can't do this anymore. I won't. The lies, the manipulation—it's too much. You've taken everything. You've taken me."

He didn't respond right away. Instead, he looked at me with something that might have been pity, or maybe that was just wishful thinking. It didn't matter. The look alone was enough to twist the knife deeper.

"You're not leaving," he finally said, and the way he said it made my skin crawl. "You're too weak for that."

I felt the heat rise in my chest, the anger, the fury that had been building up in me like a volcano about to erupt. For so long, I had tried to placate him, to make him believe that I was enough. Enough for him, enough for the magic, enough for the twisted little world he had built for us. But I wasn't. Not anymore. And I was tired of pretending that I could ever be.

"You don't get to tell me who I am anymore," I shot back, the words sharp, cutting through the thick air. "You don't control me."

There it was, the flicker of something in his eyes. Not surprise, no. He had never been surprised by anything I did. But something else. Something darker.

"Oh, but I do," he said, voice lowering, each word deliberate. "You always have been. Always will be."

The air shifted again, like the storm outside was suddenly inside, swirling between us. The space around us felt alive, vibrating with a tension I couldn't understand. The ground beneath my feet trembled, just slightly, but enough to unnerve me. I didn't know what was happening, only that it was far from over.

I swallowed hard, the weight of his words pressing down on me. But I wasn't backing down. I couldn't.

"I'm leaving," I repeated, forcing the words past the lump in my throat. This time, I didn't just speak them. I felt them, the finality of the statement. There was no going back.

Without another word, I stepped toward the door, my fingers closing around the cold handle again. I didn't look back this time. Not even when I heard him take a step forward, his boots scraping against the stone floor.

And then, I heard it. A sound that stopped me dead in my tracks. A low, guttural noise, something between a growl and a laugh. I froze, the blood draining from my face as the realization hit.

"You think you can just walk out?" he asked, and there was no mistaking the venom in his voice now. "You think this is over?"

I turned slowly, and what I saw made my heart stop in my chest. He wasn't standing there anymore, not quite.

His body was still there, but his eyes... they were different. Darker. The flickering candlelight reflected in them like the depths of a storm. And in that moment, I realized something terrible: whatever had been unleashed tonight, whatever storm had raged within us, was far from finished.

"You should never have tried to walk away," he said, his voice distorted now, more than human. "You belong to this. To me."

I stepped back, breath quickening, heart racing. The walls seemed to pulse with energy, the ground beneath my feet shaking once more as the storm outside intensified. And in the midst of it all, I felt it—the unmistakable weight of his power wrapping itself around me, squeezing, pulling.

I reached for the door again, but my hand froze halfway.

Because I didn't know if I was leaving... or if I was about to be dragged back into the darkness forever.

Chapter 22: The Memory Returned

The wind had died down, leaving only the remnants of the storm in its wake—wet streets glistening like spilled ink, and the air thick with the scent of earth and ozone. I stood in the middle of the living room, barefoot and alone, but not truly either of those things. His presence lingered in the corners of my mind, just as palpable as the way my heart still beat erratically, as if it knew something my mind couldn't yet grasp. I touched the side of my neck, where his hands had once cupped me in an effort to pull me closer, to somehow save me from the darkness that had come too fast, too fiercely. But it hadn't been enough. Nothing had been enough.

The memory hit me like a wave, crashing with such force that I stumbled back. His voice, thick with panic and desperation, echoed in my ears. "Don't leave me. Please. You have to fight, you have to stay with me." I hadn't wanted to die, not then, not ever. But there was nothing more I could have done. The world had torn itself apart around us, and we had been caught in the middle, two fools caught up in something we didn't even understand.

My hands trembled as I ran them through my hair, pulling it away from my face. The betrayal—his betrayal—it had been a wound I couldn't have seen coming. No, not him. I had trusted him, had trusted that he would never allow anything to harm me, not in the way the world had. And yet, in the end, his choices, his mistakes, had been what led to my death. The memory of it was sharp, raw, but somehow, it was a part of me now. Something that, despite the pain it caused, I couldn't let go.

But as quickly as the memory had come, another one followed. This one was softer, warmer. His face—an image of torment and sorrow—hovered in my mind. The way he had held me, even after I had slipped away, as if he could somehow stop time, stop the inevitable. He had tried to save me, not just physically, but emotionally, too. That was the part of him that haunted me the most. The way he had loved me, even after I had given him nothing but silence and distance.

I blinked, my vision blurry. I had been angry at him. Furious, even. But why? It was as though all those old feelings—the ones that had once fueled the fire of my hatred—had evaporated, leaving only the memory of the love we had shared. A love that had been corrupted, twisted, yes, but still a love. The realization nearly brought me to my knees. He hadn't betrayed me. He had been deceived, just as I had. We had been pieces on a chessboard, and neither of us had seen the hand that moved us.

I stumbled toward the kitchen, needing something to ground me, something solid. The cold tile beneath my feet was a small comfort as I opened the refrigerator and grabbed a bottle of water. I unscrewed the cap, taking a long drink, but the sensation did little to quench the dryness that had settled in my throat. It was a kind of emptiness I hadn't known before—one that filled my chest, pressing against my ribs, suffocating me. The storm had passed, but the chaos it had left in its wake still clung to me like the dampness of the air, refusing to let go.

The shadows in the corners of the room seemed to pulse with the echo of the past, the memory of his touch, his voice, still there in the quiet. How had I gotten here? How had I allowed myself to believe that he had been the architect of my pain when, in reality, he had been the one who suffered alongside me?

I set the bottle down, my fingers trailing across the countertop as I leaned forward, staring at the empty space where the old coffee maker had once stood. Would he come back for me? The thought caught me off guard. It was absurd. Foolish. He couldn't come back. But even as the rational part of my mind screamed for me to let go, my heart—a traitorous thing—held on. There were too many pieces of him still embedded in my soul, too many moments that we had shared that couldn't be erased, no matter how much I wanted them to be.

He had loved me. The thought was a mantra, a balm to my wounded spirit. It was hard to admit, even harder to face. But it was true. And somehow, despite everything, I had loved him, too.

The door creaked open, and I froze. My heart slammed into my chest. The sound was unmistakable, and for a brief, irrational moment, I wondered if I had imagined it—if I had summoned him somehow, through sheer will and desperation. But then I saw him, standing there in the doorway, his eyes wide with something I couldn't read. Him.

He hadn't changed. His hair still fell messily around his face, his clothes still worn, but the same anguish that had once defined him was there, more palpable than ever. He didn't speak, just stood there, waiting, as if the weight of the moment had kept him from moving any closer.

"I—I thought you were gone," I whispered, my voice hoarse, raw with emotion I didn't know how to control.

He took a step forward, and then another, until he was standing in front of me. "I never left. Not really. You just... you couldn't see me, could you?"

I swallowed hard, my heart racing. "You left me."

His face twisted with pain. "I never meant to."

And suddenly, in that small, cluttered kitchen, everything else fell away—the storm, the confusion, the years of resentment. All that mattered was the truth that hung between us, waiting to be acknowledged, waiting for us to finally face what had always been there.

I stared at him, at the man who had once been everything to me, and yet, for so long, had felt like a stranger. There was so much I wanted to say, so much I needed to scream, but my voice failed me, reduced to nothing more than the shaky breath between us. I watched him closely, as if searching for some hint, some crack in his façade that would explain the chaos that had unfolded between us. But there was nothing. His expression was unreadable—an open book in a language I hadn't spoken in years.

"I thought I had lost you," I whispered, the words more of a confession than a statement. It wasn't just the shock of seeing him again after all this time, but the overwhelming flood of memories, all tangled together—his hands on me, his kisses that had once been tender, and the promises we had made when we thought the world would always bend to our whims. The storm outside had been nothing compared to the storm inside me.

He didn't respond right away, just watched me with a quiet intensity that made my heart ache in a way I couldn't explain. "I never meant to hurt you," he finally said, his voice so soft it barely cut through the space between us. "I never meant for any of this. You have to believe that."

I wanted to tell him that I did believe him. That somewhere, buried beneath all the pain and confusion, I had never stopped believing. But the words felt like a lie in my throat. "You left me," I said, the bitterness creeping in, despite my best efforts to hold it back.

"I didn't leave you. I had to..." His voice faltered, and for a brief moment, I saw something in his eyes—regret, pain, and something far deeper than I had anticipated. "I had to keep you safe. Even if it meant letting you go."

The room felt smaller, suffocating, and I needed air. I pushed past him, my bare feet brushing against the cold floor as I went to the window, staring out at the night. The storm had passed, but the wreckage it left behind remained, both outside and within me. It felt like the world was holding its breath, waiting for something to shift.

He followed me, his footsteps tentative, as if unsure whether to bridge the distance between us. "I know it doesn't make sense," he said, his voice now closer, almost a whisper. "But you have to understand. We were caught in something we didn't control. We were never meant to be part of this... this war."

I turned to face him, my hand gripping the edge of the windowsill for support. "A war? You're going to tell me this was all for some cause we couldn't see?" I laughed, a bitter sound that tasted foreign in my mouth. "You didn't just walk away. You disappeared. You let me think—" I stopped myself, unable to continue. The words were too sharp, too raw, too dangerous. But he was still standing there, waiting for me to say them, as if the truth would somehow make it better.

His gaze softened, though his jaw tightened with a mix of guilt and frustration. "I was trying to protect you. You don't know what they—what they did to me. I couldn't let them get to you. I couldn't risk it."

"Risk what?" I asked, the sharpness in my voice betraying the vulnerability I felt deep inside. "What could they possibly do to me that they didn't already do?"

He took another step closer, and I could feel the tension between us coil tighter, like a rope pulled too tight. "They already took everything from us, didn't they?" His voice dropped, softer now, quieter. "But I knew that if I stayed... if I let you see me, if you found out what I'd become..." His voice faltered. "I couldn't do that to you. Not after everything we went through."

And just like that, I was back there. Back in the place where trust was nothing but a faint memory, where betrayal had left its scars on both of us. I closed my eyes briefly, letting the wave of emotion wash over me.

But then, it happened. A soft sound. A whisper. A name.

I blinked, disoriented, as my mind tried to piece together what had just happened. Had he said something? A name, perhaps? A name I hadn't heard in so long?

"I... I heard it too." His voice was barely above a whisper, but there was no mistaking the fear that clung to it. His eyes met mine, wide and uncertain, as if he wasn't sure whether the sound had come from me or from somewhere much darker.

I shook my head, a knot forming in my stomach. "What are you talking about?"

He swallowed hard, his breath shallow. "You didn't hear it?" He leaned in slightly, his voice lowering even further. "I swear to you, it was—"

And then, the lights flickered. The room seemed to pulse, a strange vibration in the air that made the hairs on the back of my neck stand up. I stepped back instinctively, my heart pounding harder than before, like a drum in my chest.

He reached for me, his fingers brushing against my arm, and for a split second, I saw something in his eyes—something raw, something desperate. "We have to leave," he said, the urgency in his voice unmistakable. "They're coming. We're not alone."

I glanced around, confusion blurring my thoughts. "Who's coming?"

He didn't answer, but the fear in his eyes said it all. Something was wrong. The storm outside was nothing compared to the storm that was about to hit us. And I wasn't sure we were ready for whatever it was.

I looked at him, the man I had once loved, and felt my heart twist. "What have we walked into, really?"

And before he could answer, the door slammed shut behind us, a force so strong that the air itself seemed to bend under the pressure. I turned to look at him, but he wasn't there anymore—he was already moving toward the door, toward whatever came next, leaving me to follow, as always.

The air was thick with something more than just the remnants of the storm. There was a shift—something palpable that hung between us, heavier than the silence that had settled in the room. He hadn't said a word as he watched me. His gaze was intense, the kind of look that makes a person question everything they think they know. I couldn't tell if it was guilt, fear, or something else entirely that made his eyes so unreadable, but whatever it was, it was a stark contrast to the man I remembered.

I followed him through the narrow hallway, the shadows stretching long against the walls, the only sound our footsteps—his measured and calm, mine ragged with emotion. As we reached the front door, I hesitated. "What do you mean, they're coming?" I tried to keep my voice steady, but it wavered despite my best efforts.

He didn't answer at first. He just stood there, hand on the door handle, staring into the darkness beyond. It was as though the world had gone still—too still, like it was holding its breath, waiting for something terrible to happen.

"Are you going to tell me what this is all about, or are we just going to run blindly into whatever's coming next?" My words were sharp, but they didn't sting. I was beyond caring about how they came out.

He turned to face me then, and there was something in his eyes that made me falter. "I didn't want to bring you into this. I never did." His words came slowly, deliberately, like he was testing them out before letting them fall. "But now... now you're already in it, and there's no turning back."

I shook my head. "I don't even know what 'it' is, okay? What exactly is it that you're so scared of?"

He opened the door just a crack, peering out into the black night beyond. The wind had picked up again, howling in a way that made the house groan with the effort to hold itself together. The world outside was a blur of rain and darkness, just a thick wall of nothingness that felt... wrong.

"Don't," I said, stepping forward, reaching for the door. "I don't want you to go out there. You don't even know what's—"

"I do," he interrupted. "I know exactly what's out there." He gave me a look, his eyes hardening, and for a moment, he seemed almost... familiar. Not the man who had betrayed me, but the one who had loved me so fiercely, so utterly. The one I had trusted before everything had fallen apart.

He pulled the door open wider and stepped outside, leaving me no choice but to follow. It felt like something was pulling at my very soul—compelling me to move, to keep walking, even when every instinct told me to stay put.

The rain lashed against my skin, and the wind bit at my exposed flesh as I stepped into the yard behind him. It was colder than I expected, colder than it should've been after the storm had passed.

"What are we doing out here?" I demanded, my voice barely audible over the howling wind.

He didn't answer immediately, instead staring out into the darkness as if searching for something, or someone. "I didn't want you to see this," he said finally, his tone heavy with regret. "But I don't have a choice anymore. Neither do you."

There was something in the air—a tension that was too thick to ignore. The hair on the back of my neck stood on end, and my stomach twisted in a knot that I couldn't undo.

"Who are they?" I asked again, more urgently this time. "Why are they after us? What do they want?"

He seemed to hesitate, his lips pressing together as though he was trying to find the words, but nothing came out. His eyes flicked back toward the door, then to the darkness beyond, and I could feel the shift in him. Something had changed. Whatever small fragment of reassurance I'd been holding onto had vanished, swept away by the weight of what was coming.

"They want everything we have," he said quietly. "They want control of what we started. Of what we both had a hand in."

I blinked, trying to make sense of his words, but they felt like shards of glass—sharp, hard, and incomprehensible. "I don't know what you're talking about. What do you mean by 'what we started'? What—"

Before I could finish, the ground beneath us trembled. It wasn't an earthquake—just a slight, unsettling shake that made the trees around us groan, their limbs stretching toward the sky like they were reaching for something. My pulse raced.

"Something's coming," he muttered under his breath. "They've found us."

I grabbed his arm, panic flaring in my chest. "Who? Who's found us?"

He didn't answer right away, his face tightening as he scanned the shadows. I followed his gaze, my heart in my throat, trying to see what he saw. And then, in the distance, I caught a flicker of movement. A shadow. But it wasn't just one. There were more. Figures, all emerging from the darkness like phantoms.

"They're here," he said, his voice grim. "Stay close."

I didn't need telling twice. Every instinct in my body screamed for me to run, to flee back inside, but something told me that wouldn't be enough. The figures were closing in, moving faster than I could've imagined. Too fast.

We turned toward the house, but before we could reach the door, a low, guttural growl rose from behind us. My blood froze in my veins as I turned around, seeing the eyes first—two burning lights in the darkness, watching us with an intensity that made my stomach drop.

"Go inside," he said urgently, his grip tightening on my arm. "Now!"

But the door slammed shut before I could even make a step toward it. The unmistakable sound of a lock snapping into place echoed through the night, leaving me with nothing but the dark, the storm, and the creatures that were slowly surrounding us.

"Move," he hissed. "We don't have much time."

And just like that, I knew. We were trapped.

Chapter 23: The Last Wish

The moon hung low in the sky, a delicate sliver of silver that seemed to hover just above the jagged cliffs, its light spilling like honey onto the windswept landscape. The air was thick with salt, the scent of the ocean mixing with the raw, earthy tang of the forest. It was the kind of night that made the world feel like it had been paused—suspended in the tension of what was about to unfold.

I stood at the edge of the cliff, my feet planted firmly in the cool, damp earth, feeling the wind tug at my hair as though it too was trying to pull me away from the decision I had made. Below me, the sea roiled in a frenzy, waves crashing against the rocks like the echo of some distant, forgotten storm. But there was no storm now—only this stillness, this quiet before the inevitable. And I knew, with every fiber of my being, that what I had to do would ripple through time and space, sending waves across everything I had ever known, everything I had ever loved.

My heart was heavy, as if the weight of a thousand years had settled in my chest, yet somehow it beat with a clarity that pierced the fog of uncertainty. The memories were clear now, restored in vivid flashes of color and sound—the laughter, the loss, the love. He had been there, always. Even when I thought I had forgotten, he had never truly left me. His touch, his voice, the warmth of his presence—it was all still there, etched into my soul.

And yet, here I was, facing him for the last time, knowing the choice I made now would sever the thread that had bound us for eternity.

"You don't have to do this." His voice was thick with emotion, a mix of desperation and sorrow that twisted my gut. He stood a few paces behind me, the shadows of the night cloaking him in a sorrowful embrace. His features were drawn, his usual confidence replaced with something raw, something vulnerable that I had never seen before. It made him more real to me than ever. But the pain in his eyes was a reminder of why I had to go through with this.

"I do," I replied softly, not turning to face him. I couldn't. Not when my resolve felt so fragile, as if a single glance might shatter it into a thousand broken pieces. "I can't leave us trapped like this. We've suffered enough."

"Don't you see?" His voice was a whisper now, low and pleading. "We've been given another chance. We don't have to end it like this. We can find another way. We always have."

I closed my eyes for a moment, the weight of his words pressing against me, but I knew what I had to do. I had already tried every other possibility. Every path had led here, to this moment, to this decision. And while my heart ached with the thought of what I would lose, I knew there was no other way. Not anymore.

The curse that had bound us for centuries was born from a wish—a wish I had made in a past life, a wish that had come with consequences I never could have foreseen. A wish that had woven our fates together in a tangled knot, a knot that only I could undo. But undoing it meant a sacrifice I was reluctant to make, one that would sever everything, even him.

He stepped closer, the sound of his boots on the soft ground barely reaching my ears. I could feel the heat of his presence behind me, feel the magnetic pull that had always existed between us, even when we were worlds apart.

"You're not just giving up your life, are you?" His words were almost too quiet to hear, but they struck me all the same, a blade to the heart. "You're giving up everything. All the time we've spent together. All the memories."

"Yes," I whispered, my voice barely audible, yet so sure. "But I can't let us live in this prison anymore. If I don't do this, we'll keep repeating the same cycle, over and over, never finding peace. I can't do that to us. Not when I know what it would cost."

He was silent for a long time, the only sound the distant crashing of the waves, as though even nature itself was holding its breath. And then, when he spoke again, his voice was tinged with a kind of quiet resignation.

"If you go through with this... there's no coming back. Not for either of us."

"I know," I said, the words tasting bitter on my tongue. "But this is the only way we can break the cycle. You know that too."

I felt him move, his presence at my side now, his hand brushing against mine. The touch was gentle, almost tentative, as if he feared I might disappear the moment he made contact.

"It's not fair," he muttered, the words jagged with pain. "It never has been."

"No," I agreed, my voice steady, though my insides were a whirlwind of emotion. "But nothing about this has been fair. Not for either of us."

He took a deep breath, his fingers curling slightly around mine before he let go. There was no more time. No more words to say. I had to do this.

Turning to face him, I saw the conflict still written on his face, the flicker of hope that maybe, just maybe, I might change my mind. But it was too late for that. There was no other choice, not if I wanted to truly set us free.

I closed my eyes, my heart thundering in my chest, and whispered the words—my final wish.

The air shifted, thickening as though the world itself were holding its breath. I felt the weight of the wish settle deep into my bones, an anchor dragging me into the past, into a life I thought I had left behind. The words I had spoken—soft, deliberate, laced with the ache of a thousand lost moments—hung in the space between us, heavier than any silence I had ever known.

I had never intended for this to be my fate. The wish I had made, those last whispered words as life slipped through my fingers, had seemed innocent enough at the time. I had only wanted us to be together, to escape the confines of circumstance, to rewrite the story of us in a world where we could be free. But freedom came with its own set of chains, chains that had bound us for centuries. And now, at the cusp of breaking them, I was the one who would have to be shackled for good.

"I wish you could understand," I murmured, my voice barely a breath in the wind. "This is the only way. There's no other path. If I don't do this, nothing will change. And we'll be stuck in this endless loop forever."

His gaze was steady, searching, as though he thought he could somehow read the words from my soul. His expression was torn between disbelief and sorrow, and I could see the way his jaw clenched, the muscles in his neck tightening with the strain of restraint. He was fighting me, fighting the truth that had already settled in the deepest corners of my heart.

"You think I haven't tried to understand?" His voice cracked just the slightest bit, a quiet edge of frustration slipping through. "We've both been living in this cycle, and I'm telling you, I won't accept this. You're talking about giving up everything—the future we could have, the life that's still ahead of us. You're willing to throw that away for some... some idea of what's right?"

I turned to face him fully, the weight of his words like a pressure on my chest. But I didn't waver. "The future we have isn't a future at all. Not like this. We're both caught in a loop of our own making, and it's only by fulfilling the wish that we can finally break free."

"Stop," he said sharply, stepping closer, the heat of his body warming the cool night air between us. "Don't say that. You don't know that. You can't. You don't know what the future holds. We've been given so many chances, so many opportunities to make things right. I won't let you go through with this. I won't."

But the certainty in his voice faltered, and I could see the flicker of doubt, the same doubt I had fought against for so long. He had always been the one to search for the hope when I had already given it up. The one who believed in second chances, even when I couldn't see how they existed. But I had lived with this curse long enough to know there was no other way.

The wind howled in the distance, a mournful sound that seemed to echo the finality of my decision. The stars above us blinked out one by one, swallowed by the thickening clouds, as though the universe itself had decided to bear witness to the moment that would unravel everything.

"I'm not asking you to understand," I said, my voice growing firmer with each word. "I'm asking you to let me do this. I'm asking you to trust me."

He flinched as if my words had struck him, his features tightening with emotion. "Trust you? After everything we've been through? You're asking me to trust you to leave me? To... to vanish? Just like that?"

I swallowed hard, my throat thick with the emotion I had been trying to suppress. "I'm not vanishing. I'll always be with you, in some way. But if I don't do this, we'll never truly be free. And neither of us will ever be able to move on."

His eyes softened, though the sadness never fully left them. "And what about me?" he asked quietly. "What happens to me when you're gone?"

The question hit me harder than I had expected. I had never allowed myself to think about the cost to him, to his heart, to everything he would lose. But it was too late to take it back. There was no changing the truth of what I had to do.

"I'm sorry," I whispered. The apology felt hollow, but I couldn't say anything else. The words, the feelings, they were all tangled together in a knot too tight to unravel.

He stepped back, his hand brushing across his face in a motion of helpless frustration. "I can't stop you, can I?" His voice was barely audible, the weight of defeat creeping into every syllable.

I shook my head, my own heart breaking with every second that passed. "No. You can't. I wish you could. But I have to do this. For both of us."

There was a long pause between us, a stillness that seemed to last forever. Then, as if some unspoken understanding passed between us, he nodded once, sharply. It wasn't acceptance—no, it was resignation. He had surrendered to the inevitable, but I knew that surrender was not the same as giving up.

"I will always love you," he said, the words low and raw, like the last thread of hope clinging to the edge of a ravine.

"I know," I said, my voice a soft echo of his. "And I'll always love you, too. But this is the only way we can truly be free."

The finality of it hung between us like a heavy fog, and though my heart screamed to stay, to turn away from the choice I had made, I held firm. For us. For the promise I had made long ago. I turned away from him then, my heart shattering with the weight of what I was about to lose.

And as I stood there, on the edge of everything, I knew—without a doubt—that this would be the last wish.

I could feel the pulse of my heart, erratic and unsteady, as the words of the wish hung in the air around us like a weight, thick and oppressive. The night seemed to thicken with it, the shadows stretching and swirling at the edges of my vision. Time was slipping away—my last moment, the one where everything could finally change, and yet, I was still tethered to him. To this place. To the life I had once known. It felt like standing on the edge of a precipice, staring down at a jagged cliff that was somehow more inviting than the safety I had once clung to.

I couldn't go back. Not now.

But that didn't stop the tremor in my hand as I held it out, reaching for the dark sky above me. The wind tugged at my clothes, whipping them around me in a storm of chaos, as though nature itself was fighting against my decision. The stars blinked above, each one a silent witness to the curse that had plagued us both for lifetimes. Each one a reminder that there was no escape, no alternative, but to face the consequences of the wish that had bound us.

"You're really going to do it, aren't you?" His voice, low and raw, reached me from behind, the sound of it like a rope pulling me back from the brink. But it wasn't enough. Not this time.

Turning to face him, I saw the pain in his eyes, the desperation that always came when he thought he could save me, when he thought there was another way. I had seen it in his gaze before—in that other life, in a hundred other lifetimes—and it had never been enough to stop the inevitable. It would never be enough.

"You know I have to," I said, my voice steady, though every inch of me screamed to turn away. But I couldn't. I wouldn't. Not now. "You've seen the signs. You've felt it, too."

He took a step forward, his gaze softening for just a moment, and then hardening again with resolve. "I can't lose you. Not again. You're asking me to walk away from everything we've built, everything we've fought for. And I can't. Not when I know there's still more to do. More chances to make it right."

I swallowed against the lump in my throat, the ache in my chest too much to bear. But it wasn't enough. It would never be enough.

"I don't want to lose you, either," I whispered, my voice cracking under the weight of the truth. "But we've been living in this cycle for so long. How many more times can we repeat the same mistakes? How many more lifetimes before we're both swallowed whole by it?"

His gaze faltered, the lines of his face etched with regret. "I don't care about mistakes. I care about you. I care about us. I'm not ready to let go of everything we have."

But the decision had already been made. I could see the world slipping through my fingers, feel the edges of the curse tightening their grip around us. I had already seen the price of breaking free, and I knew I couldn't live with the alternative. There was no more room for hope. No more time for second chances.

With a deep breath, I closed my eyes, and for the first time, I let go.

The air around me seemed to thrum with energy, the sky darkening as though the universe was holding its breath. Then, as if the world itself was in mourning, I whispered the final words. The ones that would bind everything together. The wish that had been born from love and had become a curse.

"I wish... I wish for us to be free."

The moment the words left my lips, the world seemed to tilt. A sudden gust of wind rushed through the trees, snapping branches and sending them crashing to the ground. The ground beneath me trembled, as if the very earth were protesting the weight of what I had just done. My vision blurred, the edges of everything fading into darkness as the curse unraveled, piece by piece.

And then, just as quickly as it had begun, it stopped. The stillness was suffocating. For a long, drawn-out second, there was nothing but silence. The waves, the wind, even the stars themselves seemed to have stilled in their eternal dance.

I opened my eyes, but the world around me was... different. Not wrong, but not the same. The ground beneath me felt solid, unyielding, as though I were standing on something ancient, something that had always been here, waiting for this moment. And yet, something was missing.

I looked at him.

He was standing there, frozen in place, his expression unreadable. His lips parted as if he were about to speak, but no words came. His gaze swept over me, his face pale under the moonlight. And for the briefest of moments, I saw it—the flicker of confusion. The very same uncertainty I had seen in my own heart when I had whispered the wish.

Something had changed. But what?

I took a step forward, my breath quickening as my senses screamed at me that something was terribly, terribly wrong. The air, the ground, even the sea—it felt... lighter. But not in the way it should. There was something unsettling about it, as if the universe itself had shifted and taken something important with it.

I reached for him, my heart hammering in my chest. "What's happening? What did we do?"

But as my fingers brushed against his arm, the world around us seemed to ripple. A strange, harsh light filled the sky—blinding, unearthly—and before I could process what was happening, his body was no longer solid beneath my touch. He vanished. Just like that.

"NO!" I screamed, my voice tearing through the silence, but it was too late. The space where he had been was empty. Completely empty.

I stood there, alone, in the stillness of the night, my heart shattering under the weight of the truth.

And as the world around me continued to shift, I realized with a sickening clarity—the sacrifice wasn't just mine. It never had been.

Chapter 24: The Dance of Shadows

I could feel the cool stone of the floor against my bare feet as I moved in time with him, the rhythm of our steps echoing through the chamber like a forgotten song. The scent of incense lingered thick in the air, mingling with the faint musk of ancient stone and the heady sweetness of jasmine, each breath both grounding and dizzying. Shadows stretched across the walls, their twisted forms dancing like specters caught in an eternal waltz, a dance I now realized I had been practicing all my life.

His hand brushed mine, a fleeting touch, but one that sent ripples through the delicate web of nerves that seemed to have formed between us over the past months. I had always been careful, always kept a distance, but now there was no room for hesitation. No more time for wondering if the magic that pulsed through our veins was our salvation or our undoing. His eyes met mine—dark, knowing, and as impossible to read as they had always been. In those depths, I saw everything I could never quite put into words: the silent understanding, the shared grief, the remnants of something once pure and now tangled in the mess of our history.

The wind from the open archway shifted, carrying with it the chill of the coming dawn, but it didn't touch me. It didn't touch us. We were wrapped in a cocoon of energy that seemed to suspend us in a place between worlds, neither here nor there. The spell was closing in, tightening its grip around us as we circled each other, feet silent on the stone, breath synchronized, the pulse of our hearts beating in time. It wasn't just the ritual. It wasn't just magic. It was something deeper, something older than all of us, something written in the stars long before our paths had ever crossed.

I forced my gaze away from him, my steps faltering slightly, though my body knew better than to stray from the pattern we had perfected. The flicker of candlelight danced in my peripheral vision, casting long, wavering shadows on the stone walls. The shadows were part of the spell, part of the trap. We had been warned about them—told not to let them consume us, to never look too closely into their depths, for fear that they would pull us in and keep us there. But there was no turning back now.

As the ritual's pull deepened, the air around me thickened, stifling, as though the very space we inhabited was closing in on itself. I swallowed hard, the heat in my chest rising despite the chill, the sweat gathering along the line of my jaw. I could feel the weight of centuries pressing against me, the remnants of countless others who had tried and failed, those whose names I would never know but whose stories seemed to pulse through the floorboards beneath my feet. I was just one in a long line of fools trying to outsmart fate. And yet... the ritual had to work. It had to.

My breath caught as the room shifted again, the shadows lengthening and creeping like liquid darkness. Something sharp brushed against my skin, too swift for me to track. A whisper, almost too faint to hear, curled around my ear, but when I turned, there was nothing—nothing but the shadow of him, of us. I reached out, my fingers brushing against his arm, but it wasn't him anymore. Not fully. Not in the way he had been. He was slipping away, just as I had feared. The magic had taken hold of him too, drawing him into its ever-deepening chasm.

"Don't," I whispered, though I wasn't sure if the words were for him or for myself.

He didn't reply, not with words, but with a single, small shift of his body, the barest movement that told me he had heard. He wasn't gone yet. Not entirely. But the strain was visible, pulling at him like a thousand threads unraveling. His eyes flickered to mine again, and for a moment, I saw something there—something familiar, something that made my pulse quicken. It was the same spark that had always been there, the one that had drawn me to him in the first place, the one that had kept me tethered to him when I should have run.

But I couldn't run now. Not when we were this close. Not when everything hinged on this final step, this final motion. He needed me, I knew that. But I needed him too. It wasn't just the ritual that had bound us. It was something else, something that had formed between us in the silence of those long nights, in the spaces where words failed.

The first light of dawn slipped through the archway, spilling golden warmth across the cold stone, but it was fleeting. Only a moment before the shadows seemed to fight back, swallowing it whole. The world outside remained indifferent, oblivious to the battle we fought here in the heart of this chamber, where magic collided with memory, where love met its limit. The dance was nearing its end, the final step within reach, but the cost—the cost would be more than I had ever imagined.

I wasn't sure which part of me was still holding on to him, still reaching for that spark of who we had been, but it didn't matter. The ritual was coming to its conclusion, and as I moved through the last series of steps, I could feel the pull of it, the weight of it settling over me like a shroud. It wasn't magic anymore. It was something more primal. Something I couldn't control. And I wasn't sure I wanted to.

I could hear the faint, steady rhythm of my breath mingling with his as we moved, each motion sharp and deliberate, a perfect reflection of everything that had brought us to this moment. The energy around us hummed like a tuning fork struck in the deep silence of a midnight sky, each vibration pulling at the threads of the world, tugging us both toward something greater—and yet terrifying. My pulse was erratic, my chest tight with the anticipation of what was to come. But as the shadows closed in around us, there was no fear, only the strange clarity that comes when everything is stripped away, when there is nothing left but this moment and the choice to make it count.

I stole a glance at him, but it was fleeting. His gaze was fixed ahead, unfocused but intent, as though he were staring into the very heart of the ritual. I tried not to read too much into it—the way his jaw tightened with each movement, or the fact that his hands were trembling ever so slightly, the smallest crack in his usual composure. He had always been the steady one, the constant, and I had built my world around that. But now, in the thin light of the early morning, I wasn't so sure anymore.

The shadows whispered, curling around us, twisting into shapes that were no longer familiar. They weren't just reflections of the past anymore; they were alive, breathing, pulling at the edges of reality. A breeze stirred, but it wasn't the wind. It was something else, something that didn't belong. I stopped for a moment, as though my body had remembered something that my mind hadn't—something instinctual, buried deep beneath the surface. My hand reached out, almost without thought, to steady myself, but instead of the cold stone I expected, I felt only a shifting warmth, a presence that was both terrifying and exhilarating.

"Do you feel that?" I asked, my voice almost drowned out by the sound of the ritual's hum.

He didn't answer right away, his focus still anchored to the swirling shadows, as though if he looked away for even a second, everything might collapse. But then, his eyes flickered to mine, and I saw the unspoken acknowledgment there, the flicker of something between us that was more than words. He had felt it too.

"I don't think it's just the magic anymore," he said, his voice low, carrying that same edge of uncertainty I had been trying so hard to ignore.

I nodded, unable to find the right words to explain the sensation. The air had thickened, pressing against me, as though the very atmosphere was bending to accommodate something—someone—else. The room had become too small, the walls closing in as the shadows stretched farther, filling every corner. The magic had taken on a life of its own, a force that pulsed through my veins like liquid fire, burning away every trace of doubt, every second of hesitation.

"You should stop," I said quietly, though I wasn't sure who I was speaking to—him or to myself.

But he was already shaking his head, his expression unreadable, though I could see the flicker of something behind his eyes. Regret, maybe. Or determination. Or perhaps something more complicated, something too tangled for me to untangle on my own.

"No," he replied firmly, his voice carrying the weight of a thousand unsaid things. "It has to be done. There's no turning back."

I wasn't sure if he was trying to convince me or himself, but it didn't matter. Because, in that moment, I realized I wasn't sure if I even wanted to turn back. The pull of the ritual was too strong, too undeniable. We had crossed the threshold, and there was no undoing what had already been done. It was a dangerous game, one that I had never intended to play, but here I was, dancing on the edge of it, my feet moving instinctively, as if the steps had been carved into me long ago, a rhythm I didn't remember learning but had always known.

The floor beneath us seemed to shift, a subtle movement, just enough to make me pause. It was a deep, rumbling sensation, like the earth itself was groaning in protest, but the energy we had summoned only grew stronger, pulling us both deeper into its embrace. I stumbled slightly, but he was there, his hand steady on my arm, guiding me back into the dance.

His touch was warm, too warm, and I wondered—just for a moment—if I had imagined the hesitation I'd felt in him earlier. But as his fingers tightened around my wrist, I realized it wasn't hesitation. It was fear. I had never seen him afraid before. But now, I saw it in the way he held me, in the way his breath came a little faster, the way his gaze darted nervously from one corner of the room to the other, as if he expected something—someone—to appear from the shadows at any moment.

"You're not scared, are you?" I teased lightly, trying to break the tension, but even I could hear the edge in my voice. I was trying to make light of it, trying to find some way to ground myself, but the words came out brittle, fragile, like glass on the verge of shattering.

He didn't smile, but his grip on me tightened, and I saw the corner of his mouth twitch, just for a second. "Should I be?"

I didn't answer. There was no need. The answer was in the way the shadows were closing in, in the way the air had shifted, thickening with the promise of something that could not be undone. There was no turning back now. Not for either of us.

The shadows around us began to move, swirling like smoke, their forms indistinct and formless, their whispers growing louder. The room felt as though it were collapsing inward, the edges of reality blurring until it was impossible to tell where the walls ended and where the magic began. And then, just as I thought we had reached the point of no return, the air cracked.

And for the first time in what felt like forever, everything went quiet.

The silence that followed was more deafening than the storm that had raged just moments before. It stretched out between us like a gossamer thread, so fragile it might snap with the slightest tremor. I stood there, frozen in place, my eyes still wide, unable to process what had just transpired. The shadows, once thick and suffocating, had vanished as quickly as they had come. The room had returned to its mundane, dusty quiet, the only sound the quiet thrum of my heartbeat, which felt suddenly loud, almost too loud.

And then, in the stillness, I noticed it: the change. The world had shifted, but I wasn't sure how. The air smelled different—cooler, fresher, like the first breath after a long storm. But there was something else too, something I couldn't quite put my finger on, like the scent of rain mingled with the faintest trace of metal.

His hand—still holding mine—was colder than before. It wasn't just the temperature; it was a distinct chill that reached deep into the marrow of my bones, unsettling in its finality. His eyes met mine, and for a brief moment, the fleeting touch of vulnerability in them caught me off guard. There was no hiding behind the hardened exterior anymore. He wasn't the same, not completely, and neither was I.

"You feel it too, don't you?" I asked, the words escaping before I could stop them.

He didn't immediately respond. Instead, he looked past me, out into the room, as though seeing something I couldn't. "I think we've done it," he said slowly, as though weighing each word carefully. "But at what cost, you're right. I'm not sure I want to know."

A chill passed over me, much colder than the lingering effects of the ritual. The shadows might have gone, but the weight of what we'd unleashed was still hanging in the air, palpable, pressing down on us both. We were free—at least, that's what we had agreed we would be. But this new freedom was not the triumphant release I had imagined. It was more like stepping out of one trap and finding that you had only walked into another.

I took a step back, and for the first time, I noticed that the ritual's circle—the one we had so meticulously created—was no longer intact. The symbols had bled away, fading into the stone, their sharp, angular lines no longer defined, as if the very foundation of our work had begun to unravel. My stomach twisted as I stared at the empty space where the circle had been. Was it possible that we had undone everything? Or had we merely opened a door to something far darker?

His grip on my hand tightened again, as if he had read my mind. "I can feel it too," he said, his voice tight. "Something's wrong. Something's watching us."

I stiffened, my skin prickling as the hairs on the back of my neck stood at attention. The room, once still, now hummed with a subtle but undeniable energy. The air seemed to thicken once more, pressing against me, as though the walls themselves were closing in. I glanced around, but nothing—nothing out of the ordinary. Just the flicker of candlelight, casting shadows that seemed to grow longer with every passing second. But the weight was there. That familiar, suffocating presence that told me we were not alone.

"I think... I think we've stirred something," I said, the words falling heavy between us. "Something we weren't supposed to."

He nodded, his jaw clenched, but his gaze never wavered. "It's always the things we don't expect that come back to bite us," he muttered, his eyes scanning the room. "We should have been more careful."

I looked back at him, trying to meet his steady gaze, but all I could see were the shadows. They were moving again, slow and deliberate, like something stalking us from the corners of the room. They seemed to stretch and twist, as if they were alive, reacting to our very presence.

"Do you think we're being punished?" I asked, almost joking, though the tremor in my voice betrayed me.

He didn't laugh. "No. I think we've just... awakened something. Something that doesn't play by the same rules we do."

The room felt smaller now, the air too thick to breathe. I reached out to steady myself on the cold stone of the wall, but as my hand brushed against it, the surface shifted—moved beneath my touch, as though the very structure of the place had begun to breathe, to pulse with an eerie rhythm that matched my quickening heartbeat.

"Something's changing," I whispered, pulling away as the sensation of movement under my fingertips refused to leave. It was a ripple, a subtle shift that felt more like an invitation than an accident.

Suddenly, a low, guttural sound echoed from somewhere deep within the walls. It wasn't a sound made by any living creature, but by something far older, far more ancient. The very walls of the room seemed to breathe with it, the stone groaning as though it had just awoken from a centuries-long slumber. My heart pounded in my chest, a thunderous noise that matched the resonance of whatever was stirring beneath the floor.

His grip on my wrist tightened, his breath catching in his throat. "We've done something," he murmured, eyes wide with realization. "Something... has noticed."

Before I could ask what he meant, the shadows in the room began to pulse, stretching unnaturally toward us. A low hum vibrated through the floor, shaking the ground beneath us, and the temperature dropped suddenly, sharply. My breath clouded in the air as the shadows converged at the center of the room, their forms twisting and writhing, no longer just the absence of light but something more—a presence, tangible and terrible.

And then, with a sudden rush of air, it all stopped. The room fell silent.

But the silence was the worst sound of all. Because in that stillness, something moved. Something very close.

Chapter 25: The Bound Heart

The moon hung low in the sky, casting its silver glow over the forest that stretched beyond the stone walls of the clearing. It was quiet now, the echoes of the incantations slowly fading, leaving nothing but the rustle of leaves in the breeze and the soft crackle of the fire. A quiet that, at first, seemed peaceful but soon turned uncomfortable. I could feel the weight of the silence pressing in on me, like a thick fog that threatened to choke the very air from my lungs. I had done it—I had freed him—but I wasn't sure if it was a victory or a loss.

His presence beside me, once so tangible, felt distant now. I didn't even have to look at him to know the change was there. The energy that had pulsed between us before, a constant hum of connection, had stilled. It wasn't the sort of silence you find in the absence of words, but the kind born of something deeper, something unspoken. He wasn't gone, not in the physical sense, but something was undeniably missing.

I glanced at him, my heart squeezing in a way that made my chest ache. His eyes, dark as the night around us, met mine briefly before he turned his gaze to the flames. His jaw was set tight, his posture rigid, as though the act of breathing had become a conscious effort.

"You did it," he said, his voice low, almost a whisper, though there was an edge to it that made my skin prickle. His words weren't meant to be a compliment.

I nodded, though the action felt hollow. "We did it," I corrected him softly, my gaze drifting toward the ground. "I couldn't have done it without you."

He didn't respond. His silence spoke louder than any words could. It felt like he was retreating into himself, as if I were no longer the one he shared his heart with.

The fire crackled between us, sending up little sparks that disappeared into the cool night air. I could hear the chirp of distant crickets, the occasional rustle of a creature passing through the underbrush. But none of it seemed to reach me. The world felt muted, as if the very fabric of reality had shifted beneath our feet.

I could feel it then, the subtle shift that had occurred the moment the ritual ended. A part of me had expected something different—some grand, triumphant sensation, like the heavens opening or a great light flooding the world around us. Instead, I was left with this strange, hollow ache, as though I'd given up something precious and couldn't quite figure out what it was.

I pulled my cloak tighter around my shoulders, the fabric brushing against my skin like a comfort I could barely hold onto. "What happens now?" I asked, though I wasn't sure if I was asking him or the universe itself.

His response came with a slow exhale, his breath stirring the air between us. "Now? Now we live with the consequences."

The words hit me harder than I expected. It wasn't so much the weight of his tone, but the way he said it—like he wasn't sure if he believed it himself. The uncertainty that lingered there, behind his eyes, made my pulse quicken. What had I done? Had I truly freed him, or had I simply set both of us adrift in a sea of unanswered questions?

"You sound like you regret it," I said, the words slipping out before I could stop them.

His eyes flickered to mine again, sharp and guarded. "Do you regret it?"

The question hung between us, suspended in the firelight. I didn't know how to answer. The freedom I'd fought so hard to achieve now felt like an empty promise, a phantom of hope that had evaporated into thin air. I wanted to say no, to tell him I didn't regret it, but the truth was more complicated than that. The weight of what we had shared, the bond that had once been unbreakable, had dissolved, leaving behind nothing but the faintest trace of its presence.

"I don't know," I admitted, my voice barely more than a breath. "I thought freeing you would make everything better, but now... now I don't know what to feel."

He didn't respond immediately, his gaze flicking back to the fire, watching the flames dance and flicker in the night. I could see the muscles in his shoulders tense, his hands clenched at his sides like he was struggling to hold something back.

"I never asked you to free me," he said quietly, the words hanging heavy in the air. "But you did. And now... now we have to deal with whatever comes next."

I didn't know what to say to that. I wasn't sure if he was angry, or just confused—maybe both. The silence stretched between us, thick and uncomfortable, like a wound that hadn't been fully stitched closed.

It wasn't just the ritual that had changed things. It was something deeper, something that had shifted in the very fabric of our connection. The bond we had shared had been severed, and though I could still feel the faint echo of it, it was no longer the tether that had kept us grounded to each other.

I opened my mouth to speak, but the words failed me. What could I say? What could I possibly say that would undo what had been done? Nothing. No words could fix this.

In that moment, I realized something—I had freed him, but in doing so, I had unknowingly set us both free from the one thing that had defined us. And now, standing on the precipice of something unknown, I had no idea what came next. Only that we would have to figure it out together—or not at all.

I wasn't sure how long we stood there, each of us caught in the web of unspoken words, the crackling fire the only sound between us. The world felt smaller, quieter somehow, as though the very earth beneath our feet had exhaled a long, weary sigh. I could almost hear it, the wind carrying the weight of everything we hadn't said, a soft murmur on the edge of understanding.

His eyes didn't leave the fire, but I could feel the weight of his presence in the way the air shifted around me. Something about him had changed—no, not him, but the way I saw him. He had always been a force of nature, untamable, wild, fierce in ways that both terrified and exhilarated me. But now, the force felt stilled. The sharpness that had once pulsed in his every movement, his every glance, had dulled, like a blade losing its edge.

"Is that it then?" I asked, my voice coming out too brittle, as though I was afraid that if I spoke any louder, the fragile thread holding us together would snap. "No more... no more binding? No more reason to..." I trailed off, unsure how to finish. To what? To love? To feel? I didn't know.

He didn't respond at first, his gaze still fixed on the flames as if the flickering lights held answers that I couldn't see. And then, after what felt like an eternity, he turned toward me, the movement slow, deliberate, as though it took an effort to look at me. His face was unreadable, the hardness there unfamiliar.

"It's not that simple," he said, his voice rough, like he hadn't used it in years. "Nothing ever is."

I swallowed, the taste of his words bitter in my throat. "You think I don't know that?" I countered, the words sharper than I intended, but I didn't care. "I didn't think freeing you would come with a manual, but I sure as hell didn't think it would come with this... with you looking at me like I'm a stranger."

The words hung between us, and I regretted them the moment they left my lips. I hadn't meant to hurt him—not like this.

He flinched, just barely, but I saw it, the quick tightening around his jaw. "You really think I wanted this?" His voice was quieter now, but it still held that raw edge, the kind that could slice through the thickest of walls. "You think I wanted to be... this? Someone who can't even look at the person who's supposed to matter most without wanting to tear myself apart?"

I didn't know how to respond to that, because there was so much truth in his words that it left me reeling. He was right. This wasn't what either of us had bargained for.

I stepped forward, my hands trembling, but I forced them to stay steady. "We—" I cut myself off, taking a breath, trying to gather the scattered pieces of my thoughts. "We've been through so much together. You and I. I thought we could survive anything. But now... now I don't even know who we are anymore."

He reached out then, his hand brushing against mine in a gesture so unexpected, it left my heart pounding in my chest. For a second, just a second, the world around us stilled, and I thought—maybe we were getting somewhere. But then he pulled away, just as quickly, like the very touch had burned him.

"I don't know either," he admitted, and there was something in his voice that made me feel like I had just torn open an old wound, one that had never fully healed. "You freed me, but in doing so, you've freed us both from everything we thought we knew. And now, we're both just... here. Stuck in this strange space where neither of us knows how to be anymore."

His words were the cold water I hadn't known I needed. They doused whatever fire I had been holding onto, and in its place, something even more terrifying grew—a quiet realization that maybe he wasn't the only one who had changed. Maybe we had both lost something we didn't even know we needed to survive.

I took a step back, my mind swirling in a haze of confusion and hurt. "What are you saying?" I whispered, though I already knew the answer. He had already given it to me, wrapped in layers of unsaid things and half-buried feelings. But I needed to hear it, needed to know for sure that this wasn't just some fevered dream.

"I'm saying..." He ran a hand through his hair, the motion rough and frustrated. "I'm saying that we can't just go back to what we were. Not after everything. Not after you—" He paused, his eyes meeting mine, and for a fleeting second, I saw the ghost of the man I once knew. "Not after everything we've done."

And there it was. The finality in his voice, the soft echo of something ending, of something irrevocable breaking between us. I wanted to fight it, to deny it, to scream at him that we could find a way back, that we could make it right. But something deep inside me—the part that had been tangled in the very fabric of our connection—knew that it was already too late.

The silence stretched out, dense and suffocating, until I couldn't stand it anymore. I turned, desperate to escape the weight of it, but as I took a step away, his voice stopped me.

"I don't want to lose you," he said, and his voice—low, raw, filled with a depth of emotion that he hadn't let slip before—caught me like a fist in the chest.

I closed my eyes, taking a shaky breath, the air around me heavy with his confession. "I don't want to lose you either," I whispered back, even though the words felt hollow, like they didn't belong in the world we had just created. "But I think we've already lost something we can't get back."

I didn't know what to do with the silence that had settled over us, thick and suffocating, like a storm waiting to break. The fire flickered in front of us, its bright light illuminating our faces in jagged flashes, the warmth failing to reach the coldness that had taken root between us. I could feel it in every inch of my skin—this strange distance. This change. A rift had formed, and no matter how hard I tried to reach across it, I couldn't bridge the gap.

His hand had left mine, but his fingers still lingered in the air like an echo of the touch we had shared only moments before. A touch that had once meant everything, a lifeline between two hearts, two souls bound in ways words couldn't explain. And now? Now it was just... nothing.

I wanted to scream. To shake him, to demand answers. But what answers could he give? He was as lost as I was.

"You said you didn't want to lose me," I said, my voice barely more than a breath, though the words felt heavier than they had any right to. "But I don't even know if you're still here. Not really. Not the way you used to be."

The wind picked up, howling through the trees like a chorus of ghosts, but neither of us moved. Neither of us spoke. The only sound was the crackle of the fire and the distant, rhythmic beat of my heart, a drum that seemed to grow louder with every passing second.

Finally, he turned, his eyes locking with mine. And for the briefest moment, I saw something there—something raw and untamed. "I never wanted to be this," he said, his voice thick, like he was struggling to force the words out. "But I don't know how to be anything else anymore. Not after everything we've been through."

It was the truth, one I hadn't been ready to hear. I had spent so much time trying to fix everything, trying to force us back into the molds we had once fit into. But maybe—just maybe—there was no going back.

I took a step forward, my pulse quickening, but stopped myself just before I reached him. What if the distance was insurmountable? What if trying to close that gap only made it wider?

"I don't know what to say," I whispered. The words felt empty as soon as they left my mouth, but they were all I had. "I don't even know if there's anything left to say."

He took a step toward me, slow and deliberate, and for a second, I thought maybe this was it. Maybe this was the moment where we both found our way back. But when his gaze met mine again, I saw the hesitation in his eyes.

"I wish there was," he murmured. "I wish there was a way to fix this, to fix... us. But I don't think there is."

My breath caught in my throat. It was as though the ground had suddenly been ripped out from under me, and I was falling. Falling into a chasm I hadn't known existed until this very moment.

"I don't want this to be the end," I said, my voice shaking despite my best efforts to remain calm. "I can't—"

Before I could finish, there was a sound. A rustling from the forest beyond the clearing. Low, like an animal creeping through the underbrush. But it wasn't the sound of a deer or a wolf. No, this was something... different. Something darker.

My heart skipped a beat as the air seemed to thicken, like the world itself was holding its breath.

He noticed it too. I could see the change in him, the way his muscles tensed, his eyes narrowing, the same alertness he had carried in his every movement before all of this had started.

"We're not alone," he said softly, his voice filled with a warning I could feel down to my bones.

I nodded, though my pulse was racing, every sense screaming that something was terribly, terribly wrong.

And then, as though the world itself had been waiting for this moment to shatter, a figure emerged from the trees.

At first, I couldn't make out who—or what—it was. The figure was tall, cloaked in shadows, with a presence so powerful it seemed to distort the very air around it.

"You shouldn't have done it," the figure said, the voice a low, melodic hum that seemed to wrap itself around my spine like ice.

I recoiled instinctively, though my feet remained rooted to the ground.

"You," I breathed, recognizing the voice, the presence, the way the very earth seemed to quiver in response. It couldn't be. Not after everything. Not after all we had fought to destroy.

The figure stepped forward, its form becoming clearer in the firelight.

"You think you're free?" the voice asked, a cruel laugh trailing through the words. "You think breaking the bond was the answer? How quaint."

I felt the ground beneath my feet shift, the very air around me trembling as if some ancient force had just been awakened.

"It was never going to be that simple." The figure's gaze flicked to me, its eyes glowing like embers in the dark. "You were warned. You both were warned."

I wanted to run, to turn away, to scream, but my body refused to move.

I heard him take a step beside me, his presence suddenly solid, as if he were trying to stand guard. But even he seemed unsure of what to do.

"Who are you?" he demanded, his voice sharp, filled with an edge I hadn't heard in a long time.

The figure tilted its head, as if savoring the question. "Oh, I'm nobody," it said with a smile that didn't reach its eyes. "But I know exactly who you are."

And just like that, the world around us twisted, the shadows stretching in unnatural ways, the firelight flickering like it was struggling to stay alive. My heart pounded in my chest as I realized—this wasn't over. It had only just begun.

Then, before either of us could move, the ground beneath us cracked open, and the figure vanished into the darkness below.

And with it, the last semblance of peace we had left.

Chapter 26: The Space Between Us

It wasn't until the third day of this strange, almost unbearable quiet that I realized how much I had grown to rely on the sound of his breathing beside me, the rhythm of his voice that would slip between us like a secret. Now, that same silence clung to every corner of the room, and the space where we had once been intimate felt like a vast, uncharted desert. The bed was no longer warm, but cool to the touch, and I couldn't stop my fingers from brushing the empty side where he used to sleep. I half-expected to feel a pulse, the trace of his presence still there, but there was nothing. Just the unrelenting hum of the air conditioner.

I paced the length of the room, my bare feet quiet against the hardwood floor, my eyes flitting to him now and then. He was sitting by the window, staring out at the world beyond, his fingers absentmindedly tracing the outline of the glass. His profile was a study of something unreadable—an enigmatic frown that hinted at a storm just beneath the surface, but it was a storm he refused to let anyone see. Certainly not me. Certainly not now.

"Still out there?" I asked, the words slipping out before I could stop them. I hadn't intended to break the silence, but something inside me had grown desperate for any acknowledgment, even if it was just the smallest crack in the wall between us.

He didn't answer at first, just continued to watch the horizon, the setting sun casting his face in shadow. But then, his lips parted, and his voice came out low, almost too soft to hear.

"Yeah," he murmured, the word hanging like a thick fog between us. "Just thinking."

"About what?" I asked, the question tinged with more curiosity than I meant to betray. His gaze flickered to me for a second, and then quickly back to the outside world. It was like I wasn't really there, just a blur in his peripheral vision, something he couldn't quite focus on.

"Nothing," he said after a pause, his tone too quick, too dismissive. "Just... nothing important."

I nodded, feeling my chest tighten. It was the same response I had gotten over and over again, a shield, a wall that only seemed to grow higher the longer I stood there, watching him. My mind raced to fill the gaps, to piece together the fragments of the man who had once been so open with me, so willing to share every thought, every doubt. Now, he was like a locked chest with no key, and I was left standing on the outside, searching for a way in.

"You're lying," I said before I could stop myself, the words sharp and more accusatory than I'd intended. "I can see it in your eyes."

He turned his head slowly, his expression unreadable. For a moment, the silence deepened, the air between us thick with tension. I held my breath, waiting for him to snap back, to tell me I had no right to judge him, to throw the wall up even higher. But instead, he sighed, a sound heavy with defeat, and finally spoke, though his voice was strained, almost raw.

"I don't know what to say anymore," he admitted, his gaze now focused somewhere over my shoulder, as if he couldn't quite bring himself to look me in the eye. "It's like... everything I say just makes it worse. Like we're two people who are stuck, and neither of us knows how to move forward."

The confession hit me like a cold slap, and for a moment, I didn't know how to respond. Part of me wanted to scream, to demand to know why he was pulling away, why he was doing this to us. But another part—the part that had learned over the years to stay silent, to give him space—told me to hold back, to wait for him to explain when he was ready.

And yet, no matter how hard I tried to let him speak in his own time, there was a pressure building inside me, a need to bridge the distance between us before it became permanent. Because if I didn't—if I didn't reach out now—there was a real possibility that this silence, this gulf that had formed between us, would swallow us whole. I could feel it in the air, thick and suffocating.

"I don't want this," I said softly, almost to myself. My voice trembled despite my best efforts to keep it steady. "I don't want us to be... like this. I want to fix it. I want to find a way to fix us."

He finally turned his head, and for the first time in days, our eyes met directly. His gaze was not cold, but it wasn't warm either. It was a mixture of something painful and yet tender, a vulnerability I hadn't seen in him in so long that it almost hurt to witness it now.

"Maybe we can't fix it," he said, his voice low and rough. "Maybe it's already broken."

His words sank into me, heavy and cold, like stones being dropped into a lake. I felt the sharp sting of them, like the wind was knocked out of me. "Don't say that," I whispered, my voice faltering. "Please don't say that."

But even as I begged him, I couldn't shake the feeling that something had shifted, that maybe—just maybe—he was right.

I thought maybe if I left the house for a while, the space between us would shrink. There was something about the quiet that made it feel like I was suffocating—like the walls themselves had decided to join him in their aloofness. The world outside was a balm to the rawness of the silence that hung in the air at home. Or so I thought.

I grabbed my keys from the counter, the jangle of them unnervingly loud in the stillness. He didn't even look up when I made my way to the door. I didn't want him to see how desperate I had become for him to care, for him to reach out, to do something that would bridge the gap. But I couldn't stay there any longer. Not when every breath I took felt like I was inhaling a poison of my own making.

Stepping into the cool evening air was like stepping into another world. The city felt alive, vibrant, its sounds and lights flickering like stars against the dimming sky. It had been so long since I'd allowed myself to just... be. To breathe without waiting for his voice or his touch or his disapproval.

I started walking without any destination in mind, my feet carrying me through familiar streets that felt foreign in their distance. I passed coffee shops and bars, old bookshops with cracked windows, the scent of fresh-baked bread wafting from a bakery. There was nothing to hold my attention except the overwhelming pulse of the city, each step an attempt to outrun the gnawing ache in my chest.

I didn't realize how far I had gone until I found myself standing in front of the old park near the river, the one we had always liked to visit on lazy Sunday afternoons. The swings creaked in the wind, their chains twisting, as if echoing the tension in my heart. The night had fallen fully, casting long shadows, but the lights from the city reached over the water, making the dark river glimmer with a strange beauty. It was beautiful in a way that made my chest ache, the sharp contrast between the glittering lights and the darkness pulling at the ragged edges of my thoughts.

I sat on the cold bench, pulling my coat tighter around me, not because I was cold, but because I needed the comfort of something tangible. Something that reminded me that I was still here, still breathing, still existing outside of the space we had carved between us.

And then, as if the universe had decided it was time for me to face reality, my phone buzzed in my pocket. It was a text, from him. Just one word, but it hit me like a bolt of lightning: Can we talk?

For a moment, I just stared at the screen, blinking as if the message had been written in a language I couldn't comprehend. My fingers hovered over the keys, unsure of what to do. My instinct told me to ignore it, to let him stew in his own confusion, to punish him the way he had punished me with his silence. But that wasn't who I was. Or at least, it wasn't who I used to be.

I typed back, simple and to the point: Where?

A moment later, his reply came through: Meet me at the usual place.

The usual place. I could almost hear the words in his voice, the familiar cadence that used to make my heart flutter. But now, it only caused a hollow pang of longing to well up inside me. I shoved my phone back into my pocket and stood up, the decision made before I could fully register it. I would go. Not because I thought it would fix everything, but because I had to know whether there was anything left worth saving.

The walk back through the city felt like a blur, the rhythm of my steps quickening, as if my body knew something my mind hadn't fully caught up with yet. My breath was shallow, my thoughts a constant whirl of questions and worries. What would he say? Would he apologize? Would he tell me that it was too late, that the distance between us was now permanent? And would I even be able to recognize him when I got there?

I didn't know what to expect, but I couldn't stop myself from hoping that somehow, this time, it would be different. This time, he would find me again, and we could put all of this behind us.

When I reached the small park bench by the river, the same spot where we had shared so many late-night conversations, I saw him sitting there. His figure was silhouetted against the dark expanse of water, his head slightly bowed, as if lost in thought. He didn't look up when I approached, but I could feel the tension in the air, the gravity of everything that had been left unsaid.

I stood there for a long moment, just watching him, waiting for him to acknowledge me. But he didn't. The only sound was the faint rustle of the leaves, the quiet hum of the city behind us. I swallowed hard, the lump in my throat thickening with every passing second.

"Hi," I finally said, the word coming out smaller than I'd intended, but it was enough to make him look up. His eyes were tired, but there was a softness to them, something raw and open in a way I hadn't seen in days.

"Hi," he replied, his voice low, rough. "I'm glad you came."

I nodded, unsure of what to say next. The silence between us stretched, heavy and thick, and I could feel the weight of everything that had passed between us in those quiet moments. Everything we hadn't said.

"I don't want to keep hurting you," he finally said, his voice barely above a whisper. His eyes met mine, steady but uncertain. "I never meant for any of this to happen."

I wanted to ask him what this was. What had happened? Why he had pulled away when I needed him most. But the words wouldn't come. Instead, all I could do was watch him, willing myself to believe that whatever had brought us here, we could find a way back.

The quiet stretched between us like a taut wire, pulling at the edges of my thoughts. It was as if we were two people trapped in an echo, each sound we made somehow distorted, lost to the space that had grown between us. I watched him, trying to find some flicker of recognition in his eyes, some sign that he was still there, still the man I knew. But the longer I waited, the harder it became to find the version of him I'd once known. The distance between us wasn't just physical—it had settled deep inside, wedged itself into the rhythm of our days, into every interaction, every glance.

When I had returned to the park, he had looked at me with that same weariness, the same hesitation that made the words feel fragile, almost too heavy to speak. I had thought—foolishly, it seemed—that we might find our way back to something that resembled normal, to the laughter and easy silences that had once defined us. But instead, all I had gotten was a confession wrapped in sorrow, a revelation that only added to the weight in my chest.

"I don't want to keep hurting you," he had said, his words the softest of whispers, like a confession of his own guilt. "I never meant for any of this to happen."

And in that moment, I realized the truth that I hadn't wanted to face: it had already happened. Whatever this was between us had already broken, and no matter how many apologies we exchanged, no matter how much we tried to undo the distance, it was still there, an insurmountable rift neither of us knew how to bridge.

I had wanted to scream at him, to tell him that he had meant it—that this space he had created between us wasn't some mistake, but something that had been building, little by little, until it had become impossible to ignore. But instead, I had stayed silent, watching him, feeling as though my heart was breaking all over again.

"You never meant to hurt me," I repeated, tasting the words on my tongue like ash. "But you did."

He flinched, the sound of my words hitting him harder than I had expected. His face softened, the lines of guilt deepening as he ran a hand through his hair, a gesture that felt far too familiar. But there was no warmth in the movement, no affection. It was the kind of gesture someone makes when they're trying to remember how to care, how to feel.

"I didn't want this," he said again, his voice rougher now, like the weight of his own remorse was crushing him from the inside out. "I just—I didn't know how to fix it."

I stared at him, the words hanging in the air like a promise neither of us could keep. Because, deep down, I knew that fixing it wasn't something either of us had the power to do anymore. Not after everything that had passed between us. Not after the silence that had suffocated us for so long.

"You're right," I said, my voice quiet, but steady. "We can't fix this. Maybe we never could."

His eyes widened, the shock of my words causing him to stiffen. It was as if he hadn't expected me to give up so easily, as if he still thought there was a chance for us to come back from this—whatever this was. But the truth was, I was tired. Tired of waiting for him to choose me, tired of trying to find pieces of a person who was no longer here, no longer the one I had fallen in love with.

I stood up, my legs trembling slightly as I turned away from him, my heart a slow drumbeat in my chest. "I can't keep doing this," I said, more to myself than to him. "I can't keep living like this—waiting for someone who's already gone."

I didn't look back as I started to walk away. I couldn't. I knew that if I did, I would crumble, and I wasn't sure I had anything left to give. The cool night air kissed my skin, a reminder that I was still alive, still breathing, still capable of moving forward—away from him. But even as I took step after step, the silence between us pressed in on me, heavier than anything I had ever known.

By the time I reached the street corner, I felt the sting of tears at the back of my eyes, a betrayal of the calm I had so carefully constructed. But I didn't stop. I couldn't stop, not now.

The light at the intersection turned green, and I stepped into the crosswalk, the noise of the city washing over me like a tide. My thoughts were scattered, broken fragments of what had been. And just as I reached the other side, my phone buzzed in my pocket.

I ignored it, but the vibration didn't stop. A persistent reminder that whatever was happening, whatever we were doing, it wasn't over. Not yet.

I fished my phone from my bag and glanced at the screen, my heart skipping a beat when I saw his name.

Please, don't walk away. I'm sorry. We need to talk.

It was the last thing I wanted to see. The last thing I wanted to hear. But it wasn't the apology that caught my attention. It was the need in his words. The desperation that seemed to spill out from the screen, desperate and raw.

I stood there, the weight of the city rushing around me, and for a moment, I couldn't breathe.

Then, the phone buzzed again.

I'm at the place we first met.

I froze.

The place we first met. How could I have forgotten? How could I have been so stupid?

I knew, without a doubt, that I wasn't ready for whatever conversation awaited me there. But it was also the only place I could go, the only place that felt like it might hold an answer.

And as I began walking again, I couldn't shake the feeling that what was waiting for me there—at that old, forgotten place—would change everything.

Chapter 27: The Return of the Past

The air had a biting edge to it, the kind of sharp chill that cuts through fabric and settles in the bones, especially at this hour when the day's last warmth has already surrendered to the relentless grip of evening. The sunset was painting the sky in rich shades of red and purple, an omen in its own right, but it was the man standing by the iron gates that truly unnerved me. He was draped in shadows, his form long and distorted by the low light. At first, I thought perhaps he was just another drifter, the kind that finds their way to the edge of a place like this, drawn by the tales of ghosts and riches. But no, there was something different about him. The way he stood, his hands tucked into the pockets of his coat, his gaze locked onto the windows of the mansion as if waiting for something—or someone.

I had never seen him before, but the nagging sense of familiarity tugged at me, making my pulse quicken.

I stepped out onto the veranda, the old wooden boards creaking underfoot. The distant sound of waves crashing against the cliffs below was muffled by the evening's thickening air, but it did little to calm the uneasy sensation curling in my chest. I wasn't sure if it was the stranger's presence or the memories of a past that refused to stay buried, but there was an undeniable pull to him.

"Are you lost?" I called out, my voice carrying through the stillness.

He didn't flinch, didn't even seem to acknowledge the question at first. His eyes, dark and unreadable, stayed fixed on the mansion as if the very stones held some secret only he could see. Then, without moving, his lips curled into the smallest of smiles. It wasn't a pleasant smile, but one that seemed to mock the very air around him.

"I didn't think you'd recognize me so easily." His voice was low, almost a whisper, but it sliced through the growing tension like a knife. There was a bitterness to it, an old wound buried beneath the surface that had never fully healed.

A chill swept over me. The sound of his words settled in, and I felt it—the recognition. His voice was one I hadn't heard in years, not since that night when everything had changed.

"No," I whispered, more to myself than to him. "It can't be you."

He finally turned, and in the half-light, I saw the familiar lines of his face, those same sharp cheekbones, the way his jaw tightened whenever he spoke, and the deep-set eyes that once held nothing but tenderness for me. But those eyes were different now. They were empty, hollow even, and the warmth I had once known in them was gone, replaced by something far darker.

"I'm not the man you remember," he said, his voice now laced with a twisted mix of regret and something darker—something that made the hairs on the back of my neck stand at attention. "But I'm the one you've called back."

I blinked, my mind struggling to make sense of what was happening. The air between us thickened, charged with some invisible current. I could feel it—the weight of something old and forgotten clawing its way to the surface, threatening to drown us both in its wake.

"Called back?" I said, my voice barely audible. "I don't understand."

His lips twisted, and for a moment, I saw a flash of something akin to amusement flicker across his face. "You really don't, do you?" He stepped forward, and the night seemed to press in closer around us. The stone walls of the mansion behind me felt more like a prison than a home, a silent witness to the history we both shared, a history that he seemed determined to resurrect.

"Your actions have awakened something—someone," he continued, his tone shifting, taking on a sense of urgency. "And it's not going to let you go. Not this time."

I took a step back, confusion mingling with a rising sense of fear. His words didn't make sense. But the look in his eyes—the intensity—told me that he wasn't lying. He was as much a prisoner of this place as I was, and the chains that bound him were wrapped tightly around me, too.

"What are you talking about?" My voice cracked as I tried to steady myself.

He chuckled, but it was a hollow sound, like the echo of a long-dead promise. "You think this place, this mansion, holds nothing but memories, don't you? That's what you tell yourself, over and over, to make sense of everything. But you're wrong." He took another step closer, his eyes never leaving mine. "This place is alive, and it's not the mansion that's keeping you here. It's him."

I froze. The name hovered in the air between us, unspoken but hanging heavily, suffocating the words in my throat. "No," I whispered, more to myself than to him. "That's not possible. He's—"

"Dead?" The man finished for me, his voice laced with dark humor. "You're wrong. And you'll find that out soon enough. Whatever you think you've escaped, whatever you've tried to bury, it's all coming back. He's coming back."

The air grew even colder, and I could almost hear the pounding of my own heart, loud and frantic in my ears. His words hit me like a punch to the gut, but it was the familiar weight of them that truly terrified me. The man standing before me wasn't just a stranger—he was a reminder, a living specter from a past I had desperately tried to forget.

And now it was clear: the past had never left.

The man didn't move, not an inch, but his words hung in the air between us like thick smoke, swirling and suffocating the breath from my chest. He's coming back. The words echoed in my mind, bouncing off the walls of the mansion, filling the empty space with their weight. I wanted to shake them off, pretend they didn't matter, but something in the depths of his eyes—a coldness that had no place in a living soul—told me they were true.

For a long moment, neither of us spoke. I stood there, my hands gripping the wrought-iron railing, trying to steady the pulse that was quickening in my throat. He had always been good at making silence feel like an unbearable weight, and now, standing in front of me after all this time, I was reminded of how he used to hold the power to freeze everything around me. My heart ached for the past, for the way things had been before everything had spiraled into madness. I had tried to forget, tried to bury the truth of what had happened here, in this place.

But now, standing before me, the past had returned with a vengeance.

"You think I'm lying," the man said, breaking the silence like a crack of thunder. "You think you can dismiss all of this as some strange coincidence. But you know better. You've always known better."

I shook my head, but the words stuck in my throat. The truth had a way of slipping past my defenses, gnawing at me until it had no choice but to claw its way to the surface. I wanted to argue, to scream at him that he was wrong, that nothing could ever come back, not after all this time. But instead, I found myself staring into the darkness that clung to his face, searching for any hint of humanity, any glimmer of the man I once knew.

"I don't know what you're talking about," I finally said, though the tremble in my voice betrayed me.

His laugh was soft but bitter, like the sound of leaves crunching underfoot in winter. "You don't, do you? Well, that's a blessing, I suppose. But your actions, your decisions, they've awakened something far worse than either of us ever imagined. He is here. And nothing, not even you, can stop him now."

I felt a pang in my chest, the sharp, unmistakable sting of a memory that had stayed buried, locked away for so long. It was a feeling I'd tried to outrun, tried to bury beneath layers of time and distance. But it was here now, pressing down on me with an urgency that I couldn't ignore.

I swallowed hard, stepping back as if the space between us could somehow offer me protection. "You're talking about him," I said, the words slipping out like a confession.

He nodded, a grim satisfaction flickering across his face. "You think you can keep pretending, but you're not fooling anyone. You've called him back into this world. And now, we all have to face the consequences."

I could feel the walls of the mansion pressing in around me, the weight of the past beginning to crush me once more. I had thought I could leave it behind, could build a life outside of this place, outside of the shadow that had hung over me for so long. But the more I stood there, listening to him, the more I realized how wrong I had been. This place, these walls, they never let anyone go.

"I didn't mean to," I whispered, though I wasn't sure who I was trying to convince—him or myself. "I didn't know what I was doing."

The man's eyes softened for a moment, but it wasn't sympathy that flickered there. It was something far more unsettling, something closer to pity. "It doesn't matter what you meant to do. You've awakened him. And now, we all have to suffer for it."

The words hung in the air like a curse, a weight I couldn't escape. I had always known that the past had its claws in me, but I had never imagined that it could return with such force. This wasn't just a man standing before me. He was a messenger, a herald of something darker, something that had been waiting in the wings for far too long.

"Why now?" I asked, my voice barely above a whisper. "Why after all this time?"

His smile was thin, almost predatory. "Because time doesn't heal all wounds. Some things can't be buried, no matter how hard we try. He's been waiting, you see. Waiting for you to make the wrong move. And you did."

The coldness in his voice made my stomach twist, but it was the fear that rose within me, the creeping sense of inevitability, that made me take a step back. I had hoped, all these years, that I could outrun the things I had done, the choices I had made. But it seemed that hope was as fragile as the glass in the windows behind me, ready to shatter at the slightest touch.

"I didn't want this," I said, more to myself than to him. "I didn't ask for any of this."

"You think I did?" he shot back, his voice laced with a bitterness that stung like salt in an open wound. "None of us asked for this. But it doesn't change the fact that it's happening."

I took another step back, feeling the cold stone of the mansion at my back. It felt like a trap, a cage I had wandered into willingly, believing that I could escape, believing that I could leave it all behind. But there was no escape now. No way out.

"Then what do you want from me?" I asked, finally meeting his gaze. My heart was pounding in my chest, the blood rushing in my ears, but I was done pretending that I wasn't terrified.

His smile faded, replaced by a hard, unreadable look. "You know what I want. What we both want. To survive this. To stop him before he destroys us all."

The words sent a shiver down my spine. I had hoped, for a fleeting moment, that this was some kind of mistake. That maybe, just maybe, the past could stay buried, forgotten in the dusty corners of my mind. But now, standing face to face with him, I knew the truth.

The past was never finished with me. And it was coming for me again.

I turned away from him, the weight of his words sinking deeper with each passing second. My legs felt unsteady, and for the first time in years, I wondered if it was the mansion itself, or perhaps fate, that had played me for a fool. The light from the windows spilled across the ground in pools of amber, but it felt as though the night had already swallowed me whole. I needed to retreat, to gather myself, but something kept me rooted to the spot.

His footsteps echoed as he followed me into the house, a soft rhythm that should have sounded normal but now sent a chill through the air. I couldn't shake the feeling that his presence had already seeped into the very walls of this place, as if he had always been here, waiting for me to notice him again. The house, once so familiar, felt like a stranger's skin—cold and foreign.

"You don't believe me," he said, his voice trailing behind me, a shadow that refused to let go. "But that doesn't change what's coming."

I spun around, heart hammering in my chest. "What is coming? You're not making any sense. What do you want from me?"

For a moment, he didn't respond, his gaze studying me as though weighing my every word. Then, finally, he exhaled a slow, deliberate breath, almost as if he were trying to hold back something too vast to release all at once.

"You're asking the wrong questions," he said, his tone cutting through the tension. "The question isn't what I want from you. It's what you'll do when he comes for you. And trust me, he will come."

My stomach twisted, and I couldn't bring myself to ask the question that lingered on the edge of my lips. Who is he? But I already knew the answer, didn't I? The man had been a shadow, a presence that haunted me in my sleep, in my every waking thought, and now he was coming back to finish what had been left undone. But even in the grip of fear, there was a strange relief in the recognition. It was like standing at the edge of a cliff and knowing that the fall was inevitable, but at least you understood why it was happening.

"You've seen what he can do," the man continued, as if reading my mind, his voice growing darker. "You've seen the destruction he leaves in his wake."

I felt a shiver run down my spine, but I forced myself to meet his gaze. "I've seen what happens when you let fear control you. And I'm not going to make that mistake again."

He laughed, a dry, bitter sound that barely resembled the man I once knew. "Fear doesn't have to control you. It's enough to simply survive it. But surviving him... that's a different matter entirely."

His words hung in the air like a warning, heavy and suffocating. I wanted to shout at him, to demand he explain himself, to beg him for any kind of reassurance. But I knew there was no comfort to be found here. He was right—this was bigger than both of us. It had always been bigger than us.

"Why now?" I asked, my voice barely more than a whisper. "Why come to me now, after all this time?"

He took a step forward, his eyes never leaving mine, and something flickered there—something almost like regret. "Because you've never been able to forget. You're tied to him, just like I am. Whether you want to admit it or not, your story with him is far from over."

A sharp laugh bubbled up from my chest, but it came out strangled, forced. "You're right about that. Nothing about this has ever been finished, has it?"

He didn't respond, just watched me with those unsettling eyes, and for a moment, we both seemed to fall into a silence too thick to cut through. The only sound was the distant creaking of the mansion, the wood groaning beneath the weight of whatever had been buried here for so long.

Then, as if a switch had been flipped, the air between us grew heavier, charged with an energy that hummed and crackled. It wasn't just the house that felt alive now—it was the very earth beneath our feet. Something was stirring, something ancient, something that had waited for years, biding its time in the darkness, and now it was coming closer.

Suddenly, the floor beneath us shuddered, a low, guttural rumble that vibrated through the air. The walls seemed to moan in response, as if they too were awakening from a long slumber.

The man's eyes widened, a flicker of fear passing over his face before he quickly masked it with a blank expression. "It's begun," he said, his voice tight with urgency. "We don't have much time."

My pulse quickened as I felt the temperature drop around me. The familiar warmth of the house was gone, replaced by an icy chill that seemed to cut through my bones. I wasn't sure if it was the house, the man, or something far darker at work here, but whatever it was, it felt like the world itself was shifting, cracking open, revealing something I wasn't ready to face.

"We need to leave," I said, the words coming out before I could think them through. But even as I spoke them, I knew it was too late. There was nowhere to run. Nowhere to hide.

The man took a step closer, his eyes filled with a quiet desperation. "You can't run from him. Not anymore."

I wanted to argue, to tell him that I wouldn't just sit back and let whatever this was destroy everything I had fought for. But as the rumbling grew louder, as the very ground beneath us began to shake, I realized the truth. I wasn't in control here. None of us were.

With a sharp crack, the windows shattered, sending shards of glass flying in every direction. And in that instant, I saw it. A shadow, dark and formless, creeping toward us from the farthest corner of the room. It was there and then gone, but its presence lingered in the air, suffocating everything in its path.

My breath caught in my throat as the man reached out, grabbing my arm. "We don't have much time," he repeated, his voice tight with urgency.

I tried to pull away, but his grip was like iron, unyielding and desperate. "What is that? What's happening?"

But he didn't answer. Instead, his gaze flickered to the doorway, and I followed his eyes just in time to see a figure step into the room, cloaked in shadow. And in that moment, I realized—there was no escape.

Chapter 28: The Covenant of Souls

I could feel the weight of the forest pressing in around me, the silent shadows stretching long as I stood at the edge of the clearing. The trees whispered secrets I wasn't meant to hear, their branches swaying with an eerie rhythm that seemed to beckon me into their depths. The air was thick with the scent of damp earth and wildflowers, a fragrance both intoxicating and suffocating. I had come to him, to the Watcher, desperate for answers, but as I listened to his words, the very ground beneath my feet seemed to shift.

"You've done something, something you don't fully understand," his voice rasped through the thick night air. "And in doing so, you've torn a rift—one that cannot be mended unless you complete the covenant."

I stared at him, my heart pounding in my chest, my breath shallow. The Watcher, a figure both familiar and otherworldly, stood cloaked in shadows, his features impossible to discern in the dim light. He was part of the forest, as ancient as the trees themselves, a creature who had lived longer than I could fathom. His eyes, though hidden, burned with a knowing that both terrified and fascinated me.

I had known of him, of course. All the stories told of the Watcher in the woods—the keeper of balance, the one who held the veil between the human world and whatever lay beyond. But those were just stories, the kind whispered by campfires and muttered in hushed voices when the night grew too dark.

Now, standing before him, I realized how little I knew of anything.

"The rift you've opened between our worlds isn't just an inconvenience," he continued, his voice low, dangerous in its softness. "It is a rupture that threatens everything. But there is a way to close it. A way to mend the fabric of our reality—but it requires more than just words. It requires a sacrifice."

I swallowed hard, my mind racing. A sacrifice. I had heard that word too many times lately, each time like a stone thrown into the still waters of my mind, sending ripples of uncertainty across everything I thought I understood. But this, this was different. This wasn't just a choice between life and death. This was the promise of forever, a forever I was not sure I wanted, and yet... I could already feel the pull of it, an ache deep within my bones, where the promise of his touch still lingered.

I could feel his eyes on me, even though I couldn't see them, could feel his presence enveloping me like a shroud.

"One of you must join the other, body and soul," the Watcher said, his voice dropping to a near whisper, his words heavy with the gravity of the decision. "If you complete the binding ritual, you will be united forever. But there is a price. One of you will remain here, in the mortal world, and the other will enter my realm, to live in eternity, never to return."

The words landed like stones in my chest, sinking deep, leaving ripples in their wake. I couldn't breathe. My heart stuttered in my chest, as if the very rhythm of my life had been disrupted. He was asking me to choose between worlds, between the life I had known and the one I had barely begun to understand.

"And if we don't?" I asked, my voice trembling even as I fought to keep it steady.

The Watcher was silent for a moment, his presence pressing against me, heavier now, as if the trees themselves were leaning in, waiting for my answer.

"Then the rift will grow," he said softly. "And when it does, it will consume everything. Not just the two worlds, but everything in between. The land, the sky, the very souls of those who dare cross its path. Your love, your choices—they will matter for nothing if you do not make the sacrifice. The rift will be your undoing."

A cold chill crept down my spine. I could feel the pull of the rift now, too. It was an almost physical sensation, a tightening in my chest, a hollow place where something was missing. And yet, the thought of giving up everything—the life I had known, the people I had loved, my family, my future—it was more than I could bear. To leave it all behind for a love that might not survive? To give up my mortal ties for the sake of something I couldn't even truly grasp?

But then, his face appeared in my mind. His eyes, dark and soulful, full of a depth that had touched something inside me, something I hadn't even known existed. I thought of his touch, the way it had made me feel alive in ways I had never known. And I thought of the way my heart beat when he was near, as if it knew something I couldn't yet understand.

Was it foolish to think that love could transcend all? That even in the face of impossible odds, it could survive?

"Why me?" I asked, my voice barely more than a whisper.

The Watcher seemed to consider the question before answering, his gaze distant. "Because you are the one who opened the rift. And because you are the only one who can close it."

I closed my eyes, the weight of his words settling on me like a blanket of stone. I could feel the pull of both worlds, the life I had built and the one I could never fully grasp, and I knew that I stood on the edge of something vast, something terrible, something beautiful.

The Watcher's words hung in the air, each one heavier than the last, curling around me like the damp fog that had begun to creep in from the woods. The forest, which had seemed so full of life moments ago, now felt distant and foreboding, a place that existed far beyond the realm of human understanding. I could feel the ground shifting beneath me, the earth itself conspiring to keep me here, caught between two worlds, each more impossible than the last.

A part of me wanted to run, to tear myself away from this place and from the question that lingered like a shadow over my heart. To forget everything the Watcher had said. But I couldn't. I couldn't because I knew, deep down, that the choice was mine. There would be no turning back once the ritual was done. No second chances, no rewrites.

"So, what happens after?" I forced the words out, though my throat felt tight, as though something was lodged in it, something sharp and bitter. "Once the covenant is made, what exactly do you expect from me?"

The Watcher tilted his head, the faintest glimmer of something—pity, perhaps, or maybe something far darker—flashing in his hidden gaze. "It's not what I expect, but what is required," he said, voice smooth, almost serene. "The worlds cannot coexist in this state forever. The balance must be restored. And for that to happen, one of you must choose to leave. Choose to be bound to the other, not by love, but by fate."

His words stung. Fate, I thought bitterly. A cruel joke for someone who had believed she controlled her own destiny.

I glanced back toward the distant shadows, where I could just make out the faintest outline of his figure. The man I loved. Or the man who had become so much more than that, depending on how you wanted to look at it. What would I be without him? Could I really make that choice? To sever the ties that had grounded me to this world, to the people who had shaped me into who I was?

"You're asking me to make a choice that would leave me..." I trailed off, not sure how to finish the thought. Could I even articulate it?

The Watcher didn't respond at first, and for a moment, I thought perhaps he didn't need to. He simply stepped back into the shadows, his presence fading into the forest as effortlessly as smoke dissipates into the air. I could still feel him, though, the weight of his gaze pressing against me, pulling at my very soul.

The sound of footsteps behind me snapped me out of my stupor. A moment later, his voice, low and familiar, wrapped around my heart, tugging me toward him even before I turned.

"I'm not going anywhere," he said. "Not without you."

I blinked rapidly, trying to clear the haze in my mind. It wasn't him. Or was it? The voice was unmistakable, but I hadn't heard him approach. I felt his presence before I saw him, and then I turned and there he was—standing in the clearing, just beyond the reach of the trees.

His hair was disheveled, dark curls framing a face that I thought I knew. His eyes, the same eyes that had always found me in a crowd, now seemed to search me with a desperation I wasn't used to. He had always been calm, so steady, the anchor in a storm. But now, there was a rawness in him that mirrored the chaos I felt inside.

"You heard," I whispered, unable to stop the tremor that ran through my words.

"I heard," he confirmed, his jaw tight. "And I don't care what it costs. If it means being with you, then so be it."

I took a step toward him, but my legs felt as though they might give way beneath me. I had been strong—so strong in my resolve until this moment, until the weight of the decision sank in.

"I can't—" I stopped, forcing myself to breathe deeply, the air thick with the fragrance of the woods, the smell of something old, something forgotten. "I don't want to lose you. But I can't—"

"You won't," he interrupted, his voice fierce now, a heat to it that I wasn't used to hearing. He stepped closer, until his warmth wrapped around me like a cocoon, and for the first time since the Watcher's revelation, I felt a moment of peace. "You won't lose me. Not ever. Not in the way you think."

My heart swelled at his words, but the doubt quickly crept back in. "But the Watcher said—"

"Forget what the Watcher said," he said, his voice soft now, almost tender. He reached for me, his fingers brushing against my cheek, sending a jolt of warmth through my skin. "What matters is what we choose. The covenant, the ritual—it's not about what they say it's about. It's about us. You and me. And I choose you. I always have."

I closed my eyes, my mind spinning. The world was spinning, a dizzying blur of choices and consequences, of impossible decisions that could tear everything I knew apart. Could I follow my heart? Could I be brave enough to believe that love might, in fact, transcend all the forces pulling at us?

"I can't live without you," I whispered, the truth slipping from my lips before I could stop it.

"And you won't have to," he replied, his lips brushing against my forehead in a kiss so light I barely felt it, yet it left me breathless. "But we'll do it together. However this ends, it ends with us. And that's the only truth I need."

The weight of it was like an anchor settling deep inside me, pulling me closer to him, closer to a choice I hadn't yet fully accepted but that was already taking root in my chest.

His words hung in the air between us, heavier than any raincloud I had ever felt gathering over my head. I was drowning in them, struggling to come up for air. Every part of me screamed for escape, for the familiar comfort of my own life, the routines that had given me something solid to stand on. But I wasn't standing anymore, was I? I was teetering on the edge of a precipice, and no amount of logic or second-guessing would change the fact that this was my moment of reckoning. My heart beat in time with his, both of us caught in the weight of an unspoken promise we hadn't quite made, but already couldn't take back.

He took a step toward me, a slow, deliberate movement that stirred something deep inside me. I thought I had prepared myself for this moment—had steeled myself against the inevitable—but now, facing him, everything I had told myself seemed to dissolve, like smoke in the wind.

"I've never been one for waiting," he said, the ghost of a smile curling at the edges of his lips. "But it feels like you're making me wait. Not for you, but for the answer."

I shook my head, not trusting myself to speak. If I said anything now, it would only be a lie—a desperate attempt to hold on to something that was slipping away.

"I don't know what you want me to say," I whispered instead, my voice trembling despite myself.

The smile faded from his lips, replaced by something more serious. "You don't have to say anything, not yet. But I'll ask you this—how long can we pretend that this isn't happening? That we're not in the midst of something that's bigger than both of us? You feel it, too. The pull. The thing that draws us together, no matter how hard you try to fight it. I've fought it long enough. I won't anymore."

His words tangled with the pulsing beat of my heart, each one a reminder of how close I was to losing everything. But could I really walk away? Could I really walk away from him? The truth was, I didn't want to. I wanted to stay here with him, to hold on to this moment as if it were all that mattered. And for a fleeting instant, it was all that mattered.

But the Watcher's words, the warning of the rift, continued to echo in my mind, as relentless as the crash of waves against jagged rocks. This wasn't just about love; this was about survival. The fabric of both worlds, pulled taut between us, threatened to snap at any moment.

I closed my eyes, not wanting to look at him—too afraid of what I might see. Too afraid of what my heart might decide for me.

"You're asking me to make a choice between two lives," I said, my voice tight. "To give up everything I know for a life I don't understand. And you're telling me that if I don't..."

The words caught in my throat. I didn't need to finish the sentence. He knew. He always knew.

"If you don't," he said, stepping closer now, his breath warm against my skin, "then everything we've built will burn to the ground. You'll lose more than just the world you know. You'll lose me. And everything else. It's already happening, can't you feel it? The world is starting to unravel, piece by piece."

I swallowed hard, my stomach tight with dread. The sense of foreboding was impossible to ignore now. The edges of my vision blurred, as if reality itself was beginning to bend in ways I couldn't comprehend. The air felt too thick, too close, and everything seemed so fragile, like the calm before a storm.

"Then tell me what to do," I said, barely recognizing my own voice, which had become brittle and raw. "Tell me how to stop it."

He reached out then, cupping my face in his hands with a tenderness that made my heart ache. "I can't tell you what to do. This has always been your choice, and it always will be. All I can do is be here. For whatever comes next. For whatever you decide."

His fingers, warm and familiar, traced the line of my jaw, and for a moment, the world outside seemed to fade away. There was only him and me, only this moment.

But the stillness was short-lived. A sudden noise—distant, but unmistakable—split the silence, a crack like thunder rolling over the horizon. I jerked back, my heart leaping in my chest.

"What was that?" I asked, my voice a sharp edge of panic.

His eyes darkened, and he took a step away from me, his expression clouded with something I couldn't quite read. "It's starting," he said, his voice low. "It's already too late to stop it."

Before I could ask what he meant, the ground beneath us trembled, a low rumble shaking through the earth. The trees shuddered, their branches creaking with the weight of something unseen. I looked up at him, my breath catching in my throat.

"I didn't—"

He grabbed my hand before I could finish, pulling me into the thick shadows of the woods. "It's coming," he said, urgency lacing his words. "Whatever happens now, we're out of time."

I stumbled after him, the ground beneath my feet unsteady, my mind spinning with a thousand questions that had no answers. The rift was widening. It wasn't just a tear in the fabric of reality anymore; it was a chasm, a void that threatened to swallow everything in its path.

And yet, I couldn't shake the feeling that this was only the beginning. Whatever we faced, whatever we did next, there was no escaping the fact that the covenant—whatever it was—was going to change everything.

The trees parted suddenly, and ahead of us, a figure emerged from the mist. His face was hidden, his outline barely visible in the fading light, but I knew without a doubt who it was.

And then I saw it.

A shimmer, barely perceptible at first, like the air itself had rippled. The rift. It was here.

The Watcher's grip on my hand tightened as he whispered one word, a warning, a plea.

"Run."

And before I could make sense of anything, the ground cracked open beneath us, sending us both tumbling into the abyss.

Chapter 29: The Kiss That Changed Everything

The firelight danced across his face, flickering shadows and bathing his features in an almost ethereal glow. His eyes locked onto mine, and for a moment, the world seemed to disappear. The winds outside had picked up, their howl an eerie reminder of the tempest that brewed both in nature and in our hearts. The quiet hum of the ancient room pressed in around us, a soft murmur of forgotten voices, as if the walls themselves knew what we were about to do and were holding their breath, waiting.

His fingers grazed the back of my neck, sending a shiver cascading down my spine, and I felt the weight of the moment settle over me like a heavy cloak. There had been no words for this. No need for them. The ritual had been explained in whispers, with so many assumptions, uncertainties, and unspoken fears. But here we were, poised on the edge of something vast, something incomprehensible, and neither of us dared to speak the things we both knew were lurking in the spaces between us.

I tried to steady my breathing, but it was impossible. My chest tightened, a knot of anticipation and dread coiling deep within me. This kiss—this single moment—had the power to unravel everything, to reshape the future, to rewrite the very fabric of our existence. How could something so simple carry so much weight?

"Are you ready?" His voice broke through the stillness, rough and uncertain, like he was asking me to take a leap into a void, with no promise of safety.

I nodded, though my heart was anything but steady. "I don't know if I ever will be," I whispered. "But I trust you."

It wasn't just the words. It was the feeling behind them, the raw truth that we had built our connection on for years. In a world where certainty was fleeting and every promise came with an expiration date, the trust between us had always been our anchor. And in that moment, it felt like the only thing that could guide us through the storm.

He leaned in, his breath mingling with mine. The scent of him—earthy, like damp earth after a storm, mixed with the faintest trace of woodsmoke—wrapped around me, grounding me in a way nothing else could. His lips brushed against mine, soft at first, tentative, as if he was testing the waters, feeling for any sign of resistance. But there was none. No hesitation. I met him halfway, closing the distance between us, and the kiss deepened.

Time stretched, warped, as if the very fabric of reality had bent to accommodate the intensity of that moment. His hands roamed, pulling me closer, and I responded in kind, my fingers threading through his hair, feeling the weight of his desire, his need, pressing into me. The kiss was electric, a current that sparked with every touch, every shift, every breath. But it wasn't just the physical sensation that consumed me. It was the flood of memories, of past lives, of echoes of promises whispered under different skies. The kiss was a bridge—a bridge between all that had come before and all that was yet to be. I could feel the weight of every single moment we had shared, every joy, every sorrow, every moment of connection and loss.

I pulled back, gasping for air, but he was relentless. His hands tightened around me, pulling me back into the storm of him. His lips trailed down my neck, the soft scrape of his stubble against my skin sending another wave of heat through me. "We can't undo this," he murmured against my skin, his voice thick with an emotion I couldn't quite name. "Once we begin, there's no going back."

The words were a promise and a warning, a reminder that this kiss was not just a kiss. It was a catalyst, a point of no return. But in that moment, it didn't matter. I was no longer sure what was at stake, or if there even was a future without him. His presence consumed me, filling up every empty space within me, until the thought of a world without him seemed impossible.

"I know," I whispered, the words feeling foreign in my mouth, as though they had been waiting for years to be spoken.

And then it happened—the shift, the change. A soft, almost imperceptible pulse of energy rippled through us, a wave of power that neither of us could have anticipated. The room seemed to tilt, the walls stretching and contracting as though the very air around us had been transformed. I could feel it deep in my bones, the shift in the balance between us, the blending of our souls, of our destinies. Something ancient and primal stirred within me, a recognition of the weight of what we were about to do.

He pulled away just enough to look me in the eyes, his expression unreadable, yet full of a kind of resigned acceptance. "This was always going to be our end," he said softly, his words cutting through the haze of desire. "But in the end, maybe it will be worth it."

I opened my mouth to speak, but no words came. Instead, I kissed him again, harder this time, as if the very act of kissing him could somehow anchor me to the ground, could tether me to something real. I didn't know how this would all unfold, what the consequences would be, but in that moment, it didn't matter. All that mattered was the kiss—the kiss that had changed everything.

The kiss lingered in my mind long after our lips parted, an electric aftershock that trembled through me like the fading pulse of thunder. He held me at arm's length, just enough to look at me with that intensity that could freeze time. But I wasn't frozen. Not in the slightest. No, I was caught in a storm that had swept me off my feet and sent me tumbling into a reality that felt both terrifying and inevitable.

"Do you feel that?" His voice, hoarse and raw, seemed to scrape against the air between us. He didn't need to ask, not really. I felt it. How could I not? The air between us crackled, thick with an unspoken understanding that somehow seemed both exhilarating and suffocating.

"I feel everything," I said, my words more of a breath than a sentence, and as soon as the words left my mouth, I realized how true they were. Everything. The weight of his gaze. The pull of our shared history. The ominous certainty that whatever had been set into motion tonight couldn't be undone.

He sighed, the sound so full of longing that I almost reached for him again, but something in the way his shoulders dropped stopped me. "I wish things could be different," he murmured, almost as though he were talking to himself, the soft words barely reaching my ears.

I stepped back, creating a space between us that felt uncomfortably vast. "We can't undo this, can we?" I asked, my voice steady but uncertain, because as much as I knew the answer, the part of me that still clung to hope wanted to believe in something else—something simpler.

"No," he answered immediately, the finality of the word ringing in the stillness of the room. He ran a hand through his hair, tugging at it, the raw frustration evident in the way his fingers gripped the strands. "But that doesn't mean we can't fight it."

My heart leapt in my chest, a flicker of something dangerous flaring within me. "Fight it?" I repeated, not quite sure if I had heard him right. "You think we can fight this... this fate?"

He turned to face me fully, his eyes locking with mine, unyielding and desperate. "I don't know what else we can do," he said, his voice taking on an edge, the tension coiling between us like the taut strings of a bow. "This... thing between us—it's not just about us anymore. There's too much at stake, too many lives on the line."

I swallowed, a cold shiver creeping down my spine as the weight of his words sank in. This wasn't just about us anymore. It never had been. It was about something much bigger—something ancient and unforgiving. And no matter how much I wished otherwise, I could no longer deny the gravity of it.

"Then what do we do?" I asked, stepping closer to him again, the distance between us feeling too wide, too unbearable. "What happens now?"

He ran a hand over his face, exhausted, as though the weight of everything had finally caught up with him. "We honor the pact," he said, the words laced with regret. "We don't have a choice."

I flinched, the rawness of his admission cutting through me like a blade. I had always known this moment was coming—the moment when we would face the consequences of everything we had allowed to grow between us. But knowing it and living it were two different things entirely. And no amount of preparation could have shielded me from the truth that now hung in the air between us.

"I don't want to lose you," I whispered, the words tumbling from my lips before I could stop them. It was the simple truth. The one thing I hadn't been able to say, not even to myself, until now. The one thing that had been lodged in my chest, heavy and suffocating.

He reached out, brushing a strand of hair from my face with a tenderness that made my heart ache. "I don't want to lose you either," he replied, his voice thick with emotion. "But if we don't do this, everything we've fought for—everything we've built—will fall apart. There won't be anything left."

His words hit me like a thunderclap, rattling my bones and forcing me to confront the undeniable truth: I had never really had a choice. Not when it came to him, and not when it came to the forces that had shaped our lives. The weight of our past, of everything we had both been through, pressed down on me with a suffocating force. There was no escaping it now.

But even as the reality of the situation settled in, something fierce and unrelenting stirred deep within me. It was a spark, something that refused to be extinguished by fate, by destiny, or by the cold hands of the world. I wasn't ready to surrender—not yet, not completely.

"What if we don't honor it?" I asked, my voice low and dangerous. "What if we choose each other?"

He shook his head slowly, as though he were already mourning the possibility. "It's not that simple."

"Nothing is ever simple," I snapped, frustration rising up in me like a wave. "And yet, here we are—facing something impossible, and we have to make a choice. Maybe it's time to stop running from it."

The room seemed to hold its breath as the words hung between us, suspended in the charged air. His expression softened, but there was a sadness there, a sorrow that seemed to weigh him down. "You don't know what you're asking," he said, his voice barely above a whisper.

I met his gaze, my resolve hardening, even as fear churned in my stomach. "Maybe it's time we found out."

The silence that followed was a blanket, heavy and unyielding. I could still taste him on my lips, the remnants of that kiss clinging to me like the scent of something burning—familiar yet volatile. I could feel the edges of the world beginning to fray, as if the fabric of our reality had been pulled just a little too taut. The space between us felt enormous now, the weight of what had been set in motion pressing in on both of us, suffocating in its inevitability.

"I didn't expect it to feel like this," I whispered, the words slipping out before I could stop them. It was the truth, though. I had prepared myself for the ritual, for the ancient pull of forces beyond our control, but I hadn't prepared myself for the rawness of the emotions it unleashed. Not just the desire—though that was there, burning hotter than I ever thought possible—but the pain, the grief, the realization that there might be no way out of this, no way to undo what we had done.

He stepped back, running a hand through his hair, his eyes distant, as if he was searching for something in the shadows that I couldn't see. "I didn't either," he said, the roughness in his voice betraying a deep well of frustration. "But here we are. And there's no turning back."

His words were a harsh truth, but they didn't feel like a sentence. Not yet, at least. There was something else there, something that made my pulse quicken—a strange, uneasy hope. Maybe it was the same hope that had always danced on the edge of our conversations, a fragile thing that refused to be extinguished no matter how many times we told ourselves it wasn't possible. But as I looked at him, standing there with that unshakable resolve in his eyes, I couldn't help but wonder if he still believed in it too.

"What do we do now?" I asked, my voice low and steady despite the turmoil that churned beneath the surface. "We've made our choice. But what comes after?"

He didn't answer right away, his gaze flicking over me like he was weighing something too heavy for words. Finally, he let out a slow breath and met my eyes. "I don't know," he admitted. "I've always known the cost. I've known it since the beginning. But this—" He shook his head, the words catching in his throat. "This isn't just about us anymore. This isn't just about what we want."

I crossed my arms, resisting the urge to take another step closer to him. The pull between us was still there, undeniable, but I needed to hear him out. "Then what is it about?" I asked, the frustration in my voice a thin veneer over the vulnerability I couldn't quite hide.

He took a deep breath, his chest rising and falling like a man who had long ago learned to hold his breath, to wait for the storm to pass. "It's about what's coming," he said, the words heavy with unspoken fear. "I've seen it. I've felt it. The darkness that's been creeping closer, the thing we've been avoiding for so long. And now, it's here. And we don't have the luxury of running from it anymore."

I didn't say anything at first. The weight of his words settled over me like a blanket made of stone. It wasn't just about us. It never had been. This was bigger. The storm he spoke of had been looming over us for so long that I had stopped seeing it. I had let myself believe that we could keep it at bay, that love and hope and whatever magic we still had left could be enough to shield us. But as he stood there, looking like a man who had already come to terms with the cost of it all, I realized the truth I had been avoiding: nothing would ever be enough.

I turned away, pacing the length of the small room, needing to move, to think, to make sense of everything. It was impossible to think clearly when I was standing so close to him, when every part of me was still aching with the ghost of his touch. The kiss, the ritual, the promise of forever—it was all tangled up in my chest, pulling at me from all directions.

"How do we stop it?" I asked, stopping abruptly, my voice almost a plea. "How do we stop whatever's coming?"

He didn't respond right away, but I could see the struggle in his eyes, the way the weight of the answer was too much for him to bear. He opened his mouth, but then closed it again, his jaw tightening. "We can't stop it," he said finally, the words as final as they were heartbreaking. "But we can face it. Together."

I felt the floor drop out from beneath me. "No," I said, shaking my head, as though the words themselves could change everything. "No, that's not good enough. You can't ask me to just... accept this."

"I'm not asking you to accept it," he said, his voice firm now, stronger than before. "I'm asking you to fight with me."

I stared at him for a long moment, the silence between us stretched thin. His face was set, his resolve as unshakable as the mountains in the distance. But I couldn't help the knot that twisted tighter in my stomach, the dread that coiled around my heart. Fighting with him—that was one thing. But this? Whatever it was that was coming, whatever had been set into motion—it felt like something we were too small to fight, too human to win against.

"I don't know if we can win this," I whispered, the words slipping out before I could stop them.

He didn't flinch. His gaze never wavered. "Maybe we don't have to win," he said softly. "Maybe all we need to do is survive."

I opened my mouth to respond, but before I could, the door to the room slammed open, cutting him off mid-sentence. The chill that swept in from the hallway wasn't just from the wind—it was the kind of cold that made my skin prickle and my blood run cold. Something had changed. Something had entered the room with the kind of presence that made the air thick and charged.

I turned to face the doorway, my heart pounding in my chest, every nerve on high alert. The figure standing in the doorway was tall, cloaked in shadow, but I could feel the weight of its gaze from across the room. And for the first time that night, I felt the cold fingers of fear slip around my throat.

"You're too late," the figure said, its voice low and calm, as though it had been expecting us all along.

And just like that, I knew that the game had changed again.

Chapter 30: The Choice of the Mortal

The sun was still a shy promise on the horizon, a pale streak of pink that hovered just above the trees, as though it, too, was unsure whether to rise. The air was thick with the scent of earth, damp from the night's mist. I stood there, frozen in the clearing, my heart racing to match the erratic rhythm of my breath. His voice—low, almost pleading—lingered in the coolness between us, each word like a weight pressing down on my chest.

Only one of us could survive the covenant.

His gaze, dark as the night itself, flickered to the distant woods, as though they held the answer, as though they could take away the burden of his words. The winds rustled the leaves around us, but there was no comfort to be found in their soft sighs. No wind could stir my bones the way he did, no sound could break me quite like the beat of my own heart. This wasn't supposed to be my choice.

"I don't understand," I murmured, my voice trembling, barely a whisper in the vastness of the forest.

He closed his eyes, as if searching for strength in the morning light. "I know. But the realm doesn't care about understanding. It only cares about balance. We've both been touched by it. And one of us must give way for the other."

The trees groaned, their trunks twisting and creaking, as if the very land mourned with me. My hands, still trembling from the weight of his admission, clutched the delicate fabric of my dress, the threads unraveling beneath my touch. The covenant had always been a distant thing—something others spoke of in stories or warnings—but now it was a cold, unforgiving reality.

It was strange, really, how the heart can feel both weightless and anchored at the same time. My thoughts scattered like the leaves in the wind, torn between the life I'd known and the life I'd been drawn into since the moment I first saw him.

"I don't know if I can," I said, stepping back, as though the distance between us could make the decision any easier. It didn't.

His lips twitched at the edges, the faintest hint of a smile pulling at his features. But there was something in the depths of his eyes that I couldn't quite reach—a sadness that made my heart ache in ways I never thought possible. "You'll have to. Whether you want to or not. The choice will come."

"I'm not ready," I breathed, my voice cracked from the pressure that weighed heavily on my chest.

"You will be." His words were certain, so certain that they rang with an authority I couldn't contest. But even as he spoke, there was an undeniable pull—something deep and visceral—that made me look at him with more longing than I had ever felt before. I wanted to scream, to break, to find a way out of this nightmare. But I couldn't. I was bound to him in ways no ordinary bond could explain.

I glanced up at the sky. The pale light was becoming warmer now, the color of the dawn gradually shifting to gold. Everything around us seemed to slow, as though the world itself held its breath, waiting for me to choose, to decide who would live and who would fade away.

There was a rustling behind me, the sound of footsteps approaching. But they weren't his—no, they were too light, too fleeting, too... unsure. I spun around, and my heart stopped, my pulse pounding in my ears.

A figure stood at the edge of the clearing, silhouetted against the rising sun.

The newcomer was a stranger, yet I knew the unmistakable aura of the covenant wrapped around her. She had that same glow about her—an ethereal presence that seemed to blur the edges of reality. Her face was hidden beneath the shadows of a hood, but even from a distance, I could see the flicker of something ancient in her gaze. A weight of experience, of power, and of things long lost.

"Who are you?" I demanded, though my voice barely held the steadiness I'd hoped for.

She stepped forward, her movements deliberate, her presence enough to make the earth tremble beneath my feet. "A choice must be made," she said, her voice soft yet carrying an undeniable authority. "The realms demand it."

I looked back at him, my breath catching in my throat. "You never told me... you never told me there would be someone else."

His silence was a confession in itself. The kind of confession that broke the walls I'd built around my heart, that made the sharp sting of betrayal feel like a gentle kiss.

The stranger's eyes—dark and unreadable—focused on me with a strange intensity. "You are not the only one caught between worlds. The rules of the covenant are not as clear as they once were."

I could hear the trees groaning again, the ground beneath me shifting as though it were alive with secrets. The air tasted of salt and earth, of something ancient and dangerous, as if the world itself were holding its breath for the inevitable decision.

I turned back to the man who had become the center of my universe, my heart crashing in my chest like waves against the shore. "What does this mean?" I asked, my voice hoarse. "What happens now?"

His eyes were filled with a fire, an intensity that spoke of battles fought and sacrifices made. But there was something else there now. Something I couldn't quite place.

"It means," he began slowly, "that your choice will define everything. And once it is made, there is no going back."

And with that, the air between us shifted—became charged with something heavier than the weight of a thousand lifetimes. The choice was mine. It always had been.

The silence that followed his words wasn't comforting. It was suffocating, as though the entire world had stopped spinning just to watch me unravel. The stranger—the one who appeared out of nowhere, a sliver of some otherworldly fate—stood still, her dark cloak barely fluttering in the soft breeze, her eyes fixed on me with a strange mixture of sympathy and judgment. I could practically hear the invisible clock ticking, each second taking me closer to a decision I wasn't prepared to make.

My pulse drummed in my ears as I tried to process the weight of it all. The covenant. The realms. The sacrifice. This wasn't a choice—it was a wound that would never heal, no matter which direction I turned. If I stayed, if I chose to remain tethered to him, would that be enough? Or would I suffocate under the weight of a love that couldn't be? I couldn't picture a life without him, but I also couldn't picture a life that wasn't mine to claim.

"Why now?" I asked, my voice ragged. The question didn't feel right—nothing about this felt right—but it was the only thing I could say to break the oppressive stillness. "Why is it me? Why do I have to make this choice?"

The stranger stepped closer, her eyes unreadable, and yet I could feel her presence like a thousand tiny threads pulling at me from every angle. She didn't answer immediately, her gaze sweeping over the landscape as though she were assessing the world around us.

"The realms have waited long enough," she said finally, her tone heavy, laden with meaning. "And so have you."

I didn't want to hear that. I didn't want to be reminded that this wasn't just a cruel twist of fate; it was inevitable. He had been waiting for me, just as I had been waiting for him—waiting for something I couldn't even define.

His hand reached out, fingers brushing mine, and for a moment, I almost thought I could forget about the world. Forget about the impossible choices, the torn loyalty. But reality settled in quickly, like ice on my skin. The world I knew was never going to be the same again.

"You think I don't know this?" he said, his voice raw with emotion. "That I don't wish I could change it all? That I haven't cursed the moment this started?"

His words hung in the air between us, and though I could feel the pull of them—the agony in them—there was something else. Something darker lurking beneath the surface. I stepped back, unsure if the distance would help or if it would only magnify the growing weight on my chest.

The stranger tilted her head slightly, an expression I couldn't quite place softening her features. "He's right, you know. But this isn't about what either of you want. It's about what must be."

I turned to her, a surge of frustration bubbling inside me. "That's not fair. You're telling me it's fate? That I'm just supposed to accept it?" I shook my head, an involuntary laugh escaping my lips—bitter, cruel, hollow. "This is about my life, not some mythical prophecy."

Her lips curved upward, the smallest of smiles, as though she'd expected this from me. "The realm doesn't care about fairness. The world doesn't care about your feelings."

Her words weren't a slap. They were a revelation. I stared at her, my chest tightening. No matter how much I resented her, she was right. The world had never cared about me. Or him. Not in the way we wanted. We were pawns in a game too big for us to understand, yet we were its players nonetheless.

"I don't want to lose you," I said, my voice breaking as I turned back to him. The words were raw, stripped of any pretense. A confession I hadn't allowed myself to say until now. But even as I spoke them, I knew it wasn't enough. It wasn't a simple matter of love. I had to think about what was beyond that, beyond this moment.

"I don't want to lose you either," he whispered, his voice tight with the same rawness, the same hunger for a future neither of us could have. His eyes never left mine, and for a moment, I felt the weight of every unspoken thing between us.

I was drowning in the need to choose. To take the decision out of fate's cold hands and make it my own.

The wind picked up again, swirling around us in a frenzy as if nature itself was urging me to act. The stranger's gaze flicked briefly to the trees, then back to me. "The covenant cannot wait forever. Your time is running out."

A strange pressure settled over me, not unlike the pressure in my chest as I tried to breathe through the fear and the uncertainty. The air seemed to thicken, each breath feeling heavier than the last. I didn't know what would happen next, but I could feel the world turning with every second that passed. And I—I—was the one who had to decide whether to stop it or let it happen.

The world wasn't asking for my permission. It was demanding an answer. The choice was mine, yes, but it wasn't a choice at all. It was a consequence. A consequence of love. A consequence of the worlds colliding in ways that would rip everything apart if I didn't act.

His hand, warm and steady, found mine again. I could feel the weight of it, and for a moment, it anchored me. It was the one thing in all of this that was real. The warmth of his skin. The pulse beneath his fingertips.

"I love you," he whispered, his voice rough with the weight of all we had been through, and all we still might never have.

I could feel my heart splitting in two, torn between the need to hold onto him, to stay where I was, and the undeniable truth that I couldn't keep both worlds from crumbling.

I had to choose.

And as I felt the gravity of that decision pressing down on me, I realized the answer wasn't as clear as I had once believed.

The tension between us was palpable, the air so thick with unspoken words that it was almost suffocating. I stood at the edge of the clearing, my feet barely touching the earth, as if even the ground beneath me could sense the weight of the decision I was facing. His hand, still clinging to mine, felt like a lifeline, but also a chain. A chain that bound me to something I couldn't hold onto forever.

"I never asked for this," I whispered, the words barely making it past the lump in my throat.

He exhaled slowly, as if the weight of my statement had taken some of the air out of him too. "Neither of us did," he replied. His voice was steady, but there was a tremor in the way he held me, as though he, too, was caught between the pull of worlds, between what was and what could be.

I glanced over at the stranger, her presence now seeming less like a threat and more like a reminder. A reminder that we were not the only players in this game, that fate had long ago determined the terms of this contest. "So, this is it? We're just supposed to—choose?" I nearly spat the word out. "And you're just standing there, watching us?"

The stranger's lips curled, but it wasn't a smile—it was more of a knowing curve, as though she was privy to some secret that we were still too naïve to understand. "What choice would you have, mortal?" she asked, her voice quiet but sharp. "The rules have been set for longer than you realize. This isn't about whether you're ready or not—it's about what must be."

My teeth gritted at her words. The finality of them, the certainty in her tone—it made my skin crawl. I hated how helpless she made me feel, hated how she made it seem like I had no agency in this. But even as I resisted her, I could feel the truth of it sinking in, like stones piling up at the bottom of my chest. I wasn't in control. Not really.

I turned back to him, my heart aching. "I don't want to live in a world without you," I said, the words tumbling out before I could stop them. "I don't want to make this choice. I don't want to be the one who decides who dies."

The rawness of my words hit both of us like a tidal wave. He closed his eyes briefly, as though bracing himself against the force of my pain. "You don't have to decide now," he said, his voice cracking slightly. "I'll wait. Whatever you choose, I'll wait."

And there it was—hope. The one thing that shouldn't have been in the equation. Because what he was offering wasn't just time, it was an impossible promise. A promise that, even if I chose to let go, he would still be waiting for me. But how could he wait? How could any of this be real?

I swallowed hard, trying to steady myself, to find something solid in this world that felt like it was collapsing around me. But nothing was steady. Not anymore. "I can't do this," I said, my voice cracking under the weight of the admission. "I can't make this choice."

"You have to," he said, the words quieter now, but no less firm. "Because whether you want to or not, the world will keep turning. The realms will keep shifting. And we can't stop it."

The stranger took a step forward, her eyes narrowing, but her voice still calm. "It is you who must decide. Only you can hold the balance. Only you can choose between love and sacrifice."

Love and sacrifice.

The words wrapped themselves around me, curling in my mind like smoke. Could love really sacrifice? Could it be so simple? It had never felt simple before, not when we had fought for every moment we shared, every breath that had connected us. How could it be reduced to a choice between life and death? How could he—the man I loved with everything in me—be the price for my survival?

"Do you want to save him?" she asked, her voice softer now, almost coaxing. "Do you want to keep him with you? Then you will need to give up everything. Everything that ties you to this world. Your heart. Your breath. Your life."

I felt the coldness creep in, the sharp bite of reality sinking into my bones. She wasn't asking for an answer. She was making it clear that I couldn't have it both ways. I couldn't hold on and keep him. There would be no middle ground.

But what if I didn't want to live without him? What if the world without him was a place I didn't even recognize?

"I don't want to be alone," I whispered, my voice shaking now with the full weight of what I was being asked to sacrifice.

The stranger's gaze softened, just the slightest bit. "You won't be. But you will be changed. That's the price of love."

The price of love.

The words echoed in my mind, louder than anything else. Because this wasn't just about love anymore. It was about everything we had fought for, everything we had endured, and everything we still wanted to build.

I reached for him, instinctively, but the moment my hand brushed his, something shifted. The air thickened around us, and a strange, unfamiliar pressure clamped down on my chest, like the very ground was folding beneath my feet. His hand twitched, as if reaching for me, but he didn't make contact. The world around us seemed to warp, twisting and shifting like it was a reflection in a broken mirror.

"Wait—what's happening?" My voice barely sounded like mine, distorted and distant.

The stranger's eyes widened, the faintest glimmer of surprise flashing across her otherwise composed expression. "The realms are shifting," she said, a whisper of uncertainty creeping into her voice. "It's too late to stop it."

I tried to move, but the world around me felt like it was being pulled apart, disintegrating into pieces too small to comprehend. And in the midst of it all, I heard a voice—a whisper, distant, impossibly distant.

Choose.

The choice wasn't mine to make anymore.

Chapter 31: The Final Embrace

I could feel the weight of the decision pressing against my chest, suffocating in its finality. As we stood in the doorway of the small, dimly lit room that had been our haven, the world outside felt impossibly distant, like a dream I couldn't reach. The moonlight spilled through the cracked window, casting fractured shadows across the floor, and for a fleeting moment, I wondered if this was how everything ends—quiet, soft, like the last breath of a dying star.

His hands, always so sure and steady, trembled ever so slightly as he cupped my face. I hadn't seen him so vulnerable before, not even in the darkest of hours. His brow furrowed, his lips parted as if he were searching for words that wouldn't come. And that look—God, that look—burned into my memory, a mix of longing and resignation. I could have sworn I felt his heart breaking in sync with mine.

"I never wanted this," he whispered, the words slipping between us like a confession meant for no one but the silence of the night.

I shook my head, unwilling to let the tears rise, though they hovered dangerously close. "Neither did I." My voice barely rose above a whisper, thick with the weight of our shared pain. It was as though the universe had conspired against us, throwing obstacle after obstacle in our path, and now it was asking for the final sacrifice. I couldn't say no to him. Not when it meant saving him from something far worse.

His fingers brushed my cheek, the touch light, but it was enough to send a rush of warmth flooding through me. I wished I could reach out and stop time, hold him here forever, but the reality was as unyielding as the cold that crept into the corners of the room.

"I'll be with you," he said, his voice low, like a promise he couldn't quite keep. "Always. In whatever way I can."

A choked sob threatened to escape, but I swallowed it down. “I don’t need you in whatever way you can,” I shot back, my voice sharper than I intended. “I need you here. With me. Where I can touch you, where I can hear your voice.”

He stepped back, giving me space I didn’t want, yet needed. His eyes—those eyes that had once been full of mischief and life—had turned distant, resigned. And still, there was that strength, that quiet power in the way he held himself, in the way he refused to let go of what little we had left. But even then, I could see the truth in his eyes. He knew what was coming.

“I know,” he murmured, his voice breaking as he struggled to hold it together. “I know. But sometimes we don’t get what we want. Sometimes the only choice we have is to let go.”

I wanted to scream, to rail against the unfairness of it all, but what would that accomplish? We were past the point of reasoning, past the point of change. The choice had been made, and it was final. The ache in my chest throbbed painfully with every heartbeat.

“I wish I had known you longer,” I said, the words slipping out before I could stop them. It was a foolish thing to say, one that would only add to the weight between us, but it was the truth. The thought of all the time we’d never have, all the moments we would never share, threatened to undo me.

His lips quirked into a sad, crooked smile. “You know me better than anyone,” he said softly. “And that’s all that matters.”

The tension between us grew thicker, heavier, like the air before a storm. My chest felt tight, my throat a lump of raw emotion I couldn’t express. My gaze flickered to the door, the one we’d always dreamed of walking through together.

He reached for his coat, his movements slow, deliberate. There was no hurry. He wasn’t coming back. Not in the way I wanted him to, at least.

I wanted to run after him, throw myself into his arms and beg him to stay, to reconsider, to fight for us. But there was no fight left in him. Or me. The love we shared had been tested by time and distance, by forces neither of us had understood until it was too late.

"I'll never forget you," he said, his voice tight with something more than sorrow. "No matter where I go."

I nodded, the words stuck behind my teeth. I didn't know how to say goodbye to someone who had been so much a part of me. Who was still a part of me. But I did. I turned away, forcing my legs to move, my heart to follow.

He was already out the door, his silhouette a fading memory against the night. I stood there, the empty space between us growing wider, until I felt the chill of it in my bones.

And then, for the first time in what felt like forever, I allowed myself to breathe. It was the only way forward. The only choice we had left.

It wasn't the end. I refused to let it be.

I sat there in the quiet aftermath, the silence pressing in around me like a heavy, suffocating blanket. The room felt too large, too empty now that he was gone. I could still feel the lingering warmth of his arms, the echo of his breath against my skin, but it was fading, slipping through my fingers like water. I had tried to memorize him in that last moment, cataloging every detail—the way the light from the window caught in his hair, the slight tremble of his hand as it brushed my cheek, the way his voice cracked when he told me to take care. It was too much. And yet, it wasn't enough.

The door clicked shut softly behind him, and I was left with nothing but the faintest trace of his scent in the air and the sharp sting of tears that I hadn't dared to shed.

The ache in my chest was a constant, a dull throb that reminded me of the gravity of the choice I had made. The right choice, I told myself, even though the word felt foreign, like something borrowed that didn't quite fit. It was what had to happen. What had to be done.

But as the minutes ticked by, as the world outside carried on, I found myself growing more restless. The emptiness of the room stretched into the emptiness inside me, and I knew that staying here, in the same space we had shared, would only make the pain more unbearable.

I stood up and walked over to the window, the cool glass against my fingertips a reminder that life, in its most mundane form, went on. The world below me seemed so far removed from the turmoil I felt inside. People walked by, heads down, lost in their own small dramas. I envied them. They didn't have to carry the weight of a love that had torn them in two, that had burned so brightly, so fiercely, only to flicker out in the dark.

I couldn't stay here, not in this place that felt like a tomb for the life we had planned. And so I did what I had done countless times before—I ran. But this time, it wasn't away from anything; it was away from everything that had come before.

The cool night air hit my skin like a slap as I stepped outside, the rush of it grounding me, pulling me back from the edge of myself. I couldn't let myself fall apart. I wouldn't. I wasn't the kind of person who broke, not in the way I feared. Not in the way that he had broken.

I kept walking, my footsteps quick and uneven, my mind a blur of conflicting emotions. The city around me felt strangely familiar and utterly foreign all at once. The same streets I had walked down a thousand times before now seemed alien, as though I were seeing them for the first time. The lights blurred, the sounds of the evening faded into the background, and all that remained was the beating of my heart, a rhythm I couldn't control.

I wandered aimlessly, not caring where my feet took me, just needing the distance, the space to breathe. And then, out of nowhere, I found myself in front of a small café. The sign above it flickered in the dim light, a soft invitation to anyone brave enough to step inside. I wasn't sure why I had stopped here, but I had, and the sudden urge to find solace in a cup of coffee, to hide for just a moment, was impossible to resist.

I pushed open the door, the little bell above it chiming softly as I entered. The warmth of the place enveloped me, a stark contrast to the chill outside. The smell of freshly brewed coffee and cinnamon filled the air, and I exhaled slowly, savoring the comfort of it. The small café was nearly empty, save for a couple seated in the far corner and a man behind the counter, cleaning a mug with the kind of meticulous attention that spoke of years of practice.

The man glanced up as I approached the counter, his face neutral, but his eyes sharp. "What can I get you?" he asked, his voice low, almost measured. I wasn't sure why, but something about him made me pause.

"I'll have a coffee," I said, my voice sounding too loud in the quiet space. "Black. No sugar."

He nodded and went to work, his movements smooth, practiced. The quiet buzz of the espresso machine filled the silence between us, and for a moment, I allowed myself to just be—here, in this small bubble of normalcy that I had sought without realizing it. I needed to be invisible. I needed to be someone other than the girl who had said goodbye.

When he handed me the coffee, I wrapped my fingers around the cup, the heat from it a welcome distraction. I made my way to the corner booth, sinking into the plush seat as I took a tentative sip. The rich bitterness of the coffee hit my tongue, grounding me in a way I hadn't expected. It wasn't much, but it was enough to quiet the storm inside.

The man behind the counter didn't return to his cleaning. Instead, he watched me from across the room, his gaze steady, almost as if he were waiting for something. The longer he stared, the more uncomfortable I felt, but I wasn't sure why. There was nothing about him that stood out—he was just a man, tall and lean, with dark hair and an easy way about him. But his eyes held something—an intensity that felt too sharp, too perceptive.

Finally, he approached my table. "You look like you've had a long night," he said, his voice soft but laced with an understanding I hadn't expected.

I glanced up at him, startled by his observation. "Don't we all?" I said, forcing a smile, but it felt like a thin mask over the truth.

His lips twitched, a small, knowing smile. "Not everyone, no."

I didn't know how to respond to that. But then he sat down across from me, uninvited, and I couldn't bring myself to tell him to leave. Maybe it was the quiet of the room, or maybe it was the way his presence seemed to fill the empty spaces inside me. Either way, I found myself drawn to him, curious about the strange connection that seemed to spark between us.

He studied me for a moment, then spoke again, his tone a little lighter, a little more teasing. "You know, if you're trying to disappear, you're doing a terrible job of it."

I met his gaze, and for the briefest of moments, I wondered if he could see the crack in my heart, the jagged tear that had widened with every word he hadn't said, every moment he had waited too long to speak. His eyes were soft, holding something between resignation and a kind of quiet desperation. I wasn't sure if he was waiting for me to stop him, to tell him I'd made a mistake, but I wouldn't. I couldn't. Not when I knew the truth, even though it felt like betrayal carved into my bones.

He leaned forward then, just slightly, as if on instinct, his lips brushing the air near my ear. It was a simple gesture, one I'd once taken for granted, but now it sent a jolt of raw, aching awareness through me. My breath caught in my throat, and I almost reached for him. Almost. But I didn't. I wasn't sure if I could pull him closer, or if doing so would make the final break worse.

"Don't make this harder than it already is," he whispered.

It wasn't the words that held the power, but the weight of them. They were the last promise he would ever make to me, an unspoken truth that we both understood too well.

I nodded, the motion slow, deliberate. "I won't." The words were mine, but they didn't feel real. They were like a coat too big for me, one that didn't fit and never would. I'd been living in a lie for so long that now, when faced with the cold reality of what had to happen, I almost didn't know who I was anymore.

I turned to leave, the door closing behind me with the finality of a gunshot echoing in an empty room.

But the streets outside, the city that never seemed to rest, didn't feel like home. It didn't feel like anything. My feet carried me on autopilot, moving through the crowd, through the noise, through everything that had once felt like it mattered. The rhythm of life seemed distant, foreign, like I was watching from the wrong side of a glass. Nothing felt like it was mine. Not the trees swaying under the weight of the coming rain, not the flickering streetlamps casting their soft shadows on the pavement, not even the cars honking as they sped past. I couldn't shake the feeling that something was off. Something had shifted in a way I couldn't explain, but I knew it was there. It was like the world itself was holding its breath, waiting for the inevitable.

And then, there he was. Standing at the corner, just a shadow in the growing twilight, his figure almost indistinguishable from the rest of the city's noise. But I knew it was him, even before he stepped forward, before his eyes locked with mine.

"You're making a habit of this," he said, his voice low, almost playful, though the intensity in his gaze told me he wasn't fooling around.

I stopped short, surprised by his sudden appearance. "I didn't expect you to follow me."

His lips quirked up, a smile that didn't quite reach his eyes. "Well, you didn't exactly leave me with a choice, did you?"

I crossed my arms, taking a cautious step back. "I thought we agreed to—"

"I don't care what we agreed to," he interrupted, his tone sharp now. "I'm not letting you walk away from this, from us. Not like this."

There it was again, that familiar weight of his words pressing down on me, making me feel like a ship anchored too long in the storm. Part of me wanted to run, to flee into the safety of the night and the distance, but another part—one I hadn't acknowledged until now—wanted to stay and hear him out. I wasn't sure which side was winning, but I couldn't ignore the pull between us, even as I fought against it.

"Do you really think you can change my mind?" I said, the words sharper than I meant. "Do you think you can just walk in and—what? Fix this? Fix me?"

He shook his head slowly, his eyes never leaving mine. "I'm not here to fix anything. I'm here to make sure you don't do something you'll regret. Because, for all the things you think you want, for all the decisions you think you've made, you don't know what's waiting for you on the other side."

"I don't need you to tell me what I don't know." The words were bitter in my mouth, like I was swallowing glass. "I've made my choice."

"But you haven't, not really," he countered. "You're running. You're always running, hiding behind your decisions and your walls, but they're not enough anymore. I'm not enough, maybe, but don't pretend this is the answer."

His words hit me like a slap, sharp and jarring. I hadn't expected him to say that, and yet, there it was, hanging between us like a terrible truth. The walls I had built, the ones I'd relied on for so long to keep myself safe, were starting to crumble, piece by piece.

"I'm not running," I said, more to convince myself than him. "I'm moving on. Letting go."

"By doing what?" he asked, his voice soft now, as though the fight had left him. "By pretending we were never real?"

My breath hitched in my throat, and I looked away. "I can't do this anymore," I whispered, more to the wind than to him. "I can't live in the memory of what we were, always chasing something that doesn't exist."

There was a long silence, one that stretched between us, heavy and full of things we couldn't say. And then, in the quiet, I felt the air shift again. Something was wrong. I couldn't pinpoint what it was, but it felt like the earth had shifted beneath my feet, like we were both standing on the edge of something.

And then, without warning, I heard it. The low hum of an engine. The screech of tires. And before I could process it, the world around me exploded in noise, a blur of movement that left me gasping for air.

Something was happening. Something that would change everything.

And I wasn't sure if I was ready to face it.

Chapter 32: The World Without Him

The morning light crept slowly across the floor, stretching its golden fingers across the room as if reluctant to touch the cold hardwood beneath. I pulled the covers tighter around me, though I knew they wouldn't offer warmth—not today, not anymore. I had learned to live in the hollow spaces, where the air felt thinner and the silence louder. His absence was a constant companion, clinging to the edges of my thoughts like a faint, unshakable perfume. It had been two months since he left, but it still felt like yesterday.

I sat on the edge of the bed, staring at the clock on the nightstand. The ticking was louder now, somehow. I could feel it in my bones, a constant reminder that time was marching on, indifferent to the way my heart kept breaking in the quietest moments. The sun had risen early that morning, its rays slipping through the curtains, but it was still too early for me to want to face the day. I wasn't sure what I was waiting for—maybe I was hoping for a sign. Something that would tell me I wasn't alone in the way I felt. But the world outside seemed to spin just fine without me, and that irritated me more than I cared to admit.

I finally dragged myself up, the weight of the morning pressing on my chest like a lead blanket. I didn't bother with the mirror as I shuffled across the room to the window. It was easier not to look at myself—at the tired eyes, the pale skin, the way my hair had become an afterthought. He had always liked it when I let it fall loose around my shoulders, but now it felt like too much of an effort. The reflection staring back at me had grown unfamiliar, as though the person I had been before he left was a stranger.

I watched the garden below, the once perfectly manicured lawns now overgrown with weeds. Everything seemed to fall apart without him, even the things that had once thrived under my hands. The roses, which had once been his favorite, were now tangled with thorns, their petals faded and brittle. I reached for the glass of water on the windowsill, but my fingers hesitated just before I touched it. The same way my mind hesitated whenever a thought of him crept in.

I had never imagined a world without him. It was a concept I had dismissed as impossible, a cruel trick my heart refused to entertain. But here I was, walking through this strange version of life, a version that felt both familiar and foreign. The house was still grand, still impressive with its marble floors and antique furniture, but it felt like a shell—empty and hollow, its grandeur a mockery of the life we had built.

The coffee pot gurgled in the kitchen, the scent of freshly brewed coffee slipping under the door like an old friend. I made my way downstairs, each step a reminder of the routine that had carried on without him. The kitchen was as it always had been—well-worn, cozy, and full of memories that made the air thick with longing. I poured the coffee, the warmth of the mug a small comfort, and then I sank into the chair by the window, my eyes instinctively drifting toward the garden once more.

The housekeeper had taken the liberty of keeping the place in order, of course. There was always something to tidy, something to polish, but no amount of dusting could chase away the loneliness that clung to the walls. No matter how many cups of coffee I drank or how many times I adjusted the cushions on the couch, nothing would bring him back.

My fingers wrapped around the edge of the coffee cup, the ceramic smooth and cool against my skin. My thoughts wandered, as they always did. To the day he left. To the look in his eyes when he turned to walk out the door. It hadn't been anger or even sadness. It had been something else—a quiet resolve, as if he knew exactly what was happening, as if he had already made his peace with it.

I hadn't, though. I wasn't sure I ever would.

The morning was slipping away, the light changing, the shadows stretching across the floor as if they were coming to claim me. I forced myself to stand, the mug still warm in my hands, and walked over to the door. There was no plan, no grand gesture waiting for me outside. Just the world moving on without me, indifferent and endless. But for a moment, I allowed myself to wonder if there was still a chance, if the world could somehow be made whole again. A fleeting thought, really. A moment of weakness that passed as quickly as it had come.

I stepped outside into the garden, my footsteps muffled by the thick grass that had overtaken the paths. The air was cool, but it didn't soothe the heat that still lingered in my chest. I took a deep breath, willing myself to feel something other than this ache, but the silence only deepened the weight of my grief. I had thought that time would make it easier. That eventually, the hole he left in me would heal. But time, it seemed, only made the wound more complicated, more painful. It was like trying to put together a broken piece of glass—every attempt to fix it only left more jagged edges.

I closed my eyes, the faint rustling of the leaves the only sound in the stillness. If I listened closely enough, I could almost hear him. His laugh, his voice calling my name, the way his fingers had brushed against mine like a promise. But when I opened my eyes again, the garden was empty. And I was left standing in the quiet, alone with my thoughts.

The world outside carried on, its daily rhythms continuing as if I hadn't been left behind in the wreckage of what we had built. The newspaper was always on the doorstep by eight o'clock, the mail came at noon, and even the sun managed to rise with the same unyielding punctuality. Everything in the world moved forward, indifferent to the fact that inside, the clock seemed to be frozen in a moment that had never quite passed. I kept telling myself that eventually, I would start feeling like me again. Eventually, I would return to the life I had known before him, before us. But it didn't happen that way.

I found myself sitting more often than not, staring out the window, watching the cars that passed in the distance, the people who seemed so ordinary, so untouched by the strange curse I had found myself under. They had their lives—busy, full, and moving in directions that didn't feel like a dead-end road. They weren't stuck in the quiet ruins of a love that had both held and destroyed me.

He was everywhere, in ways I hadn't even expected. It wasn't just in the rooms where we had laughed or whispered secrets in the dark. No, it was the little things, the absurd ones, that came out of nowhere and hit me with the force of a wave. A sudden gust of wind would catch me by surprise, and I would almost swear I heard his voice behind me, just a murmur, just enough to make my heart stop before reality would come crashing in. Or the moment when I reached for the remote and his favorite show was on—something I had always avoided but now couldn't escape. It wasn't just reminders of him; it was the reminders of who I was when we were together. And I didn't like who I was becoming without him.

One morning, I found myself walking through the house without even thinking, my bare feet making quiet sounds against the floor as I moved toward the study. It was a room I hadn't been in much since he left. The desk was cluttered with papers I hadn't touched and books I hadn't read, their spines cracked, their pages curling from neglect. I ran my fingers across the wooden surface, tracing the lines of the desk as though I could pick up pieces of him in the dust. Maybe he had touched the papers like this, or maybe he had leaned on this very spot when he thought I wasn't looking. The idea made something cold stir in my chest.

The chair creaked under me as I sat, my fingers settling on the keyboard, half-tempted to type something—anything—to fill the silence. But I didn't. Instead, I found myself just staring at the screen, watching the cursor blink at me like a metronome, reminding me that time was still moving forward, no matter how much I wanted to stall it.

I sat there for hours, or maybe it was minutes, I didn't keep track. Eventually, I decided I was done pretending that I could fill my time with distractions. There was a life out there beyond the four walls of the mansion. A life I had forgotten how to live. And so, I pulled on a jacket, forced myself to leave the study, and headed out the door.

The air outside was crisp, the kind that clings to your skin and bites at your fingers. I inhaled deeply, trying to find something that resembled clarity. The grass crunched beneath my shoes, and I found myself walking without direction, as if my feet were leading me to answers that only the earth could provide. The estate stretched out behind me, its boundaries marked by overgrown hedges and a stone wall that had begun to crumble in places.

I wandered for what felt like hours, my mind a dull thrum of thoughts that refused to settle. I passed the old oak tree where we used to sit together, and for the briefest moment, I could see him again, his face framed by the branches, his eyes filled with something I couldn't quite decipher at the time but now understood as hope. We had talked there, about everything and nothing, like the world had no power to break us. But time, as it always does, had the last laugh.

The town was quieter than usual when I arrived. Most of the shops were closed, the streets empty except for a few cars that seemed to drift past in a haze. I didn't know why I had come here. Maybe because it felt like a place where life hadn't quite caught up with me, where the world hadn't turned into a place full of ghosts. I walked toward the small café on the corner, where we had spent lazy mornings, sipping coffee and pretending the world didn't exist beyond that little corner of the world.

The bell above the door jingled as I entered, and the barista behind the counter smiled at me, though it didn't quite reach his eyes. I couldn't blame him. People had started to avoid me, or at least, that's how it felt. They didn't say anything, of course. But I could see it in the way they looked away, in the way they hurried past me on the street. There was something about grief that made other people uncomfortable, as though it was contagious.

"Morning," I said, my voice sounding like it hadn't been used in days.

He nodded, the smile still in place. "The usual?"

"Yes, please." I took a seat by the window, trying to ignore the weight of the world outside. It was a stupid thing, coming here. A place where everything had once been so simple, so full of possibility. Now, it felt hollow. As though even the air had lost its warmth. The coffee arrived in front of me, its scent familiar, but not comforting. It was just another reminder of what had been, of how even the smallest of things could never remain the same once the world had shattered.

As I took a sip, I noticed a familiar face across the room. Someone I hadn't expected to see—someone who had been a part of the old world, a part of the life I was struggling to leave behind. For a moment, I wondered if it was an illusion, my mind playing tricks on me, but no. There she was. I hadn't seen her in years, not since before he left.

Her gaze met mine, and I saw the same questions in her eyes that I had been asking myself for months. What happened? How did we get here? Was it possible to go back, or were we both stuck in the wreckage of something we couldn't fix?

She smiled, that same knowing smile, and stood up to join me. The sound of her footsteps was louder than I expected.

She walked toward me, her steps deliberate, as though she were measuring each one against the weight of the years between us. I had known her long enough to see the subtle shift in her posture, the way her shoulders had squared a little more firmly, the sharpness in her eyes that hadn't been there before. Life had done something to her—something I wasn't sure I wanted to understand. But there she was, right in front of me, a ghost from the past that I wasn't sure I was ready to confront.

"Well, look who's still here," she said, her voice laced with something that could have been amusement, but it didn't quite reach her eyes.

I stood up slowly, the weight of her gaze pressing against me like the heat of the sun on a summer day. "I could say the same about you."

She raised an eyebrow, the familiar, mischievous glint flickering for just a moment. "I didn't expect you to be so... alone."

The words stung, but I kept my face neutral, my hands clenched tightly around the coffee cup. "People change. You know that."

She didn't reply right away, instead sitting down across from me. She ordered a coffee, the same as mine, the same as we had shared countless times before. A strange, almost nostalgic silence settled between us, thick and uncomfortable.

I hated that it was like this. I hated how time had slipped away from us, how it had molded us into these versions of ourselves that were familiar, but just out of reach. She hadn't seen me in months, not since everything had collapsed. And yet, she still looked the same in all the ways that mattered: sharp, confident, a woman who wasn't afraid to say whatever was on her mind. A woman who probably hadn't experienced the kind of soul-shattering loss that had left me hollow, constantly searching for pieces of myself in places that didn't exist anymore.

"So, what now?" Her tone was casual, but there was an edge to it—something that suggested she already knew what I would say, that she was waiting for me to offer her the answers to questions neither of us were ready to ask.

"I'm not sure," I replied, trying to keep my voice steady. "I'm just... living."

She leaned back in her chair, her eyes scanning the room with that look of someone who had seen too much, too fast. "Living. Right." She smiled a little, but it wasn't kind. "Is that what you call this?"

I met her gaze, the sting of her words lingering, but I couldn't let her see how deeply they had cut. "What do you want from me, Sarah?"

She shrugged, her fingers drumming on the table, the sound sharp and quick. "I want you to stop pretending. We both know you're not living, not really. Not since he left."

I could feel the walls in my chest tighten, a familiar ache rising in my throat. I hadn't expected her to be gentle with me, but her bluntness stung nonetheless. I opened my mouth to respond, but the words stuck, lodged in the space between my lungs and my tongue.

"Don't talk to me about pretending," I finally said, the words escaping with more force than I intended. "You're not exactly living either."

Her face hardened, the corners of her mouth turning down slightly. She didn't reply, but I could see it in her eyes—the recognition that I was right. She wasn't fooling anyone, least of all herself.

For a moment, the air between us thickened, the silence pulsing with tension. Then, as if trying to shake off the weight of the moment, she broke the stillness with a sharp laugh. It was humorless. A little bitter. "I came here for a reason, you know. It wasn't just to make small talk."

I raised an eyebrow, feeling the spark of curiosity flicker despite myself. "What reason?"

She leaned forward slightly, her voice dropping to a whisper. "You've been keeping something from me."

My heart skipped a beat, my pulse quickening as I leaned in, unable to stop myself. "What are you talking about?"

Sarah's eyes flicked to the side, her lips curling into something that was almost a smile but not quite. "You've been hiding it. I know you have. The truth about what really happened. About why he left."

I froze.

A sudden chill gripped me, spreading down my spine like a cold hand. For a moment, it was as if the world around us disappeared entirely. The clinking of cups, the murmur of voices, even the sunlight outside—all of it faded into nothing.

My voice was barely a whisper, the words slipping out like a secret I had buried too deep to remember. "You don't know what you're talking about."

Her gaze didn't waver. "Oh, I think I do. You think you've been clever, hiding behind your grief, your silence, but you're not fooling anyone. You've been running from the truth for months."

My chest tightened, the weight of her words pressing down on me, suffocating me. I had thought I could keep it buried, keep it hidden away where no one could reach it. But here she was, digging into the place I had locked away in the deepest corner of my mind.

I wanted to stand up, to walk away, but my body refused to move. It was as if I were frozen, trapped in a moment that had been building for far too long. The world outside, the quiet, ordinary world that had once been so easy to ignore, seemed to press in on me, forcing me to face something I had never wanted to admit.

The truth.

Sarah was still watching me, her eyes unwavering, and I could feel her pulling at the edges of the mask I had carefully constructed, one piece at a time. I could feel the weight of what I had done, what had happened, and for the first time since it all began, I wasn't sure I could hide from it any longer.

Just then, the door to the café swung open, a gust of wind blowing in, scattering napkins and rustling the curtains by the window. I barely noticed it at first. But when I did, my blood ran cold.

A man stood in the doorway. A man I never thought I would see again.

Chapter 33: The Return of the Watcher

I stood in the middle of my living room, staring at the man who shouldn't be here. My pulse hammered in my ears, and my hands trembled, clutching the coffee mug like it was the only thing anchoring me to this world. I could feel the old ache in my chest, that familiar pang, like a taut string pulled too tight. He was here. Again.

I had thought I'd buried it—buried him—under the weight of my days. Time had passed, after all. The calendar pages had turned like they always do, and in the quiet hum of life, I had convinced myself I was moving forward. It hadn't been easy, but I had managed. I'd filled my hours with work, with obligations, with the mundane chatter of daily life, and even with joy—genuine joy, too, which surprised me. Still, every so often, when the night stretched too long or the silence grew too thick, his absence felt like a slow and relentless tide pulling at my ankles, dragging me back into the deep.

But I had learned to swim in the shallows, to breathe without him, to exist in a world where he didn't.

And then he appeared in my doorway, as solid as he had been in life, as if he hadn't been gone a day.

His eyes—those eyes I had thought I would never see again—met mine, and everything in me stilled. They were the same: dark, fathomless, searching, like they could see right into the very marrow of my bones. But this time, there was something different in them. Something heavy. A weariness that hadn't been there before.

"I didn't expect to find you here," I said, my voice barely a whisper, as though speaking too loudly might shatter the fragile tension between us.

He didn't smile, not the way he used to. There was no teasing, no warmth in his gaze, just the cold weight of something unspeakable. "I didn't expect to be here either," he said, his voice low and rough, like it had been carved from stone.

I swallowed hard, unsure whether to step toward him or run in the opposite direction. Everything in me screamed to go, to turn my back on him and pretend that he wasn't standing there, a ghost made flesh. But my feet were rooted to the floor, and the more I tried to tear my gaze away, the more I found myself unable to.

"Why are you here?" My throat felt tight as I spoke, each word feeling like it might choke me.

His expression hardened, his jaw tightening, and I saw the familiar flicker of pain flash across his face before he masked it. "Because of you. Because you called me."

I blinked, unsure if I had heard him correctly. "I—what?"

"You called me." He repeated the words, each one falling from his lips like a stone sinking into a pool. "You've been calling me back. You, with your thoughts, your memories. Your love." He paused, his eyes darkening with something I couldn't place, something sharp and dangerous. "You don't understand, do you?"

I didn't understand. But the icy tendrils of fear were beginning to curl around my heart, squeezing tight. "What are you saying?"

"I'm saying," he said, his voice low, almost pained, "that you've pulled me back into this world. Your love—your desperate, foolish love—it's been calling to me, pulling me from the other side." He stepped closer, and I instinctively took a step back, only to find my heels brushing against the edge of the couch.

"You're—what? You're dead," I said, the words tasting like ash in my mouth. "You've been dead. I buried you. I..." I swallowed hard again. "You left me."

"I didn't leave you," he snapped, his voice rising with a raw edge. "You let me go. There's a difference."

The accusation in his tone made my heart constrict, but I wasn't sure which hurt more—the weight of his words or the truth I knew was buried somewhere deep inside me. Yes, I had let him go. I had buried him with the hope that maybe, just maybe, I could finally stop feeling like I was drowning in a sea of his absence.

But what he was telling me now—that my love had somehow reached across the boundary between life and death—was a truth that felt impossible to process. It was too much, too unreal. And yet, there he was, standing in front of me, as real as any man could be.

"You're wrong," I said, shaking my head as though I could somehow shake the truth out of the air. "I'm not calling you. I can't. You're not real."

He gave a bitter laugh, his eyes flicking to the space where I stood. "You think you can move on so easily, don't you?" His voice softened, and for a moment, there was a vulnerability there that caught me off guard. "But I'm bound to you. You've called me back, and if you don't sever the tie, if you don't let me go once and for all, I'll be stuck. I'll be trapped in this place between, never fully here, never fully gone."

I felt a chill sweep through me, colder than anything the winter winds could ever bring. "You're asking me to forget you?"

"I'm asking you to free me," he said, his voice strained. "If you don't, you'll destroy both of us."

I didn't know what to say, or even if I could say anything at all. The man I had loved, the man I had buried, was asking me to do the unthinkable. To sever the bond between us—not for me, but for him.

I looked at him, standing there in the dim light of my living room, and realized that I didn't know how to let go. Not of him, not of this.

I could feel the walls of my apartment closing in, as if the space had shrunk to accommodate the weight of the decision hanging between us. The flickering lamp above cast long, uncertain shadows across the room, making everything feel out of place—distorted, like we were trapped in some kind of half-dream. Maybe we were.

"What happens if I don't do it?" I asked, even though I already knew the answer. It wasn't a question to be answered. It was a last-ditch attempt to delay the inevitable.

He met my gaze, the intensity in his eyes almost unbearable. "If you don't let go, I will never move on. I'll be stuck here, forever caught between this world and the next. A shadow of what I was. A shadow of you."

The words hung in the air like a low hum, vibrating with the tension between us. I wanted to argue with him. I wanted to shout that I couldn't let him go, that this—this impossible situation—wasn't fair. But the truth was too raw, too painful. Somewhere, deep down, I knew he was right.

"I didn't ask for this," I muttered, my hands balling into fists at my sides. "I didn't ask for you to come back and—"

"And neither did I," he cut in, his voice sharper than I'd ever heard it before. "I didn't ask for any of this. But here we are."

There was a pause. A long, stretching silence where all the words we both wanted to say were too tangled up in our throats. He stepped closer to me, his eyes searching mine like he was looking for a crack in the armor I had carefully built around myself.

I wasn't sure if I was breathing.

"I don't know what you want from me," I said quietly, feeling suddenly small, vulnerable. "I've already let you go. I've buried you. I've kept living."

His lips pressed together into a thin line, his jaw working as if he were holding back something—something more than the sorrow that clung to him like a shroud.

"Then why is it so hard?" he whispered. "Why is it so hard to let go of me? Why is it so hard for you to move on?"

I swallowed, feeling a lump form in my throat. The truth was, it wasn't hard to let go of him. It had been hard to live without him. To fill the hollow where he used to be, to pretend I was whole when

I felt like a part of me was always missing. I had loved him, loved him in a way that had cracked something deep inside me. The love we shared wasn't something that faded. It wasn't something that could be erased.

And so, I had let it linger, unspoken, lingering in the corners of my mind, in the spaces where no one else could reach.

But it had never been enough, had it?

Not enough to keep him here, not enough to pull him back from the abyss.

I felt him shift, his presence closing in, filling up the room with the weight of what we were both avoiding.

"You don't have to do this," he said, his voice softer now. "But I can't keep existing like this. I'm not alive, and I'm not dead. I'm something... in between. And it's killing me."

I wanted to tell him that I understood. That I got it—that it was killing me, too. But somehow, the words got stuck.

"We were happy once," I said, my voice cracking. "You and me. We had something real."

"And you think this is real?" He gestured vaguely between us. "This... whatever this is? This is not real. This is not what we had."

I took a step back, his words like a slap to the face. "What are you trying to say? That it was all a lie? That none of it mattered?"

His eyes darkened with frustration, the lines of his face tightening as though he were forcing himself to say something that tore him apart. "No. What I'm saying is that it doesn't matter anymore. What mattered once—what was—is gone. And if we keep holding on to it, we'll both be lost."

The sting of his words stung more than I was willing to admit, but they were true. He was right. We were standing at the edge of something we couldn't undo, a choice that was too big to ignore. If I didn't let go, I would keep him tethered to this world, this place, this ghost of a life. I would keep him from ever moving on, from ever finding peace.

And if I did let go?

I had no idea what that would do to me.

The silence between us deepened, thickening with the weight of the decision I had to make. I glanced at him, his face still so familiar, so beloved, but now it was bruised with something darker, something I couldn't quite place.

"Tell me what to do," I said, my voice barely audible. "Tell me how to fix this."

He shook his head slowly. "I can't fix this for you. I can't make the decision for you."

I closed my eyes, pressing my fingers to my temples as though the pressure of it all could make it go away. The weight of his gaze, the heaviness of his presence, it was all too much. The love between us, the memories, the ghosts of what we once had—it was all pulling at me like a current I couldn't escape.

"You have to choose," he said softly. "You have to choose whether to let me go. To cut the tie, to sever the bond. If you don't, I'll be stuck in this half-life forever."

His words hit me like a shock to the chest, and I staggered back, suddenly unsure whether I could stand under the weight of this impossible choice. The love I had for him, the love I thought I had buried, was dragging me under. And I couldn't tell whether it was saving me or destroying me.

"Please..." I whispered, more to myself than to him. "Please, just let me think."

But he didn't answer. Instead, he just stood there, watching me with those dark eyes—waiting for me to make the decision. Waiting for me to choose whether to save him—or destroy us both.

I should have known better than to think I could outrun this moment. The choice, the heaviness of it, had always been lurking at the edge of my thoughts, a silent whisper in the back of my mind, telling me that the end would come in a way I couldn't predict, couldn't control. And now here it was, with him standing in front of me, his eyes full of that familiar longing. The very longing that had once kept me awake at night, burning with desire, now felt like a shackle. And I was the one holding the key.

The room had grown colder, and I could feel it creeping through the walls, curling around my skin like the ghost of winter itself. His presence was suffocating in the best and worst ways. I could see the struggle in his eyes, the tension that pulled at every line of his body, as if he were fighting a battle he didn't want to fight. But he was fighting it. And so was I.

"I can't do this," I said, the words coming out like an apology. "I don't know how to do this."

"Then don't," he said, his voice softer now, almost coaxing. "Don't do anything. Just let me go."

But the words felt like a betrayal. To let go of him would be to let go of everything we had shared—everything that had once felt so real, so right. The memories of us were as vivid as the day we had created them: the laughter, the warmth, the feeling of his hand in mine as we walked through the world, side by side. How could I throw that away? How could I possibly choose to sever it all for something that, deep down, felt so impossible to erase?

"I can't," I said, my voice breaking. "I can't choose. Not between you and everything we had."

He stepped forward, his hand outstretched, but it wasn't the reach for comfort I'd once known. It was something more desperate, more final, like he was trying to close the gap between us in one last attempt to make me see reason. His eyes held mine with an intensity I hadn't felt in years, and for a moment, I thought I might drown in them.

"You don't have to choose me," he said, his voice low. "You don't have to choose anything. Just let me go. It's the only way."

"But what if I'm not ready?" I asked, my throat tightening as the words escaped me. "What if I never am?"

"You don't have a choice, do you?" He laughed, but it wasn't a sound of joy. It was brittle, jagged, like a laugh that had been born from desperation. "You've been living with a ghost, haven't you? The ghost of what we were. You think you can keep holding on to it forever, but I'm telling you—it's killing me."

The words hit me like a physical blow. It wasn't that I didn't know the truth, but hearing him say it, seeing the torment in his face, made it all the more real. The bond between us had been a tether, a tie that had bound us together even after his death. I had thought it was something beautiful—something that defied the rules of life and death, something that proved that love was stronger than anything.

But now, as he stood before me, torn between the world of the living and the dead, I realized that I had been holding on to a beautiful lie. A lie that had kept him here, but had prevented him from truly living.

"I never wanted to hurt you," I whispered, the words slipping out before I could stop them. "I never wanted to keep you here. I thought... I thought if I loved you enough, you would be okay."

He shook his head, a faint smile flickering at the corners of his lips, though it didn't reach his eyes. "You've been loving me enough for both of us. But love can't save me now."

The words stung more than I was ready to admit. How could I have been so naive? How could I have believed that my love alone could save him, could fix something that wasn't broken, but was simply... gone?

But still, a part of me—an irrational, stubborn part of me—didn't want to let go. Didn't want to accept that what we had was just a memory now, something I could hold in my heart but never again in my arms.

"What happens to you if I do this?" I asked, the question trembling in my voice. I couldn't stop myself. I needed to know.

He exhaled slowly, his gaze softening. "I'll be free. Free to move on, to go wherever I need to go. And you?" His eyes flicked to mine. "You'll be free, too. You'll be free of the pain, the guilt, the endless wondering whether you could have done more. You'll be able to live again."

I wanted to believe him. God, I wanted to believe that this was the right thing to do, that I could finally close this chapter, lay down the weight that had been pulling me under for so long. But part of me was still too afraid.

"Then what happens to us?" I asked. "What happens to everything we had?"

His expression hardened, the distance between us growing. "We were good, once. But we can't go back, not now. Not like this."

"Then I'll never see you again?" My voice was barely a whisper, the thought of never hearing his voice, never feeling his touch, enough to crack something inside me. "This is it?"

"This is it," he said softly.

And then, before I could say another word, I felt it—a cold rush of air, like the breath of something unseen. Something more than just a chill from the open window, something deep and ancient and raw. The air seemed to thicken, the shadows creeping in from the corners of the room, and I could hear the faintest hum—a sound so soft it was almost imperceptible, like a vibration in the floorboards.

And then, just as quickly as it had begun, everything stopped.

The silence was deafening.

"Do you feel that?" I whispered, my heart racing as the hairs on the back of my neck stood up.

He looked at me, his face gone pale. "No. No, that's not—"

Before he could finish, the ground beneath our feet trembled. The room shifted, the walls bending and warping as if reality itself was cracking open.

And then—everything went black.

Chapter 34: The Severing of Love

The air around me hummed with an unsettling stillness, the kind of quiet that presses down on your chest, making it difficult to breathe, as though the world itself were holding its breath in anticipation. The moonlight filtered through the dense canopy above, casting pale, fractured light that danced in slow motion across the moss-covered stones. Each one seemed to sigh beneath my weight as I stepped forward, my bare feet sinking into the earth with a reluctant softness. A whisper of wind rustled the leaves, brushing against my skin like a forgotten touch, and for a moment, I thought it was him—his hand, perhaps, reaching for me one last time. But when I turned, there was nothing. Only the cold, empty space between us, now wider than any distance could ever account for.

"Are you sure?" The Watcher's voice broke through the silence, its rasp low and measured. He stood just out of reach, his shadow stretching far behind him, swallowed by the darkness that clung to the forest like a secret. His eyes—once so bright, filled with a hunger that mirrored my own—were now clouded, uncertain, as though even he, a creature of the night, could feel the weight of the moment.

"I'm sure," I whispered, my voice cracking under the pressure of the decision. The words tasted bitter, as though they didn't belong in my mouth, but they were true. The ritual had to be done. He had to be free.

I had promised him that I would never be the thing that held him back. That I would never be the anchor to his wings. But standing here now, with the ritual about to unfold, I wasn't so sure I could keep my promise.

The Watcher nodded, and his silhouette seemed to shimmer as the wind picked up again. There was something ancient about him, like the very earth he stood on had molded him into being, a creature carved from the same stone and rooted in the same soil.

His presence felt too old, too distant, as if he were of a time long gone, yet somehow still tethered to this world. The Watcher knew all too well what this ritual entailed. He had seen it before. He had witnessed the lives unravel and the hearts break. He had been the one to perform it, over and over again, with a detached efficiency that made my stomach churn.

"I'll guide you through it," he said, stepping forward with a quiet grace that was almost haunting. "It's not easy, but you must remember, you're doing this for him. For both of you."

For him. The thought sliced through my chest with the force of a blade, sharp and unforgiving.

The Watcher moved toward the center of the clearing, where the ritual circle had been carefully marked out with runes—symbols of binding, symbols of release. Their intricate curves and sharp edges glowed faintly in the moonlight, as though alive with some secret magic. I knew what they meant. I had studied them, understood them, but now, standing at the precipice of what would be the end of everything, they felt alien to me. My mind swirled with the weight of what I was about to do. How could I sever something that had been so deeply woven into the fabric of my being?

"You will feel it," the Watcher said, his voice softening as he caught the look of doubt on my face. "The severing. It will tear at you, but in the end, it will set you free."

The words echoed in my mind like the toll of a distant bell. Free. The irony stung. How could I feel free when I was about to lose the one thing that had kept me tethered to this world? The one thing that had made me feel whole.

I nodded, though I could feel my heart twist in my chest like a vine being yanked from the soil. The Watcher gestured for me to join him at the center of the circle, where the ground seemed to hum beneath our feet. The air felt charged, electric with the promise of change, of loss. I took a step forward, my body moving almost of its own accord, as though the ritual were not a choice at all, but an inevitability.

As I stood in the circle, the Watcher began to chant in a language I didn't understand. It was a low, guttural sound, like the earth itself had risen to speak. The words curled around me, slipping into my ears and tugging at my thoughts. There was no time to second guess. No time to turn back. The ritual had begun, and I was too far gone to stop it.

The space between us seemed to grow thinner, like the world itself was closing in. My mind, clouded with confusion and dread, began to quiet as the chanting grew louder, each word a call to something deep within me. And then, I felt it—a pull, sharp and sudden, as though an invisible thread had been tied around my chest and was being pulled taut. It was the bond—the last trace of him—that tethered us together. I could feel him, as though he were standing beside me, his warmth a ghost against my skin.

And then, in that fleeting moment, I understood. This wasn't just a ritual for him. It was for me, too. This severing wasn't just a cutting of cords between two people. It was the tearing apart of everything that had made me who I was, the destruction of the very thing that had defined my existence. The love we had shared—so bright, so fierce—was now being laid bare, ready to be sacrificed on the altar of freedom.

The ground beneath me shifted, and the sky above seemed to darken as if the heavens themselves were bearing witness to the act. The Watcher's chant rose to a crescendo, a final, unearthly note that rattled the bones and pulled the soul. I closed my eyes, bracing myself for the pain.

And then it came. A searing, unimaginable ache that tore through my chest like a jagged shard of glass. My breath hitched in my throat, and I staggered, my knees threatening to buckle beneath me. The bond—the thread—was snapping.

I opened my eyes. The Watcher was gone, and so was the forest. There was nothing but emptiness, stretching out before me like a vast, uncharted sea. And as the severing took its final, brutal toll, I understood that there would be no returning from this.

The pain was a living thing, crawling through my veins, unrelenting, biting at every inch of me until I thought I might splinter apart. But even then, I knew something worse was coming. The severing was not the end, not truly. No, it was merely the beginning of what I had to become without him, of what I had to endure in his absence. That sharp, searing tear through the fabric of my soul, the one that had left me gasping for breath, was nothing compared to the hollow space that yawned open in my chest. And still, I stood there, unable to move, unwilling to face the quiet void of a life without him.

The clearing had grown eerily still, too quiet in a way that was almost suffocating. The shadows had deepened, the trees looming like silent sentinels, their branches reaching like fingers—perhaps searching, perhaps waiting. I didn't know. I only knew that something was wrong. It wasn't the ritual. It wasn't the severing. It was the absence, the deep ache that felt like it was expanding with every passing second.

I wasn't sure how long I had stood there, motionless, staring at the spot where he had been, where I had last felt the heat of his presence. But when I finally turned, my legs shaky, my body heavy with the weight of what had just occurred, the clearing wasn't the same. The air was thick with an unsettling tension, and the shadows, once familiar, now seemed to stretch and twist unnaturally, curling in on themselves like something that no longer belonged.

And then I saw it.

In the distance, a figure stepped from the trees—tall, cloaked in darkness, their form indistinct but undeniable. I could feel them before I could see them clearly, the weight of their gaze pressing down on me, drawing me in despite every instinct that screamed for me to run. My breath caught in my throat. The air seemed to thicken further, the once peaceful sounds of the forest stilled in their tracks.

"What is this?" I whispered to myself, my voice trembling despite my attempts to keep it steady. Was this part of the ritual? Had I, in my desperate desire to be free, inadvertently invited something darker, something worse, into this already twisted world?

The figure drew closer, and with each step, the air seemed to grow colder, more suffocating, as though something—some presence—had slipped in between the spaces where the severing had left a void. I couldn't see their face, but I could feel their eyes—eyes that seemed to penetrate the very core of me, peeling back the layers of my thoughts with a sharpness that left me breathless.

"I see you," the figure said, their voice low, smooth, and unsettlingly familiar, though not in any way I could place. "I see what you've done."

I froze, my pulse hammering in my ears. I knew that voice, but where had I heard it before? It was like an echo from a dream, something that teased at the edges of memory but refused to solidify into anything more tangible. I wanted to step back, but my feet were rooted to the ground as if the earth itself were refusing to let me go.

"What do you want?" I managed to ask, the words barely leaving my lips, my throat tight.

The figure tilted their head slightly, their silhouette shifting as they stepped into a patch of moonlight. And then I saw it. Or rather, I saw them—a face that was too familiar to be a stranger and too foreign to be a comfort. The sharp angles of their jaw, the dark, knowing eyes, and the curve of their lips that twisted into a smile that sent a chill skittering down my spine.

"You didn't think it would be so simple, did you?" the figure said, a sharp edge to their words. "Did you really think severing the bond would rid you of me?"

And then, as if to answer my unspoken question, they lifted their hand, and the world around us seemed to shudder. I could feel the earth tremble beneath my feet, the trees groaning in protest, the very air thickening as though it had turned to something solid. The figure's smile deepened, their eyes gleaming with a cold, knowing light. I didn't know who or what they were, but I felt their presence like a tightening noose around my chest.

"Don't you remember?" they asked, their voice like the hiss of a whisper in a forgotten dream. "You didn't just sever the bond between you and him. You severed everything. And now—now you've left a hole that's begging to be filled."

My mind reeled. I had severed the bond. I had let go. That was supposed to be the end of it. The ritual had been clean, efficient, final. But this—this... this wasn't what I had expected.

"Who are you?" I breathed, but the words felt inadequate, too small for the storm brewing in my chest.

The figure took another step forward, the shadows around them seeming to cling to their form like a second skin. "You'll learn soon enough. But for now, let's just say I am what happens when you forget who you are."

The words stung, too real and too close to home. I didn't know if I was more afraid of what the figure was or what they knew about me. There was something about their gaze, something about the way they seemed to understand me in a way no one had ever before, that unsettled me in a way I couldn't articulate.

But then, the earth shifted again, and the clearing seemed to warp around me. The shadows deepened, pulling at me like quicksand, dragging me into a void I wasn't ready to face. And then, before I could react, before I could even gather my wits to fight, the figure reached out, their hand hovering inches from my skin.

"You think you're free?" they asked, their voice dripping with venom. "You've only just begun to understand what it means to be trapped."

The figure's hand hovered just above my skin, and I could feel the tension crackling in the air, thick enough to cut through with a blade. My chest tightened, my breath quickening as the shadows around me deepened. The space between us felt like a chasm, a divide far more significant than any physical distance could convey. The ground seemed to pull away from me, as though the earth itself were trying to reclaim me, drag me back into the dark.

I stared at the figure's outstretched hand, a part of me longing to reach for it, to understand what they wanted, but another part of me—larger, stronger—was rooted in place, unwilling to give in. I didn't know who they were, didn't understand what they represented, but I knew I didn't want to find out.

"You have no idea what you've done," they said, the words dripping like honey, sweet and deadly all at once. "You think the severing was the end? That cutting the bond would release you from everything, from the past, from the ties that bind you? How quaint." Their smile widened, a predatory gleam lighting their eyes. "You've opened the door to something far more dangerous."

I shook my head, unwilling to listen, unwilling to acknowledge the terrifying possibility that they might be right. I had done everything the Watcher had told me to do. I had sacrificed everything for him—my heart, my love, my very soul. And yet here I was, staring at this... this thing—this entity that shouldn't have existed.

"What do you want from me?" I managed to rasp, my voice shaky, as if the mere act of speaking might unravel the last thread of my sanity.

"Oh, nothing, darling," the figure purred, taking a step closer. The darkness around them seemed to bleed, leaking into the edges of my vision. "I already have everything I need." They waved a hand dismissively, as if the world itself were nothing more than a passing inconvenience. "What you've done, what you've unleashed—it's already too late. You will understand. You'll have no choice."

I opened my mouth to protest, to demand what exactly that was supposed to mean, but the words caught in my throat as the air around us thickened, suddenly damp, suffocating. I couldn't breathe. My vision blurred as the darkness seemed to spill from the trees, creeping toward me like an insidious fog. The figure's silhouette was the only thing clear in the nightmare unfolding, their eyes never leaving mine, their smile widening with every breath I took, each inhale a mistake, each exhale a misstep.

And then the ground beneath my feet gave way.

I stumbled, catching myself just in time, my hands scraping across the damp earth. But I didn't have time to recover. The darkness surged forward, surrounding me, swallowing up everything. I could no longer see the figure, no longer hear their mocking laughter. All I could hear was the sound of my own heartbeat pounding in my ears as I tried to stand. The earth groaned beneath me, the trees creaking in a way that was unnatural, like they were alive with something other than nature.

Something was wrong. Something far beyond what I had imagined.

I pushed against the oppressive weight of the darkness, trying to steady myself, but it felt as though I was wading through water, each movement sluggish and futile. I could barely see now, the world reduced to vague shapes and shadows. My mind screamed for clarity, for direction, for anything that would make sense of this madness.

The silence returned then, heavy and thick, broken only by the sound of my ragged breathing. But it was different this time. It wasn't the peaceful quiet of the forest, the kind that made you feel at one with nature. No, this silence was suffocating, an absence of everything that should have been. I couldn't sense the wind, couldn't hear the rustle of leaves or the distant call of night creatures. There was only an overwhelming, crushing stillness.

And then, a whisper. Barely audible at first, as if it were a trick of my mind, a figment born of the growing panic gnawing at me. But it grew louder, sharper, until it was unmistakable.

"You cannot escape."

I froze, the words lancing through the air like a blade, piercing the suffocating quiet. The voice was his. My heart skipped a beat, and I spun around, eyes wide with disbelief.

"No." I shook my head violently. The ritual had been clear. The severing had been a sacrifice for him to be free. He couldn't be here. He couldn't—he shouldn't—still have a hold on me.

But as I turned in circles, trying to make sense of the disorienting shift in reality, I saw it—him. Him. His figure was outlined against the thickening darkness, his expression unreadable, his form more shadow than substance, but unmistakable. My heart thudded painfully in my chest.

"No..." I whispered, my voice cracking. "You—You can't be here. I—I let you go."

His eyes, glowing faintly in the near-total blackness, met mine. And for the briefest moment, I thought I saw something flicker there—a hint of sorrow. But it was gone before I could fully grasp it.

"I never left," he said, his voice soft but full of an emotion that made my skin crawl. "Not really."

The words sank into me, twisting like thorns, digging deeper, as though each syllable carried with it the weight of a thousand promises broken, a thousand moments wasted.

"How?" I gasped, stepping back, the edges of reality trembling around me. "How is this possible?"

He didn't answer. Instead, he reached for me, his hand emerging from the shadows like a thing alive, a tendril of darkness that curled toward me with terrifying speed.

"Because," he said, and his voice was no longer just his own. It shifted, like the very essence of him had fractured. "You never truly let me go."

I backed away, but the world around me twisted, and the shadows closed in tighter. There was no escape. Not now. Not ever.

And then, before I could understand what was happening, his fingers brushed my skin. The moment they touched me, the ground beneath me crumbled entirely. And I fell.

Into darkness.

Chapter 35: The Dream of Forever

The air around me was thick with the scent of fresh rain, the kind that clings to everything it touches, transforming even the most ordinary objects into something exquisite. I stood in the middle of the street, the darkened sky above me heavy with the promise of another storm. The cobblestones beneath my feet were slick, catching the glint of the streetlamps as they flickered and hummed in the distance. There was something about the night, something that pulled me forward even though I knew I shouldn't be here. I shouldn't be anywhere anymore, and yet—here I was.

A soft laugh escaped me, surprising me as it broke the silence. What was I doing? What was I supposed to be doing? The answers had never been clear. Not when we first met, not when we stumbled through the maze of emotions and compromises, not even now, when he had become more of a memory than anything else.

I pulled my jacket tighter around me, but it did nothing to stave off the chill crawling into my bones. The rain had begun, light at first, like a whisper. I hadn't expected it to arrive so soon, but it didn't matter. It had a way of erasing everything, washing away the past until there was nothing left but the present. And right now, the present felt as empty as my own heart.

The sound of footsteps echoed from behind me, soft and steady. I didn't turn. I knew who it was before I even had to check. You could say I had gotten used to this, to the way he always managed to show up at the most inconvenient moments, the way his presence was always just a breath away.

"You know," he said, voice low and warm, laced with that familiar wry humor, "you're not supposed to be out here. You promised."

I could almost feel the smirk that tugged at the corners of his mouth. There was something about him, something that kept pulling me back, even when I knew I should let go.

"I didn't promise anything," I replied, my voice steadier than I felt. "You know how I feel about promises."

His laugh came, soft and understanding, like we were two people who knew each other in ways that didn't need explaining. He was standing right behind me now, so close I could almost feel the warmth of his body, even though I didn't turn. I never turned. Not anymore.

"Then what are you doing here?" he asked, and there was a tenderness in his voice that didn't belong in this moment. It wasn't something I was ready to face.

"I'm trying to make sense of it," I said, the words spilling out before I could stop them. "Trying to figure out if this is it. If we're it. If... if I'm done." The last word came out in a whisper, barely audible, lost in the quiet hum of the world around us.

He didn't respond right away. For a moment, I thought he might just leave me here, standing alone in the rain, but of course, he didn't. He never did. Not really.

He stepped closer, so close I could feel the pressure of his presence without ever needing to look at him. "You're not done," he said, his voice firm but gentle. "You're still here, aren't you?"

I didn't have a response for that. Because I was still here. I always had been, in some way or another, stuck in this place between what I wanted and what I couldn't have. Between what he had promised me and what I could never seem to believe.

"What if I don't know how to do this anymore?" I said, my voice breaking on the words. "What if I've forgotten how to be the person I used to be?"

He didn't move, didn't even breathe for a moment. Then, slowly, he reached out, his hand grazing my shoulder in a touch so light I almost thought it was just the rain playing tricks on me. "You never had to be that person," he said, the words simple, but they rang in my chest like the sound of an old, familiar song. "You just had to be you. That's all I've ever wanted."

The tears came then, unbidden, like a flood that I hadn't expected to break free. I didn't want to cry, didn't want to feel anything, but there they were—streaking down my face in the rain. He didn't say anything. Didn't try to comfort me, didn't try to fix anything. He just stood there, silent and steady, like he had always been.

"I don't know how to say goodbye," I whispered, the words barely hanging on. "Not to you. Not to us."

"You don't have to," he said softly, finally stepping forward so I could feel the warmth of his presence envelop me, even though I didn't turn. "Not yet. Not if you're not ready."

And in that moment, something shifted, something I didn't have the words for. The world felt different, lighter somehow, even though the rain fell harder. The promise of goodbye hung between us, but it wasn't as heavy as it had been before. It was just another part of the journey, just another chapter that we hadn't written yet.

The rain continued to fall, but I wasn't alone anymore. And for the first time in weeks, I didn't feel the cold creeping into my bones. I felt something else. Something warm. Something that might, just might, be the start of something new.

The days blurred together in a haze of muted light and soft rain, each one passing with the same weightlessness as the last. The world outside my window seemed to exist in a kind of suspended animation, where the sound of the world was muffled, the colors faded, and everything seemed slightly unreal. I woke every morning with the same knot in my stomach, an old habit I couldn't shake, but also with a quiet certainty that the dreams were not a mere escape.

They were something more. They were a map, a breadcrumb trail, leading me somewhere I had yet to understand.

I made coffee every morning, the kind of coffee that had no pretense. No fancy milk or sugar, just black and strong, the kind of drink that kept me tethered to the present. It was the small rituals like this that kept my feet on the ground, even when everything else felt like it was slipping away. I sat by the window, watching the drizzle fall in thin, gentle streams, listening to the rhythmic tapping against the glass. It was in these quiet moments that I could almost feel him beside me again. It was fleeting, but it was real.

I never told anyone about the dreams. Not even my closest friends, not even my mother. They wouldn't understand. They couldn't. How could anyone who had never lived through something like this understand what it was like to lose someone and then, against all odds, have them come back to you in fragments, in fleeting moments, like a shadow dancing just beyond reach?

But there was something else, something I hadn't told anyone. Something I was only just beginning to realize. He wasn't just visiting me in my dreams. He was there when I wasn't asleep, too. A fleeting glance out of the corner of my eye, a soft touch I could almost feel on my shoulder, the whisper of a voice when the world was silent. It was as if he had become part of the air I breathed, like he was everywhere and nowhere all at once.

I couldn't explain it. I didn't even want to try. I just let it happen. I let myself believe that maybe, just maybe, this was how it was supposed to be. That we were still connected, even if the distance between us had grown so vast it seemed impossible to bridge. There were days, though, when I wondered if the connection was real, or if it was my mind playing tricks on me, trying to hold onto something that wasn't there anymore.

But then, one evening, something shifted.

It was late, and the air was thick with the scent of damp earth and the sharp tang of wet pavement. I was sitting on the couch, a book open on my lap, though I hadn't read a word in over an hour. I was listening to the sounds of the world outside—the creaking of the house settling, the distant hum of a car passing by—and trying to quiet the racing thoughts in my head when I felt it. A shift. A presence. It was subtle at first, barely noticeable, like the hairs on the back of my neck standing at attention.

I looked up from my book, and there he was.

Not as a ghost or a figment of my imagination, but there, in the doorway. His figure was bathed in the soft glow of the hallway light, his silhouette familiar and comforting, though just a little too unreal. His face was shadowed, but his eyes... I could see his eyes. And they were the same, though different, like they held the weight of everything we had gone through, everything we had been.

"Are you real?" The question escaped my lips before I could stop it, a soft whisper, barely a sound.

He didn't answer right away. Instead, he took a step closer, the floorboards creaking under his weight, and I held my breath, as though if I exhaled, he might disappear. But he didn't. He stood there, as solid as the wall behind him, watching me with a gaze that was both comforting and heartbreaking all at once.

"I think I am," he said finally, his voice as familiar as the sound of rain on a windowpane, as if we had never been apart. "But maybe it's up to you to decide."

I shook my head, feeling the sting of tears prick at the corners of my eyes. I hadn't cried in weeks, but now, in this moment, it felt like I was being undone all over again. "I don't understand," I whispered. "How can you be here?"

His lips quirked into that half-smile that always made my heart do strange things. "Maybe I'm not. Maybe I'm just a memory. Or maybe I'm something else entirely. Something that doesn't belong to time or space."

I wanted to argue, to demand answers, but the words wouldn't come. Instead, I stood up slowly, my legs unsteady, and took a step toward him, as if drawn by some invisible force I couldn't resist. He didn't move, didn't reach for me, but his gaze never wavered, and in that moment, I knew—deep down—I had always known.

"You shouldn't be here," I said softly, my voice trembling. "You've... you've moved on. I should, too."

"I never left," he replied, his voice a gentle comfort against the turmoil inside me. "I was just waiting. Waiting for you to be ready."

And just like that, I understood. This wasn't about goodbye. This was about the space between us, the silence that had stretched too thin. This was about the moments we had shared and the ones we hadn't yet lived. He hadn't moved on, not really. And neither had I. Not completely. We were still tangled up in each other, our souls bound by something deeper than time.

In that quiet moment, standing in the glow of the hallway light, everything that had felt broken and impossible suddenly made sense.

I stood frozen, as if caught in some delicate web spun from the very air between us. His words hung there, lingering in the quiet, softer than I could manage, but undeniably real. The world outside felt suspended, as though it too had caught its breath, waiting for something I wasn't entirely ready to face. The faint hum of the streetlight outside, the smell of the rain-soaked earth, the stillness—everything held its weight, pressing down on me, keeping me from fleeing the one place I'd sworn never to return.

"You don't belong here," I said again, the words tasting more fragile each time I uttered them. My feet didn't want to move, didn't want to take the next step, but my heart? My heart, as it had always done, refused to listen to reason. It was pulling me toward him, a quiet urgency that couldn't be denied.

His eyes softened, a faint glimmer in their depths. "I never left, not really. Not from you."

I didn't want to believe him. I didn't want to let myself fall back into this place, into this madness that had once consumed me. It wasn't fair. It wasn't fair to either of us, was it? I had spent months convincing myself that I had let go, that I had said my goodbyes, that I had closed the door, locked it, and thrown away the key.

But here he was. Standing in front of me.

He took a step forward, his presence filling the small room, closing the distance between us with quiet, inexorable certainty. The air shifted around him, like the weight of the past finally catching up to us, and for a second, I wasn't sure which way to turn, which direction to face. I opened my mouth to speak, but the words wouldn't come.

"You can't still be here," I managed finally, the words slipping through like a painful admission. "It's impossible."

He smiled then, that crooked, half-smile that had once made me weak in the knees, and it tore at something deep inside me. "Impossible is a funny word, don't you think? Especially when it's used for things that feel too real to be true."

I wanted to argue with him. I wanted to shout at him that he was a ghost, a figment of my overworked imagination, a cruel trick my mind had decided to play on me. But when I reached for those words, they evaporated, leaving behind only the ache, only the overwhelming truth of his presence.

"What are you, then?" I asked, the question slipping out as quietly as the rain that continued to fall outside. "If you're not a memory or a ghost, what are you?"

He didn't respond immediately, his gaze growing thoughtful, almost distant, as if he were searching for the right answer in a sea of unspoken things. When his eyes met mine again, there was something in them—something I couldn't place, but it sent a chill down my spine.

"I don't know. I don't know what I am anymore," he said softly, his voice tinged with something that sounded almost like regret. "I've never been sure of anything, not really. But I do know this... I'm here. And I think I always will be, in some way."

I took a step back, shaking my head, a lump rising in my throat that I couldn't swallow down. "No. That's not... That's not what I meant."

"You mean you don't want to hear it," he countered, his tone gentle, teasing, and yet cutting all the same. "You want me to go. To disappear again, just like before."

I opened my mouth to argue, but the words were too thick, too tangled to escape. I couldn't bring myself to say it out loud. Couldn't admit that part of me—the part that I had tried so desperately to bury—wanted him here, wanted him with me. I didn't know how to live in a world where he wasn't a part of it, but I also didn't know how to keep him here without unraveling everything I had fought to rebuild.

"You're wrong," I said finally, my voice barely above a whisper. "I don't want you to go. I don't know what I want."

For a long moment, he said nothing, simply watched me with that calm, steady gaze of his, as if waiting for me to come to terms with something he already knew. I could feel the weight of his gaze as it settled on me, felt it like a hand on my chest, pressing gently, but insistently, at the very core of me.

"I don't want to leave," he said quietly. "But I won't stay if you're not ready."

"Ready for what?" I shot back, the words sharper than I intended, a tremor of frustration breaking through. "What am I supposed to be ready for? For you to be here, and for me to keep pretending that none of this is... is wrong?"

He stepped forward again, closing the gap that remained between us. His hand, warm and familiar, brushed against my arm, and I froze, my breath hitching in my chest.

"I'm not asking you to pretend. I'm asking you to feel. To trust that what we had... what we still have..." He paused, his gaze catching mine with an intensity that almost made me flinch. "It doesn't end just because you think it does."

The words hung in the air like a promise, but I wasn't sure I could believe in it anymore. How could I? How could I trust anything when my whole world had been turned upside down and inside out in the blink of an eye?

"I can't keep doing this," I said, the words tumbling out before I could stop them. "I can't keep waiting for something that's never going to happen."

But then, just as I turned to walk away, I heard it—the soft click of the door behind me. The one that had been locked, the one I hadn't touched in days. And when I turned back, I saw it. Or rather, him. Standing there in the doorway.

"Then maybe you don't have to."

Chapter 36: The Whisper of the Wind

It was the oddest thing, how the wind would whisper his name when I least expected it. I'd be walking down the street, lost in my thoughts, when I'd feel it—a sudden, cool breeze tugging at the edges of my jacket, like the hand of someone unseen. And there it would be, that familiar shiver at the back of my neck, like his voice calling out to me. I'd pause, listening, half-expecting to hear him step up behind me, the scent of his cologne faint in the air. But there was only the soft rustling of leaves in the trees, a peaceful, gentle sound. Almost like the wind was smiling at me, sharing an old secret that only I could understand.

I wasn't sure when I'd started seeing him in everything—the glint of the afternoon sun as it kissed the top of a mountain, the ripple of water in a stream, the way the city lights blinked in the distance, as if they too were holding a vigil for him. At first, I'd dismissed it as nothing more than memories sneaking in, clinging to the edges of my thoughts. But after a while, I began to wonder if it was more than that. Maybe there was something... else. Something beyond what I could explain with mere logic.

Some people called it coincidence. Others called it fate. I called it him. He wasn't gone, not completely. Not in the way people think of loss, like a shadow slipping away from the light. No, he was with me still. In the quiet moments, when I found myself grinning for no reason, when I was lost in the middle of a thought and felt a sudden warmth, it was as if he were right there beside me, laughing or just listening in that way he used to.

The apartment was quieter now, a little emptier. I'd rearranged the furniture, hoping that might shake things up, make me feel less... heavy with memories. But I knew it didn't matter. Nothing ever really changes in a home, not when the most important parts of it live inside you. And as much as I tried to pretend I wasn't listening for his footsteps on the stairs, I was. It didn't matter that he wasn't coming back, I was always waiting for the knock on the door or the sound of his voice, light and teasing, asking if I was ready for our next adventure. We'd made a thousand plans, dreams that would never see the light of day. Or so I thought.

I spent a lot of time in the café near the corner, the one where the barista knows my order without having to ask. It was a place I frequented when I needed to disappear, to blend in with the quiet clatter of dishes and the hum of conversation. The people there never questioned the faraway look in my eyes. They didn't know the half of it. If I could have explained it, I would have. But how do you describe a love so profound it seems to swallow you whole, only to leave you with the sensation that you're always searching for something just out of reach? How do you explain that the void you thought would swallow you up has instead left behind a space filled with echoes and remnants of what was?

I ran into him at the café one afternoon. Not him, of course, but someone who felt like him. I didn't believe in signs, not really, but when the man behind the counter called out, "Jenna? Your coffee's ready," and I turned to find him standing there—tall, broad-shouldered, with the kind of smile that was so much like his it caught me off guard—I almost didn't know how to react. I was frozen for a moment, my hand still halfway to the counter, my breath caught in my throat.

His eyes were different, though. They weren't his. But something about the way he looked at me, with that same sense of recognition, that flicker of something... too familiar, it made my heart stutter.

"I think you dropped this," he said, and I glanced down to find a napkin in his hand, a folded corner peeking out from under his fingers. The world seemed to pause as I reached for it, my fingertips grazing his. For the briefest of moments, the space between us felt like nothing. Like I could close my eyes, reach out, and find myself right back in that place with him—before everything changed.

But then, the moment passed. I pulled my hand away, taking the napkin, and forced a smile. "Thanks," I managed, my voice coming out a little too soft, a little too uncertain.

He smiled back, a small, knowing smile that hinted at something I couldn't place. "It's no trouble. Have a good day, Jenna."

I nodded, backing away from the counter with a strange weight in my chest. What had just happened? Was I imagining things, or had he really just felt like him, in a way I couldn't shake? It wasn't his face or his voice, but something in the air around him—something I couldn't quite put my finger on. It lingered as I sat back down at my table, absently stirring my coffee and wondering if the universe was playing tricks on me.

But then, I had to laugh at myself. It was absurd, really. How could I possibly be searching for echoes in a room full of strangers? Still, I couldn't help but feel a spark of something—something that reminded me of the way it had been, and made me wonder if maybe, just maybe, the whispers of the past were more than just memories trying to hold on.

It started as a dull ache in my chest, the kind you try to ignore while going through the motions of a normal day. But then it bloomed, unexpectedly, when I found myself standing in front of the old bookstore on Maple Street, its windows cracked just enough to let the musty scent of old paper escape. I had not intended to come here, but somehow, my feet had carried me this way, as though there was some invisible tether pulling me toward it. It was a place I had once visited with him, just to wander through the aisles, exchanging thoughts on the stories in the books like they were our own secret language.

The bell above the door jingled as I stepped inside, and the familiar creak of the wooden floorboards beneath my boots seemed to whisper his name again. The air was thick with the scent of leather-bound novels, dust, and the faint trace of espresso from the small coffee cart in the corner. For a moment, I thought I might hear his voice too—low, teasing, asking if I was going to get lost in the pages of yet another book. But there was only silence, heavy and unyielding, as though the walls themselves held their breath, waiting.

I wandered deeper into the store, the dim light casting shadows along the rows of bookshelves. My fingers brushed against the spines as I passed, each one a memory of our time together—books we'd both loved, debated, and argued over until late into the night. But now, standing there, surrounded by their quiet, dusty presence, it was almost unbearable. I had made peace with the fact that he was gone, or at least I had tried to. But every corner, every familiar crevice of our shared spaces held pieces of him that I wasn't sure how to leave behind.

At the back of the store, near the corner where the cozy armchair used to be, I paused. It was empty now, just a vacant space, though I could still picture it clearly. His long legs stretched out, a book in his hand, his glasses perched on the edge of his nose as he read with that intense concentration that always amused me. He had loved being surrounded by books, like it was a safe cocoon, but the funny thing was, he never actually finished anything. He would get halfway through a book and then put it down, often with no intention of picking it back up again. I used to tease him about it, but now... now, it was as if I couldn't finish the story, either.

I shook my head, trying to shake the fog of memories that threatened to pull me under. As I turned to leave, my eyes caught a slim volume tucked away on the shelf, half-hidden behind a stack of novels. The spine was faded, the edges worn, but something about it stopped me. It wasn't a book I recognized, not one we'd ever talked about. But something about it felt... familiar. Almost like a secret, like it had been waiting for me.

I picked it up without thinking, feeling the cool leather against my skin as I flipped through the yellowed pages. A note, tucked inside, fluttered to the floor. Kneeling, I reached for it, unfolding the piece of paper carefully. The handwriting was sharp, precise, and—strangely—his.

"I'll always be with you," it said, a message that stopped my heart for a beat, as though his voice had echoed from the past, threading through time to find me. My fingers trembled as I read it again, but this time, I felt a prickling sensation on the back of my neck. The sensation of being watched.

I stood up too quickly, clutching the book in my hands, trying to shake the feeling of being caught in a moment I couldn't understand. And then I heard it—soft, low, almost like a whisper on the wind—"Jenna."

I spun around, my breath caught in my throat. But there was no one there. The store was empty, just the musty shelves, the heavy air, and the echo of my own footsteps. I waited, listening for anything else, but all I could hear was the soft rustling of the pages in my hands.

Maybe I was losing my mind. It wouldn't have been the first time. I was so used to him being a presence in my thoughts, lingering in the corners of my mind, that it almost seemed natural for him to show up again, to leave me little signs like this. But I wasn't sure how to interpret it. Was it just the grief, making me see things that weren't there? Or was it something more?

I tried to calm my racing pulse, tucking the book under my arm and walking to the door. The bell jingled again as I stepped outside, the cool breeze of the evening hitting my face. It was almost as if the air had shifted, turning colder, more insistent. The wind caught at my hair, tugging it across my face, and as I pushed it back, I thought I heard a voice again. Faint, soft... but unmistakable.

"Jenna."

My heart lurched, and I froze, standing on the threshold of the bookstore, my eyes darting around the empty street. But there was no one. Only the whisper of the wind, playing with the leaves that had gathered by the curb, swirling them around in a dance of their own.

It wasn't possible, was it? Could it really be him? The thought clung to me like a veil, and for the first time in what felt like forever, I didn't want to leave. I didn't want to walk away from the place where, even in his absence, it felt like he was still here.

I took a deep breath, glancing back at the bookstore. The windows stared back at me, dark and empty, as if to remind me that there were no more answers to be found here. Or maybe there were. Maybe I had to start listening more carefully.

The next few days passed in a haze, like a dream I couldn't quite wake up from. I kept trying to convince myself that I had imagined it—the whispers, the sudden jolt of recognition in that bookstore. The problem was, I knew better. It wasn't like the random flicker of a thought or a passing memory. It was something else, something that refused to stay locked in the past, no matter how much I wanted to move on.

I thought about it every time I stepped outside, every time the wind tugged at my hair or the trees swayed just a little too purposefully. It was like there was something, some thread, weaving through the air around me. I could feel it, but I couldn't hold onto it long enough to understand it.

That night, I stood at the window of my apartment, watching the city below. The lights twinkled like distant stars, too far away to touch, yet close enough that I could imagine reaching out and grabbing one. It felt like a metaphor for the way I had been living—always reaching for something that seemed just beyond my grasp.

The phone rang, breaking my reverie. I glanced at the screen, frowning when I saw the unfamiliar number. But the moment I picked up, something in the tone of the voice on the other end made my stomach flip.

"Jenna? It's Ryan," the voice said. The words hit me like a jolt of electricity, and for a second, I didn't know how to respond. Ryan was someone I hadn't spoken to in months. He had been one of his closest friends, someone who knew us both. I hadn't seen him since the funeral, since everything had shattered into pieces.

"I didn't mean to—uh, surprise you," Ryan stammered. "But there's something I think you should know."

I waited, feeling my pulse quicken, my breath shallow. I wanted to hang up, but I couldn't bring myself to. My mind was racing, and I was suddenly acutely aware of every breath, every sound.

"Jenna, I know this is going to sound crazy, but I think you need to see something. It's about him. About... what happened."

I froze, the phone growing heavy in my hand. "What are you talking about?" My voice was barely above a whisper, though I couldn't have explained why I was so terrified.

"Just... trust me. I'll text you the address. Please come, it's important."

And then the line went dead, leaving me staring at the phone like it might sprout wings and fly away. I blinked, shaking my head in disbelief. What could possibly be important enough for him to track me down after all this time? Was it possible he had some kind of information? Something I didn't know, something that might explain the... strange feelings I'd been having? The whispers? The sudden flashes of him?

I couldn't ignore it. I didn't know what I was walking into, but I couldn't turn away from it either. I grabbed my coat and headed out, trying not to let my mind run wild with the possibilities.

Ryan's place was on the outskirts of the city, in a quieter, older neighborhood that I had only ever driven through on my way to somewhere else. The houses here were smaller, tucked into cozy corners, as if time had forgotten them. I pulled up in front of a house that looked more like a fortress than a home—tall, looming, with iron gates surrounding the yard. My heart skipped when I saw the lights in the window flicker. Not a normal kind of flicker. The kind that made my breath catch.

I rang the doorbell, and Ryan answered almost immediately. His face was pale, his eyes wide, like he hadn't been sleeping. There was something frantic about the way he looked at me, as though he had been expecting this moment for a long time and wasn't sure what to do with it once it finally came.

"Come in," he said, stepping aside to let me through. I hesitated, glancing back toward the street as if expecting to see something—or someone—lurking in the shadows. But there was nothing, just the quiet hum of the night around me.

Inside, the house was eerily silent. The walls were covered in framed photographs, some faded and yellowed with age, others sharp and clear. Most of them were of him, of the moments we had shared. I glanced at them, feeling a pang in my chest as memories—unwelcome, uninvited—flooded back.

"Why are we here, Ryan?" I asked, trying to keep my voice steady, though I could feel the tension in my throat.

Ryan swallowed hard, his gaze darting around the room like he wasn't sure where to start. "I know this sounds crazy, but... you're not going to believe this. I didn't want to tell you before, but now... I have to. You need to hear it."

He reached for a thick folder on the coffee table, one I hadn't noticed before. It was heavy, the kind of folder that would hold secrets—old letters, hidden notes, something that could change everything.

I sat down, heart hammering in my chest as I watched him flip it open, revealing a series of photographs and papers—nothing out of the ordinary at first glance, just pieces of a life I thought was gone.

Ryan picked up one of the photos and handed it to me. My fingers trembled as I took it, the image freezing my blood.

It was a picture of him—my him—but this time, he wasn't standing in a field of golden light. He wasn't laughing, or smiling, or lost in the moment like he used to be. No, in this photo, his eyes were wide and terrified, his hands gripping the edge of a table, his face shadowed by something I couldn't quite make out.

I looked up at Ryan, my voice barely a breath. "Where did you get this?"

Ryan didn't answer right away. Instead, he reached for another photo, and then another, his hands shaking. "Jenna, there's more. You need to see everything."

And just like that, I felt the world tilt beneath me. Something was unraveling, something I wasn't prepared for, and the wind was still whispering.